Dr. Cerulean's Guide to Traversing Time & Dimensions in 13 Simple Steps

MATEYO JAKOBI

DEDICATION

This book is for Mace.

Prelude: Every Word You Are About To Read Is Absolutely True

There is one thing you need to know before you immerse yourself into this adventure: Every word you are about to read in this story is *absolutely true.*

For example, the word "flummoxed" is a very true word, as it has a definition and purpose in language.

It is another word for "perplexed" or "confused."

Used in a sentence, one might say, "This manuscript has me absolutely flummoxed."

Also, the word "grimblenox" is a true word, although it has no definition and its purpose in language is wholly unclear. It became a true word the moment it found its way out of this author's imagination and onto the page in front of you.

Used in a sentence, one might use it in its capacity as a noun to describe a length of time: "I haven't been this flummoxed in a grimblenox."

"I'm grimblenoxing after reading this ridiculous book," one might declare, using the word as a verb, you see.

Why, it could even be used as an adjective if placed in the proper portion of a sentence: "Is this one of those grimblenox authors I've read about in all the modern books?"

Or, one could simply shout, "Grimblenox!" if one is in the market for a new and flummoxing interjection.

So know, reader, that every word you are about to read is absolutely true.

Post-Prelude: Also, All The Events Depicted In This Manuscript Absolutely Happened

Oh, and one more thing you'll need to know: Everything you're about to read *actually happened*.

Each scene, incident, situation, circumstance, development, occurrence, mishap, adventure, experience, bout, rout, defeat, arrival and departure have happened exactly as they are described here – and in the order in which they are presented.

Any scholars who wish to prove otherwise may proceed with providing evidence to the contrary.

☐

Pre-Prologue: This Is How The Story Ends

Particles whipped by a hot wind swept the woman's face. The tiny granules sprayed like shattered glass into her eyes. She found herself now in a vast desert, with nothing but dunes as far as the eye could see. This was an ancient place, and countless structures, bodies, and a vast array of all other unfound and forgotten things had been hidden here by time and sand.

She had not chosen this place, and she was there through no conscious effort of her own. The woman, though, had been here before, and she was going to make the best of a very bad situation.

There were thousands of miles of desert in any given direction, but she had certain powers that most other people could only dream of obtaining. Any normal person would likely die out here. Not this woman, though.

She squinted at the sun. Her skin and hair were both so fair that they bordered on being white. The radiation from above could not burn her skin, though. It was impervious to such things. The only discomfort she felt was from the heavy, black dress she was wearing.

Her magical abilities had been nearly drained, true, but there was enough left to guide her to a hidden chamber in this very desert where she'd buried the head of an incredibly powerful and incredibly dangerous woman. She needed to get to this location now.

On the other side of the planet, another woman set foot into a crumbling city. This woman was far younger than the fair-skinned witch in the desert, though the two looked as though they could have been about the same age.

The woman in the city, her complexion the color of cocoa, her hair black and wet, had just emerged from the ocean, and she was now on a mission to find someone she'd lost, someone she loved, someone she hoped was still alive amid the destruction.

If she could find her lost lover, she vowed the two would escape from this place and begin anew. The two would travel back to her parent's home, perhaps, in the valley past the mountains. She hadn't heard from them in years, and she could hope they were alive still. And even if they weren't, which she suspected was the case, she could still put down new roots and never look back.

And as these individuals set about on their respective journeys, somewhere in another dimension, a man pondered the very nature of existence. He teetered on the brink of madness having been through what could only be described as hell, returning from the nightmare with knowledge no man should have.

He made a decision then to end the cycle, one that could have been revolving for eternity for all he knew. That decision was a drastic one, and he guessed it could lead to things far worse than he'd already experienced. But he chose to hope that his decision would instead set everything right.

On the other side of his world, a guillotine blade fell with a metallic swish, and a woman's head rolled to the dusty ground.

And somewhere between those two dimensions – somewhere between all dimensions – the Engine of Existence churned out life and time and power and space, but no one could see that this entity, the battery that powers all that is – *The Core* – was now damaged.

It wouldn't be long before it either burned out completely, or was snatched by the thing that lurked beyond the fine and nearly impenetrable border between existence and the void.

Dear reader, as time travelers, sometimes we have no say in the order in which we witness events happening. You'll do well to keep this in mind as you study Dr. Cerulean's Guide to Traversing Time and Dimensions.

Prologue: This Is How The Story Begins

If ten young men of age, thin, gangly and awkward, were lined up one next to the other and marched in front of you, you would most likely be unable to discern Bratticus L. Magleby from the other nine, save but for a single defining factor.

He was 20 years old, although years had a nasty habit of differing in length, so sometimes he wondered if he was perhaps 24 or maybe 18. He was unusually tall for his age (although it is common knowledge that most men of any age can be – and usually are – many various heights). His hair was the color of graveyard dirt. Or perhaps it was the color of a beaver's fur. It depends on where the light catches it as the wind blows, and whether or not you're inclined to make remarks on minuscule variations on shades of brown.

His skin was tan in some places, but very pasty in others – the two usually coinciding with where the sun did and did not shine.

However, if you were having a conversation with young Mr. Magleby, or perhaps engaging in a contest in which the two of you must stare into each other's eyes without blinking, you would have noticed something particularly peculiar.

Bratticus's eyes were the most unique eyes of anyone in his university. Come to think of it, his eyes were probably the most unique in his entire galaxy. At first glance, they appeared to be nearly black, but upon closer inspection, one could see the edges of his pupils barely defined against irises that were dark blue and purple, flecked with strands of gold and white.

One could, and often did, get lost in his eyes, as if looking into a dark galaxy being manipulated by a black hole. And as a black hole pulls in matter and light, so could Bratticus's eyes. A person who wasn't careful would find him or herself sapped of their faculties by gazing into the infinity of young Mr. Magleby's eyes for a moment too long.

It was for this reason that Bratticus L. Magleby made it a habit of averting his gaze whilst engaging in conversation. And it was because of this that many people, upon first meeting young Mr. Magleby, assumed he was either shy or had something to hide.

As it turns out, both those assumptions were often true, although the latter was far more true than anyone could have known. Bratticus did have something to hide, but the odd thing about it was he wasn't sure exactly what that thing was he was hiding. He only knew it had to be hidden.

This thing, whatever it was, that he felt needed to be hidden was all the more puzzling because his past was not a mystery to him – as is sometimes the case when stories are written. He knew his family. He had no enigmatic memory loss. He was not an orphan. In fact both his parents were still quite alive and quite well, living comfortably in a three-story house overlooking a pond on which swam a single, rebellious goose that left his flock in his younger years after deciding none of the other geese truly understood him.

That, though, is a different story altogether, and I'll thank you, dear reader, to not stray from the subject at hand.

He – Bratticus, not the goose - was an educated young man. But despite his two-year stint at university in which he learned all matter of mathematics, equations, statistics, computations, calculations, and other subjects dealing in numbers, symbols, and letters and symbols that substitute numbers, it was those hypnotizing eyes that secured his employment once he'd completed his degree.

While traveling by train home from college, Bratticus was reading The Perfunctory Post (a newspaper that never included news one might actually care about) when he came across a paid notice that piqued his interest.

The notice read as follows:

"Wanted: One freshly-graduated student versed in mathematics, equations, statistics, computations, calculations, and other subjects dealing in numbers, symbols, and letters and symbols that substitute numbers. Room and board to be covered in full. Payment to be made in form of scientific experience. Small stipend to be included should the applicant's duties be adequately performed. Larger stipend to be included should those adequate duties be performed beyond adequacy. Applicants should inquire at the Apothecary of Dr. Gustopher Cramden Cerulean, MPharmS, MD, PhD, LDLP, ASAP, which may be found at the end of End Lane, in the City of Bell, in the County of Muss, in the State of Konfuson."

Bratticus clipped the notice, willfully ignoring the curiously specific qualifications requested, and, after arriving home and having supper with his parents, purchased another train ticket to the City of Bell in the County of Muss in the State of Konfuson. When he met the man at the specified location exactly one year before our story begins, the man, whose own face was hidden behind an impressive handlebar mustache and a pair of dark goggles, took a single glance at Bratticus's eyes and hired him on the spot.

Step 1: Choose A Fixed Point In Space And Time In Which To Establish A Home Base

"In order to properly traverse time and dimensions, one must first have a point of origin from which to travel and which to return. There is no room for time traveling Nomads, as it is physically impossible for two items of equal density to switch from reality to the next and stay put."

— Dr. Gustopher C. Cerulean, as quoted in the copious notes of Bratticus L. Magleby.

Chapter 1

If you happened upon the City of Bell in the County of Muss in the State of Konfuson some time just after the blossoms began to open on the cherry trees and some time just before the cherries themselves were plucked from the branches, you may have noticed something peculiar above the apothecary of one Dr. Gustopher Cramden Cerulean, MPharmS, MD, PhD, LDLP, ASAP.

The good doctor, of whom little was truly known, was often called upon to whip up a quick unguent for the flu or a tonic for a sudden case of objectionable offspring (the remedy, of course, followed by a prescription of one to five years at a fine boarding school across the sea).

Dr. Cerulean was also the man to seek when one's ice box began to falter or one's high-wheel bicycle began to drift automatically toward the

Mile and one Meter Ravine, which in that particular year had swallowed no less than 10 riders when their penny-farthings suddenly and without warning sprouted their own faculties.

You can't mistake the good doctor, to be sure. He stands at the height of seven feet and a few odd inches (some of those inches even odder than others). It is currently unclear how many of those feet are due to his slick, stovepipe hat. And if you're in the habit of adding haberdashery to a man's height, and I'll keep my judgments to myself if you're the sort, then you'll most likely want to add another six to eight inches for the cerulean feather plucked from some exotic bird, which Dr. Cerulean kept situated in his hatband.

That the feather's color and the doctor's surname share a title is purely coincidental, I assure you. (By the way, it will serve you well, dear reader, to keep the word "coincidence" packed into a nice, comfortable storage area in your brain. Make sure that the "coincidence" you choose is sturdy, because we'll be using it in new and robust ways and I wouldn't want your "coincidence" to get chipped or ruined altogether.)

And unlike a gun when introduced in the first act of a play, Dr. Cerulean's cerulean feather will not come into play in the final scenes of this story. This I promise, so put it out of your mind.

While Dr. Cerulean's breadth was certainly impressive, his width was a little less intimidating. The most graceful of spiders was envious of the doctor's spindly limbs; his stride was equal to at least two of any healthy man's – and three of any unhealthy man's. His branch-like fingers were always hidden beneath the shiny black of his laboratory gloves, and the equally shiny black patent leather boots similarly protected his feet and shins.

His face was the biggest mystery of all. The half above his nose was always hidden behind teacup-sized goggles, with lenses as dark as his gloves and boots. The half below his nose was always hidden behind one of the most impressive handlebar mustaches on this side of the Ridiculing River.

The rapidity of the Ridiculing River, by the way, was nothing to laugh at. But we're not discussing bodies of water at this moment, so please stop inquiring about them.

His suit was the color of red wine. Or perhaps it was the color of blood. It all depends on whether or not it's bright outside, and whether or not you're inclined to make remarks on minuscule variations on shades of red.

His tiepin was a dark bluish-purple pearl that was nearly black, and his waistcoat was merry yellow. Attached to one buttonhole in that waistcoat was a watch fob. Now, Dr. Cerulean was a straightforward man in terms of watch fobs, so he'd attach nothing else to the end of it than a pocket watch.

The watch was an especially intriguing ornament. It was brass, and the doctor wound it exactly seven times a day, with exactly the same amount of time passing between winds. The hands were carved from ivory, and the clock face had 13 numbers. Some said such a watch was useless, but I've yet to meet a person who hasn't admitted that there are, at least, 13 hours in every day. Most people will admit there are even more.

The doctor's laboratory, housed behind the apothecary door, was indeed a unique one. It was an apothecary, yes, but it was simultaneously a laboratory, a garage, a factory, and a taxidermy museum. The exterior of the structure was huge and ramshackle, the building cobbled together from a series of bricks, stones, planks, shake, pitch, pipe, clay, cement, wire, mortar and all other manner of bric-a-brac. It stood an impressive ten stories tall, at least, a height that was all the more exaggerated thanks to the building's location atop a grassy hill.

The parlor to this monstrous structure was barely five feet in length and width. It also served as Cerulean's waiting room. It housed four ornate chairs – two against each wall on the right and left sides of the door – upholstered in the finest of velvet and studded with shiny brass tacks that had to be polished no less than two times per day. The windows were mantled by purple drapes embroidered with golden dragons, which in turn enveloped green curtains embroidered with silver unicorns, which in turn veiled orange slatted blinds (which had been painted blue). From the ceiling hung two elegant crystal chandeliers, one gas and one electric. The gas chandelier was never lit because it hung so low that it touched the ornate chairs, and Dr. Cerulean was nothing if not vigilant when it came to preventing the scorching of ornate chairs. The electric chandelier was never lit because, when it was installed, Dr. Cerulean forgot to order the proper wiring and switches for its adequate function, so it just hung there without casting a single photon. The floor of the waiting room was covered by an elaborate crimson rug with long yellow fringe, its weaved illustrations depicting a great medieval battle between Protestants and Catholics. And centered in the midst of all the chairs, drapes, curtains, blinds, chandeliers and rug was a baroque mahogany coffee table with six legs and a stained glass top, atop which sat an ivory 8-armed candelabra (although where the candles themselves were, I just don't know).

Because the waiting room was pitch black and too full of furniture to even enter, people simply used the side entrance to come and go.

From the exterior of the apothecary, one would assume it was a mansion – perhaps even a castle - with many levels filled with an abundance of rooms. But upon entering (whether through the easy access of the side entrance or through the parlor for the more adventurous sorts), one was often amazed to find that, instead of a large building filled with many small or medium-sized rooms, it was large building with one gigantic room, like some sort of cathedral designed by a very unenthusiastic architect.

The one, large room was comprised of a maze of workspaces, full of machines, contraptions, gizmos, devices, appliances, inventions, doodahs, jiggers, gubbins, hickeys, and a certain cylinder the doctor had forbidden Bratt to touch that housed a single, suspended atom. All of this took up the bulk of the laboratory. In the far southeast corner was Dr. Cerulean's four-post bed, chifforobe and chamber pot. In the far southwest corner was Bratticus Magleby's humble bed and dresser. In the far northwest corner was the dining area, complete with a table, four chairs, an icebox, a pantry and a counter on which to slice beets and grind herbs. The far northeast corner was a mystery, as neither Bratticus nor the doctor had ever fully explored it, and in fact both of them were a bit afraid to venture there.

The ceiling stretched up for what seemed like a mile, though I won't say it's a mile as I've been advised against using hyperbole. But on the brightest day, when each window was open, Bratticus (or Bratt, as he'd come to be known in his year of employment) was still unable to see the workings high above. Since there were no stairs to the top, it was impossible for him to know exactly what was up there, though he knew for certain there were, at least, bats because it was his duty to clean up the droppings every Thursday morning.

Here I am blathering on about the talents, accessories and workspace of the clever Dr. Cerulean, when I've alluded to something peculiar above his secluded apothecary, on which I've yet to elaborate. I apologize, as my wandering attention is a malady even the good doctor could not correct.

Chapter 2

The Peculiarity hung above the apothecary for exactly one hour just as the sun was rising on this particular day.

This anomaly was circular and hovered what appeared to be mere inches away from the highest gable of the doctor's structure. It was perhaps two feet in diameter (or three, if your shoe size was a bit smaller). It floated unaided, suspended in the air like a nefarious balloon. One might mistake it for the morning sun rising above the building's roof — if the morning sun were black and cast off not light but pulses of odious fear, and if the sun was not a gaseous mass burning at the center of a star system but were instead an opening to an unfathomable place where something terrible awaited even the most nihilistic mind.

Suns, however, don't look like that.

The thing, this very hole in the very sky, was in stark contrast to the lightly bluing atmosphere around it. This circular window to the space beyond looked out into a darkness that was so pure in its absence of color that one could assume it was what something looked like when something was nothing.

The air around The Peculiarity was wobbling slightly, as the horizon does on a hot day. If one were to observe this, one might imagine that this apparent puncture were radiating some sort of heat. However, the effect was actually created by the molecules and atoms and particles at The Peculiarity's edges being pulled through into the void, where they were efficiently erased from their place in this time and space.

It was horrifying. The longer it hovered, the larger it grew. If one were to watch it, which at this juncture in time no one actually was, one might have seen what looked like an octopus tentacle - though far more enormous than even the most giant of cephalopods lurking in the ocean, make its way gingerly round the edge of The Peculiarity.

But did any person in the City of Bell care to look up and witness this terrifying sight? No, none of them did. Only one person knew of the existence of this puncture in a piece of reality above the apothecary. The rest of the town's citizens remained blissfully unaware.

Chapter 3

Now, the good people of Bell in the state of Konfuson were by no means simple, but I wouldn't classify them as highly-educated, either, with the exception of Dr. Cerulean and his apprentice, Bratt, of course.

Bellians were a well-kept people, wealthy through a combination of various trusts, savings, good investments and insurance scams. A good Bellian wouldn't leave his or her house with a single button or hair out of place. The men's starched collars were always stiff as a tin roof, and sharp enough to shave with. The women's necks, on the other hand, were either festooned with bright rubies or fluttering with layers of lace.

The smallest of details were always attended to when it came to a Bellian's fashion. A woman's parasol would always match her stocking buttons (even though it was illegal for a female in Bell to expose her stocking buttons). And a male would always match his tiepin to his eye color.

The fact was Bellians put so much effort into their appearances that they paid little attention to many other things of consequence. They considered academia far beneath them; they believed those who would devote their time to learning instead of dressing smartly clearly had their priorities out of order.

So perhaps it was Cerulean's manner of dress, or his many degrees, or any other number of the doctor's quirky mannerisms or knowledge that made people ignore the hole above his home, but ignore it they did. Dr. Cerulean was the man you went to for a cough or to have your gadget fixed, but beyond that, the people of Bell didn't put much stock in the doctor's talents, and certainly none of them paid much attention to the things that often hovered above his apothecary — which happened more often than you might think.

But had a Bellian seen the swirling void and found it concerning, and had a Bellian knocked on the door to the side entrance of the apothecary that day to get to the bottom of things, that Bellian would have been truly amazed. That is assuming the mirror that was hung on the wall just by the door, naturally, didn't interrupt the citizen's attention. (Bellians, when in the presence of mirrors, had the habit of spending extended amounts of time preening and fixing mis-tipped hats that hadn't moved a centimeter since they'd been placed earlier that day).

Barring any mirror-related aversions, that Bellian would have discovered that Dr. Cerulean was clever enough to construct a contraption with the sole purpose of traversing time, space and dimensions.

That The Peculiarity above the apothecary and The Contraption within the apothecary were both active at exactly the same time was quite the coincidence indeed.

Chapter 4

Cerulean and Bratt had been working to perfect the device in the year the young man had been employed.

After some trouble with this contraption, having worked on it both day and night leading up to the time the vortex to an infinity of terrors had appeared, the blasted machine rudely malfunctioned and transported Dr. Cerulean to place of which Bratt was unaware. In a move arguably even ruder, the machine refused to bring the doctor back. It opted instead to stop working altogether.

It was at that time, another coincidence, perhaps, that the peculiar, circular, nightmarish oddity above the apothecary vanished like mist as the sun crested in the eastern sky.

Bratt, with two years of fine university schooling and an entire year under the tutelage of the brilliant doctor, had spent the next several days on a series of events to bring the doctor back home.

It wasn't just because Bratt considered Cerulean a friend. And it wasn't just because he hadn't yet collected the stipend he was owed. No, young Bratticus L. Magleby had to find Dr. Gustopher Cramden Cerulean because when the doctor was sent away, someone came through in his place. And Bratt knew he had to find a way to get her back to where she came from before she killed again. ☐

Step 2: Study And Understand The Basic Laws Of Parallel Dimensions And How To Travel To And Fro

"Think of all of existence as a weighing scale, and each universe as a weighing platform. Each universe balances out perfectly, and if one item is moved from one universe to another, the scales tip and the entire engine of existence begins to wobble. Therefore, when one travels from Dimension A to Dimension B, one must always calculate and trade places with another object of equal mass."

— Dr. Gustopher C. Cerulean, as quoted in the copious notes of Bratticus L. Magleby.

Chapter 5

Time and dimensions are funny things, and universes have a way of balancing each other out.

Bratt recalled Dr. Cerulean speaking on the subject through his impressive handlebar mustache while tightening the spoke of a wheel on his time and dimension altering contraption. The various nuts, bolts, gears, buttons, handles, clasps, rigs, trappings, levers, widgets and all manner of apparatuses reflected off Cerulean's black mirrored goggles as he fidgeted with each one.

The machine itself looked like the offspring of some unholy marriage between a clock tower and a submarine.

Standing just short of eight feet tall, the device had the look of circular coffin stood on end, a cylinder composed of copper and held in place with iron rivets. Along each side was a series of eight nickel-plated tubes that jutted out horizontally. Each of these tubes folded to the back of the machine where they connected to an ionization container, which move particles about without having to use rubber hoses.

Rubber hoses are famous for being unable to time travel, as everyone knows.

The capsule was designed to hold only one person. As a safety precaution, though, the door did not latch shut. Cerulean made note that a person should not have to be forced to be projected to another dimension against his will, so anyone who found himself inside its walls either accidentally or nefariously, should be able to leave without issue. And should a human of more robust stature be making the trek into the cylinder, he should not have to die of asphyxiation as his body is crammed into the device in a manner similar to a butcher forcing ground meat into sausage casing.

The Contraption was powered by electricity, which was generated by a series of plates attached to the roof of the apothecary. The plates, as was explained to Bratt, each contained cells that absorbed sunlight somehow, which then converted the radiation from the sunlight into usable power that was piped into the doctor's laboratory and stored in enormous, spherical batteries.

It was all very complicated, but of course it was much more efficient than what the far less-advanced State of D'Nyle did for energy.

If you were to travel to the State of D'Nyle, you'd notice millions of unsightly holes across the entire country. These holes, you see, were dug to access a flammable sludge that had been created over millennia of organic materials decomposing and pressurizing. D'Nyleons would then ignite this oily substance to light their homes and power their transportation. This in turn created an abundance of pollution that was pumped directly into the atmosphere. So not only was the land they lived on completely destroyed, but so was the air they breathed. I know it sounds ridiculous, and it may be the most unbelievable aspect of this entire story, but you'll have to believe me, dear reader. Now matter how absurd it seems, the people of the State of D'Nyle lived that way willingly.

This isn't a social studies lesson on the State of D'Nyle, though, so would you be so kind as to stay with the narrative?

Bratt performed his duties diligently while attempting to soak in every bit of information Dr. Cerulean was willing to impart upon him. Every day working in his presence might as well have been an entire semester at university.

And universities were hard to come by in the State of Konfuson. In fact, I know of none. You would have to travel hundreds of miles east to where Bratt obtained his own degree in the neighboring country, the State of Schok, where you'd be surprised how steep the tuition was.

When the two had set to work building The Contraption one-year prior, Dr. Cerulean had explained dimensional displacement to Bratt by comparing it to placing a ripe pumpkin being placed into a washbasin filled to the brim with water.

Now, why any person of sound mind would choose to fill a washbasin to the brim with water and then proceed to place a ripe pumpkin in it is well beyond me. But it illustrated the point satisfactorily: The space cannot be occupied simultaneously by the mass and density of the ripe pumpkin *and* the mass and density of the washbasin water. Therefore, one must literally move out of the way of the other.

The result of this example, when demonstrated literally, is a very wet floor. And if you're the sort who demands to see physical evidence of such an experiment, as young Bratticus was, then you'll be sure not to use an overly-ripe pumpkin, and do not conduct such experiments atop a priceless Persian rug that has been passed down through generations. That is, unless you desire a newly soiled heirloom that smells of rotten pumpkin water.

Between you and me, though, the rug was blasphemously ugly, and it was high time Mr. Magleby was rid of it.

But talk of rugs and pumpkins and washbasins should be saved for another day, and I don't know why you insist on exploring such subject matter at a time when we should be discussing dimensional displacement.

Dimensions will compensate for matter moving about from one area to another by exchanging things of equal mass and density. I'm told matter can move freely between existences on its own, given the correct circumstances, but as is often the case with nearly any activity whether or not it involves inter-dimensional travel, there has to be a catalyst. An action must be taken so a reaction can occur. Someone has to push the swing if one wants to be pushed in a swing. A candle must be lit if one wants light from a candle. A story must be written if an author wants to surreptitiously reveal the actual blueprints for dimensional travel while veiling it in plot and humor so only the brightest readers could decode it.

Besides, the natural circumstances in which time and dimensional travel can happen are very rare.

After much scientific exploration, we know that people and items can travel to other dimensions under these conditions: The moon must be exactly 363,101 kilometers and 12 centimeters away from the highest point on the planet. The sun must be simultaneously exactly 152 million kilometers and one-half centimeter away from the lowest point on the planet. Both must occur on exactly the 13th hour of 13th day of the 13th year following an exact planetary alignment that includes not only the celestial bodies known to us but also the 15 additional planets beyond them – which have yet to be discovered.

Dr. Cerulean, being the clever man that he was, instead created a machine designed to imitate those circumstances exactly, thus allowing for the movement of matter from dimension to dimension and from timeline to timeline at the will of the operator.

It's all rather rudimentary, I'm told, and so any confusion incurred is strictly the fault of the reader.

Furthermore, Dr. Cerulean's contraption was designed in such a way that the operator could choose the thing of equal mass that the traveler would be trading places with.

And the key to keeping everything in order was to have a line, like a fishing reel, attached to the home base so the traveler could return at will. Perhaps it was more like a beacon, or maybe a powerful magnet, but this aspect kept the traveler attached to the dimension from which he originated.

According to Cerulean's design, each traveler would need to travel with a certain object that was connected through space and time to their dimension of origin. That connection is made up by a chain of unseen dark particles that, when gathered in mass quantities, can bend light itself. This dark matter, as some would come to call it, is the secret to traversing time and dimensions.

Light, made of photons, is the road in time we are traveling on. We, made of atoms, are the vehicles. For all that our vehicles are capable of, they can only drive forward in time. It's true, some of us drive faster than others toward our final destination, whatever it may be. But oddly, we are unable to stray from time. We cannot turn or reverse. We can only move forward.

So what's the solution? Why, instead of trying to make a vehicle drive in an area it cannot, you simply move the road.

Using the unseen dark particles, the doctor devised a way to bend space and time certain degrees and certain directions so a traveler moving forward would simply intersect with another a nearby timeline. It's at that intersection the switch between equal-massed objects must be made.

No matter how far the original traveler drives upon the new road, he has his beacon. Once activated, it signals the contraption back home to bend his original timeline back into the correct path.

So yes, you could visit your future or past self, if you so desired. It would just happen that your future or past self would be one traveling on a separate road than you. You most definitely cannot change your own past, but you could quite easily change the past of your counterpart a few dimensions away.

You see? Simple.

Chapter 6

Dr. Cerulean's brass pocket watch, which had 13 hours upon its face, was his beacon. Springing the latch to the front cover was all it took to activate this machine, allowing him to return home safe and sound from wherever or whenever he traveled.

That was the plan for the trial run that fateful day: have a quick pop over to a parallel universe for a quick look around and then be back before Bratt can finish making tea and fry bread.

And when the good doctor switched the main breaker that afternoon, his calculations were set perfectly, and he'd set his path to intersect with another object of his same mass and density so as not to tip the scales of existence.

He was to trade places with a stack of soiled socks and a bundle of sticks cut at such a length that they were deemed unusable. Finding something of equal density and mass is tricky business, and frankly you have to take what's available. Cerulean's machine had been programmed to scan for such items, and if sticks and socks were the best option, then sticks and socks it was to be.

Cerulean stepped into the cylinder and quietly closed the door. Outside, unbeknownst to Bratt, The Peculiarity churned overhead. Bratt could see the doctor's goggles and enormous mustache through the porthole.

On that fateful day, just before the cherries in Bell had been plucked from their branches, and just as The Pecularity appeared above the apothecary's roof, the machine sprang into action.

And as the sun began to rise in the east, the lanky form of Dr. Gustopher C. Cerulean was sucked into the core of the sparking machine, and another form was spit out in his place. And it wasn't a stack of soiled socks and a bundle of sticks cut at such a length that they were deemed unusable.

Chapter 7

The door of the cylinder stood bent and ajar, three hinges completely, well, unhinged. A panel to the left of the pod sparked and sizzled. The glass in the porthole was shattered, and spilling out of capsule like a sack of wet, angry flour was a woman.

What she lacked in height, the woman made up for in girth. Now, dear reader, I am definitely no mathematician, and I've ruined many cakes by either over or underestimating the amount of baking powder needed for the batter, but upon initial inspection, I would have guessed the woman was not equal in both mass and density to Dr. Cerulean. Bratt, however, was a mathematician. And he knew straight away that the globulous thing before him would have easily tipped the scales should she be weighed against Cerulean.

Upon first glance, Bratt knew he would need an exact copy of himself if he wanted to hug this strange woman and have the ability to clasp his hands around her body, as it would have taken two of him to get the job done in one try.

Her hair was pulled tightly into a severe bun, which pushed her pink and pointy hat forward across her brow. Her eyes remained hidden, but her scowling mouth was all too clear as she worked to uncork herself from the machine's doorway.

Her dress with the far-too-puffy puffed shoulders was the color of grass. Or perhaps it was the color of spinach. It all depended on where the shadows fell in the room and whether or not you're inclined to make remarks on minuscule variations on the shades of green.

Bratt could see one boot from beneath her petticoats, the tip of which was as pointed as her hat, and it drew circles in the air in an attempt to get some sort of foothold as the woman wiggled about. The other foot was still somewhere inside the contraption. Both her hands grasped the doorjamb, and her black fingernails made an awful scraping noise against the metal.

Bratt's teeth went on edge at both the sound and the sight.

"Where am I?! What happened?!" the lady squawked. "Get me out of here!"

The words spewed from her mouth not unlike the time the

contents of Bratt's stomach spewed from his gullet after consuming a bottle of Dr. Cerulean's Laudanum, Cocaine and Opium Children's Anti-Hysteria Medicament.

I wish I could say it was out of a sense of chivalry, but it was more an attempt to put an end to the shrieking and scratching that Bratt finally stepped forward and helped tug the repugnant creature from the machine. After much heaving – and some hoeing – Bratt was able to extract the woman, and she tumbled onto the apothecary floor in a jumble of skirts, petticoats and bustles. With an effort that was uncomfortable to watch, she righted herself, replaced her fallen hat, and turned her scowl toward Bratt.

The buxom little being trotted with purpose directly up to Bratt, and had his eyes been where his nipples currently resided, he would have been face to face with the disgruntled little woman.

"Where *am* I?" she screeched again.

"Miss," Bratt said with a stammer, "you - you're in the laboratory of the great Dr. Gustopher Cram–"

"Quiet you!" She belched as she spun around, taking in her surroundings.

She eyed the doctor's shelves, crammed with all variations of bottles, flasks, jars, and jugs. Her gaze then landed upon the doctor's workspace, overflowing with all manner of tools, devices, gadgets, and instruments. Her attention then shifted to the contraption, covered in wheels, springs, gears and buttons. Then her sour little face turned back to Bratt.

"A wizard, are you?"

"No miss, if I may, my name is Bratticus L–"

"Do you know what you've done?" She screeched. "I was just seconds, mere seconds away from finally destroying that rotten niece of mine! Do you know what that means?!"

"I can't say that I do.""The House of Vermilion would finally be mine! After all these years waiting and plotting and –" she paused abruptly, staring up into Bratt's eyes. "IT. WAS. TO. BE. MINE!"

The woman punctuated this statement with a flap of her arms, her palms striking her bountiful hips with each word spoken.

She huffed in her place, her skirts bellowing below her rotund waistline, giving Bratt the impression that perhaps she was a great toad beneath all the layers of fabric. As this woman did hail from an alternate dimension, for all Bratt knew, she may very well have been a giant toad beneath all those layers of fabric. But in Bell, it was against the law for a woman to lift her skirts to reveal even her stocking buttons, so to avoid any scrapes with the local law enforcement, Bratt didn't press her for evidence.

I will inform you here, dear reader, that this woman did *not* come from an alternate universe. In fact, her home was on the other side of the world on which Bratt currently lived – an exact line through the world from this point to that, to be precise. Bratt, though, did not know this. And the woman did not know this either.

Their planet was quite similar to the one upon which you currently reside. It had a center of gravity, its surface was covered with a large percentage of water, and a layer of ozone kept oxygen and other gases from leaking out into the vastness of space.

There was one defining difference from their world and yours, though. Your world is a sphere, while theirs was lenticular. Essentially, there were two sides to their planet, as there are two sides to a coin. Since the point of gravity on this particular planet all but disappeared at the very edges, most folks didn't do much traveling to the other side.

So while it was true that Bratt and this woman shared the same world, those worlds were so far removed from each other that believing they existed in separate dimensions was, all things considered, a fair way of looking at it.

"Miss," he said, since it seemed clear her fit was momentarily at an end, "I am the apprentice to the very clever Dr. Gustopher Cramden Cerulean, who has created the machine you see before you here – the very machine that has brought you to this place."

Here Bratt pointed at the contraption as to diminish any amount of confusion.

"It was designed to send matter to and from parallel dimensions and timelines, and it appears the device has malfunctioned, sending the good doctor to wherever it is you've just come from, and it has brought you here in his stead."

"So, I've replaced the local wizard and now I have to deal with his dumpy sidekick?"

She kicked a wayward wrench, which lay near the machine. The tool was a heavy one, and the woman's pointed boot did not protect her toes as a pointed boot should.

Boots from Bell, might I add, were sturdy and would surely have stood up to just such a kicking. But that's neither here nor there.

She kicked, and then she screamed.

"Damn!" She erupted, grasping for her foot but failing miserably due to her corpulent figure. "Damn!"

In her attempt to reach her boot, she toppled head over heels. Bratt immediately turned his face away from the commotion for fear of glancing either a stocking button or a giant toad, but luckily her petticoats were plenty. Instead of any amount of leg, he only saw what appeared to be a blossoming cabbage of fabrics, each layer greener than the last. Protruding from the kerfuffle of cloth were the tips of her two pointed boots, barely visible among the verdant material.

Bratt may have been an apprentice, but that didn't make him any less of a gentleman. So despite the woman's surly demeanor, he ran to her aide.

"Miss," he said, helping her back to her feet (the act was not unlike rolling an oversized and heavier-than-ordinary ball across a sandy beach).

"It's MADAME!" she bellowed as she revolved into the upright position. "Madame Vermilion! Nearly the head of the House of Vermilion!

Nearly the ruler of the State of D'Kay! And you've put my queendom in jeopardy!"

Here she paused, an expression on her face as if she'd just remembered where she placed her front-door key.

"Oh!" she said, bringing the back of her hand to her forehead with drama. "What shall I do?"

Her irritability melted away just a bit, and she pulled a blindingly pink handkerchief from her sleeve, using it to dab her eyes – although Bratt hadn't actually seen any tears.

"Please," she said, sauntering to his side and gingerly tugging at his overcoat. "Please, young sir, won't you help me get back home?"

He straightened up. Of course this bothersome woman with her irksome voice and exasperating attitude was an annoyance. But how was he to know this type of behavior wasn't simply the epitome of grace and etiquette from her dimension? Besides, he couldn't exactly blame her for her gruff and insolent conduct. She had just been ripped from her world, where she'd been in the act of destroying that niece of hers, after all. And it seemed like it was a task she'd been working on for some time.

Chapter 8

"Madame Vermilion, please allow me to brew you a cup of tea," Bratt said taking her hand. "I am not the inventor of this machine, but I have taken copious notes on its construction, and I watched as the good doctor tightened every bolt and soldered every joint. I believe – with some work – I may be able to activate it correctly and return you to your House of Vermilion."

She curtsied in a way only a walking wrecking ball can, a smile appearing on her pursed lips. It occurred to Bratt that this woman's smile was possibly even more frightening than her scowl.

He escorted her to the dining area of Dr. Cerulean's abode and pulled a chair out for the poor, disheveled woman. He said a small prayer that the chair would hold as she sat, and he tucked her into her place as best she could.

As the tea was brewing, Bratt contemplated the contraption. It had malfunctioned, as rude contraptions are wont to do. But the time had come for him to assert himself and put to use the knowledge he'd been gleaning from the good doctor over the past year. And as far as he could tell, he only had the panel to fix and the door to the capsule to repair.

He gazed at Vermilion. Her impatience was palpable.

Bratt poured the tea and sat.

"My name is Bratticus L. Magleby," he said, realizing his formal introduction had been so rudely interrupted moments before. "The 'L' doesn't stand for anything. It was simply put there because my parents felt it was the perfect letter to offset the syllables of my given name and my surname."

"Veramilicent Vermilion," she responded, plucking the teacup from his hand and slurping the beverage. She made a sour face after tasting the tea. "My parents are both dead, and it certainly took far more effort than it should have!"

Bratticus raised one eyebrow, waiting for her to elaborate.

"And just exactly how long will it take you to put me back where I belong?" she asked.

"I dare say it shouldn't take more than a day or two, assuming everything I do is correct," he answered.

"How long are the days here?" She asked.

"They're usually from about the time the sun rises to about the time the sun sets," he said.His answer, as practical as it was, didn't seem to satisfy her. But by the looks of her face and the size of her body, he got the impression Madame Vermilion wasn't satisfied by a great many things.

"This tea is disgusting," she said.

As he was about to apologize, the woman did something he

considered at least marginally interesting. She stirred the tea with one pointed, black nail, and the liquid sizzled, turning from dark brown to gold. The bubbling ceased, and she brought the cup to her lips once more.

"Ahhhhhhh."

The noise of relief was not unlike the sound he imagined she'd make when unbuckling whatever girdle was holding her midsection together.

"Sparkling wine," she said, smacking her lips. "A far better alternative to whatever that sludge was, don't you think?"

His mouth was agape, and as he was about to inquire as to the sort of alchemy she'd harnessed to change tea into wine, a dead bat from the high rafters above came crashing down to the floor with a sickening thud. Bratt started, but Madame Vermilion was as cool as a cucumber, cucumbers famously being the relaxed vegetables that they are.

Between the tea-to-alcohol trick and the suddenly dead bat, Bratt must have been exuding a visual air of confusion.

"Don't worry about that," she said, motioning to the poor departed creature on the floor. "It's collateral damage from the spell."

"The spell?"

"Yes, you stupid boy. You can't muster the power to turn tea into wine out of nowhere! That energy has to come from something! Do you not know how the world works? And it's such a small teacup, so it goes without saying I'd only need a small creature."

"We have wine!" he replied in exasperation, pointing to a very robust wine rack Dr. Cerulean kept stocked should he ever be asked to christen a boat. "Did the bat really need to die?"

The fat little wretch didn't seem to care a bit.

"Please," she said. "Just be glad it wasn't a barrel of tea I was transforming. Otherwise it would have been your life at stake!"

She chuckled at the thought, her enormous bosoms bouncing into her chin.

Bratt, for one, didn't find the humor in the situation. There would be no way in hell or on earth he'd be willing to waste that much tea to make an entire barrel, as good tea was incredibly hard to come by in Bell. Tealeaves were only native to the State of D'mand where the supply was always slim. He also didn't find the humor in turning a barrel of perfectly good tea into wine, as there was an overabundance of the stuff in Bell, grapes being the number one export, and grape stomping being the number one recreational activity. Lastly, he didn't find the humor in his life being the price for such a silly act.

Once he was done combing through the reasons he didn't find the thought of turning barrels of tea into wine humorous, he began to ponder the weight of the situation.

Since there's no such thing as magic, he thought, this woman had to be an alchemist. The only reasonable explanation is that her fingernails are painted with some solution that was a catalyst to the science. And apparently to power the alchemy, she had to pull the life from some poor creature nearby.

"So, you're an alchemist," he proclaimed.

"No," she fired back. "I'm a witch. Why do you think I wear this hat? Only witches wear pointed hats, you daft moron. Don't you read?"

Bratt put himself in check, reminding himself that this woman hailed from another dimension, where sorcery was apparently indeed real and hats apparently defined a person's occupation.

What Bratt didn't realize was that it was on the other side of his own world that sorcery was real and hats defined a person's occupation. It was all a lesson in how little people can actually know about the very planet on which they live when their planet is shaped in such a way that traveling to the other side is nearly impossible.

Interlude 1: Madame Veramilicent Vermilion, A Brief History

I'll issue you a warning, dear reader. What may seem absolutely normal to you in your world would be completely ridiculous to someone from another dimension.

On the side of the planet from which Madame Vermilion hails, things are quite different from what you're probably used to. I'll ask you to please set aside your judgments of things you believe are silly. After all, there might be a reader somewhere who is observing you right now through the pages of yet another story, judging everything you do.

It's not a pleasant feeling, being judged by an unseen reader, now is it?

Chapter 9

The State of D'Kay wasn't always in such bad shape. It sat at the very apex on this side of the almond-shaped world, though this island nation, along with hundreds of other island nations, was not the "main land."

While the main land, a huge continent just near enough the lenticular planet's edge to be adventurous, had the largest population of people by far, it was the State of D'Kay that boasted the most satisfied population of people.

Birds used to sing, flowers used to bloom, and the social structure of the country was so well-off that political races were hardly any fun to follow.

Politicians in the State of D'Kay rarely said a negative word about each other when it came time for the population to cast their votes. Perhaps it was because each politician had a sterling record, which no other woman could possibly contest. Perhaps it was because each politician had plans for the future that were inarguably brilliant.

The most likely reason, I think, is because the only politicians to run for the office of Prime Minister (with the exception of one time, which shall be explained momentarily) were Margaret and Adelaide Vermilion, twin sisters who bounced ruling D'Kay back and forth as if it were a shuttlecock in a game of badminton. The two rarely had a negative word to say to each other on any given day, let alone during political elections.

D'Kay had established term limits for its ministers when its Founding Mothers first drew up the document that declared independence from the State of D'Klyne. It was written that no woman should serve as Prime Minister consecutively for more than 10 years. But since an intermittent ministry was not expressly forbidden, it gave a previous minister the power to run again, once her ministry had been over for exactly 10 years.

It's still unclear whether the Vermilion sisters initially planned to take control of D'Kay, but they did, and the reason they were so successful was because they were, in essence, the perfect leaders.

Every woman, man, child, and domestic pet was charged a 20 percent tax on income and 10 percent tax on all goods and services. All tax dollars went directly to social programs and infrastructure, keeping the good people of D'Kay very satisfied indeed.

No money was spent on military, as D'Kay had no need for one. The small army the D'Kayans prepared for the war they expected when declaring their independence from D'Klyne more than 200 years prior was very modest indeed. And had D'Klyne decided to take physical action, the D'Kay army would have been decimated in a single day.

After all, the military at the time only included all six markswomen from the Rimshaw Township Archery Circus, and half the members of Trail Blazer Troop 221, all of whom were no older than 12.

But D'Klyne accepted the document and allowed D'Kay to form its own nation. The State of D'Klyne, as it turned out, was in a serious state of collapse, and the leaders had been glad to lighten their loads.

D'Kay was an island nation, with an incredibly successful export of wine decanters, which were hand-blown at the Demantis factory in the center of the island. These wine carafes were sought far and wide, with every neighboring nation ordering them daily. They aired wine flawlessly, oxygenating each drop to perfection and creating a taste unobtainable through any other form of decanting. Since wine grapes were so bitter in D'Kay and every surrounding island nation, perfect wine aeration was an absolute must. And once the aeration was complete and the last drop drank, the decanter would shatter, thus ensuring a constant need for the containers.

The secret was in the way the head glassblower, Madame Dee, created them. I would reveal it to you now, but it is a secret.

Needless to say, D'Kay's Demantis destructing Drink Decanters done by Dee were desirable, and because no other glassblower had the talent of Madame Dee, no nation dared invade for fear of losing the all-too-important decanter factory.

This may sound silly to you, but think for a moment what it must be like in D'Kay, where without the aid of such decanters, one would have to use magic to make wine taste delicious. And what other option was there? Abstain from wine? The idea is laughable.

But why you're insisting I tell you about the island's manufacturing and exports and bitterness of wine is an enigma to me, as it has almost nothing to do with the brief history of Madame Veramilicent Vermilion. It would be much appreciated if you could please remain on topic.

Chapter 10

All was well on the island. The people were happy. The

infrastructure was sound. There was peace. It was all due to the Vermilion Twins, who, in their 50 years of overseeing D'Kay, had created the closest thing to a living paradise on the lens-shaped world.

It is of note that a year in the State of D'Kay was much shorter than a regular year, as the citizens had become so efficient in their daily tasks that at least six months' worth of time was effectively shaved away. So the twins, although being at least 70 years old, didn't look a day over 35.

Their kindness, beauty, level-headedness, perfect posture and good taste in music made them the adoration of all citizens.

The people of D'Kay would have amended their founding document to allow for the Vermilion Sisters to serve simultaneously as co-ministers, if the original document weren't so ironclad. (I'm told there was an excellent blacksmith who worked to release the document once, but the iron quality was simply too great.)

All the while the State of D'Kay flourished, the Vermilion Twins' aunt sat brooding in her secluded house atop the narrow cliff overlooking the sea behind the House of Vermilion. The aunt's home was stately – built for the extended family of the minister of D'Kay. It stood no less than five stories tall, and no more than six. Its roof was garnished with half a dozen gables, each gable punctuated with a wrought-iron lighting rod. From a distance, it gave the home the impression of having a tall, black crown.

The aunt, herself, had run for the position of minister many, many years ago – the one time the Vermilion Sisters had been challenged – but she failed quite miserably. Her political platform differed slightly from her socially-minded nieces. For starters, she considered D'Kay's lack of an army to be quite reprehensible, and she declared that her first priority would be to redirect taxes from social programs toward building what she described as the world's greatest army, guarding the perimeter of D'Kay against any invasion.

She did not appreciate it when it was pointed out to her that a navy, or at best a coast guard, would be better suited to D'Kay since, as I've mentioned, the nation was an island. And she appreciated it even less when it was pointed out to her that an army or a navy or a coast guard was moot considering there were no countries wishing to war with D'Kay, for fear of losing the important decanter factory.

But the truth of the matter was the Vermilion Twins' aunt didn't actually wish for the protection of D'Kay. She didn't wish to lead a successful nation. She didn't want to see her state flourish economically. No, in fact, she wished to rule the country and, had her political aspirations been fulfilled, she would have used her newly-formed army to force the D'Kayans into submission, compelling them to bow to her every whim.

Since the civilians of the island were considered the most efficient – able to live an entire year in only six months, after all – the Vermilion Twin's aunt believed she could form a most proficient army. Her plan was to use that army to conquer the surrounding islands, and eventually the mainlands, giving her reign over the entire side of the planet.

Her motivation, I'm told, was that her mother was too strict on her as a child.

Let the aunt's tale be a lesson to those of you who are rearing children. Always allow them to eat candy, never restrict them with bedtime hours, and forego any schooling that displeases them, lest you be responsible in their later years for a monster who wishes to dominate the world.

Chapter 11

In D'Kay, if the Prime Minister were to perish, in the interim until the next election, the duties would be handed over to the next minister in the line of succession, which was the Minister of Decanter Production. In the case that the Minister of Decanter Production met her demise, the Minister of Adroitness would assume the responsibilities. After that it went to the Minister of Smooth Pavement Surfaces (whose job was incredibly important, as smooth pavement surfaces led to much quicker and safer commutes). And then to the Minister of Puffed Sleeves, then the Minister of Fish Mongers, then the Minister of Breads and Cheeses, then the Minister of Orange Sweets, then the Minister of Sweet Oranges, and so on and so forth. If, for some reason, no ministers were left to assume responsibility, the power of the Prime Minister would go to the recently-perished Prime Minister's next of kin by blood.

Men were not allowed to hold office in the State of D'Kay, as their place was in the home and not in the workforce.

It was a comfort to the people to know that, should every minister on the island bite the dust, the power would return to one of the two Vermilion Sisters.

Unless, of course, both the women were dead.

When the Vermilions' aunt's political campaign failed so spectacularly, she set to work on a plan that would legally put her in charge, since she had not the desire to wait another ten years for the next election nor the ability to win one even if she tried.

Ironically, it would take her two full political cycles to do the deed, but she successfully managed to methodically murder each minister masterfully – with magic.

You see, unlike magic in your realm, magic on the island of D'Kay actually exists. However, it came at a price.

There were two ways to gain magical skills in the State of D'Kay, the first being many hours of practice, years of study, and an incredibly hefty sum of money for access to the magical texts (and additional late fees if they weren't returned in a timely manner). The second way was far easier: Kill a person who already possesses magical abilities and eat her heart.

The second option, although simpler than years of study, practice, and fines, was nearly impossible because the Vermilions' aunt knew of no one with the exact magical skills she required, nor did she have an adequate recipe for cooking human hearts.

The aunt, therefore, had no choice.

She scraped up her savings (of which there were plenty) and diligently began learning the craft of sorcery, devoting decades of laboring sedulously at honing the magical arts. She shut herself away in the stately home on the cliff, drawing every window shade as she cast spells over her fire, brewed cauldrons of potions, and perfected her cackling techniques.

Granted, cackling isn't necessarily a requirement for one in D'Kay to become a master witch, and in fact her cackling had nothing to do with magic at all. She practiced so she could effectively laugh when her plans came to fruition and she found herself the head of the House of Vermilion, and thus the ruler of D'Kay.

Now, magic is more scientific than you might imagine. Think of a magic spell as a recipe. In order to create a cake, after all, one would have to add a series of ingredients together, and then alter said ingredients by beating them and heating them. A cake doesn't just happen, and I feel a great deal of sorrow for you if you're only learning this now.

For a spell to have its intended effect, one must create the correct circumstances. There are certain movements of the fingers, for example, as well as certain words muttered under the breath. Sometimes, there has to be a potion or powder. But there must *always* be a source of energy. Therein lies the true talent of a D'Kayan magician.

For it is she who knows how to transfer the energy of a nearby living being – the final action needed for the formula. It is, essentially, the baking of the cake.

And as a larger cake needs more heat, so a larger spell needs more energy.

I'm sure you'll recall the incident with the poor, dead bat, which was aptly detailed in the previous chapter. Thus, for the sake of time, I'll direct you back to that instance rather than provide a new example. There's simply no reason we should rehash the workings of magic when we've clearly more important things to discuss.

To properly charge her magical workings, the Vermilions' aunt had used the life power of the passing mountain goats, which often wandered onto her particular cliff to nibble the yellow tulips off her back porch.

The yellow tulips, I might add, were not placed there by the aunt, and she suspected the bulbs had been planted year after year by some detestable scoundrel from the city below who hoped to sour her day with the sight of such a cheerfully pedaled flower.

She had absent-mindedly begun to cast magic without knowledge of where the energy was being drawn, since the mountain goats were plentiful and their bodies, once sapped of life, would simply tumble off the cliff into the waters below. With no physical evidence of the spell's aftereffects, it was easy for the Vermilions' aunt to forget the price to conjure such power.

Beneath the cliff of the aunt's stately home, which looked out over the sea, there was a near-constant deluge of dying goats.

I'm told that a band of undereducated fishermen, who frequented the bay beside the high cliff with the stately home, would dredge the waters with their nets and pull the goats' bodies from the depths. They cogitated deeply on these strange, furry, horned, four-legged fish, but didn't dwell too much on their appearance, as their meat was delicious and was not unlike the lamb chops served from the butchers just up the lane.

When she finally and completely mastered the science of magic, the Vermilions' aunt purchased for herself a pointed pink hat, which was indicative of any great witch. It was the hat, after all, that announced to others that they were in the presence of power and should behave accordingly.

She would not don the embellishment, though, until her task was complete, lest she spoil the element of surprise. So she took her new status symbol, wrapped in its magnificent hatbox, and stowed it away in a broom cupboard in her stately home on the cliff.

After the years of labor and the single day of hat-purchasing, she was finally ready to begin her work.

Chapter 12

The Vermilions' aunt intended to put her magic to use by killing straightaway the Minister of Decanter Production, so she joined a group of tourists taking one of the twice-daily tours of the Demantis Decanter Factory.

While touring the facility, she conjured a spell to cause the Minister of Decanter Production to trip on a pair of errant copper pliers, which were used in the factory to handle the heated glass during the special procedures that gave the decanter its unique ability to aerate bitter wine before shattering completely. The sudden loss of balance would cause the minister to topple headfirst into the great furnace, which kept the glass malleable so it could be sculpted into various pleasing shapes.

The spell was a success, as the aunt had been practicing for many, many years.

However, it was the old woman's first attempt at magic outside her own home, and it had slipped her mind that her usually goat-powered spells needed to draw energy from something nearby.

The energy for the spell that would cause a pair of copper pliers to appear in just the right spot, and the energy for a spell that would cause a Minister of Decanter Production to topple in just the right direction, would have to come from some living thing nearby. You may find this surprising, but mountain goats are often scarce inside glass blowing facilities.

The aunt was reminded of this when a woman standing not 15 paces away from the Minister of Decanter Production fell down dead just as the minister plummeted to her own death into the fiery abysm of the factory's furnace.

The sight of the minister tripping on an errant pair of copper pliers might have been comical, had it not resulted in her horrendous demise.

The Minister of Decanter Production loved to style her snowy hair into a swirl atop her head, and on that day she was wearing a golden, honeycombed pattern dress with puffed sleeves as big as butterfly wings (butterflies in D'Kay being about the size of small horses). So when she tripped and fell, the whole incident looked not unlike a giant swirl of vanilla ice cream inside a toasted waffle falling comically into an oven and then screaming in agony while it burned alive.

Had it been a serving of ice cream and not an actual human being, it would have been hilarious.

The woman whose life was sacrificed so that the Minister of Decanter Production might die a fiery death, on the other hand, expired silently. The magic was quick and efficient – as most things were in D'Kay – and so the poor, deceased woman had no time to react to her own death.

None who ran to the yet-to-be-identified woman's body suspected magic. It appeared her heart had simply stopped beating while witnessing the horrific death of the Minister of Decanter Production.

The aunt didn't care about killing an innocent bystander, but she was worried someone might become wise to the cause of death. But her fear of being found out was transitorily eclipsed by a piece of more important news, announced by a factory worker who had rushed to the now deceased bystander.

"Oh dear!" cried the woman. "The Minister of Smooth Pavement Surfaces has died!"

The Vermilion's aunt hadn't known what the Minister of Smooth Pavement Surfaces looked like, as the Minister of Smooth Pavement Surfaces was very boring. Therefore, she was never interviewed or photographed for the local news services.

Had the aunt read that morning's edition, though, she would have known that the Minister of Decanter Production had invited the Minister of Smooth Pavement Surfaces to the factory that day to inspect the structure's pristine floors.

The happy accident set the stage for the many murders to follow.

Chapter 13

Did you know that a book's chapter can be as long or as short as the author wants?

Chapter 14

D'Kayans who took one of the daily newspapers (*The D'Kayan Body* if you preferred gossip, and *Truth D'Kay* if you wanted strictly facts) would notice a disturbing trend in the weeks following the Demantis Disaster, as it was deemed in the press.

The ministers throughout D'Kay seemed to have the unfortunate habit of dying in twos. One would experience a horrifying and bizarre fatality, which included crushing by large sacks of refined sugar at a local bakery, decapitation by the propellers of a capsized cruise liner, gouging by a wayward javelin at the university games, drowning in a vat of bitter wine at an area distillery, and spinal snapping from the wings of a newly-christened windmill. And with every grisly accident, another minister nearby seemingly died of shock.

With so many D'Kayans having at least a suitable education, it's no small wonder none of them figured witchcraft was behind the series of deaths. The fact is that the time it took to master magic in D'Kay was so long and so expensive that very few people actually pursued it as a line of work. Had magicians in this land been a bit more plentiful, then people most likely would have recognized the mystic arts in the pattern of deaths.

But that's neither here nor there as soon the only two women left in the line of governance were Margaret and Adelaide Vermilion. And this left just one more spell for their aunt to cast.

Chapter 15

It was at dinner, in the House of Vermilion, where the sisters and their aunt gathered somberly around the table. They were joined by the sisters' subordinate husbands, whose names are too unimportant to recount here. (A husband's purpose was to keep the house tidy, keep the children in line, and keep quiet.)

There had been so much death in such high positions that any amount of elation would be downright rude. So where the sisters would usually be laughing and carrying on, making light of Adelaide's husband's allergies ("Really dear, is there anything you *can* eat?") and commenting on Margaret's husband's inability to show happiness in his face ("Darling, you'd be so much handsomer if you smiled more"), they instead filled the time with grave discussions on the state of the State of D'Kay.

"The only course of action now is to begin appointing new ministers," said current Prime Minister Adelaide, who reverently poured herself a glass of wine. Her husband gingerly touched his own wine glass, hoping for a second helping as well. Adelaide refused, shaking her head at him scornfully. (She didn't like his ideas of independence when he consumed too much alcohol, you see.)

"I agree," said Margaret as she helped herself to a cut of the strange fish the cook had prepared. It had tasted deliciously like lamb chops.

Margaret pulled the plate away from her husband as he tried to lance a second helping, though. (She could see he had gained a couple of pounds, and she wasn't about to encourage a couple more.)

"And let's hope this cloud of bad luck lifts soon," she said, "or else the entire State of D'kay will fall into a state of disarray."

Their aunt stifled a small chuckle. Luckily, neither sister nor husband noticed her suppressed bouncing.

As the conversation continued, she decided now was as good as any to cast the final spell, putting her ultimately into the highest-ranking position in D'Kay.

She reflected a moment on how she'd wield her new power, and smiled at the thought of invading neighboring islands and conquering the main land. And who knows? Perhaps her army would be so powerful that they could find a way to get to the other side of the biconvex planet and conquer it, too.

She moved her fingers about in just the right way, and she muttered some words just audibly enough to be heard by the aunt alone. She drew in her breath, and focused on Margaret. The aunt felt her face go flush as the energy began to draw from nearby Adelaide.

The unexpected happened then, as the unexpected often does, and things went awry very quickly indeed.

Chapter 16

Adelaide's husband began gasping, and then choking. His face turned a very pale color of blue, a totally unbecoming look for this man.

You see, Adelaide's husband had all manner of allergies. The only meat to which he was not allergic was fish. The cook of the House of the Prime Minister was ordered to only purchase main course meats from the fishmonger so as to avoid any unpleasant allergic reactions.

Every other cut of beef, veal, turkey, quail, chicken, grouse, goose, duck, swan, pork, venison, wild boar, black bear, grey wolf, marmot, lamb, and goat caused his throat to swell shut, his skin to break out in a raised and red rash, and his body to stop functioning altogether.

It was a mystery why this dinner caused his allergy to flare as it did, as Adelaide Vermilion made doubly sure these fish filets that tasted so deliciously like lamb chops came from the fishmonger. The cook had promised they had, and may her "kitchen knives rust and her soup ladle never pour" if she was lying.

Adelaide jumped from her seat and ran to her husband's side.

As he choked and gasped for air, Adelaide reached into the pocket of her stately jacket with the puffed sleeves and removed a vial and a needle. She was about to administer medicine that had always done the trick when her husband went into fits of allergic reactions.

In one swift and elegant move, she uncorked the vial, drank its contents, and then shoved the needle into her husband's throat, puncturing the liquid that had gathered, opening a hole for him to breath, and causing green pus to spray from his neck.

The liquid in the vial, I'm told, was one of the House of Vermilion's finest spirits, which Adelaide was very fond of in times of stress.

But the needle, which usually opened a big enough hole to drain the affronting juice and allow for oxygen to enter the trachea, didn't do the job this time around. Nor did it work a second time. Or a third, fourth or fifth.

Soon, poor Adelaide's husband was dead, either from asphyxia or being stabbed countless times in the throat. It was all a jumble of magic and meat and needles and pus, and whether the allergic reaction was the cause of the mismanaged magic, or the magic was thrown off because of the unsuccessful attempt to combat the allergic reaction, one way or another, the spell ended up missing the mark and landed on Adelaide's poor husband instead.

But while Adelaide's husband was now dead and cold in his dinner chair, which the aunt found very disappointing indeed, the energy needed for the magic had still been culled from the nearest living creature – which just so happened to be Adelaide herself.

Adelaide's eyes went dead, and she slumped face first into her husband's dinner plate.

It was chaos. Margaret's husband screamed (men were prone to hysteria), and members of the Prime Minister's Secret Service were ushered in to examine the scene, ask questions, and try their hardest to appear as important as possible.

f course the aunt couldn't finish the deed that night. It would be suspicious if the remaining two heads of state, along with their servile husbands, all died at one dinner. Naturally, the suspect would be the person who survived – namely the Vermilion's aunt.

So she decided to bide her time just a little while longer.

Chapter 17

Days passed, and the State of D'Kay went into mourning. They'd lost not only their Prime Minister, but also the ministers of every other branch of government in the nation. There were, what seemed to be, an endless procession of funerals. Minister after minister was honored in her own service, each one requiring the shutting down of factories, the closing of schools, and the docking of boats.

Production came to a screeching halt, and as days turned to weeks, and weeks to months, D'Kay's financial standing began to drop. Countries across the sea ran out of Dee's Decanters, and with no more exports of the bottles, folks had to drink their wine poured straight from the bottle. It was then the people of neighboring lands realized the wine they were drinking wasn't actually bitter at all, and the decanter popularity was due instead to both one of the most successful ad campaigns in the region's history, and a slightly devious decanter company.

As this side of the world learned that D'Kay's decanters were a dupe (which was in fact news to even the D'Kayans), the island fell into disrepair.

There was no trade, no income, no taxes, no infrastructure funds and no social programs. The fishermen couldn't afford bate, so the fish monger closed shop. The butcher's cattle died, so the store was shuttered. Even the school had to shut down, as there was no money to buy the gas to keep the lamps lit.

It was at this time that D'Kay's years tripled in length, and their weeks went from seven days to twelve. The hours in each day grew exponentially, until it wasn't uncommon for the sun to stay sweltering in the sky long enough for the D'Kayan Body to print five issues (which eventually also petered out due to the cost of ink).

It would have been wise for the Vermilions' aunt to take action far sooner, but Margaret, having now assumed the position of Prime Minister, had secreted herself away in the House of Vermilion, barring the doors and locking the windows.

She had, since the fateful dinner where her sister and her sister's husband had both lost their lives, done the math, as it were. And while she hadn't pinpointed her own aunt as the culprit, she'd come to the conclusion that someone was using magic, and that someone's target was the governing body of the State of D'Kay.

With Margaret Vermilion hunkered down in the fortress of her house, her aunt had no way of accessing her to finish what she'd started.

She could have used magic to enter the house, but there were no more mountain goats or cattle from which to draw energy. If she could convince someone to accompany her to Margret's house, she'd have energy enough to break the bolts on the doors *and* the windows.

D'Kayans had, at this point, lost their will to do anything at all – especially go on random strolls with curmudgeonly old women.

So with no choice left, she decided she would simply have to set the House of Vermilion on fire, although it was a shame because the architecture was quite grand, and she had hoped to reside within its walls once the task of deposing her niece was out of the way.

So she set off to her own stately home to gather lumber, kindling, and a match.

But she never made it up the path. An unseen figure had been tailing her all day. That person, with a heavy stone in hand, walked dutifully up behind the Vermilion's aunt and swiftly cracked the back of her skull.

The Vermilion's aunt fell down dead.

Chapter 18

Here I am going to educate you on two things, as I'm sure you're rather confused at this point.

First, it's a known fact, that twins are hereditary in D'Kay. Margaret and Adelaide, had they had daughters of their own, would have had at least one set of twins in the bunch. And while their mother didn't have a twin, they did have two older aunts who were born on the same day just moments apart.

Second, it was not the story of Madame Veramilicent Vermilion we have been following this entire time, but her twin sister, Vida's.

And as you may or may not have guessed at this point, it was in fact Veramilicent who had plucked the rock from the path leading up to the stately home on the cliff, and it was she who strode purposefully up behind her twin sister, and it was she who took the stone and cracked it upon Vida's skull, killing her instantly.

You see, Veramilicent, too, wished to reign as a queen over D'Kay. But she was far lazier than her sister, though she preferred the term "smarter."

Vera took leave of the stately home on the cliff some many years ago, indicating to her sister that she desired to see the other lands across the sea. This left the heavy lifting to Vida, who spent the time and money gaining the powers of an accomplished witch. This left the dirty deeds to Vida, who used her magic to dispose of nearly every minister in the land.

While Vida was learning and killing, Veramilicent was going about her daily life as normally as she could, renting a room from the school's headmistress in the town below the House of Vermilion and staying generally out of sight.

Vera had intended on letting Vida take the role of Prime Minister before she made her move, but it was clear Vida had gone as far as she could. So she'd have to take her twin sister by surprise and kill her from behind. She found the perfect opportunity on the very day we're discussing now.

Mind you, Veramilicent was unaware of Vida's plans to kill their niece in an act of arson, so had Vera practiced just an ounce more of patience, she could have bashed her sister's brains in after the arson and become the next ruler of the land.

Chapter 19

There were two ways to gain magical skills in the State of D'Kay, in case you have forgotten. The first way is through many hours of practice, years of study, and an incredibly hefty sum of money for access to the magical texts.

The second way was to kill a person who already possessed magical abilities and eat her heart.

So that's what Veramilicent did.

She wouldn't discover until later the full price of this action, and she never considered for a moment that her sister might have guessed that Veramilicent might attempt this exact operation.

Mind you, Vida knew her sister quite well, and it had crossed her mind multiple times during her magical erudition that Vera just might try to kill her and consume her heart.

Vida had put a contingency plan into place, in a manner of speaking. It was a plan Vera would discover at a later time, even if she wouldn't recognize it.

Vera dragged her twin sister's bloody corpse into the stately home on the cliff where she resolutely cut out her heart and set it to boil with a sprig of rosemary and a clove of garlic, both of which she'd been saving in a satchel for nearly 20 years just for the occasion. Unlike her sister, Veramilicent actually *did* have a recipe for cooking heart, and she'd been holding onto the ingredients for decades.

The rosemary and garlic were dry and brittle and neither had much flavor, but the only recipe for cooking human heart that Veramilicent was able to find called for both, so both were added to the pot.

As the clock struck the hour, Vera took Vida's heart off the stove and placed it on a glazed terracotta dinner plate that was painted with bluebells and green ivy. She took a knife and a fork from the cupboard. She sat at the dining room table.

With small and polite bites, Vera consumed the entire heart, not leaving a single ventricle or valve uneaten. The power within the heart began to disseminate while Veramilicent's digestive tract went to work.

She didn't know it then, but she would eventually become the most powerful witch in all of existence, and it would destroy her.

Veramilicent Vermilion then stood up, quietly took the plate to the kitchen sink, washed it thoroughly, dried it with a freshly-pressed dish towel, placed the plate on the shelf above the chopping block, marched to the broom cupboard down the hall, opened the door, pulled down the magnificent hat box, removed the pointed pink hat, and placed it upon her head.

She stepped into the parlor, gathered a bundle of firewood, a basket of kindling, and a single match from the chestnut box on the mantle and set off down the lane to the House of Vermilion, where she intended to set fire to the home, kill her niece, and become ruler of the State of D'Kay.

She would have succeeded, too, if it hadn't been for a crack of blue electricity at that very moment, which struck her in the back and sucked her into a rip through time.

The next thing she knew, she was spilling out of the now busted capsule of a contraption in the laboratory of Dr. Gustopher C. Cerulean.

Step 3: Make Plans For Possible Early Onset Errors And Malfunctions

"In the study of traversing time and dimensions, it has become abundantly clear that if something can go wrong, it absolutely will. This is of course no fault of the builder or the operator of the machine. It is instead dimensions branching off from dimensions, creating new timelines, which could not have been created had something not gone afoul. The remedy to this is to simply be prepared to make repairs to the machine, and be prepared to entertain any new guests who might appear as a result of some malfunction.

– Dr. Gustopher C. Cerulean, as quoted in the copious notes of Bratticus L. Magleby.

Chapter 20

The Mayor of Bell, the Honorable Rudolf Baron MacBritches, or Rudy as friend, enemy, stranger and acquaintance called him, may not have been a man of action, per se, but he was a man of fashion. That was something that solidified his place in the high esteem of nearly every Bellian.

Rudy MacBritches' eyes were the color of emeralds, his tiepin an actual emerald. They were large – both eyes and tiepin – and were offset in a most complimentary way by the ember-red of his beard and eyebrows. Atop the shockingly carmine hair sat a purple bowler hat, which was accented by a green floral print hatband (rumored to be manufactured by a non-Bellian haberdasher, which was quite the scandal).

The city's leader was a huge man with shoulders as wide a kitchen table. Bratt had been told the mayor once lifted an entire steam engine above his head for a full six seconds, beating Kunfuson's previous record of five and one-half seconds. That record had apparently also been set by the mayor.

The fact that it was the mayor himself who told Bratt this with no accompanying evidence is completely beside the point.

MacBritches' shoulders, impressive as they were, were often a hindrance when the mayor wished to walk through doors. Since he wasn't in the habit of walking sideways, the City Hall, MacBritches' home, and the houses of all his closest friends and family had to be modified – the doorways widened at the top to properly accommodate the bulky Bell leader.

It gave select doors along the neat and tidy streets of Bell the appearance of coffin lids, which served a dual purpose as the shape tended to keep door-to-door proselytizers from neighboring cities at bay.

Any time the mayor found the occasion to call upon a home that didn't have a doorway fit to his specific shoulder needs, the occupants were required to set a full table on the front lawn, complete with bread plate, dinner plate, salad plate, table fork, salad fork, ice cream fork, soup spoon, caviar spoon, egg spoon, butter knife, steak knife, pilsner glass, wine glass, and tea cup – even if there was to be no food.

It was those wishing to fall into the good graces of Mayor MacBritches that kept both the local cutlery stores and the local carpenters in booming business.

He was a sharp man, both in dress and in form. The edges and creases on his body and his clothes were straight as rulers.

His green and purple three-piece was striped, giving him the appearance of a very large candy wrapper. His knickers buckled just below the knee, his calves adorned with a silvery silk stocking that plunged into two immaculately polished high heels, each accented with a large, emerald-studded buckle.

One might say he looked like an enormous leprechaun. But don't let's be silly. There's no such thing as leprechauns.

He was never without his most unique walking stick, which appeared to be a great green cobra, straightened out in some manner, its head curled into a handle. In its eyes sat two diamonds, which glittered beautifully along with his tiepin and shoe buckles.

The paralyzed snake wasn't to aid his walking, as MacBritches' muscular thighs were capable of supporting at least three mayors total. Instead, he would use the cane to rap children upon the head for kicking dirt on his polished heels.

In town, Mayor MacBritches was known as the second-tallest man, a runner-up to one Dr. Gustopher C. Cerulean, who was clever enough to take the title in such a competition. Bratticus, as I've described to you, was also a tall man, but his dress and demeanor made him appear smaller to others, so folks simply didn't believe the evidence when it was presented to them.

Oddly, it doesn't matter in which dimension you live or on which planet you tread, there are always groups of people who could have mountains of evidence dumped at their feet and they'd choose to ignore it altogether than admit they were ever wrong.

Had Bratticus L. Magleby poured attention into every buttonhole and seam he presented to the world every day, perhaps the fine people of Bell would be more inclined to acknowledge his elevation.

"Yes, but who paid for the measuring tape?" you'd often hear when the proof of Bratt's height was placed in the face of an average Bellian. "This is all a hoax to further line the pockets of those who make measuring tapes!"

But we're not discussing Bell's Annual Tournament of the Tallest Gentleman right now, so I'll thank you not to inquire further. Besides, I'm certain the competition is rigged. The winner – always Dr. Cerulean – only receives a cask of wine, while the runner-up – Rudy MacBritches – always wins a cash prize and a weekend getaway at the nearby resort nation, the State of Rappose.

So please, if you must satisfy your urge to read about immovable idiocy of people who refuse to acknowledge things even when mountains of evidence are dumped at their feet, then look elsewhere. I suggest reading about your elected officials in the local newspaper.

Chapter 21

The City Hall, where the mayor spent at least four hours per day, was more than four kilometers from the front entrance of Dr. Cerulean's apothecary, and it was at least four and one-sixteenth kilometers from the side entrance. It would take a man with Bratt's leg length nearly 20 minutes to stroll at a leisurely pace from the side entrance of the apothecary to the coffin-shaped door of town hall.

If he were to have pressed some particularly strong black coffee before leaving, perhaps he could make the trek in 15 without breaking into a run.

It was on this particular morning, the day after one Dr. Gustopher Cramden Cerulean was sucked into the core of a device that is capable of sending a man across time and dimensions, that Bratticus found himself working to replace some damage done when said doctor was lost to who knows where when he activated said machine. It was Bratt's priority, as he had to find Dr. Cerulean, wherever he was, whenever he was, and return him home.

One Madame Veramilicent Vermilion, who traveled to Bratt's home from her own, was busying herself about the doctor's workspace, looking through every last book, register, record, publication, album, log, tome, chronicle, ledger, account, catalog, notebook and receipt she could get her hands on. It was hard to say exactly what her goal was, but as long as she was out of Bratt's hair, then he was satisfied.

Between you and me, though, and I'll thank you not to repeat this to anyone, Bratticus's own copious notes in what seem to be endless volumes were always hidden in a chamber beneath his bed. The floor in his area of the large room was paved with river stone, one of which came loose when he tapped it at just the right angle with just the right force. Beneath it was a surprisingly large chamber – big enough for Bratt to fit into if he so desired.

However, he had no purpose in spending time crouched in hidden chambers below his bed, and the idea of anyone doing this purposefully is, quite frankly, preposterous.

Instead of hiding himself, he had found a better use for the hidden chamber beneath his bed. There were, give or take a few, nearly 100 notebooks filled with the accounts of his life, his many sketches and diagrams, and the detailed workings of Dr. Cerulean.

Suffice to say, Madame Vermilion did not see Bratt's notes. And because he was absolutely sure she wouldn't find them, he was happy enough to let her peruse the doctor's library, as it mostly contained varieties of recipes on bread pudding, clippings of town gossip from the local newspaper (The Bell Chime), and a remarkably lengthy book of dirty limericks.

As he worked to repair the contraption, Vermilion left his peripheral vision for no less than five minutes – he knew this because he'd glanced at his pocket watch to check the time, as lunch was just five minutes away. When the time came to eat, he scanned the workspace for Vermilion, but she was nowhere to be found.

He did a lap around the giant room.

She was not in his bed quarter, and even though he knew with certainty that a woman of her shape would never fit beneath his bed, he still took a glance at his hidden chamber to make doubly sure his notes were safe. They were.

She was not in the dining quarter, where he would have liked to have sat and eaten the loaf of bread before it became stale. She was not in Dr. Cerulean's quarter, where his bed sheets lay crumpled on the mattress (it was here that Vermilion insisted on sleeping, against Bratt's demands).

He knew for certain she wasn't in the northeast quarter, as she had remarked on it not but an hour before.

"There's an eerie mojo from that space," she declared, pointing a stubby digit in the northeast direction. "I'll never go there."

Bratt understood what she meant, but he might have begun to explore the northeast corner nevertheless had it not been for the side entrance. He distinctly remembered closing and bolting it the night before so as to dissuade a gaze of raccoons from making mischief inside (the little devils loved to spin the gears on Dr. Cerulean's machines in the dead of night, for some reason).

But now it stood open, and the daylight spilled in.

Chapter 22

Bratticus ran to the door and peeked outside. The sun was high, the immediate area radiated green and gold in its light.

Dr. Cerulean's apothecary was secluded from the rest of Bell, built on a grassy hill to the north of town. The side entrance faced the doctor's garden, filled with herbs, vegetables, spices, grasses, weeds, flowers, shrubs, clovers, endives, caraways, grains, inhalants, mosses and all manner of flora. A small meadow stretched beyond where Cerulean kept three goats and a llama. Beyond the meadow was a dense forest.

If one exited the side entrance and followed the garden path to the front of the apothecary, the road to town was visible, as was the town itself.

Bratt walked to the front of the apothecary and peered downward toward Bell.

While the City Hall was a great many steps away from the apothecary on the hill, he could still make out a round figure at the steps of the mayor's entrance, a bright pink hat perched atop it. It was Madame Vermilion. There wasn't another citizen of Bell so adipose or so short or so inclined to wear a pointy, pink hat.

He could only assume Vermilion made the trip so quickly from the side entrance to the steps of City Hall by rolling the entire way, as she made the journey in the time it took Bratt to notice she was gone and to check three of the four corners of Cerulean's laboratory.

Knowing what he did about her objectionable past, he didn't think it a good idea for Vermilion to be hobnobbing with the Bellians, particularly Mayor MacBritches. Who knew how long he'd have if she decided she wanted his position?

Bratt turned on his heels and ran back to the side door. He slammed it shut and then took off on foot in a full sprint toward Bell.

Had he paused to take in his surroundings, he might have noticed the doctor's prize llama, Gertrude, the poor chap dead as a doornail. Mind you, Cerulean was not in the habit of naming his livestock based on their genders. He named his livestock based on the name that would suit them best. In Gertrude's case, that name happened to be Gertrude. But Bratt's present attentions were not on llamas nor their names nor their current states of being.

Chapter 23

He thought he'd made the trip from the apothecary to City Hall in record time, considering how his clothes were drenched in sweat. His breath was as short as Madame Vermilion herself. But by the sight he saw after he opened the doors to City Hall, one might have thought it had taken him half a day.

There was Mayor MacBritches, leaning over an oak desk reserved for reception duties. He was grinning and chatting with Vermilion, who herself was seated in a plush armchair reserved for reception sitting. The two didn't even notice Bratt, despite his dripping and panting.

"I never knew he had any siblings at all!" MacBritches chuffed.

"Yes, well, this is the first time I've come to visit him. He usually makes the trip over to my neck of the woods," Vermilion chortled.

"My! If it isn't young Bratt!" MacBritches boomed when he glanced Bratticus's rumpled form. He straightened himself up and smiled a smile that had far too many teeth. "I've just met Dr. Cerulean's sister. What a magnificent creature she is!"

Vermilion turned to Bratt and batted her eyelashes, which gave the impression that two panicked spiders were trying to escape her eyelids. For what he knew of the woman, that might have been exactly the case.

"Yes," she crooned, "And Bratticus here has been a most gracious help as I keep an eye on the doctor's apothecary while he's away."

"I'm surprised you didn't come to tell me that old Gustopher was taking a sabbatical," MacBritches scolded Bratt playfully, pointing a gigantic, pink finger at his nose. "What if my coal boat had sprung a gasket? I would have made the trek to the apothecary for nothing!"

The mayor's coal boat was quite an invention, indeed. When stoked with enough fuel, it could reach speeds that rivaled any spooked horse, skidding across the waters of the Ridiculing River as a stone might when let loose at just the right speed and angle.

However, this is neither a lesson on coal boats nor the physical properties of surface tension, which allows for stones, coins and other objects of similar shapes to skip across water. I'm sure there's plenty in Bratt's notebooks on those subjects if you desire further knowledge in that area.

Bratt held his tongue for a moment and thought. Cerulean hadn't sworn him to any level of secrecy on the matter of traversing time and dimensions, and he couldn't stand by and allow some witch from another dimension, (though, as we've established, she was actually from the other side of the almond-shaped world) to lie, bald-faced, to the perfectly quaffed visage of the town leader.

"The doctor is not on sabbatical," Bratticus stated as he straightened his spine and narrowed his eyes at Vermilion, hoping his gaze of disapproval met its mark accurately. "He has been sucked into another dimension, and this woman –" here, he pointed an accusatory finger at her fat little face "– has taken his place."

Vermilion paid no mind to Bratt's pointing and merely smirked in his general direction.

"Yes, yes," MacBritches replied with a chuckle, turning his face back to Vermilion, his eyes sparkling. "I expect the doctor will return from his trip with all matter of stories and souvenirs. We shan't long for that return too greatly, though, if it means losing his fine specimen of a sister."

Now it was MacBritches' turn to bat his eyelids.

The mayor had ignored every word Bratt had said. This was not like him, as Rudy MacBritches was constantly listening to every bit of gossip he could wrap his freckled ears around, lest he miss a bit of juicy natter.

For example, Rudy couldn't help but to eavesdrop on information about the town's florist, Champs Bremière, and his latest affair with one of the many and beautiful Priazza Sisters (all of whom happened to be town pollsters, by the way). Or he might miss word about Champs Bremière wife's latest attempt at mistress disposal.

The mayor had also honed his skill at reading between the lines of town gossipers, since it was the only way to gauge his approval levels. The town's pollsters, you see, had an unusual habit of disappearing, for some reason.

Vermilion, through a side-glance that was not unlike that of a crocodile eyeing a zebra at the edge of a watering hole, saw Bratt's confusion at the mayor's inability to register his remarks.

The corner of her mouth turned up just enough to turn her dark red lips into a slanted grin. This, thought Bratt, was more unnerving than a crocodile smile.

Bratt gambled a bit with his next move. He knew Vermilion could easily dispose of him through her magical prowess, but he also knew her abilities could not get her back home. She needed him to fix the contraption, so he took a chance.

"Did you not hear me, MacBritches?" he belted. "This woman is a murderess and a witch! She is not the doctor's sister, nor is she a fine specimen of anything! Her motivations are malicious, and it is my goal to send her back to where she came from before she can wreak havoc on this town!"

"Oh, of course my boy!" MacBritches righted himself and, with a laugh, slapped a large, manicured hand on Bratt's back, nearly sending him toppling. The impact caused a spattering of Bratt's sweat to spray across MacBritches' impeccable suit, which on any normal day would have sent the mayor into fits. "There's no need to tell me when Dr. Cerulean will return. I'll make sure to keep his beautiful sister entertained in the meantime!"

This was not like the Honorable Rudolph Baron MacBritches at all.

Now, Bratticus L. Magleby had been daft before – every person in existence has been at some time in life. It's part of the human condition. Each of us has, at one point or another, licked a winter lamppost or urinated upon an electrified fence. It's how we learn, dammit! And yes, this was a moment where Bratt's daftness had resurfaced.

He hadn't encountered an evil witch before, so he was still learning about the matters surrounding such a foul creature. While you may have surmised Vermilion had cast some sort of an enchantment upon Bell's dapper mayor, the notion had yet to occur to Bratt. He'd had quite the exciting several days, and his mind wasn't exactly in tip-top form.

"Now, Bratt," MacBritches boomed, "be on your way! Someone has to keep track of the apothecary! Miss Vermilion and I have much to do! I've made it my purpose to escort this beautiful young lady on a tour of our fine hamlet!"

Stupefied and mouth agape, he watched helplessly as MacBritches bowed, allowing Vermilion to waddle out the front door. He followed behind, caught up to her, and allowed her to loop her swollen arm through his own. She glanced back at Bratt and winked.

Bratt didn't even try and suppress his shudder.

Chapter 24

Madame Vermilion had spent decades biding her time while her sister, Vida, did all the heavy lifting by disposing of any and all political enemies in the State of D'Kay.

To put it bluntly, what little patience she had in this new world was now spent.

The day had just begun in this new land when she found herself half-stuck in the doctor's contraption. By the time she'd been properly extricated and finally given a cup of something to drink (though she'd preferred sparkling wine to tea, and thus cast her magic spell), the sun had moved to the half-day mark.

That lily-livered apprentice had set to work tinkering on his infernal machine shortly after the drinks had been poured and just moments after he had disposed of the dead bat that had fallen from the laboratory's rafters.

She had first busied herself with a self-guided tour around the interior of the apothecary. She made mental notes of where everything was, paying special attention to any shelves and cupboards that housed books, documents, newspapers, journals, or any other sort of recorded materials.

The sun was getting closer to the western horizon, and Vermilion asked if she could "pretty please with chunks of chocolate" take a walk around the grounds outside. The apprentice was a pushover, and he agreed on the condition that he accompanies her.

That was just fine, she'd said, and the two spent the next hour walking around the enormous building outside.

Vermilion admired it. The trees and grass were a blinding green that didn't so much as shine in the sunlight as they did reflect it and illuminate everything with an electric chartreuse glow. There were even wildflowers of all shapes, sizes and colors, which she also found pleasant.

Her twin sister, Vida, was never fond of flowers, she remembered, and specifically hated yellow tulips. Vera, though, had no quarrel with budding plants of the annual or perennial sort.

She took note of the two goats and the stately llama, which all grazed peacefully in a tiny meadow beyond a garden full of vegetables and herbs.

At the base of the hill behind the building was a vast horizon of green forest, interrupted in a few places with jutting, black rock formations that looked to be the remnants of ancient volcanoes. Beyond the forest was a wide river – the Ridiculing River, in fact, the path of which made a sort of horseshoe shape around the vast grounds surrounding Dr. Cerulean's apothecary. On the east side, beyond the river, was a mountain range of spectacular height. The day was clear, but still, the peaks of the mountains had a few clouds tufted around the tops.

The reason for this was the eastern mountains easily caught clouds due to the peak's porous and sharp igneous rocks. And frankly, once a cloud was caught on the rough stones, it was hard for it to escape.

It was the city, though, which stretched out below the front of Dr. Cerulean's apothecary, that had Vermilion's interest most piqued.

It was dense in areas and sprawling in others. The cobblestone streets winded about through buildings of all sizes, making it almost appear as though a giant damask quilt had been laid across a hilly landscape. The main roads, large and wide, were all lined with cherry trees. She could see the river jutted directly up to one side of the city, where there were a series of docks and boardwalks, a few boats, and at least one long, stone bridge connecting to a road that squiggled off into the distance.

It was alive. It was a thousand times more desirable than the dump D'Kay had become.

That night, Vermilion insisted she sleep on the elegant, four-poster bed rather than the tiny cot the mealy little lab assistant had wheeled out for her. He protested at first, but she soon wore him down. She slept comfortably.

The next day, after putting herself together in the mirror (her eye and lip makeup had stayed quite nicely, thank goodness), she began to read. She read everything she could get her hands on, paying special attention to newspaper clippings. The pushover Mr. Magleby didn't even try to stop her. He just kept tinkering with the machine as Vermilion drank in information from every document she could set her eyes on.

Soon, she knew as much as she needed to know about the basic workings of this world and the City of Bell below. It was quite remarkable, she realized, how similar this world was to her own – if the effects of Vida's murders hadn't ravaged it, that is.

Why, even the language was the same.

Vermilion made up her mind then and there that D'Kay was a disaster, and she'd much rather be queen of a prosperous land, and this prosperous land would do so nicely. And thus her plans to become ruler of the State of Konfuson, beginning with the City of Bell, began.

She slipped out the side door of the apothecary as the young man twiddled about. Vermilion had realized he could have easily caught up to her if he noticed she'd left within the next three-quarters of an hour, so she conjured up a little speed spell to get her to the City Hall as quick as a flash (perhaps even quicker) where she could set her plan in motion.

That was the second time she'd used magic since gaining the powers from eating her sister's heart.

Chapter 25

Bratticus was, first and foremost, the very loyal apprentice to Dr. Cerulean. He was not, nor had he ever been, a detective. So it did not occur to him to check the mayor's office for signs of the City Hall's receptionist, Mrs. Hilda Von Cree, who had filed paperwork, dusted bookshelves, and turned away solicitors for every Bellian Mayor for the past five decades. It was true, she was an old woman, but she was spry in her age. Von Cree had at least one more term in her, if not two. Had Bratt had the wherewithal to go searching for her, he would have found her, dead, sitting in the mayor's chair, with no sign of a struggle.

He only found out about the receptionist's death when he read the evening edition of that day's The Bell Chime. It stated that Von Cree had died peacefully in her sleep, and hadn't it been nice that she'd died at work, which was one of her favorite places to nap.

The article was peppered with quotes from various elected officials who declared they'd expected old Von Cree to be stoking the bureaucratic fires for years to come. But there was no foul play suspected, and the coroner declared her heart had simply stopped. The townsfolk attributed it to old age, and Von Cree was buried in the city cemetery the following week.

Bratt had seen neither hide nor hair of Vermilion since he left City Hall that day. She'd gone off gallivanting with MacBritches, leaving him to fix the machine. He'd drudged back up the grassy hill after his encounter with the twitterpated mayor, and his resolve had strengthened to repair Cerulean's contraption.

It was when he approached the side entrance that he noticed poor Gertrude the llama, and it was then he began to do the math.

As a mathematician, it was a wonder he hadn't begun earlier. But until we've had to endure witchcraft and dimensional travel, with all responsibility for bringing our employers back from the recesses of space and time landing squarely upon our shoulders, we should not point the finger of blame.

Vermilion hadn't an athletic bone in her body, Bratt thought. She hadn't raced to town in less than five minutes. She'd magicked herself there, using the power from poor Gertrude. His anger boiled, as the llama was of the friendly sort and had kept the doctor and Bratt in sweaters all winter. However, he hadn't come to the conclusion that the mayor had been under some enchantment until he'd read the news of old Von Cree's death.

After placing that evening's copy of The Bell Chime down, Bratt knew Vermilion had used Von Cree to cast a spell on MacBritches, making him, and he shuddered to even imagine the notion, her love slave.

It was Madame Vermilion's third spell.

Bratt found himself unable to finish his supper at the very thought of MacBritches and Vermilion engaged in some act of carnal intimacy, and he tried desperately to put the image out of his head.

His mind clouded with repulsive images, Bratt was finding it difficult to figure out Vermilion's end game. What purpose did it serve to glamorize the mayor? She, after all, wanted to return back to her own State of D'kay, where she was on her way to ruling as queen. She'd begged Bratt to help her get home. Why would she suck the life out of both an essential work animal *and* Cerulean's llama to magic herself into the life of Mayor Rudy MacBritches?

What was her goal?

He sat pondering, seated on a stool beside the doctor's machine. The sun had set hours ago, and he could hear the raccoons pawing at the side door, wishing to get a good gear spin in if they could.

Chapter 26

Bratt was plotting, or at least attempting to do so, if it weren't for the annoying noises coming from the door. What was his next plan? How could he go about retrieving Vermilion from the enchanted clutches of MacBritches? Could he get her back to where she came from? And what of Cerulean? Was he in that place now, attempting to find a way back? Was he rubbing shoulders with the D'Kayans? Or was he being treated as a second-class citizen, as men in D'Kay were best suited for domestic chores only?

It was nearly impossible. The scratching at the door was aggravating!

Then Bratt noticed it wasn't a raccoon's nimble fingers making an etching sound. It was more of a rapping. As if some dwarf or fairy creature hidden in the dark woods beyond the fields had decided to come peddling wares at the side entrance to the apothecary.

This is only a parallelism, mind you. There's no such thing as dwarves or fairies – at least, not in this dimension.

Now that his attention was focused, he was aware that it was indeed a knocking. It was firmer than he'd originally heard, in fact. Nay, by the time his faculties were gathered enough to notice the sound, it was more of a pounding.

Could it be Vermilion, returned after a day of frolic and chaos? The door was bolted, and she didn't have a key. She could magic her way right in, Bratt was sure, and she wouldn't think twice about one of the doctor's beloved goats, the price surely to be paid for her witchcraft. No, this rapping wasn't hers. It was distinctly taller.

It was dark outside. Bratt was a young man who had seen very little of his world having barely ventured beyond the limits of his hometown, his university, and of Bell. But the past day two days had shown him many things he'd never thought possible, and he was positive he would be seeing many more impossible things. So of course he was hesitant to answer the door, although the rapping had changed to a banging at this time – desperate and angry. He was, not to put too fine a point on it, scared.

It was a feeling he'd only felt when gazing into the mysterious northeast corner of Dr. Cerulean's cavernous laboratory. It was a feeling of dread. But, as the new master of the apothecary, if only temporarily, it was his duty to answer doors and deal with whoever may be on the other side, be it solicitor, proselytizer, or uniformed girl selling cookies.

By the sound and strength of the now booming pounding, he doubted his late-night visitor was the latter.

He stood from his seat beside Cerulean's machine. It was many yards to the side entrance, and he began to walk. As he drew closer to the door, his trepidation doubled. His heart began to skip beats. He approached the entrance, slowly, mind you, and placed his hand upon the latch. It vibrated violently with the bang, bang, bang of the fist on the other side.

He drew in a deep breath. He flipped the bolt to the left. He turned the handle to the right. He opened the door.

There, in the inky night beyond the threshold, stood a young man with desperation and fury in his eyes. His clothes were odd – like nothing Bratt had ever seen before. His white shirt collar short and rounded, although he wore no tie. His overcoat was as black as the night itself, and it clung tightly to his body. His pants, boots and gloves were the same color. In fact, there wasn't a stitch of pigment in his attire, the entire outfit consisting of only blacks and whites. It would not have gone over well in the fashion-conscious city below.

In his hand he clutched a walking cane adorned with a bizarre, silver handle.

His coloring was very much like Bratt's. He stood at exactly Bratt's height and exactly Bratt's width. His posture wasn't exactly noteworthy –

his shoulders slumped forward slightly, in the exact same manner as Bratt's.

His eyes were the color of dark velvet flecked with snow. Or perhaps they were the color of spilled fountain pen ink dusted with gold. It all depends on whether or not they're lit by the moon or by a porch gas lamp, and whether or not you're inclined to make remarks on minuscule variations of the galaxy itself.

Bratticus L. Magleby knew this the man at the door. It was Bratticus L. Magleby.

Step 4: Make Preparations Should You Meet Another Traveler Of Time And Dimensions

"To assume that we are the only scientists to master the art of traversing time and dimensions is to assume that only one fish lives in the sea or only one busybody attends weekly church services. In an infinite number of universes, mathematically speaking, there are likely an infinite number of time travelers – possibly even more."

— Dr. Gustopher C. Cerulean, as quoted in the copious notes of Bratticus L. Magleby.

Chapter 27

Bratticus had for a moment the strangest sensation of glancing in the mirror, and he even turned to the one hung by the entrance to make doubly sure he was still himself.

"Well, well," said the man with a sneer, making Bratt wonder if his own face was that callous when he found himself unamused at something imbecilic.

He was dumbfounded as his doppelgänger shouldered past him and into Cerulean's lab. It was here he noticed his double's coat was wet, and it dripped a pathway from the side porch to the doctor's workbench, where he had finally stopped and turned around to face Bratt.

Bratt turned and looked out at the night sky. There wasn't a cloud.

Without further examination of the grounds outside the apothecary, he gingerly shut the door and faced this other version of himself.

One million and one scenarios played out in Bratt's head as to what could have brought this other Bratt to the side door of Dr. Cerulean's Apothecary, although 999,999 of those scenarios were highly implausible.

At this point in time, knowing what he knew of displacement and interdimensional travel, Bratt came to two possible conclusions: Either this was a version of himself from a time in the future, or this was a long-lost twin brother who had finally found him after years of searching. Bratt was, unfortunately, not in a position to telegram his parents to verify if the latter scenario were true.

"Who are you?" Bratticus demanded in what amounted to the most undemanding voice he'd ever mustered.

"I am you," the man answered with unperplexed composure.

Thus, Bratt's first assumption was correct.

"From the another dimension," Bratt stated, hoping to impress his double with his knowledge of time travel for some strange reason.

Bratt's double scoffed.

"I am the you from exactly three and two-thirds seconds away from here," he declared, pointing a finger at the ground.

"But how can that be?" Bratt asked. "Traveling backward on the path of time is impossible."

"I see," he responded, shaking his head. "So I've come to a place where my intellect is about as bright as the wallpaper in this room."

"But this room has no wallpaper," Bratt pointed out.

"You make my point exactly," he said brusquely before continuing. "Where is the doctor's machine? Do you know how it works?"

"There," Bratt said reluctantly, pointing beyond a cluster of chifforobes to the contraption. "I know of time displacement. In order for one to move about in dimensions he must bend time and trade places with an object of equal mass and —"

"I see this is where you are in your understanding," Bratt's counterpart said sardonically.

He spun toward the contraption, his wet coat spraying Bratt with water in the process. It occurred to him that he was quite rude, and he made a mental note to treat himself better if he ever met himself again.

"Is it complete?" Bratt's double called back over his shoulder. "Can it send someone across dimensions?"

"Yes," Bratt answered with a slight shout, tying to make his voice heard over the maze of furniture. He took a moment to close and latch the side door (raccoons, you know) before sprinting to catch up with himself. "Dr. Cerulean has already traveled, but I'm unsure how to get him back."

Bratt wiped the water from his face with a trembling hand as he caught up to himself.

The double, who at this point had reached the doctor's device and was eyeing it, turned his face toward Bratt and cocked an eyebrow upward.

"Already, you say?"

"Yes, and the machine is broken. I am trying to get it fixed quickly because —"

"Because someone from another dimension has found her way here and is now wreaking havoc in yours?"

"Y-yes. Yes! You see —"

"Dammit all," he said, stamping his foot slightly. He turned his attention back at the machine. He seemed to be searching for something particular.

Bratt had questions. So many questions.

"See here, uh, B-Bratticus," he said with a stammer, "you need to start explaining. Why are you here? What's this business of three and two-thirds seconds? ... Why are you wet?"

"I see your gears spinning, but they're not spinning fast enough," he replied. "First of all, if you think everyone has the same name no matter the dimension in which they exist, then, my lusterless little lookalike, your comprehension of science and philosophy is far inferior than I'd originally surmised."

Here he looked Bratt up and down.

"And, believe it or not, I didn't think that much of you to begin with."

Bratt's double began grabbing at mechanisms on the machine, unscrewing screws and unwashing washers.

"Hey - uh - YOU!" Bratt blurted, "I just fixed that!"

"My name is October," he answered curtly from the other side of the machine. "And if you know what's good for you, you'll stand away as I find ... aha! YES!"

Bratt was dumbstruck. This man — who shared the same name as his father's brother, coincidentally — had barged into the apothecary, soaking wet, no less, dressed down Bratt as if he were a servant before promptly prodding Dr. Cerulean's device as if he were at a butcher shop trying to decide which goose to purchase. But before Bratt could gather the courage to confront October, the man returned to his side, a small, silver globe clutched in his fingers.

"Good. This one is still intact, thank heaven." He paused and appeared to ponder something. "Or hell. I suppose it all depends upon your point of view of things, right?"

October's tone had become slightly less vexatious now that he had the item he'd been looking for. Bratt could see the object shining dully in the laboratory light. It was spherical, although it appeared to be punctured and scored at even intervals across one side.

Bratt recognized it as the contraption's filter, a device used to focus the essence of dark matter into a single line of energy.

Chapter 28

"Yesterday — your yesterday, I mean — something happened," October said as he gazed at the little silver ball. "Not just here, but everywhere — across all dimensions. It's as if the single source of power that drives all of our timelines was temporarily shut off. It only takes a moment in the dark before you trip over something and land somewhere you didn't mean to land. And when the light comes back on, you find yourself face-first into a chamber pot."

He looked from the orb to Bratt.

"That's the only way I can explain the phenomenon to someone with a feebler mind than my own," he stated.

Bratt, tired as he was of the insults, was too engrossed to interrupt.

"When the lights came back on, we'd all stumbled into places we didn't belong. If you think the issue in your existence is bad, you wouldn't believe the one I just left if I told you, which I won't.

"I've been traveling for at least a year of my life trying to find the source of this anomaly. I've been touring clusters of existences, but I can't get to the base of the thing. I think I'm close, though. In fact, my calculations show this specific timeline is the closest I've been so far to the root of The Peculiarity.

"And The Peculiarity is doing things I cannot even describe," October added.

"This 'Peculiarity,'" Bratt said, "Is it happening in every timeline, then?"

October pursed his lips and squinted his eyes, as if he were trying to avoid some dust storm of stupidity that had just erupted from Bratticus.

"Young man," October began slowly, speaking to him as if he were a child despite the fact that the two were most likely the same age, "Are you aware how quickly light travels?"

"Yes, it's something the doctor and I have been —"

"So how far away would you assume I am, in terms of differences, from you? How different is my upbringing? My education? My love life? My reading habits? Sleep schedule? Breakfast routine? Place of employment?" Here he looked Bratticus up and down again. "Sense of fashion?"

"Well, I suppose it'd be —"

"Exactly three and two-thirds seconds. Do you know how far light travels in exactly three and two-thirds seconds?"

Bratt began calculating in his head. As a mathematician, this was a question he knew with certainty he could answer. But it appeared October had the answer at the ready."

"That distance is 1,607,734.66 kilometers, give or take a few millimeters. So to answer your question, no, the things you've experienced in the past 24 hours and the things I have experienced in the past 24 hours *do not* happen in every timeline. However, they do happen in the cluster of timelines in which you reside, where light branches off only minutely due to nearly insignificant choices being made, creating minuscule differences barely noticeable, if at all."

The sentence was a long one, and October paused for a breath before continuing.

"This world may mirror the next world, which is less than one trillionth of a picosecond away from yours, in every single aspect. The only difference you'd find is that some woman in the town below is wearing purple bloomers instead of blue."

Bratt's eyes widened slightly at the thought, and he became exhausted just thinking about the type of field research October was apparently undertaking.

"Stop blushing. It's a purely hypothetical scenario," October responded to the look he saw cross Bratt's face. "Look, the point I'm making is that I believe this hiccup in time originated in your dimension — or a dimension close to yours — because I'm unable to get beyond these 24 hours, no matter which dimension in this cluster I jump to."

"It must have been the machine," Bratt answered quickly and, he hoped, helpfully. "When the doctor enacted the dimensional jump, it must have set off a reaction beyond this laboratory!"

October sighed and lifted his walking stick with the interesting handle into Bratt's line of sight. Bratt could now see it was a contraption; the silver handle itself looked more like the grip and clasp on one of the levers protruding from Dr. Cerulean's machine. Coiled around the collar was a transparent tube in which he could see a rotating collection of what appeared to be particles of light, though they weren't bright enough to be seen from several feet away. The transparent tube then ran the length of the shaft, disappearing into an eyelet just above the heel.

"Do you believe your Dr. Cerulean is the only scientist to experiment with traveling from universe to universe? And do you think he was the only one to fail? My dear boy," here he nodded at the walking stick, "this is a device of my own making, which allows me to travel dimensions at will."

"So Cerulean was not the first?"

"Nor the last. My machine is just one of many used by dozens of travelers. Those dozens equal an infinite number if you count each cosmic ray in their multitude of realities in which they reside."

Bratticus eyed October's walking stick device.

"And what of the displacement? Does yours —"

"My machine is able to handle the displacement correctly, save for one time when my mass switched places with a barrel of freshly-wrapped taffy. It was difficult rebalancing when I arrived home considering one of my colleague's sons had eaten five pieces of the candy. Luckily the thumb on his left hand equaled exactly five pieces of wrapped taffy, so now the boy has eight fingers and one thumb. He learned the important lesson of asking before eating someone else's taffy, and time and space remained balanced. Until now, that is."

October turned his gaze to Dr. Cerulean's contraption.

"My device is more practical, when you think of it. Mobile. Stylish. Probably far easier to use. But I must admit. Dr. Cerulean's machine handles dimensional displacement a little better. Since mine does not include a containment unit, it often switches the things around me with items from the places I've traveled."

He gazed at the doctor's invention a moment longer.

"Oh," he said, turning back to Bratt. "That reminds me. I hope you enjoy your new pond to the side of your laboratory."

October used the brief pause in the conversation to dramatically wring the water from one of his sleeves, creating what amounted to a pond inside the apothecary.

"I was in a dreadful hurricane when I left," he said. "So, naturally, a fair amount of water came with me."

Somewhere, in another dimension, a poor soul who's home had just barely survived a hurricane was now figuring out why there was a perfect circle of grass and a dead llama on his roof.

Chapter 28

"So it was not Cerulean's machine that set off this, this Peculiarity?"

"No," October answered. "However, I believe it was The Peculiarity that happened at precisely the same time Dr. Cerulean traveled, possibly causing his transport to malfunction. My theory is that this is the reason that woman, Vermicelli or whatever, landed in your universe.

"But things are worse in other places. Whole cities have been spirited away, leaving, well, I can't explain it. Leaving nothing. In other places, things have been moved about. Big things. Moons have rolled off their planes of existence and right onto planes in which the very idea of a moon is unfathomable. And in at least one case, a perfectly habitable planet found itself in a completely new galaxy with a dying star. The people on that world, I dare say, have but a thousand years left before they're consumed by a supernova."

"And," he paused, a somber look creeping onto his face, "I've already seen damage that can't be undone. And I fear if someone doesn't get to the bottom of this, our infinite universes will be unable to reconcile."

"Existence," said Bratt, "will cease to exist."

"More or less," responded October in a matter-of-fact tone one wouldn't expect from a man describing an end to all time and space.

Dear reader, while it was true that October knew many things Bratt didn't, it was also true there was much knowledge contained in Bratticus's mind that October could never fathom. October, though, was raised by a very smug pomposity of professors, who felt knowledge and skill were nothing unless they were bandied about like a poodle in a dog and pony show.

The thing about dog and pony shows is they feature not just dogs, but also ponies. And a barking dog, while impressive and intimidating, could easily be trampled accidentally by a large and silent mare who was merely walking to receive her winnings at the Semi-Annual Bosters and Flang Amazing Prize Pony and Pooch Extravaganza and Raffle.

Any Bellian would be more than happy to educate you on the logistics of the Semi-Annual Bosters and Flang Amazing Prize Pony and Pooch Extravaganza and Raffle. (It was one of the many ostentatious events held in Bell each year.) The ponies were just as important as the pooches, despite the fact that they were completely different animals altogether.

But we're not here to discuss matters of equine, canine, shows and raffles. I'll thank you very much for staying on topic.

With the grace of a magician, October palmed the tiny silver globe he'd removed from Cerulean's contraption. He then opened a panel just beneath the handle of his walking stick. From it, he withdrew a tiny sphere, which was nearly identical to the component he removed from Dr.

Cerulean's machine. Scored and punctured in intervals on one side, smooth on the other. This one, however, was pewter in color and appeared to have been scorched.

Bratt was astounded. The doctor's filter, which made dimension-hopping possible in the first place, was identical to the one October had plucked from his own machine. The only difference was that October's had been used up and was no longer functional.

October chucked the marble-sized object over his shoulder. Bratt watched as it gathered shreds of metal filings from the unswept floor with each bounce, making it appear more and more like a tiny, mechanical hedgehog the farther away it got. It bounced its third and final time, landing it on Cerulean's workbench. It clanked to the canister that housed the suspended atom and clung tight.

"Magnetization," October said as he plugged Cerulean's filter into the socket left vacant by his own. It fit perfectly. "The process has a tendency to realign the atoms to create a fairly powerful magnet."

Bratt, of course, knew this, having helped build the machine and the filter. He didn't respond, though. Instead, he crossed to the workbench and picked the cylinder up delicately. He hoped the magnet hadn't had an effect on what was inside. While Cerulean hadn't given him all the details on this particular contraption, he did know two things specifically.

One was that the energy a tiny little atom could release would be magnificent and could power a million dimension-traversing machines simultaneously. The second was that the power could have an after effect to anyone unfortunate enough to be near it when it's activated. At least these were the things the doctor had told him.

He looked down at the metal canister, now with its own little metallic, magnetic growth. It appeared to be stable.

"What is that?" October nodded to the cylinder.

"A device of Dr. Cerulean's," Bratt responded. He was determining whether to remove the magnet, unsure if it would disturb the canister's delicate inner workings. "It's a source of energy, although it can only be used once, I'm told."

October, though he asked the question, didn't pay much attention to the answer, as is often the way of bullheaded men.

Bratt was going to tell him that it housed an atom, which could be pulled apart and create a reaction with the power of a very tiny sun. Seeing his apathy, though, he instead decided to ask October a question of his own.

"Why on earth would the doctor's component fit your machine exactly?"

October's eyes met Bratt's, and Bratt could see he wanted to reveal something.

"All I can tell you right now," October said hesitantly, "is that Dr. Cerulean is not who he says he is."

There suddenly came a gentle rapping on the apothecary's side door.

Interlude 2: October F. Magleby, A Brief History

I'll issue you a warning, dear reader. Every tiny decision you make creates a diverting path in your life. Those two paths will then diverge when your two counterparts make two separate decisions. So yes, somewhere in time and space there is a version of you who pilots an enormous airship and holds lavish parties in the middle of the sky.

These alternate timelines most often break apart, millisecond by millisecond, from tiny decisions such as choosing the purple socks over the green pair or choosing to eat stew for dinner instead of a baked potato.

Some decisions and actions, though, can have extreme consequences and send two timelines shooting off from each other in near opposite directions. This is an example of just such a case.

Chapter 29

You will never be able to find the Village of Wax for two reasons.

First, it is because it's in a very hidden and remote location. To get it to it, one must journey through the Forcible Forest, which is so dense the very leaves have their own gravitational pull. It makes traveling through it very dangerous indeed, considering the constant barrage of objects being flung into its gravimetric field. One then must ascend the Mephistophelean Mountain, with cliffs so sheer that a man could easily check his hair in the reflection of the stone during the 3,000-meter ascent. Finally, one would have to find a way to traverse the giant Lake Lysergia atop the huge mountain, in which the Village of Wax sits comfortably on an island in the very center.

Lysergia was the color of peacock feathers, or perhaps it was the color of a melted turquoise stone. It all depended on the temperature of the water and whether or not you're inclined to make remarks on minuscule variations on shades of blue.

The same volcanic anomaly that created gravitational flora and glassy mountains also generated gasses so toxic that they acidified the lake. The people of Wax found the lake water served multiple uses, including keeping their silver polished with just a single splash, dabbing a drop to remove unwanted facial blemishes, and submersing murder victims to get rid of evidence.

The second reason you'll never be able to find the village of Wax is because the volcano beneath has long since violently erupted, blasting even the memories of the forest, the cliffs, the lake, and the village into oblivion.

Of course, our story takes place just before that fateful geological event.

Monsieur Bartholomew Benoit Magleby and his wife, Madeleine, had recently inherited a cozy cottage in the Village of Wax after Bart's accident-prone uncle Oggie tripped on an untied shoelace and fell headfirst into Lake Lysergia. This was a stroke of good luck – for the Maglebys, at least – as Madeleine was pregnant and had wanted to find a safe place to raise her child. In a not totally unrelated motivation, the two were also happy enough to seize the opportunity to go where their creditors most likely would not be able to reach them.

Wax was a retirement village, for all intents and purposes. People were not born there. They only moved there (usually with much difficulty and plenty of help from friends with asinine amounts of rope) when they'd had enough of their lives in the hustle and bustle of their own cities.

The Maglebys, having lived in just such a hustling and bustling city full of businessmen and banks constantly wanting their loaned money back, decided to make it their home. Neither Bart nor Madelaine, after all, were volcanologists, so neither understood the inherent danger of relocating to such a place as the Village of Wax. Once the cottage's deed had been placed into Bartholomew's hand, he and his wife packed their belongings and took their hot air balloon to the top of Mephistophelean Mountain.

Fate had smiled upon them since they'd never had the occasion to use their hot air balloon. Bart had purchased it on a whim several years ago, and the couple had only missed two payments on it so far, so it was one of their few possessions left to have not been repossessed.

Wax was a perfect place to call home. The streets were wide enough for a team of six horses, harnessed side by side, to pull grand carriages from one side of the island to the other. Never you mind that there were no horses on Wax. It should satisfy you enough to know that, if there were, they'd have more than enough room on the roads.

The buildings were low and friendly, and Wax did not include a single structure that was more than two stories tall. This, more or less, made all the residents feel comfortable knowing none of them could show off any ridiculous riches by building a huge mansion or multi-level shop. Wax was inhabited by humans, though, so it should be noted there were a few braggadocios residents with ridiculous riches who would have loved to build towering mansions or brownstone skyscrapers. Unfortunately, every time they tried, the weight of their structures sank into the rock beneath them, which was incredibly pliable, for some strange reason.

It was because of this that there were at least five buildings on the island with basements as deep as cathedrals are tall. It was a shame none of those underground rooms were much use, though, as they had the tendency to fill with the same vibrant blue waters that surrounded the island.

The noxious gasses from the magma-filled caverns beneath Mephistophelean Mountain also imbued all who lived there with a constant state of euphoria.

The citizen's lives, like the oxygen around them, were light. There were very few arguments, as the people could never quite remember what it was they were fighting about in the first place. Everyone, in fact, seemed happy at nearly all times, and it wasn't uncommon for the villagers to break out in laughter no matter the occasion.

They'd always find something to giggle about during conversations with each other or conversations with themselves. There'd be sudden bursts of chuckling from people walking down the street in pairs or alone. It was common to hear chortling from inside the water closet, and you could guarantee a good cackle or two from anyone who looked in a mirror. There were constant guffaws during meals, and no one could escape breakfast, lunch or dinner without having sprayed tea from their noses or be sprayed upon by someone else's nose tea.

People laughed when they slept, they laughed during philosophical contemplation, they laughed when they were injured, and they laughed while attending funerals.

Whether it was the elevation of the village, the width of the roads, the size of the buildings or the geological anesthetic, something about Wax sparked vigor in Bartholomew he hadn't felt in years. After only one week living in their newly inherited cottage, their first child was conceived.

Nine months later, give or take a few days, the boy was born. He was a healthy baby, and Madeleine lived through the birth, which I can't say was common for mothers during those days. Madeleine felt no pain at all during the process, and, as a matter of fact, laughed through the entire ordeal, as did the midwife, the doctor, and Bartholomew, who laughed even while passing out from the sight of the parturition.

The child, who was born laughing, was a very healthy 4.5 kilograms. He hadn't any hair on his head to speak of just yet, but his skin glowed a healthy pink and his eyes were nearly the same enchanting blue color as the Lake Lysergia itself.

Chapter 30

You'll be wondering why a writer would dedicate so many words to the description of a person's eyes, telling the reader in previous chapters that they looked like galaxies orbiting black holes and they were hypnotic and intense, only to then inform the reader that they were a simple color of blue at the time of birth. It just so happened that, on the day of the babe's birth, there appeared above Mephistophelean Mountain a peculiar sight. It, as you'll see, has everything to do with the color of the infant's eyes.

The Peculiarity hung above the mountain for exactly one hour. It was circular, flat, and hovered mere inches away from the highest peak. It was perhaps two feet in diameter (or one, if your shoe size was a little larger). It stood upright, and one might mistake it for the evening sun setting above the mountain's summit — if the evening sun had the appearance of water emptying into a lifeless void, beyond which something terrible awaited even the most nihilistic mind.

Suns, however, don't look like that. So no one in Wax would have made that mistake, had anyone actually seen the oddity.

Instead, the villagers were too concerned with the sudden appearance of fire in places fire should not be. Mr. and Mrs. Wheeler were incredibly distraught as they went to turn in early that evening only to find their bed completely engulfed in flames. Old Countess Opal was scolding her man servant for burning her toast yet again, believing it was his fault that the whole house was currently aflame. And Claude Van Hart, bless his bottom, at first thought he must have eaten something entirely too spicy the previous day. He was the first official casualty of the Mephisthelean Mountain eruption when he gathered that day's newspaper, walked into the water closet, had a seat, and was then promptly launched through the roof and off the mountain altogether.

He laughed for his entire trip and only stopped laughing when his body was flattened upon the floor of the Forcible Forest.

At the Magleby residence, however, the new parents had stopped finding all these situations so funny. They could see out their window that the waters of the lake were literally boiling. Homes around them were bursting into flames. The wide roads that gave so many of the residents so much joy were now beginning to run red with glowing lava.

They could leave, of course, but a hot air balloon takes time to inflate. And even if time was on their side, getting a hot air balloon to work properly when the air surrounding it is even hotter can be a bit of a struggle.

It was at that moment, however, that a strange man burst into the

Magleby's front door. He was tall and thin and wore dark goggles over his eyes.

"Quick!" the man exclaimed, "You must get out! The balloon is at the ready!"

"But who –" Madeleine began to ask, her babe clutched in her arms.

"There's no time Maddy!" Bartholomew shouted. "Follow him!"

Bart ran up to the man.

"You say the balloon is ready?"

"Yes."

"And it will fly in this heat?"

"I have added an extra piece of equipment that will allow flight. Now hurry!"

"Who are you, stranger?"

"Get to the balloon, you fool!"

Madeleine, Bartholomew, the babe and the stranger fled the house. True to his word, the stranger had the Magleby's balloon fully inflated in the family's back yard. Bart took the baby from Madeleine's arms and instructed her to enter the gondola. Once she was inside, he handed the child to her and climbed inside himself.

The stranger opened a panel on the basket's side and flipped a switch. There came a sound like something you'd hear if you put a seashell up to your ear, and the seashell suddenly blew bursts of flames at thousands of kilometers per hour onto the side of your face.

The balloon began to rise. The stranger only stood there.

"Aren't you coming?" shouted Bart above the sounds of the balloon gondola.

"I'll be fine!" the stranger shouted back. It was then Bart saw the man reach into his breast pocket and pull out a pocket watch. The man appeared to fiddle with the watch's latch, though the thing's cover was not opening.

Madeleine, who was also watching the stranger, noticed another man exiting their home. He looked very similar to the gentleman who just helped them escape certain death. Why, he even wore the same goggles. The second man appeared to be looking for something. When he turned his head toward the rising balloon and the stranger with the pocket watch, Madeleine could tell the second stranger had found what he'd been looking for.

There was a mad dash. Before the Maglebys knew it, the two men were fighting. Bart thought he heard something to the effect of, "You have to let them die!" but it very well could have been "You had the apple pie!" After all, the gadgets that had been applied to the balloon were quite a barrier to eavesdropping on the conversations of dueling strangers.

With fires and fights and gadgets and strangers being such a distraction, no one looked up to see what was going on so near to the balloon. No one, that is, except the baby.

The child opened his blue eyes, gazed toward the sky, and looked directly into The Peculiarity. Something beyond The Peculiarity looked back.

Like the ancient myth of Medusa, the child was transformed when he looked into the gaping maw of oblivion. Only instead of turning to stone, he was transformed in another way. His eyes immediately darkened, and had the baby continued to watch the thing that watched him back, perhaps even more of him would have been transformed. Circumstances being what they were, though, the baby's attention was drawn away in a split second by the cacophony around him.

It is here that the timeline of October and Bratticus split. Yes, there are arguably infinite timelines, each with a Brattics or October, each one created by a small event or decision with just enough cosmic force that it causes the light upon which they're traveling to bend ever so slightly away from its previous ray. But we're learning about a major event right now, and this story would but much too long for reading if we were to delve into every minute splinter of time.

Chapter 31

The gondola was now exactly 2.289 meters off the ground.

"Bratticus! Stop!" Madeleine heard one of the men yell.

Then one of the men broke free from the struggle and ran to the balloon. It was he – the man who set the scene for the family to escape. The man still held the pocket watch, and he was furiously clicking the latch release as he ran. His face was panicked. Madeleine placed the child gently on the gondola floor. She and Bart reached for the man's arms in hopes of pulling up. The stranger jumped, but he barely missed the basket. The balloon's engines took full force at that moment, and the family flew safely into the sky.

The two men stood below, watching as Bartholomew, Madeleine, and their new baby, disappeared.

The Forcible Forest at the base of the mountain burst into a blue and white inferno. The glassy stone of Mephistophelean Mountain glowed a brassy color and then began cracking. The turquoise waters of Lysergia Lake disintegrated into a toxic mist. And, within seconds, the Magleby family's brief home was destroyed when the mountain erupted into a chaotic form of fire and stone.

The Maglebys watched in sadness and in awe at this sight. They didn't even see The Peculiarity and the giant, reptilian eye that drifted into the anomalous oculus. It blinked a huge, dark grey lid over rusty orange sclera, electric green pupil, and a black iris in the shape of a vertical almond. The peculiarity then slowly disappeared into the mist and smoke of the eruption.

Bart and Madeleine, who landed safely more than 200 kilometers away, never understood exactly what happened. But they did know this man, Bratticus, they'd heard him called, had known somehow that the village of Wax was going to be destroyed that day. He had saved them, and, had it not been for the sudden appearance of another stranger, they might have been able to save him, too.

Bartholomew steered the balloon to safety, getting the vessel as far away as possible from the now vaporized Mephistophelian Mountain.

The two would eventually sell the balloon, using the money as a down payment for a new home. Their creditors from the past had assumed the Maglebys, like everyone else in the Village of Wax, had died in the dramatic explosion that could be seen for miles around and would be told of for years to come.

Things being what they were at that time, nobody came looking for Bartholomew and Madeleine again, and the two made a pact to pay all bills on time lest they have to escape to yet another doomed village and eventually rely on some magical stranger to save them at the last minute.

In honor of the gentleman who'd ensured their child would live and they would get a second change at living a normal life, they named the babe Bratticus.

Chapter 32

The gondola was now exactly 2.289 meters off the ground.

"Bratticus! Stop!" Madelaine heard one of the men yell.

Then one of the men broke free from the struggle and ran to the balloon. It was he – the man who set the scene for the family to escape. Madeleine placed the child gently on the gondola floor. She and Bart reached for the man's arms. The stranger jumped and grabbed hold of the two outstretched hands. The balloon's engines took full force at that moment, and the stranger's weight pulled Madeleine and Bart from the basket. Only the baby remained inside.

Madeleine realized then that it was *not* the man who had saved them. It was the second stranger – the one who had appeared at the door after the Magelbys had boarded the gondola. He had purposefully pulled them from the vehicle.

The two men were identical, both Madeleine and Bart could now see.

The three fell to the hot earth below, and Madeleine screamed. Bart made a mad dash toward where the basket had been, jumping into the air in a completely futile attempt to reach his son, who was now far above them.

Dammit!" said one of the strangers.

"Oh, dammit yourself!" said the other.

"This shouldn't have even been attempted!" the first man replied.

"You'll thank me later," the second man said with a sneer.

Bartholomew and Madeleine looked on in abject horror from the balloon that held their baby to the two men and then back to the balloon. They were completely unable to speak.

The two men, whom the Maglebys decided must have been twin brothers, noticed the gaze of the man and woman beside them.

"I'm sorry, mother," said one stranger.

"It's about to blow," said the other. "Are you staying? Or do you have plans for the future?"

"Fine."

The two men stared at each other. The second man reached into his pocket and withdrew a pocket watch. It was identical to the watch the first man held. They punched the latch releases at the same time, and as they did, they each stepped away from each other.

One of the strangers appeared to be sucked into a sphere of blue electricity. He was gone.

The other stranger, though, seemed to be having trouble. He clicked, and clicked, clicked. The pocket watch did nothing more than sit there telling time. His face panicked as he looked toward Bartholomew and Madeleine.

The Forcible Forest at the base of the mountain burst into a blue and white inferno. The glassy stone of Mephistophelean Mountain glowed a brassy color and then began cracking. The turquoise waters of Lysergia Lake disintegrated into a toxic mist. And, within seconds, Madelaine and Bartholomew were killed when the mountain erupted into a chaotic form of fire and stone. They didn't see the stranger, whose pocket watch latch release finally deployed, as he, too, was gone in an instant in a ball of blue electricity.

Chapter 33

The child and the balloon eventually landed safely more than 200 kilometers away. The vehicle was discovered by a group of scholars from Ansford-Upon-Uptonshire-On-Tees University who were out having a picnic and enjoying the view of a distant volcanic eruption.

How this baby in a balloon came to land upon their potato salad was a complete mystery. One of the gentlemen rifled through the belongings packed inside the gondola while another perused the balloon and its addition of some sort of motor.

The scholars used the occasion to practice some of their newest interjections.

"Fiercely fascinating!" said Professor Friday F. Jones, reading a piece of paper through his pair of ridiculously thick spectacles. "The only piece of information I could discover as to this bairn's identity is a deed for a home atop the Mephistophelean Mountain in the name of one 'October Magleby.'"

"Well, clobber my clock!" blustered Emeritus Professor Horoatio Q. Jones through a billowy, white beard. "The very mountain that has just been blasted to Kingdom Come?"

"Googly gadzooks!" exclaimed Associate Professor Thaddeus G. Jones, his thin, black mustache looking like a circumflex over the "o" of his mouth. "This balloon has been upgraded with all manner of devices, beyond any scientific machinery I've ever encountered!"

"Alabaster academia!" said Adjunct Professor Percival A. Jones as he cradled the curious child in his arms, "the baby has the most peculiar eyes. I dare say he must become our charge. Serendipity is science, as we all know and have proved many times over."

"Oh, tits," said Assistant Professor Reginald T. Jones despondently. "I spent half a day on that potato salad."

The only man in attendance who didn't speak was Headmaster Purpureous P. Jones, who watched the scene unabashed. He was tall and wore an umber-colored turf top hat. On his hands were immaculately white kit gloves, and a fanciful, green cravat covered his neck. Headmaster Jones wore a long tailcoat the color of tangerines. Or perhaps it was the color of a begonia. It all depended on how much volcanic dust had dimmed the sunlight, and whether or not you're inclined to make remarks on miniscule variations on shades of orange.

His face was hidden behind an impressive salt-and-pepper beard. Upon his nose was a pair of gold wire, purple-tinted spectacles. His eyes were completely imperceptible behind the dark glass.

Step 5: Find Alternate Sources Of Energy Whenever And Wherever Possible

"When traversing time and dimensions, one will often encounter obstacles that require on-the-spot improvisation. In such instances, one must look to one's surroundings and utilize any and all tools available at that time. This could come from all manner of commodities, including but not limited to extraordinary powers of certain individuals and their possessions."

— Dr. Gustopher C. Cerulean, as quoted in the copious notes of Bratticus L. Magleby.

Chapter 33

If you've never been under the sea on a Wednesday during springtime, just before the sun rises, I highly recommend it. It's a tranquil place to gather one's thoughts among a bevy of ocean life that are, usually, apathetic to your affairs and therefore will keep any secrets you might let slip.

Of course, you'll want to do so in a safe manner. One cannot simply dive into an ocean on a Wednesday during springtime, just before the sun rises, without the proper equipment. Otherwise, any number of unfortunate incidents may occur, including dying by hypothermia, dying by drowning, dying by strangulation from giant squid, and, if you're unfortunate to be near a whaler with very poor eyesight, dying by harpooning.

It just so happened that Miss Molly St. Mercalli, who had a fear of being harpooned, owned exactly the right equipment. Her steel submersible – named The Presidio – was 30 feet long with an enormous window on one side made of glass a foot thick to allow occupants to stare in awe at whatever may be on the other side.

The submarine was painted red so as not to confuse any nearsighted whalers. It could hold 10 people, a dining table, a buffet, and a phonograph. It was the perfect place to host underwater dinner parties, if Molly wanted to host underwater dinner parties, which she did not.

Where a buffet might go, Molly instead placed a bureau filled with an abundance of ingredients contained in flasks, bottles, vials, jugs, pouches, bowls, sacks, flagons, bins, cans, bags and cigar boxes.

In the area a phonograph might be placed, Molly instead had a round table covered in a velvety black cloth. Atop the black cloth were placed two candles (unlit unless absolutely necessary) and a crystal orb that would capture sunlight and spray it into rainbow curvatures upon nearby surfaces (that is, if the crystal orb were in the sunlight, which it was not, because it was currently in a submersible beneath the sea).

And where a dinner table would have fit quite nicely, Molly instead had a large slab of black obsidian, the surface of which was as reflective as a freshly polished mirror. It was roughly the length and breadth of a coffin, although it was never intended to have someone buried in it – mostly because it was a slab of obsidian, and trying to bury a body inside a slab of obsidian is, frankly, impractical.

Upon the sides of the stone were carved multifarious runes, symbols, marks, icons, notations, ciphers, numerals, integers, cryptograms, and the letters "MsM + VS 4 EVER," which were inside a crudely-etched heart. It was a remnant of a romance with an up-and-coming alchemist. The alchemist had completely and utterly forgotten Molly when she ascended to the top of her class and was hired immediately upon graduation. It was mostly due to the amnesia concoction she'd brewed for her in order to quell her infatuation. She had ambitions far beyond romance and alchemy, thank you very much.

Though Molly still found herself thinking about the woman every now and again, imagining a life that could have been.

Upon Molly's stone was placed an ever-changing collection of items, depending on the project she was undertaking. Today, she'd placed upon it a cherry, a bluebird's feather, a bit of red wool, a broken pocket watch, and a purple pin. The items were arranged around a large, flat, wooden disk upon which was carved a five-pointed star.

Molly was bent over the altar, her arms on either side of the trinkets, her head bowed in exasperation. Two people stood behind her, watching. She had been working for days attempting to fix something, but the problem was she didn't know what it was she was trying to fix.

She only knew she had to do something about it.

Molly's black hair hung only slightly across her face. It was cropped to her neckline, straight and severe. She had long ago disregarded the popular style of piling the hair upon the head and holding it in place with all manner of pins and combs. She'd found the pins and combs would often fall upon her altar, which then spoiled her spells, with unintended consequences to follow. One of her ruined spells ended up getting the president of her nation assassinated. (She felt little guilt over this, though, as the man who succeeded him was far better at the job.)

Molly's skin was the color of chocolate, and her eyes were the color of mint. Or perhaps they were the color of moss. It all depended on how bright the bulbs burned inside her submersible, and whether or not you're inclined to make remarks on minuscule variations on shades of green.

Those eyes pored over the items placed at the star's tips. Cherry. Feather. Pocket watch. Cloth. Pin. They were pieces to a puzzle, although Molly felt like she was attempting to assemble an image without having any idea what the image was and using components from different puzzles. It was all rather, well, puzzling.

"Well?" asked a gruff voice opposite her.

A stone-faced man, stoic in the way one is when someone is trying to compensate for other, less unimpressive traits, stood behind her. His dark eyes peered through wire-rimmed glasses; his square jaw was tufted with muttonchops. Standing beside him was a tall woman, dressed in an expensive black dress. She had long, white hair that was gathered loosely at the nape of her neck – fashionable and effortless. She wore an ebony-colored Merry Widow hat with a black rose held in place by a hatpin adorned with a single, large black sapphire. Even in the perfectly still air of The Presidio's interior, the gathered strands of her moon-colored hair waved slightly as though they were underwater.

"Give her a moment, Byzantium. Molly knows what she's doing," said the woman in words that sounded simultaneously soothing and unnerving.

The woman's imposing and intimidating demeanor was matched only by her startling beauty. She was neither young nor old, and in fact her exact age was never truly known and was completely impossible to decipher by her appearance. And one found out very quickly that attempting to guess the woman's age came with almost immediate consequences. In fact, you'd be hard-pressed to find any survivor who tried to estimate the age of Mistress Artemis Vix.

Molly made brief eye contact with Vix, and then glanced at Byzantium Screech.

Truth be told, she didn't like either one of them, particularly Mr. Screech, whose gruff disposition seemed to dissipate any time he didn't have Vix to shield him from any actual malice. If he were to encounter a ruffian in the dead of night while ascending alone up Lombard Street, chances are he'd be discovered the next morning, shivering in a fetal position minus any cash and precious metals he'd had on his person the evening before.

Of course such a thing would likely never happen. Mr. Screech had an uncanny ability to hide himself, even when people were looking directly at him. It was his own little magical talent that had averted midnight muggings on more than one occasion.

Still, there was an amount of respect to be paid to Mr. Screech. Molly's where and when was not like the State of D'kay, where women were the ruling gender in society, in government, and in household. Luckily for

Molly, Mr. Screech was still in her submersible, doing work for Mistress Vix. And Mistress Vix did not adhere to the social rules of Molly's time and place

Molly sighed.

The electric engines of The Presidio whirred softly beneath her feet. They were of Molly's own design. Imbued with just a modicum of magic, Molly was able to steer the craft trough any ocean, sea, or bay she wanted across the globe with no more effort than a focus of her willpower.

The low, hypnotic buzzing brought her comfort.

She glanced up and through the enormous window, seeing the dark ocean through the thick glass. The Presidio was submerged just deep enough that anyone who might be passing overhead on a ship would not see them. But it wasn't so deep as to miss the rippling scars of white and blue caused by the sun's early-morning rays cutting the singular black sea into zillions of tiny, undulating bodies of water, each a different shade of green, gray, blue and black. It was a phenomenon Molly loved, and it was only moments before the sun would set it in motion. This, too, brought her comfort.

She'd been tasked with discovering an event that had caused a certain amount of chaos through a very important society to which she belonged.

One might call this very important society a coven. It was a group of very influential people who used extraordinary powers to bend the world to their will.

However, the group's members had in a matter of days lost powers they'd been honing for years. Soon, each person in the coven was left with just one or two skills that they'd apparently been born with.

Unlike the States of Konfuson and D'Kay, Molly's where and when required no loss of life in order to generate magic. Instead, magic in her world was created with ingredients – as one would use ingredients to bake a cake, as we've established. But instead of using someone or something else's energy to push the spell into action, magic in Molly's realm was catalyzed by the power of one's own mind.

The ingredients for these spells – feathers, candles, incense, water, salt, etc. – were rapidly losing potency, though, and the coven found it having less control than they once had over the world's affairs. Molly, using her natural and unmatched skills of scrying and her talent for unveiling mysteries, had discovered the drain of power was due to a single event. However, she'd been unable to pinpoint when and where it had happened.

Whatever it was, it had nearly drained the extra magical abilities of everyone in Molly's coven save for one person: Mistress Vix. It was a mystery to everyone except for Vix as to why she was spared.

As for Molly, she still retained her uncanny ability to see the future – or at least to see possible futures – as well as discover truths and root out lies. It was her one natural ability. Mr. Screech, too, retained his natural ability to become unseen.

Molly, though, was also a tinkerer, and had the power of science on her side. She used her knowledge to her advantage any time she could. Mr. Screech, though, was little more than a man-sized chameleon at this point.

So it was decided that Molly and Vix, accompanied by Mr. Screech, who in his years as a hanger-on more or less became Vix's personal secretary, set voyage in The Presidio away from the city so as to be as far away as possible from any wayward energies, magical or otherwise, that might interfere with Molly's ability to figure out what the hell was going on.

Chapter 34

Molly closed her eyes and drew in a breath. Leaning over the star, she pursed her lips as though she was about to kiss it, but instead blew the air, slow and steady, onto its center.

She then dipped her thumb and fore fingers into a bowl of salt that lay to the right of the star disc, pinching out a few granules. With her other hand, she dipped her fore and index fingers into a small bowl of water, set off to the left. She brought the two elements back to the star, dropping them simultaneously into the center.

The lines of the pentacle immediately glowed a bluish-white, lighting the faces of the three sorcerers looking down upon the altar.

"I'm still having difficulty finding where this event happened that's disturbed the Fabric," said Molly, straightening herself up (the damn corsets were always so uncomfortable when one was leaning over altars for too long). "And the timing is very cloudy. What has me boggled is that –"

Molly paused and once again bent over the star. This time, she traced the edges, stopping at each of the objects, over which she placed her palm face down and then made a circular, clockwise motion as if she were polishing silver.

"It can't be," she stated.

"What is it, woman?" Mr. Screech demanded.

Here, Artemis Vix spoke softly, although her voice reverberated in both Mr. Screech's and Molly's skulls, drowning out whatever the man might have said next.

"There are two events," she said.

Molly looked up and nodded, saying, "Simply put, yes. Two events happening simultaneously." She looked back to the altar. "One is magic. One is not."

Molly St. Mercalli was a junior member of the coven, though she'd been working up the ranks ever since she'd shown a proclivity for casting spells at a level even some of the senior council members had yet to attain. She'd caught the attention of Mistress Vix when she built a magnetic device that generated electricity. Attached to the magician's wrist, it was compact and provided an unlimited supply of energy to aid in the working magic, thus boosting spells for optimum effect. It was the same concept she'd used on the motors powering her submarine, and one of the myriads of Molly's inventions that utilized both magic and science to create a force more potent than either on its own.

This made Molly incredibly efficacious. More so, in fact, than Artemis Vix herself, when it came to certain things. Neither Molly nor Vix knew this fact, though, as one-upmanship among witches was generally frowned upon in polite society.

Mr. Screech stepped to the altar and looked down upon the items, lit pleasantly by the soft blue light from the glowing star. The same blue light also lit his face from below, though an antonym of "pleasant" would be a far better descriptor for the effect.

"Two events?" he asked. "How?"

Molly couldn't hold her tongue.

"Well," she said, speaking slowly while using over-exaggerated tones, "when one event happens over here," she pointed to one side of the room, "and another over here," she pointed again to the other, "and they happen at the same time, that means there are two events."

Screech looked as though he were ready to pounce. Molly stood in defiance. Mistress Vix stepped away from the black stone, leaned against the nearest wall, folded her arms and looked on in amusement.

"Well, this certainly is an excellent use of our time," she said.

"My apologies," Molly said, though there wasn't a trace of sincerity in her words.

She turned her attention back to the star.

"There's another witch," Molly said, pointing to the cherry, "She killed her sister and consumed her heart."

Molly squinted, and then tutted.

"Well, not only was this lazy," she said, "but it was also stupid. Her sister foresaw something like this happening. It appears she placed an enchantment on her own heart, so this second witch cursed herself the moment she took her sister's powers."

"A curse powerful enough to rip the Fabric?" Mr. Screech scoffed.

"No," Molly answered. "In fact, I don't think the curse has

anything to do with it. But it is lucky for us. I could track a cursed witch across a thousand seas. I can see she's affected somehow by the disturbance."

Molly then turned her attention on the broken pocket watch.

"A scientist," she said, indicating the watch, "he's ... he's a sort of catalyst to one of the events. I can see he's created a way to travel across the Fabric by," she paused a moment, squinting again at her pentagram, " ... by folding it?"Molly looked up and into the eyes of Vix, who was still leaning casually against the wall of The Presidio. Vix blinked but said nothing.

Molly turned her attention back to the star.

"I can see the witch and the scientist will cross paths," she said before pausing and studying the items on the altar. "No, that's wrong. The scientist will ... he will travel on a fold of the Fabric over the witch, and she will fall into the place he once occupied. ... I think."

She paused and arched her eyebrow. Her magic must have been flawed because it showed the scientist was in multiple places at the same time. She didn't reveal this last tidbit aloud.

The Coven had tasked themselves with enforcing a sort of decorum among the myriad magical beings scattered across the world. While a witch was generally left to his or her own devices, which may be good or evil or neutral, sometimes a sorcerer would conjure something incredibly dangerous to the Fabric of Existence, as the Coven called it. You may have a different name for it than the Coven did. After all, there are probably as many names for the plane upon which all things are as there are things that exist upon that plane.

The Coven made it their duty to rein in any petulant prestidigitators and ensure they didn't wreak havoc on other, more responsible witches, who usually only used their magic to benefit themselves without risk to other magical persons.

"If I could get to the witch before the event, I might not be able to stop it, but I could be there when it happens and perhaps ... prevent it," Molly said.

"What riddle are you spinning, girl?" Screech barked. "You're making as much sense as a pig in the president's parlor."

"How noble of you to volunteer," answered Vix, seemingly ignoring Mr. Screech's swine simile. "But what, pray tell, could any single person, magical or otherwise, do to prevent a tear in the Fabric?"

"Let's gather the Coven, then," Molly said.

"There are three of us here," answered Screech. "Three is good enough."

"Three would be good enough," Vix replied, "If the three witches were in top form. I believe two among us perhaps don't possess the proclivities to adequately attack the event we're attempting to remedy, yes?"

Mr. Screech's magical abilities didn't hold a candle to that of Mistress Vix's even on his best day and her worst – and he knew it. It also didn't hold a candle to Molly's, but he didn't know that. As far as magical abilities go, he was, not to put too fine a point on it, almost average.

"Well that's ... I ..." Mr. Screech stammered, "It's all very well and good, but you don't even know where this witch is, or where this scientist is, or even when this event took place, or is taking place, or will take place!"

He pulled his pocket square from his coat and dabbed beneath his ears where sweat had suddenly begun to appear. His usually bristly mutton chops began to sag slightly under the water's weight, giving his facial hair the appearance of black mold.

Molly rolled her eyes and turned to the crystal orb in the corner.

"It's true," she said. "I don't know where the witch nor the scientist are located. But I can tell you they're not anywhere near here. They're in a place I've never visited either in person or in astral projection."

She cupped the back of the orb, palming the smooth surface and turning the entire sphere the color of flesh with distortions of lacy black nets, a magnified view of Molly's fingerless, black lace gloves. Upon seeing the fine, dark material through the orb, she quickly took her hands away and removed the gloves. She tied the two together by their ribbons and secured them to her bodice before replacing her hands on the crystal.

"Scientifically speaking, the event has already happened," she said. "Something that has not happened surely can't have an effect on us. Something that has not happened cannot suck the very powers we've honed over years."

She leaned close to the ball, stopping centimeters away from the glass. The rotund vision of her warped hand became foggy as her breath moistened the surface. With her left hand, she drew a deosil spiral in the fog, starting in the center and working the line outward.

"But perhaps it *hasn't* happened yet."

Mistress Vix cleared her throat.

"Very well," Vix said, straightening up. "We'll convene the Coven. What exactly is your plan of attack, dear Molly?"

Chapter 35

"We'll need three more *accomplished* witches," she answered, placing an extra emphasis on the word "accomplished." "We'll definitely need to recruit one of the witches with a penchant for traveling spells. I dare say we must get to a place neither my submersible, nor your train," here she nodded at Vix, "nor your zeppelin," she acknowledged Screech, "can take us."

Mr. Screech frowned. A drop of sweat fell from his left ear. He dabbed again with his hanky.

"Very well," Vix said, eyeing the grouchy man whose cheek plumage was slowly wilting. "I can think of one or two. We'll contact them once we arrive back at the bay. What is it we must do?"

Molly sighed.

"We'll each need to harness an element and bring them together. We have to open a line of sight to wherever this cursed witch resides. I can do that. We need to remove her. Bring her here. That's where we'll need a sturdy transportation spell."

"A transportation?" Mr. Screech scoffed. "The very idea. It's only been done once before! And it took five senior Coven members to do it! And, if you recall, only three-quarters of Dr. Ocherous came back. For God's sake, his left arm and half his face are probably still gallivanting about in Venice as we speak!"

Vix eyed Mr. Screech and then turned her attention back to Molly.

"What Mr. Screech lacks in magical ability he makes up for in knowledge," she said. "He's correct. It would take five very talented conjurers to successfully execute a transportation. And even then, the slightest mishap could send bits of a person to the world's edge. Perhaps farther."

"That's the only plan I've got," Molly said.

"Well then," Vix shrugged slightly, glancing sideways at the now very perturbed Byzantium Screech. "It appears we may have no other choice. Let's hope my choice of witches are up to the task."

Molly moved back to the star. She picked up the pocket watch and the cherry and placed them at the center. She focused on the two items.

"I don't know exactly where they are," she said. "But I know that they're there. I can sense them. If I can keep their energies in my sight, we can bring one - or maybe both - through to us."

What Molly didn't know is that the magic deed would have been impossible, as the magic on her world only extended to the borders of her existence. Vix, on the other hand, had her suspicions, but even she was unaware of the vast void that lay between her universe and the place where the event would occur.

Luckily, since it meant Molly would not have to face the council after her plan would have gone horribly wrong, something happened at that exact moment that changed everything in the three witches' lives forever.

Chapter 36

Molly began to open her mouth to add an additional comment, but what that comment was will never be known. There was a sudden flash inside the submersible. A great arc of electricity boomed near the glass orb, and several light bulbs popped overhead in response. Mr. Screech screeched.

At that exact moment, a form appeared in the lightning. Molly, her hands held to her face to shade them from the painful brightness, saw it suddenly. There, where her crystal orb had once been, was a stack of soiled socks and a bundle of sticks that appeared to be cut at such a length that they would be utterly unusable.

The orb and the table upon which it sat was now gone entirely.

The three witches stared in confusion, but they didn't stare long. The arcs of energy zapped about through the interior of The Presidio and began to electrify the whirring, enchanted engines. Magic and science, when paired, can create much power. And when magic and science collide, it can also create much destruction.

It was then all the magical energy contained within Molly's undersea vehicle burst, creating an explosion that reverberated into the very ocean floor. The Presidio appeared to implode.

As the sun began to paint the sky the colors of the morning, the earth quaked from the sheer force of the explosion, and a nearby city called San Francisco cracked and crumbled in the magic's wake.

I'm told that scientists there blamed the seismic anomaly on tectonic plates floating about on lakes of molten rock. In fact, women and men of knowledge on that particular plane of existence nearly always found tectonic plates to blame whenever the earth shook beneath them. They were correct nearly 45% of the time. Of course, none of them had traveled below these molten lakes before and weren't aware of the gigantic, ugly, naked trolls that made the core of the planet their home.

It's common knowledge, of course, that trolls' homes are in a constant state of renovation. Since they wear no clothes, they spend no time deciding what outfit to put on each day and whether or not it makes their backsides look big. Trolls' backsides were always big, and since they were always exposed, there was never time spent trying to disguise it as anything other than a giant, ugly, troll bum. This, in turn, left much free time in their lives, and they spent their vanity efforts on home structure and interior design instead.

So any time a family of trolls had to blast a wall or install a new chandelier, the humans living miles above would often feel the tremors from the construction. Had the men and women above truly understood what was happening, remedying it might have been as easy as a knock on one of the thousands of stone doors that led to the trolls' domain, and a quick, "Do you mind keeping it down?" in a voice a bit louder than usual.

This, however, is not a story of naked subterranean dwellers and their decorating habits, and I'm finding it quite tiresome that you insist on diverting your attention away from the matters on which we're focusing.

Step 6: Traversing Dimensions Does Have Repercussions, But Do Not Label All Mishaps As Having Stemmed From Such Travels

"Traversing time and dimensions is risky business, and it will, no doubt, lead to repercussions both good and bad. However, just because an unfortunate fate has befallen one, it does not necessarily mean one has been the victim of time traveling mishaps. Travelers would do well to remember that correlation does not equal causation."

— Dr. Gustopher C. Cerulean, as quoted in the copious notes of Bratticus L. Magleby.

Chapter 37

Below the apothecary of one Dr. Gustopher Cramden Cerulean lay the City of Bell where, for the first time since anyone could remember, things weren't quite as nicely-buttoned as townsfolk were used to.

Gregar Rumpkin, who'd dedicated his entire life to candle making (as did his father before him and his father's father before him), suddenly found himself feverish and decided it was best if he vacationed for the foreseeable future in a more pleasant and arctic climate. He had since boarded the S.S. Merryweather and joined a group of tourists setting to sea to study the migration patterns of penguins.

This was perplexing because Mr. Rumpkin famously hated the cold and was often seen bundled in all manner of overcoats, waistcoats, morning coats, frock coats, dress coats, trench coats, dinner jackets, shooting jackets, evening jackets, Chesterfields, cloaks, furs, capes and mackintoshes, even during the high summer heat. In the wintertime, he'd adorn himself with layers of thick clothing and work double shifts in the candle shop, scarcely leaving the vicinity of the fires that heated the many boiling waxes.

Rumpkin's apprentice, Robert Dipwick, mixed an incorrect concoction in his master's absence, which subsequently caused a giant vat of paraffin to bubble over, coating the floor of the Rumpkin's Candle, Candle Holder and Wax Fruit Emporium, and running down the street outside. This was odd given that Dipwick was one of the most skilled wick dippers to the east or the west of the Ridiculing River.

Outside, Grace Golightly, the most skilled ice skater in the State of Konfuson, suddenly found she was unable to keep her balance on the now slippery surface of the wax-coated cobblestone lane. Mayhew Muttersmunch, the city's most accomplished cricket player, was unable to catch Miss Golightly as she barreled backward onto her backside.

As Miss Golightly's arms flailed, her hand basket pitched an impressive several yards, which in its turn startled Mrs. Ratherty's Clydesdale, which then raced away pulling Mrs. Ratherty's Candies and Cocaine cart ("For Your Little One's Health and Happiness," the sign read).

Just up the street, Bobbert Finn was working in his boot shop. His craftsmanship was known far and wide, and all the best Bellians wore footwear cobbled by Mr. Finn. He took great pride in his work, and he never let a boot, shoe, Oxford, pump, Mary Jane, low-heel, boudoir slipper, or stiletto off his workbench that didn't have every seam aligned, every stitch tightened, and not a buckle, strap or lace out of place.

"I put my heart and *sole* into my work," he'd chuckle to customers when they arrived to retrieve their footwear.

Every new customer of Bobbert Finn usually chuckled back at the cobbler's droll comment the first and second times. The joke, however, did get tiresome after purchasing more than three pairs of boots. But, his craftsmanship was unrivaled, so the quip was deemed a necessary evil among Bellians who wore shoes – which happened to be most of them.

Only the hero Captain Periwinkle Wallace, who lost both his legs during the very brief war with the State of Schok, never found reason to patronize Bobbert Finn's shop after his wartime injuries.

The war with the State of Schok, by the way, ended so quickly that it surprised everyone. There were no casualties, although a multitude of sailors on both sides lost a variety of fingers, hands, legs, arms, feet, toes, noses, ears, and a few unmentionable extremities after each state's ship was overturned in rough sea waters. The men, all of whom were fantastic swimmers, were safe until they encountered a school of very irritable tuna. I've heard the fish were ravenous, having not eaten for weeks, but I think the more logical explanation was that the tuna had simply had enough after years of seeing their brothers and sisters caught, killed, and canned before being spread on bread or crackers and enjoyed during picnics. The fish merely wanted to give the men a taste of their own medicine.

The men were happy to have lived through the ordeal. Those who still had hands shook them, and each navy swam back to its respective shores and declared that everyone was a winner, and why can't we use words to work out our differences anyway?

I also have it on good authority that one of the tuna was seen swimming away dabbing a clump of cracker crumbs off its cheek with its pectoral fin. Suffice to say, none of the sailors ever touched a fish sandwich again. However, this is not a tale of vindictive sea creatures and the proper way to win wars, and I'll thank you very much to stick to the point of the story.

Bobbert Finn, on that pell-mell day in Bell, found that each left boot he crafted was perfection save but for the inner side seam. As his nimble fingers fed the leathers through his machine, he found himself in sudden and uncontrollable sneezing fits just as the footwear was about to be complete. No less than seven boots had a final centimeter of seam that lagged slightly to the right. It was pure anarchy.

In a fit of frustration, he took each of the abominations one by one to the bank of the Ridiculing River and angrily chucked them in. He punctuated each throw with a very coarse word, which differed with each style of shoe.

Gibson Gold, who had just celebrated his eighth birthday, was about to launch his new toy wooden boat nearby when he heard approximately seven new and extravagant words. He was so excited to add them to his vocabulary that he completely forgot his boat and ran off to tell them to all his friends.

The words spread like wildfire among the city's youngsters. One little girl, Lucille Lumboxen, known for her smiling and pink face framed by golden hair that hung in ringlets, had to be removed from the premises of the town's tavern after she walked by the establishment singing a song she'd just invented using the dictionary of words she'd just learned. Tavern owner Petunia Bea Bracken had to shoo the adorable little cherub away from the building after the lyrics offended nearly every customer inside.

Only the sailors sitting at the table near the entrance of the pub seemed unperturbed by the adorable little angel's repulsive language. It could be because none of them had ears, having lost them to the school of ravenous tuna.

Down of the river, the Widow Josephine Gaye, who'd taken up her late husband's talent for catching the largest sturgeon in the waters, had caught nothing that day save for seven boots, all of which were for left feet only; two gloves, one made of lace and one made of leather; a soaked copy of last week's The Bell Chime, and a pair of handlebars from a penny farthing. The Widow Josephine Gaye was particularly saddened that the bell attached to the handlebars was too rusted to chime.

At the residence of Mayor Rudy MacBritches, Madame Vermillion found herself in probably the most chaotic scene of all.

The mayor had poured two glasses of his finest whiskey, lit a romantic fire in the living room's fireplace (distinguished from a regular fire only by its creator's intent), and insisted Vermillion sit next to him on his chaise lounge while he regaled her with tales of heroics and chivalry from his past. Madame Vermillion, as revolted as she was, found herself powerless. She'd seemed to have lost all magical ability.

Chapter 38

The day prior, after deciding she'd make the State of Konfuson her new conquest, Vermilion had spirited her way to the City of Bell where she was more pleased than she thought she'd be. The shops were open, the trees were blooming, and time was functioning at more or less a regular speed. And look! Here was the Town Hall, unshuttered and in perfect working order.

She had entered and admired the fine drapes, the plush carpets, the mahogany paneling, and she imagined herself ruling over a pleasant place like this rather than the sad decaying state from which she'd left.

It was there that she encountered the town's leader. And it was then she decided to use some magic to put herself in control.

She drew energy from an elderly spinster who appeared about at the end of her rope already and cast a spell to transfer the power of the elected office from the ape-shaped buffoon in the green and purple jacket to herself.

The spell did not work. Or at least it did not work as intended.

Instead, the mayor fell head-over-diamond-studded-heels for the portly witch. His infatuation only seemed to grow with each moment. No matter what Madame Vermillion did, no matter how many spells she attempted to cast, no matter how she struggled to break free of the mayor's embrace, she simply could not.

Little did she know her spell also set off a wave of discombobulation across Bell, pushing all sorts of things off kilter. Menial tasks that would have otherwise been executed perfectly and without second thought were now being bungled and botched. Folks found themselves completely out of character, going places they'd never go, saying things they'd never say, and doing things they'd never do.

You see, Madame Veramilicent Vermillion may have thought she was clever by letting her twin sister put in the hard work before stealing her power. But you should know, dear reader, that hard work has its benefits. One such benefit is the ability to know things. In Vera's many years working to perfect her skills, she'd guessed her slightly less-scrupled sister might take advantage of her. She knew that, if Vera could somehow catch her off guard, her sister could easily cut out her heart and gain all the magic she'd accumulated over days and months and years of study and practice.

Vera, in her wisdom, however evil it may have been, placed a spell on her own heart. If anyone were to kill her and eat it, that person would be able to conjure exactly three spells. Upon the third spell, the magic would backfire drastically in a way most annoying.

And, as a pièce de résistance, once the slipshod spell was cast, the consumer of the heart would lose more of her power with every piece of magic she conjured, and every piece of magic would be less and less effective.

Chapter 39

Veramilicent Vermilion had, upon arriving in the State of Konfuson, turned a cup of tea into sparkling wine. This was her first spell. She'd then sucked the life from Gertrude the Llama to transport herself to town. This was spell number two. And finally, she'd conjured a bit of magic attempting to become mayor. It was the fateful third spell.

Vermilion did not know of the curse, though. She hadn't a clue as to what was happening, or why.

Vida, for her part, did not foresee the residual effect her curse would have on the environment around her sister. At this point in the story, though, Vida is dead, so she most likely cared very little about the pandemonium caused by her sister's infelicitous magic.

The citizens of Bell, though, cared very much, although they too had no idea from where their troubles had suddenly stemmed. And upon the hill where a certain apothecary loomed gimcrack and precarious over the city, a group of people, strangers but moments ago, were about to feel the sting as well.

Interlude 3: Molly St. Mercalli, A Brief History

I'll issue you a warning, dear reader. You mustn't forget that every person in this narrative has an extensive history dating back to the days they were born. Some of them even have histories that date back further.

Sometimes, a history may seem completely pointless to a story. Sometimes, a history is imperative. The history of Miss Molly St. Mercalli lands somewhere in the middle.

Chapter 40

Somewhere between San Francisco, where Molly St. Mercalli had made her home, and Chicago, from where Molly's mother hailed, sat a city nestled between mountains where Molly was born.

The city, humble and new, had been built in a very strange place indeed. The travelers who'd settled the area chose to do so near a giant lake that was saltier than any ocean, with waters unsuitable for any use. It could not water crops. Humans or animals could not drink it. And it most certainly couldn't be bathed in, as it had the nasty tendency of depositing more things into the nooks and crannies of one's body than it washed away.

The lake sat in a basin with no outlet. It was, more or less, a graveyard for rivers and streams – a place where life flowed in but did not flow out.

Its stinking shores were covered in the corpses of countless brine shrimp. Its stagnant waters were buzzing with the wretched sound of brine flies. And because the area was a veritable insect smorgasbord, the bushes surrounding the lake were usually covered in the webs of spiders that had decided they didn't want to do much work to catch their supper.

In fact, spiders on the shores of the great lake had so many leftovers that they often found themselves packing them up and taking them to their neighbors in the next bush to see if they'd like some. Those neighbors, of course, would already have more than enough food themselves. It was a shame, really, because they'd all heard that spiders were starving in Africa somewhere, and they shouldn't actually let any of this food go to waste (although how that helped African spiders from starving was a mystery). So spiders at the lake grew fat and large.

The brine flies, for their part, were not happy that so many of their family members were being consumed by spiders, so they took extra steps to lay as many eggs as possible in an attempt to overwhelm the gluttonous arachnids.

And the brine shrimp were just content reproducing and dying, happy enough that they had the opportunity to contribute to the overall atmosphere.

All this made the lake a very unpleasant place for humans. Yet, it was here a group decided to make their home.

Chapter 41

For Gwendolyn Mace and her brother, Emerson, it was the perfect location. Although for them, it wasn't because some pioneer leader told them to stay. Had they been with a wagon train that had no intention of even pausing in the area, they still would have bid farewell to their travel companions and stopped.

As mentioned in the previous chapter, this great, salty lake was essentially a watery graveyard. But as any witch knows, graveyards are powerful places that house many important elements to magic.

While the salty lake was entirely unpleasant, it was still a gathering pool for all the energies washed down mountains and through valleys. And since the lake had no outlet, those energies were constantly piling up, and they had long since overflowed beyond the body of water.

If one were to put on a pair of glasses that had the ability to see these energies, one would see an ocean in that area between mountains, glowing with the essence of nature itself. (Those glasses, consequentially, would later be invented by Gwendolyn's daughter.) It was really quite the cache for people like Gwendolyn and Emerson, who knew exactly how to use the stored forces for their own benefits.

The Mace siblings were not twins, but they were born on the same day and during consecutive years from the same parents. Yet, they looked nothing alike.

Emerson had hair the color of hay and his skin was tanned to a level of gold that made him look almost metallic. He always smelled of honey, even when he hadn't eaten any, and his eyes looked like giant drops of Xanthus nectar. As a result, he was often shooing bees away from his face.

Gwendolyn, on the other hand, had hair the color of coal, and her skin was as pale as polished silver and as soft as a dandelion. Her eyes were startling and amethystine, giving off a radiant violet reflection in the dark. She smelled of lilies and orchids, two flowers commonly placed at graves.

The only commonality between the two was their stature – just tall enough that they could be noticed in a crowd should they want to be noticed, and just short enough that they could easily disappear in a crowd should they choose to disappear. Their build was slight, their waists slender. Gwendolyn's shoulders appeared to be rolling like gentle waters from her neck, while Emerson's frame had a slightly rockier build. Standing side-by-side, one couldn't help but imagine they were two parts of a 24-hour cycle, completely different but each absolutely necessary for the other to exist. Without day, there is no night, and vice versa.

Their ages were a mystery to everyone but them. Depending on the circumstances, they could appear to be anywhere between 20 and 40 years old, though they usually seemed to be on the younger side of the spectrum.

It should be noted that, had the two been entirely truthful with the parties in which they traveled, they probably would have been shunned at best – and at worst, stoned or hanged. The two, after all, were witches. And if the people in the party in which they traveled paid extra attention, they might have figured it out for themselves.

Chapter 42

During the arduous journey, many in the group had died or lost limbs in the bitter cold. Dozens more starved to the point of rotting, their bodies barely alive but stinking of death. Gwendolyn and Emerson traveled the same distance with the same equipment as everyone else. They ate the same foods when foods were available. They drank the same water and encountered the same beasts of the wild. Yet neither ever fell ill. Their skin never turned sallow. They never thinned nor broke any bones. They sustained no snakebites nor stumbled down ravines (as old Joshua Young did on several occasions).

If the others weren't so busy trying not to die, they just might have observed the Mace siblings having quite an easier go at the trek than everyone else.

While being a witch doesn't necessarily protect one from the perils of pioneering across treacherous terrains, knowing the proper spells and charms and when to deploy them certainly does.

It was lucky, then, that as the brother and sister were preparing to leave Chicago, they happened upon a drunken politician. He was easily dispatched, and since Chicago had more than its fair share of drunken politicians, he wasn't missed. His teeth were then ground into a fine powder and mixed with the dirt from a graveyard. Gwendolyn sewed the concoction into matching pouches made of the dead man's skin. Emerson ran the two trinkets through a puff of sage smoke and then dipped them each in wax. The siblings wore their pouches around their necks throughout the journey, and it essentially kept them free from harm.

But there were fewer magical ingredients to be found in the bustling city, and the items they were able to forage were tainted with villainous, corrupt residue that had seeped into the very dirt beneath their feet.

They needed to find a new place. It needed to be a place untouched by all but those who were native to the land. Such a place would have much to offer two witches. When they heard of groups of religious people seeking better lives in a far away valley that just so happened to have a veritable repository of everything they could ever want and more, they made their plans, killed their politician, and then packed their bags.

Chapter 43

So it was in the valley the two settled, taking extra care to build their homes as far away from the others as possible.

While most of the travelers who chose to stay constructed houses and shops and farms on the flattest part of the valley floor, the Mace siblings chose a cozy spot up a nearby canyon to establish themselves. In a clearing with a stream cutting directly down the middle, the two built comfortable houses on either side of the water. Each house had a little cobblestone walkway from the front door, and the two joined at the stream with a little stone bridge.

Gwendolyn lived on the east side of the stream. The surrounding mountain peaks and tall pine and aspen trees allowed for her house to stay almost exclusively in shadow, save for a few hours in the evening. Emerson's home was on the west side in an area where the morning sun's first rays poured onto his doorstep and kept light shining on his property until it set.

This was the power of the siblings. Light and dark. Black and white. Cold and warm. And, yes, good and evil. Neither can exist without each other, and both can only exist when they work well together. After all, none of us would look forward to long days of carefree frolic in cool river waters if there weren't a bitter winter to make us long for the heat.

Conversely, none of us would be pining for drifts of snow and cozy nights in front of fireplaces if there weren't a scorching summer to make us wish for a picturesque winter.

The two were shielded from the general population by trees and boulders, where they were free to build fires, brew potions, chant into the night, and other general witchy activities that would have them drawn and quartered had they done it in full view of the religious folk below.

At every new moon, the two would ride horses to the lakeside, each of them filling a vile with the disgusting water, which they would then place in their garden as the moon waxed to full. Having collected the energies of the sun, the moon and the earth, as well as all the static power in the liquid itself, the lake water would then be used to add extra potency to spells. Emerson once had to use his entire flask when a young man from town came proselytizing and found Gwendolyn carving runic symbols in a tree while repeating mystical words. As the man began to flee in terror, Emerson uncorked the bottle and flung the entire contents into the boy's face. Emerson then whispered three times, "erunt cacus obliviscatur, erunt cacus obliviscatur, erunt cacus obliviscatur," before swiping his right hand downward across the young man's face in a move similar to a respectful undertaker closing the eyes of the dead.

The young man's expression went blank and he returned to the settlement, stinking of dead brine shrimp. He remembered nothing from that afternoon, and went on to believe his memory was probably washed away by beings from another world (which, I might add, eventually happened to him, though that's a tale for a completely different manuscript).

Chapter 44

Gwendolyn and Emerson did not age much outwardly, though they did grow old in years. As the city below them continued to expand both in size and in population, the siblings eventually found new inhabitants with whom they made friends. Ultimately, both of them even found companionship with foreigners.

Emerson discovered a beautiful woman with golden hair named Queron Vester who arrived in the city quite by accident. Her father in Denmark arranged for her to travel to the Americas and marry a Louisiana man who would have kept her (and her father) very comfortable for the rest of their lives.

She spoke not a lick of English, and she was unable to read any signs, so while she was supposed to purchase a ticket to New Orleans, she'd accidentally procured a train ride to a place called Promontory. When the little man with the giant mustache behind the bars at the ticket booth handed her the slip of paper, she looked at the word "Promontory" and thought to herself that it looked an awful lot like the word "Louisiana" and congratulated herself on a job well done.

If you are unfamiliar with Scandinavian languages, I challenge you to look at two words of similar length and see how well you fare. If you were tasked with finding your way to Hedensted-Løsning and you, instead, found yourself on a boat to Hedehusene-Fløng, who could blame you? So I'll thank you to leave your judgments of young Queron to yourself.

When on the train, Queron noticed the geography failed to become a place of swamps and vampires (as was the rumor), and instead became a place of desolation and unbearable heat. When she arrived at Promontory, she first decided that anyone who actively chose to live in such a place must be completely out of his mind. She then decided she had to find someone to help her.

Not a soul at the station was able to communicate with her, but she eventually found herself on a coach into the city near the salty lake where she happened to bump into Emerson Mace.

Emerson had been sitting by a stream that ran near his and Gwendolyn's houses just the day before when an acorn fell from the runic tree and thumped him on the back of the neck. As all witches know, this means there's an appointment you must keep that you probably don't know about. Without much more information, he mounted a horse and traveled into town the next day in hopes of figuring out whom it was he was supposed to meet and what it was they were supposed to be accomplishing.

It turned out his appointment was with his future wife.

Chapter 45

Emerson did not speak Danish, but he was a witch, so he made it work. He brought Queron back to the clearing and introduced her to his sister, and the three of them got on famously. Each of them learned to speak each other's language, and it wasn't long before Queron Vester Mace was casting spells to rival even the greatest witch.

Gwendolyn was happy for the two of them, and unlike many of the women in the growing city below, she didn't feel a pang of jealousy nor a longing for a husband of her own. She was a very independent woman, and love and marriage had never even breached the horizon of her world of personal priorities.

That changed one day, though, when a handsome man happened upon the two homes while hunting an errant buck that had fled up the canyon.

He was tall, handsome and aloof – the man, not the buck. It was a trio of fine characteristic passed down from his Italian father and Ethiopian mother. Upon meeting the trio in the canyon, he smiled a warm and enchanting smile, one that imbued all who met him with an immediate ease. It was specifically his mother who passed down this particular talent. There was actual magic in that smile.

The man never knew he had magical powers that manifested themselves through his facial expressions, but it was that smile that had managed to keep him safe and free during a time when people who looked the way he did were hardly ever safe and free.

But even if the man had known he possessed these remarkable powers, it still would have been that magical smile he'd use most. He was a kind and generous person by nature, and his smile came naturally and often.

Now, witches had a certain immunity to the actual magical abilities of this man's smile, and Gwen was indifferent to this stranger. However, there was something about him that lit a small but manageable fire in her heart. Emerson, also not affected by those spellbinding teeth, took an immediate liking to the man, who introduced himself as Vincenzo St. Mercalli, and invited him to stay for supper. The deer had long since escaped, after all, and Vincenzo needed to eat.

Gwendolyn, upon hearing his Italian name, wondered if she could possibly render him unconscious so she could shave his head. (The hair of an Italian man is a key ingredient for the banishment of leg cramps, as everyone knows.)

Chapter 45

The man had only recently fled from the city of Firenze, where he admitted he was wanted for an incident in which he'd managed to convince local authorities to stop a public execution and let the offending prisoner go.

Vincenzo didn't actually know the prisoner, but he had thought public executions were in total poor taste. With his pleasant smile he'd persuaded the three carabinieri guards to do the dirty deed somewhere else. Not knowing the strength of his own powers, though, the carabinieri laid down their weapons, unshackled the prisoner, and then set about finding a nearby bar where they could all drink to the health and happiness of the man they'd just set free.

The crowd that had gathered to watch a man be hanged in the piazza all applauded, having a collective and sudden urge to do a kind deed. The citizens dispersed, each going his or her own way to hopefully make someone else's day a little better.

The prisoner, by the way, had been sentenced to death for insulting King Umberto's ridiculous mustache. It's unclear what ever happened to the mustache-hating prisoner, but it's this author's hope that he lived a long and happy life somewhere and kept his mouth shut when encountering facial hair worn on regal faces.

An old woman pulling a cart of tomatoes witnessed Vincenzo's actions and was appalled. Of course she knew this was some sort magic, as old women are quite deft in recognizing magic. It also helped that she, too, was a witch, and therefore was not glamorized like the rest of the crowd.

She trotted as fast as she could to the carabinieri, who were happily drinking at an outdoor table in the piazza. She informed them they'd just been enchanted by that man over there, and the prisoner who dared to criticize dear King Umberto had turned tail and disappeared.

She snapped her fingers thrice, one for each guard, to wake them from their happy little trances.

The carabinieri, now out of range of Vincenzo's smile, paused in the act of drinking their beers, looking as though they were posing for a painting. Vincenzo, seeing the authorities had, for some reason, changed their minds about his persuasive argument not moments ago, decided it was his turn to run.

The guards slammed their beers on the table, making quite a mess for the barista to clean up, and began to give chase. The old woman nodded in approval, returned to her cart of tomatoes, and continued walking the streets of Firenze.

Now, Vincenzo was not only tall and handsome, and not only could he place persuasion spells upon people with just a glance, but he was also extremely clever. And though the carabinieri had soon fanned out across the city in search of him, he'd managed to slip away, quite easily, in fact. The next day, he was safely on a coach to Porto di Livorno, where he would board a ship bound for the Americas.

As luck would have it, he made friends with everyone on board.

This story, which poured from his mouth like waters through a broken dam, was one he wouldn't have usually offered to strangers upon their first meeting. Vincenzo's wine, his meal and his tobacco, you see, had each been spiked with just a bit of truth serum — each of the three witches adding his or her own drop.

Had the Maces coordinated their efforts before dinner, they might have known each had the same plan and would have saved a little potion should any local politicians find their way to their homes begging for votes.

But Gwendolyn, Emerson and Queron knew Vincenzo's story to be true because each was now completely out of truth serum.

Chapter 45

They discovered Vincenzo St. Mercalli was, indeed, a fine man with fine intentions. And it was no more than a few days before he had forged a strong friendship with Maces. Since Vincenzo was new to the valley, he had yet to build a home and was currently camped in a canvas tent at the base of the canyon.

As you might have guessed, dear reader, it wasn't long before plans were made that Mr. Mercalli should build his home in the clearing and live alongside Queron, Emerson and Gwendolyn.

And thus, the two cottages in the clearing became three.

Vincenzo was the first to fall in love. It was a deep love, which was utterly unrequited by Gwendolyn. She had snuffed out that fire of infatuation within her heart, dousing it by convincing herself that love and marriage would only lead to control and misery. She'd seen it in her own parents, and she was not about to tread down the same road of agony they did.

Disliking Vincenzo, though, was a task not even the very powerful Gwendolyn could undertake. Even if he'd not an ounce of magical blood in his body, he was still the most gracious and humble and kind person she'd ever met. After several months, her own hardened heart melted, and she couldn't help but fall in love with him, too.

The two married, one of the cottages went dark and was only used for storage, and Gwen now had access to an endless supply of Italian hair – and she never suffered another leg cramp from that day forward.

Before long, both couples welcomed children of their own, which was mathematically astounding as the babies were born on the exact same day within 13 minutes of each other.

Emerson and Queron named their baby boy Archimedes.

Gwendolyn and Vincenzo named their daughter Molly.

The families thrived, the children were happy, and their parents were content. It wasn't until Molly's 16th year that a woman from a coven, *The Coven*, appeared in the canyon. She arrived in a bright blue steam engine that came to rest mere inches from the families' property. This was quite a feat, since no tracks existed on which to convey the vessel, and train tracks couldn't have been built in the area at all without several years of dynamiting and hundreds of determined workers.

Gwendolyn and Emerson recognized the woman at once. She was the leader of a very secretive group of witches to which their own parents once belonged. If you were a member or knew about the existence of the organization, you simply called it The Coven. Those outside the organization, though, who only heard of it in passing and invented wild theories about its functions, often referred to it as The Illuminati.

Now, we shan't speak that word again, lest this author find himself in a very precarious situation involving a secret society of witches who, above all else, hate being called by that name.

Chapter 46

The organization, which was hundreds, perhaps even thousands of years old, went about on recruiting missions to gather the most powerful among the magical peoples of the planet.

The leader of this society collected magical things, you see. She had relics from across lands, across seas, and across time, from grails of certain levels of holiness to waters from fountains of certain youthfulness. That desire to collect – and use – magic also extended to people.

Eventually word made it to the society's organizer that both Gwendolyn and Emerson Mace had children, and a certain society leader couldn't help but come investigate.

What happened that day is a conundrum, and what magic was used is a mystery – even to this storyteller. But by the time the sun had set on the day the bright blue train appeared in the canyon near the valley with the stinking salty lake, the Maces and the St. Mercallis were watching their children board a passenger coach on a steam engine. It was a train that, as Queron, Emerson, Gwendolyn and Vincenzo would all later agree when they reminisced about the events of that day, had definitely not arrived as any normal train would, although when it exited (somehow getting completely turned around while no one was looking), there were a pair of shining, very distinct tracks on which it rolled. Those rails appeared only long enough for the train to move across them, and they vanished from sight as the last wheel on the last car rolled away.

Gwendolyn, Vincenzo, Emerson and Queron continued their life in the canyon, though they never saw their firstborn children again.

However, both families had more babies, who in turn grew into healthy human adults. Those children found love and companionship with others among the city, and eventually had children of their own. As witches are wont to be, some were good, some were evil. Some were powerful, and some were weak. Some were beautiful, and some were ugly. Some were successful with little effort, and others barely survived with many struggles. After many generations, some didn't even know their lineage and weren't aware of their own potential.

I am happy to report, though, that their stories, each and every one of them, are astounding. Some of their tales are tragic, and some of them lived happily ever after. All of their stories are adventurous. A few are frightening enough to turn one's hair white, and if one's hair is already white, the stories may very well turn one's hair completely invisible.

Perhaps those stories can be told in another time and in another place.

Step 7: Take Copious Notes Along The Way, As Really Anything Could Happen

"While we have examined traversing time and dimensions from a theoretical standpoint, there will still be much to learn once the traveling has begun. In fact, through a nearly mind-numbing amount of calculations, I have surmised that the travels of one person can likely affect the lives of hundreds, thousands, or perhaps even millions of others. Therefore, it is suggested one takes along a book and fountain pen to record the results of such interactions."

– Dr. Gustopher C. Cerulean, as quoted in the copious notes of Bratticus L. Magleby.

Chapter 47

This step is your story, dear reader. There's a crucial element to this entire chronicle of magic, murder, machines, and mathematics, and that is the moment your reality is bent by the events in this manuscript. I am not as adept at mathematical equations as Bratticus L. Magleby, so I could be off on the exact time frame. However, the moment you find yourself trading places with a crystal orb sitting on a black cloth, please use this space to make note of your experience.

Step 8: Make Allies In Your Travels

"One can never have too many friends."

– Dr. Gustopher C. Cerulean, as quoted in the copious notes of Bratticus L. Magleby.

Chapter 48

The pond outside the apothecary just beyond the vegetable garden of one Dr. Gustopher Cramden Cerulean was pleasant to look at. Had it been there longer, many a resident of the City of Bell might have made regular strolls to it on a summer day. There would have been much holding of hands and much feeding of ducks had it been at the disposal of Bellians for some time.

However, the pond had not been there for long. And in fact, it had only recently appeared in its entirety when it traveled from exactly three and two-thirds seconds from an alternate dimension, which just so happened to be a mere 15 minutes ago. And any courting couples or duck feeders likely would have not found the pond to be a source of enjoyment at that very moment considering it was clogged by a 30-foot-long, bright red submersible (30-foot-long, bright red submersibles being legendary duck scarers and romance killers).

Besides, the hour was late, the moon had risen, and those with a penchant for feeding ducks were all fast asleep. Citizens of Bell who were eager for romance, however, were quite awake at this time of night, but rest assured their current activities most certainly did not include holding hands next to a pond.

The pond, as it turns out, was not that deep. The submarine that was now stuck within its shallow waters had the appearance of a large, red whale playing about in a puddle of water.

If anyone had been present to witness the sudden appearance of the mechanical beast, they would have noticed a hatch opening where the whale's blowhole should have been. And instead of an impressive burst of seawater, out climbed three very disheveled persons who, despite their waistcoats, petticoats, overcoats, fob chains, necklaces, brooches, lace, ribbons, frocks, socks, watches and rings, were embarrassingly plain compared to the ostentatiously fashionable residents of Bell.

It turned out the only witnesses to the sudden appearance of the mechanical monstrosity, though, was a gaze of raccoons that were stopping for a sip of water before attempting to sneak into the apothecary. And nearly all of them were able to flee safely before the submarine landed.

But this is not a tale of flattened raccoons, and it will serve you quite well to keep your attention on matters at hand and not on the compressions of procyon lotor by apparating subaqueous vehicles, thank you very much.

From the hatch first appeared a young and annoyed-looking woman with cropped black hair (even the thought of short hair on a woman would have driven those in Bell with the strongest constitutions to swoon in surprise). She was followed by an older man who wore a very sour expression indeed. The last to emerge was a woman who might have looked the most at home in Bell, although she lacked the specific array of colored accouterment to successfully pull it off. She had a look of wary bemusement, as if she might have expected something like this but wasn't sure of the extent of the situation.

The three stood atop Molly's submarine and surveyed the scene. Before them was erected a grandiose monstrosity, so tall that its roof could not be seen from their vantage point. Windows of all shapes and sizes reflected the glowing of the moon, and the structure appeared to be the conglomeration of many smaller buildings. From this side, at least, there was only one door. It was simple, unpainted, and seemed a bit out of place against the facade consisting of a garish hodgepodge of materials.

"What is this?" grouched Mr. Screech, adjusting his eyeglasses even as his once perfectly-slicked hair had managed to take on the appearance of a frightened peacock.

"It appears that we have docked," Molly said.

Chapter 49

Miss Molly St. Mercalli looked away from the structure. They were situated upon a hill. At the bottom of one side was a line of wild trees and bushes that lined a wide and meandering canyon. No, it wasn't a canyon, she realized. It was the darkness of a river. To the side opposite the building was the line of a forest at the edge of what could only be described as an empty llama enclosure. Two goats were asleep at the very edge of the fence, neither of them smart enough to awake upon the arrival of a undersea vehicle.

Down the front hill was a sprawling city with winding roads lined with blossoming cherry trees. Its street lamps lit the town like a giant birthday cake. The river - no doubt the same that could be seen on the opposite side of the hill - snaked along the outer rim of the city.

"Indeed," said Mistress Vix, who had completely regained her composure and was looking as prim and as pressed as if she had just stepped out of her home before an afternoon tea with the local society women. That Vix would never associate with society women of any stature outside The Coven was completely beside the point.

"Interesting that we should be spirited away to this pond," Molly said. "The Presidio is enchanted to seek waters with depth to allow freedom of movement. There appears to be a more-than-adequate river just there." She pointed to the body of water beyond the glowing city.

"Yes, but, you also didn't command your vessel to seek out any other waters at all, correct?" Vix said, walking toward the ladder attached to the side of the submersible. She looked back over her shoulder. "Is it even possible for you to move your submersible at this point?"

Vix already knew the answer to that question, and she didn't wait for Molly to reply before mounting the ladder and climbing down toward the grass below that particular section of the submarine. Molly followed.

"Will someone please explain what the bloody hell is going on here!" Mr. Screech bellowed, his tousled hairs vibrating with his anger. His voice echoed slightly in the dark, and he peered around in fear at the sound of his own shout being reverberated.

It's strange, isn't it, how echoes are magnified in the dark?

"Can't you see?" Vix was already out of sight, although her voice wafted gently up and over the side of The Presidio. "Molly's spell worked."

Molly, who had just begun climbing, stopped in her tracks. She turned and looked down the ladder toward where Vix was now standing. The master sorceress was slowly strolling toward the door of the building while examining the area around her. Molly looked up at Screech whose look of rage had faltered and was now a look of befuddlement. Molly wondered if her face bore a similar expression.

"You had better ready your gloves, Molly" Vix said as she approached the door, casting a momentary backward glance. "Just in case."

Molly landed on the moist grass, which was a good 15 feet away from the edge of the pond. Her black boots sunk into the moist turf slightly, and she had to steady herself on the edge of The Presidio. She wondered if she'd ever reach a point where magic took care of every tiny annoyance – such as keeping one's balance when dismounting one's magical submarine – as it apparently had for Mistress Vix.

What Molly did *not* notice, though, were the patches of what appeared to be scorched grass that Vix left behind with each step. Vix apparently did not notice, either.

Chapter 50

Molly untied the pair of black, lace gloves she had secured to her bodice. She tugged them onto her hands and hastily tied each with a flimsy knot. They were fancier than anything else Molly wore and looked only slightly out of place compared to the rest of her attire.

Molly was soon at Vix's side. They both turned to look at the submersible, upon which Mr. Screech was still perched, looking more like a confounded owl behind his moon-reflecting spectacles than he ever had before.

"Are you coming?" Vix asked with an air of amusement.

"I ... I think someone had best keep an eye on the ship, don't you think?" Mr. Screech called back from the top of The Presidio. "There, uh, appears to be a pair of goats just yonder, and, um, we wouldn't want any of them head butting The Presidio's hull, now would we?"

That The Presidio's hull was quite impossible to damage thanks to several enchantments placed on it by both Molly and Vix is entirely beside the point.

"Fine, then," Vix said with no desire to cosset this fragile excuse of a man at this time. She turned back to the door. "Do ensure Molly's craft is safe from rampaging goats."

The two women had reached the door. Vix brought her hand up to the wood and gently rapped. A pack of distant coyotes called to the moon.

Suddenly realizing he'd been left alone in this strange, new environment, Mr. Screech appeared to have second thoughts about guarding The Presidio from wayward goats. He scrambled from his position atop the vessel and was able to make his way behind the two witches before the side door opened.

Peering out from within the warmly-lit chamber were two faces, identical, both wearing expressions of perplexion.

All parties were silent, as each waited for the other to begin speaking. Finally, one of the men inside spoke.

"The, uh, the doctor is indisposed at this moment," the man in the forefront, whose name was Bratticus L. Magleby, said as he pulled a pocket watch from his waistcoat and checked the time. "But I would be more than happy to relay a message."

The man behind him, October was his name, narrowed his eyes.

"This doctor," Molly said, "is a scientist, yes?"

October spoke.

"What is this about?" He eyed the trio of witches, his dark and hypnotic eyes mystifying in the resplendent glow from inside the apothecary. "Are you ... spell casters?"

The three witches stood silently. A good deal of confirmation can be made through silence, dear reader. Sometimes a lack of words can mean as little as a simple "yes." But sometimes the absence of speaking up can lead to much greater - or entirely more horrible - things. In this particular case, and just for the time being, the silence indicated the former.

The latter was quickly on its way, though.

Here it was October's turn to look at his pocket watch.

"You're early," he said as he snapped the cover shut. "Very early. Well, that's either very good or very bad."

October spun away from the door and made his way back toward the doctor's machine.

Bratt watched him before returning his attention to the three new strangers. He was getting quite annoyed as now there were multiple people who seemed to know what was going on while he, the temporary keeper of the apothecary, seemed to be the only one still in the dark.

With the second man now gone from the doorway, Molly could see more of the structure's interior. It appeared to be one giant room. The light from the lamps near the door, and even the lamps that were placed on the variety of tables, desks, bureaus, counters, shelves, panels, buffets, cupboards, trays, and cabinets, did not penetrate to the outermost walls of the colossal room.

The northeast corner, Molly could see (or, rather, couldn't see), was bathed in a titanic blackness that she believed would stubbornly stay put even if all the lamps in the room had been moved to that section. Something was over there that Molly was happy enough to ignore.

"Well, I guess come in," Bratt said, his voice sounding very flustered indeed. "But hurry it up. There are raccoons about."

Chapter 51

This is the part of our story where the characters introduce themselves to each other and give a brief explanation of where they're from and where they're going and their general philosophy on life. As an omnipresent observer, you already know all these things and more. We'll be spared the niceties of the "how do you do's" and the "nice to meet you's" for two reasons. First, you know more about nearly all of these people's lives and goals than they're willing to share with each other. Second, none of them asked "How do you do" nor stated that it was "Nice to meet you."

The three witches explained to the two scientists how an event had disrupted time and space (they called it The Fabric) in a way that was draining magic in their world. Bratt explained to the three witches how he had been deluged by the meeting of five new acquaintances and the loss of one mentor amid the conundrumysticalities that had unfolded in a matter of hours.

Conundrumysticalities, as everyone knows, are enigmatic and supernatural events over which no one person or group of persons has any iota of control.

Molly explained her knowledge came from her own ability to peer across time. Bratt explained that Dr. Cerulean had actually *traveled* across time. Vix explained that she sensed some great rupture had happened, and it was up to the gathered individuals to do something about it. And Mr. Screech explained that he was in complete agreement with Mistress Vix.

Only one of the people seated at the table that late hour - the abstruse October Magleby - had refused to reveal where he'd gleaned his knowledge of events currently happening to both those present inside the apothecary *and* those reading the words upon this page. What was an absolute certainty to everyone, though, was that October knew things he was not revealing at that time - and likely wouldn't reveal at any time in the future.

"So I'm to understand Madame Vermilion *and* Dr. Cerulean are the cause of whatever's happening here?" Bratt said to the group, now seated at the dining table.

"We believe so," Vix said, casting a glance toward the now tight-lipped October.

October, for his part, rolled his eyes at Bratt's question. Had he not just explained this fact to his alternate dimensional counterpart not moments ago?

Vix did not like October nor his secret keeping. There was a spell she could use to extract information from his mind, but it involved looking into the eyes of the person upon whom the spell is being worked. However, she could feel her magic didn't work the same way here as it did in the place from which they'd come. At this moment she was unsure she'd be able to properly execute the spell, yes, but she was also fearful of looking into October's dark eyes, a feature she saw he shared with Bratticus.

Vix, in her wisdom, had made an educated guess on to why the men's eyes looked the way they did. If her assumption was correct, those eyes had impenetrable powers. Even if magic here worked the same way it did in Vix's realm, she wouldn't dare attempt to permeate those eyes.

She looked toward Molly, whose gloved hands lay folded daintily upon the tabletop. The two women's eyes met, and Vix's glance darted quickly to Molly's gloves and then back to her face in a clear message: Use them.

October noticed the exchange and slanted his eyes in suspicion.

"Well, she's running amok in the city," Bratt said scowling as he spoke of Vermilion. He had not noticed Vix and Molly's interaction – or October's reaction. "She uses the power of life as the battery for her magic.

Disgusting."

Vix's attention piqued.

"Could you explain?" she said.

Bratt recounted the events leading up to that moment, detailing how Madame Vermilion left death in her wake even as the spells she cast created a bedlam he'd never before witnessed. Molly's expression shifted to one of disappointed understanding.

Had Molly have seen the scorched turf left in Vix's footprints before the group entered the apothecary, she would have now realized why the grass had died beneath the sorceress's feet: The minor magics Artemis Vix habitually used to keep her clothes free of wrinkles, her nose flawlessly powdered, and her balance perfectly maintained on wet grass, was being drawn from living things around her.

She hadn't noticed, though, but she had come to understand that magic in this realm came not from the power within a witch, but from the power of things within the vicinity. This meant she couldn't - or at least shouldn't - use her magic gloves.

Vix, in her turn, was glad she hadn't attempted her spell to reveal the truth. It no doubt would have left one of the four people before her either dead or comatose. In the grand scheme of things, she actually didn't care much about whose life was ended and when, but at this moment, she believed everyone at the table was necessary in the mission to fix whatever had been broken — and to help her find a very rare magical prize indeed.

Mr. Screech had stayed silent the entire conversation save for his intermittent agreements with Vix. He continued that silence now.

Vix stood.

"Very well," she said. "I believe it's time to find this Madame Vermilion."

The others, who had silently been wondering when the conversation would end and the group would go about trying to locate the tiny but rotund witch in Bell below, also stood. As Molly rose from her chair, the device strapped to her left arm momentarily caught on the arm rest.

She was suddenly reminded of the thing that had set her apart from the rest of the witches in The Coven.

Chapter 52

Her epiphany was brief, as the group had already begun to walk toward the door.

On her wrist was her device, a mechanism housed in a layer of leather that had been enchanted to contain the electromagnetic energy inside. Considering the events at hand, she'd all but forgotten it.

Her gauntlet contained some clockwork, a bit of flint, and a flat, rectangular magnet that she had carved from a meteor. Its sole purpose was to add extra energy to Molly's magic, as a dose of cocaine might add extra energy to a youngster on his way to grammar school. Yes, the child could get to the schoolhouse and learn quite well on his own, but that metering of medicine would give him the drive to continue his studies for hours after the bell had rung.

The device had served her well. It had taken her many times to get it right, though. The magnet inside had the tendency to attach to any piece of metal and never let go. She had finally had the idea to house it within a pocket of bewitched leather one day when she witnessed a curmudgeonly, crotchety, weather-worn woman shouting at a grocery store clerk for not having enough red beans in stock. There was such power being expelled from a piece of old cowhide, Molly had thought at the time.

That revelation had led her to create the gauntlet's case, which held all the magnet's powers in place and extracted them as needed.

She had been so pleased with her invention's effectiveness that she used the rest of her meteor and at least half a cow to craft several identical devices to gift to other witches in The Coven.

However, being an astute observer of the human condition, Molly reconsidered her decision to hand out these magical enhancers. After all, who knew which of today's allies would become tomorrow's enemies? Now the extra gauntlets - three in total, to be precise - were locked in a cupboard hidden in the floor of Molly's submersible.

That Bratt and Molly both had a penchant for hiding things in chambers hidden in floors was, as this humble storyteller warned you, a coincidence.

As you are likely well aware, flashbacks and memories can happen in a nanosecond, and this diminutive deluge of data happened faster than it took you to read this sentence. Don't think Molly slow simply because you're unable to read as fast as she can think. She was already mulling over the possibilities and probable consequences of using her invention as a substitute for life in order to generate her magic.

In fact, in the time it took you to read this entire paragraph, she had already formulated no less than 13 scenarios of varying degrees of abhorrence that involved using her gauntlet to fuel her spells - the least of them being that her machine worked perfectly and no one died, of course.

The most dreadful of the 13 cannot even be mentioned on these pages due to the sheer terror it would undoubtedly cause to anyone who read the words, or even thought of reading the words, for that matter.

All these thoughts and more were accomplished in less time than it took for Molly to straighten herself up after momentarily snagging her machine on the armrest of the chair.

She was so quick at both thinking thoughts *and* unsnagging instruments that she was able to make it to the side door of the apothecary effortlessly before Mr. Screech had even pushed in his chair.

Chapter 53

The gas lamps were doused, and the electric lamps were switched off.

The group gathered themselves, waiting a moment longer as Bratt fetched his overcoat. October, who was still slightly damp, didn't seem to care a sniff about coats. The witches three hadn't arrived with any sort of outerwear to speak of besides the articles of clothing already buttoned, fastened, stitched, zippered, clasped, tied, and pinned to their bodies.

The five stepped out into the cool night air. The sound of skittering raccoons permeated the stillness. Bratt, the last to leave the building, produced an iron key from his jacket. How odd, he thought as he inserted the key into the lock and felt it clink into the tumbler, that he should be standing here with four strangers - one of whom was another version of himself - outside the apothecary of Dr. Gustopher Cramden Cerulean, as he locked the building tight in preparation for a midnight stroll to the city below in search of a globular little witch who could be the impetus to bringing the doctor back and putting all this twaddle to an end.

He took a mental breath following the run-on sentence his mind had just produced.

He jiggled the handle to ensure the door was latched tightly and turned around. The three witches were watching Bratt and appeared to be waiting not patiently, but politely. October, though, had his eyes on something else. Bratt followed his line of sight.

There, where once Gertrude the loyal llama had lived his carefree life, was the 30-foot-long, bright red ship the three travelers had spoken of. Its hull, still wet in places, reflected the moon and gave it the appearance of stars strewn across a little, crimson, submarine-shaped universe.

"Don't just stand there gaping," Molly said. "We have work to do."

As the five began the trek down the grassy hill and to the city below, Bratt wondered what else would pop up at the side door of the apothecary before this night was through.

Interlude 4: Artemis Vix, A Brief History

I'll issue you a warning, dear reader. Mistress Artemis Vix, though young in appearance, was far, far, *far* older than you might have guessed. So in order to properly understand her, we'll have to look into the depths of the past – farther back into history than we've gone before in this story.

Please make appropriate preparations for such a journey.

Chapter 53

To set the scene of the origin of Artemis Vix, you'll need to look around you right now. Picture everything as it is, and you'll see the world of Mistress Vix. The only differences are that her story began about 500 years prior to your even existing, it happened in a land far away from your own, and it probably didn't involve anything you see around you right now.

She was one of several brides of an incredible king. "Incredible," in this situation, is a pejorative term, as one might look upon the destruction after a war as "incredible," or how one might utter "incredible" under one's breath if someone were to cut in front of one in a line.

These are both examples of the pejorative "incredible" on opposite ends of the pejorative "incredible" scale. But they both quite accurately describe the king of this nation, as does every other derogatory version of the word "incredible" on said scale.

Vix's husband was many things, but one thing he was not was a vampire - although he did go down in history as one. The fact of the matter is there are many creatures that suck the life out of others to strengthen their own power. Why, we already know of the witch Vermilion, who worked in just such a way. There are also politicians, ex-spouses, certain co-workers, as well the cousin in every family who constantly finds himself between jobs and is in need of a few dollars just to get him through the next week or so.

But of all these soul-draining individuals, there's not a literal bloodthirsty vampire among them because there is no such thing as a supernatural creature that stalks about in the shadows before seducing prey, puncturing that prey's arteries, and then draining the poor person dry.

Well, to be blunt, there *are* creatures like that, although none of them resided in the universe where Artemis Vix lived as a wife to an incredible king.

Her husband, for his part, helped Vix become the powerful sorceress into which she eventually evolved. When he took her as his first wife, she was only a minor magician who dabbled in petite prestidigitations. Her specialty was boiling water - a feat she could complete almost as fast as it took to boil water the traditional way.

She was satisfied not having any actual beneficial powers. After all, she was well taken care of. She had servants. She lived in a castle. She could boil water. Life was good.

Chapter 54

Artemis Vix's husband started developing an interesting habit. With each passing day of their marriage, he became more enthralled with the act of killing the people with whom he disagreed. This was usually – and forgive the pun, dear reader – overkill as the average life expectancy during that time was between 30 to 40 years old. It was likely most of the people with whom the king quarreled would have died on their own if the ruler would have simply exercised some patience.

If the king had a conflict with someone, he'd have the person killed and then placed on a pike for everyone to see. He considered it proof that you cannot win an argument with the ruler of the country. The fact that he'd place entire towns on pikes at a time, leaving no one left to actually get the message to not challenge the king, was completely beside the point.

You might not be aware (or you might be completely aware) that killing hundreds of people at a time and raising them on pikes works up quite an appetite. So following the king's winning of arguments, he'd have his servants lay him out a delicious lunch on a table. Of course, the king would always face away from the carnage so as not to spoil his meal.

Why anyone would want to picnic while hundreds of people with whom you've had disagreements hang dripping from poles is a mystery. But I dare say there are certain quirks we each have that other people don't quite understand, so let's withhold our judgments, shall we?

One fine, spring morning, Artemis was joining her husband at one of these picnics. As she made her way through the jungle of poles and corpses, a drop of blood from one of the unfortunate persons punctured high on a pike landed on a small ruby ring on the fifth finger of Vix's left hand. She was displeased, as any person might be in such a situation. She thanked her husband for inviting her to the meal but informed him she'd have to excuse herself.

She turned away from the table that had been placed in the center of the village in which her husband had come to disagree with people. It was a quaint hamlet with a main road made of cobblestone, which was lined on either side by buildings with thatched roofs. Beyond the buildings on either side were the forests that continued to shrink more and more each year as residents of the country cut down trees to build and to burn.

Vix thought she'd seen a pond or a river shimmering in the sunlight through the thick wall of leaves on the eastern edge of the forest. She looked down at the ring, which had lost its luster beneath the thin layer of blood.

The ruby ring was the only trinket of her mother's that she owned.Her mother, by the way, was a staggeringly accomplished witch who had been hanged, drowned, crushed with boulders, burned at the stake, shot with arrows, drawn and quartered, and buried in consecrated dirt for her magical efforts. Her mother found all these things quite annoying and often wished the superstitious peasants would just knock it off already.

Artemis Vix navigated around several poles with a variety of folks dangling from them. She began walking toward where she'd seen the water earlier so she could wash the ring.

After a short trek through the nearby grove of trees, Vix came upon a lake that had yet to be spoiled by the river of blood no doubt making its way from her husband's picnic. She went to her knees at the water's edge and dipped her left hand into the cold water. It was early spring, and this lake had most likely been ice not but a week before. Vix shivered as she rubbed the stone beneath the water with her right hand, attempting to rid it of the blood. It was then the ruby came loose and floated gently to the sand at the bed of the shallow lake.

Startled by this (her mother's enchanted jewelry never, absolutely *never* broke), Artemis Vix removed her hand from the lake and stared down at the ruby as it sparkled in the water. She lifted her hand up and inspected the ring. The gold settings appeared to have been bent outward, and one of the prongs had snapped altogether. It was as if someone tried to force a much larger jewel into the tiny setting.

Vix turned her attention back to the ruby, its image distorted by the rippling waters.

Had the gemstone grown?

She plunged her hand back into the frigid water and retrieved the stone, the biting cold sending another shiver up her arms and through her body. She held it in her left hand and prodded it gently with the index finger of her right, turning it over in her wet, almost numb palm.

Yes, the ruby was bigger. It was *noticeably* bigger.

Vix looked back over her shoulder in the direction from which she'd come. She couldn't see her husband or his skewered aggressors beyond the trees. She began to do the math, realizing that somehow the blood of some speared stranger had made her mother's ruby grow large enough that it had broken free of its setting. She only returned her attention to the water when she felt a sudden heat emanating from its direction.

It was a surprising feeling considering both her hands had been nearly anesthetized because of the lake's cold water. She directed her attention back toward the recently icy lake to see it was now bubbling and steaming. Her mouth dropped open in shock.

There before her, where the icy waters of spring had once pooled, was now a lake of boiling water.

Had she done this? Of course she had. It was the one spell she could actually accomplish, though she never guessed she could turn an entire lake to steam - especially a lake so cold.

Vix stayed on her knees a moment longer as she held her hands above the heat of the water, the rapid change in temperature causing her arms to break out in gooseflesh. After feeling had properly returned to the tips of her fingers, Vix palmed the ruby and made the journey back to her husband's picnic place at nearly double the speed in which she'd left.

Her husband didn't notice her right away. He was fully engrossed in his food – a nice piece of fish that had been pulverized, mixed with an emulsion of oils, vinegar and eggs, and spread on a piece of bread. Besides, it wasn't easy to see an approaching wife amid the small forest of townsfolk that had been placed on the poles.

Upon arriving, she immediately began dabbing her ruby into pools of blood and holding out her hand so the fresher blood that was dripping from the bodies could pool in her palm where the gemstone sat.

Here, her husband finally noticed her.

"Oh really," Vlad said in mid mastication. "My dear, that cannot be thanitary."

His "s's" came out as "th's" due to his two large front teeth that made him look not unlike a mule when he smiled.

Vix ignored him at first. She had to confirm her suspicion that somehow the blood had both caused the stone to grow and simultaneously imbued her with stronger magical powers than she'd ever experienced.

"Arty!" Vlad called, daintily dabbing the corners of his mouth with a frilly handkerchief. "Thweety bunth! What are you doing? I dare thay you're going to ruin that lovely dreth!"

"Something has happened to my mother's ruby," Artemis called as she reached up and dabbed the gem onto the fingers of a particularly bloody hand. "It grew!" She stood on tiptoe and wiped blood from the chin of a nasty looking nobleman and then plopped the crimson substance onto the ruby.

She hurried to her husband's table and stretched her arm out to show him the stone.

"Pumpkin, pleathe!" Vlad said, bringing the handkerchief to his mouth and turning away from his wife's hand, which was so covered in blood that it appeared she was wearing a long, red glove. "Not near the food!"

Vix pulled out her chair (her husband winced when he saw the bloody fingerprints she left on its polished surface) and resumed her position at the table. Vlad reached to the center of the table, where a lovely stuffed quail with a delectable shaved radish garnish sat on a bronze plate. With a queasy look, he pulled the food away from Vix's side of the dining area.

"Honeythuckle," Vlad said, turning away again from the sight of his blood-spattered wife, "you know I can't thtand the thight of blood when I'm eating!" He brought the handkerchief back to his face to politely hide a tiny wretch.

"Yes, I'm sorry dear, but please, look at the ruby!" She held it up between her thumb and forefinger. Some blood dripped onto her lap, and Vlad wretched again.

She was right. The gem had been no bigger than a ladybug not but 10 minutes ago. Now, in her hand, she held a stone the size of a scarab. Another drop of blood fell from Vix's hand, this time landing on the table itself.

"Oh dear," Vlad said as his face turned the same color as the peppered leek soup in the lovely painted terracotta bowl on the table. He momentarily disappeared behind his end of the table and vomited.

His watery eyes and a pale nose came back into view over the wooden horizon. His mouth remained hidden. "Well, that wath a wathte of fine cuithine."

"I apologize, Vladdy," Vix said. "But I hope you see the significance of this."

"Thignificanthe, yeth," he said with a frail burp. "We'll have to get your ruby rethet on a new ring."

"Dearest, watch this," Vix said. She clutched the ruby in her left hand and with her right index finger pointed to the nearest goblet of wine. It began to boil immediately."

"Oh, thugarplum!" he said with a forced enthusiasm, retaining his position half-hidden by the table. "Well done! You've learned a thpell to make mulled wine! I'm very proud!"

His tone wasn't sarcastic, but one of a mother congratulating her young son on creating a piece of art that would surely be hung on the ice box - even if the subject of the art was completely and utterly indiscernible.

"Vlad," Vix said with an air of exasperation, "I was able to boil the waters of an entire lake just a moment ago. It happened after the ruby absorbed that first drop of blood."

She held the gem up to the light. It was caked with coagulating gunk, and it did not sparkle. She continued holding it to the light nonetheless.

"This gem has given my magical powers strength," she said in awe. "It is feeding off the blood of these people."

"Bunny bear," Vlad said, now fully seated again, his eyes averted from the bloody stone. "I'm very happy about thith newth. But ith it pothible to perhapth uthe your newfound abilitieth thomewhere elth? It'th about time for dethert, and I'd love to be able to enjoy my papanathi thomewhat."

"I'm sorry, love," she arose from her seat and strode around the table to where her husband sat. She bent over and gently kissed him on the forehead. "I'll take a horse back to the castle and leave you to your picnic."

"Thank you, my thunshine," Vlad replied, holding back yet another wretch. "I'll thee you back at home."

Chapter 55

Over the ensuing years, Artemis Vix used the blood of her husband's victims to power the stone, which in turn powered her. She found it gave her more and more magical strength, and she was able to undertake the most difficult of spells. She was even able to do magic of which her mother could only dream.

Vix's mother, by the way, did not openly confess her jealousy of her daughter over this. However, she did send fewer and fewer Winter Solstice dinner invitations to Vix, and the time came when the two didn't see each other at all. Secretly, Vix's mother was angry she'd ever given the ring away. Why, if she'd known what that stupid ruby was capable of, she would have kept it for herself.

Over many years, Vix continued to accompany her husband on his post-massacre picnics. The ruby grew to the size of a sparrow, and then to the size of a robin. Eventually the gem was the size of a baby, with shards of red rock jutting out at random intervals. It looked nothing like the precisely cut jewel that once adorned her finger.

Even without her mother's tutelage, Artemis Vix used her blood ruby to become, arguably, the most powerful person on the planet. But she had little desire to rule countries - or the world, for that matter. Her husband was happy enough to continue his reign of terror over the people of his land. Vix, for her part, began to study the art of magic itself.

What Artemix Vix didn't realize was that all the life that had been squirreled away inside the gem was also adding years of life to her own. She had unknowingly consumed the years lived from each and every person whose blood had fed the ruby.

That figure, dear reader, was a massive sum. If you wish to know the exact number, you'd be better off having a mathematician – such as Bratticus L. Magleby – provide for you a more accurate calculation.

Years passed, as years usually do, and Vix was left a widow when her husband killed. By then, though, it hadn't mattered much to Vix considering she hadn't seen him in at least a decade after he made the unforgivable mistake of being captured and imprisoned by his enemies.

She had long since moved on from her position as wife to the king, embarking on a worldwide journey of discovery.

After finding that she had mastered all she could in her little country, Artemis Vix set out to find new magic in new lands. On her travels she found there were other people who could also harness mystical powers. From tribes in jungles to royal advisors to politicians to urchins, there appeared to be all forms of magic in countless classes of people.

Every time she found a person who showed extraordinary abilities, she stopped, established a home, and set about learning. In the process, she began amassing a collection of enchanted items, including talismans, wands, crystal balls, poppets, gris-gris bags, seer stones, amulets, dolls possessed by demons, marbles possessed by angels, several magic hats, and a quill that imbued its operator with the ability to write continuously without having to eat or sleep – and without having to re-dip into an inkwell.

Vix usually spent years at a time in a single town, studying the crafts of the local sorcerers, shamans, priestesses, magicians, witches, and general populations who weren't even aware they showed magical aptitude, all the while adding to her stockpile of objets d'art. When communities began showing signs of suspicion at Artemis Vix's uncanny ability to remain young, she would pack up her ever-increasing collection of ensorcelled equipment and paranormal paraphernalia and leave.

This practice was simple enough the first few times, but after a couple of centuries, Vix found it harder and harder to both find places to store her collection of curiosities and adequately move them about when the time came for her to leave. Although magic could help in her tasks some of the time, it wasn't always the answer - especially since many of the items in her agglomeration of curios were enchanted, thus making them impervious to outside powers.

Why, the Inforcible Fetish, a devious little doll she'd acquired during a 20-year stint on a tropical island, took at least two Clydesdale horses to move it about. Moving across the globe was becoming infeasible.

Chapter 56

There was a time when Artemis Vix almost had to leave her entire collection of curiousities behind when her studies set in motion a series of very gruesome events.

She'd traveled by ship across the sea to a land that had yet to be spoiled by the actions (and inactions) of colonizers. Artemis Vix built herself a cottage on the edge of a new and burgeoning town, complete with an expansive chamber beneath the stones of the home's foundation in which to store her enchanted items.

Chambers beneath floors are the coincidental choice for hiding things throughout this story, you see.

The funny thing about the predicament in which she found herself was that it actually didn't involve magic at all. The townsfolk got it into their heads that Artemis Vix was an evil witch (a "bride of Satan," as one particularly disagreeable housewife liked to call her) not because they discovered her doing magic, not because they found her treasure of thaumaturgical trinkets, and not even because they noticed she had the uncanny inability to age.

No, they labeled her a witch because she was a woman who lived alone during the same time a crop of corn withered and a cow died.

Never you mind that the corn was killed by the inept farmer's complete ignorance on the practice of keeping crops alive. And never you mind that his cow died because it was old and didn't own a ruby that inoculated it against the ravages of time like *some people* in this tale.

For this, Vix was hanged.

Of course, she couldn't actually die, but she did have to pretend. If you think faking lifelessness while strung up on the gallows as an entire town watches is easy, then you've clearly never had to shoulder such a burden.

Luckily, the town doctor was as inept (if not moreso) than the farmer, and he declared Artemis Vix dead without even checking for a pulse. She was cut down, wrapped in a burlap sack, and thrown into the nearest river. Her little cottage was set aflame, and the townsfolk went about finding another woman to blame for their own incompetency.

After a few frustrating moments, Vix was able to free herself from the sack and make her way ashore. While she hadn't spoken to her mother in at least 200 years, she thought of her at that moment and empathized.

From afar, Artemis Vix could see the smoke rising from her burning cottage. She was saddened that her handiwork was now going up in flames, but she didn't worry about the secrets stashed beneath the foundation. Magical objects, you see, can be hidden, lost, or disguised, but they can't be destroyed unless their power has been completely used up. And none of the objects beneath her cottage were even close to being drained.

However, she couldn't simply stroll back into town and inform everyone that she'd be out of their hair just as soon as she collected her store of mystical items from a secret cellar beneath the ashes of her house, thank you very much. Yes, she would survive every attempt the townsfolk made on her life, but she couldn't risk revealing the collection beneath the stones. There were more than a few objects that could do some serious damage if they fell into the wrong hands – say an imbecilic farmer, for instance.

Unless there was a way she could quickly gather her things and be off before a mob of the willfully ignorant had a chance to steal away even one of the pieces of the collection, Vix had to bide her time. However, there was one thing she couldn't leave behind: her mother's ruby.

Luckily, it was easy enough to retrieve from the grotto beneath the rubble of her former home. Getting one piece of her collection would be simple in the cover of night, since the people in the little village were deathly afraid of literally everything once the sun had set. She only had to wait until darkness fell to silently slink to the remnants of the cottage, remove the chunk of black slate that served as a doorway to the chamber below, walk down a small set of stairs, and pick up her gem.

As she walked back up the stairs, she briefly considered placing the Inforcible Fetish atop the stone that led into the cell. It would ensure no one could even accidentally stumble upon her treasure. However, one thing she did not have handy was a pair of Clydesdale horses to move the little doll, so she contented herself with replacing the doorway and covering it with soot.

And it was there the cellar remained, undisturbed, for many years.

Chapter 57

Vix was wary of this new land, and she didn't want to expose herself to another round of angry mobs finding interesting ways to dispose of witches. She'd seen how bitter it had made her own mother, after all. However, she also didn't want to stray too far away from the site lest some unwitting contractor come along, attempt to build a new structure, discover what lies beneath the foundation, and unleash a curse that would leave anyone within 100 kilometers of the site completely unable to see the color purple.

She didn't so much care about the folks in the town when it came to observing shades of color. But there were at least six native tribes within such a curse's perimeter that she was quite fond of.

So she, and her ruby, waited. She crafted herself a quaint little dwelling in a mound in the forest. She wasn't invisible, mind you, so every now and again a hunter or a lost child would come across her humble abode. She may not have had all the magical tools at her disposal that she might have before she was lynched, but she still had the ruby. Luckily, it had enough power to help people forget they'd seen this woman.

Although, magic that makes people forget is never really absolute. If you've ever walked into a room and everything is in such a place that you feel as if this exact moment has already happened before, that's a sure sign that someone has placed a forgetting spell on you. If you ever encounter this situation, you can guarantee there's an enchantress or a warlock in your life who's trying to control you in some way.

But we're not currently discussing which of your friends and family are secretly plotting against you and using forces beyond which your comprehension reaches, so I'll thank you to put it out of your mind and keep on topic.

Since memories cannot be fully erased by magic, those hunters and lost children would return to their various lodges and homes with tales of a witch in the woods. They could never pinpoint the spot in which they'd discovered her, and since they couldn't actually remember what she looked like, they simply made things up and recounted stories that they believed would entertain their audiences. (It's a shameful practice, to be blunt.)

Over time, a local legend grew, and the incredibly superstitious and ridiculously under-educated masses found themselves steering clear of the so-called haunted woods. By extent, the village in which Vix once resided eventually became a ghost town. And soon enough, if you can count half a century as "soon enough," there wasn't a single soul left in the town to bother her.

She was now clear to repossess her possessions. But as Artemis Vix unearthed the chamber that had now been hidden for so long, she became wary. What if something like this happened again? She, just like everyone else who has ever lived, didn't know how long her life would actually be, and she didn't want to gamble on another house where she might be found out. There was too much power in her collection. She either had to find a way to stay mobile or she would have to divide and hide her accumulation of occultic riches, piece by piece, around the globe.

Altruism is a strong force, but greed is stronger. So while Vix didn't want the amassed magical items to be used for evil, she also didn't want to let go of the power she'd collected over centuries.

Thankfully, the answer to many of Mistress Vix's maladies came not from the mystical arts, but from the mind of an inventor. After more than 400 years of life and nearly 150 years after she realized she couldn't risk staying in one place for too long, a device was created that could both move many items across wide expanses, and serve as a place to live. As soon as Mistress Artemis Vix heard tell of this incredible contraption, she immediately went about securing a locomotive for herself.

Step 9: Prepare Yourself For Changes That Might Occur As A Result Of Your Travels

"While it's true that one cannot alter one's own history through traversing time and dimensions, it's entirely possible to alter one's present by stirring up too much mischief amidst your travels. Mischief can come in the form of many things, not most of which is, which is."*

— Dr. Gustopher C. Cerulean, as quoted in the copious notes of Bratticus L. Magleby.

* After reflection on recent events, it's far more likely the doctor said, "Which is, witches." — Annotation by Bratticus L. Magleby.

Chapter 58

"What an … interesting little town."

Molly St. Mercalli was the first to speak as the group arrived at the first street sign on the edge of the City of Bell. The signpost, which usually informed travelers that they were about to enter Cherry Tree Lane, was currently aflame. This was unfortunate because it made the letters totally illegible and would, no doubt, lead to more than a few frustrated travelers attempting to find the regionally-famous road with the regionally-notable cherry trees, which folks from around the region traveled to in order to witness the trees' spectacular springtime blossoms.

That any frustrated traveler would rely on a sign and not the obvious street lined with blossoming cherry trees before them is utterly off topic. Those blossoms, however, were now all dead, and the trees instead were covered with a variety of fetid fungi. The huge, fanlike sprouts were giving off a pungent odor so offensive that each member of the group momentarily eyed each other, believing one of them had passed wind so noxious that surely something had to be medically amiss.

From above the city, it had appeared the streetlamps were glowing in the night. Now that they were within its borders, though, the scientists and witches saw that none of the street lamps were lit at all. The warm light they'd witnessed from the hill was in fact the signposts - all of which were burning.

The group walked up Cherry Tree Lane, all of them holding hands and handkerchiefs across their noses to hold the smell of the trees at bay. Every few meters they'd happen upon a misshapen pillar of some sort. At first, Bratt thought they were perhaps large, black cocoons. Upon closer inspection, though, he found them to be made of scales, as if dark snakes had suddenly formed on the streets of Bell, except they had neither tails nor heads to speak of.

These pillars were anywhere between approximately 154 centimeters to 190 centimeters tall, and were, generally speaking, human-shaped.

Bratt stopped himself from thinking the worst, and as he mulled over a list of more pleasant thoughts, he nearly walked directly into a body of water.

The road stopped abruptly at the small river, which all three witches and one of the scientists considered an odd choice considering the road continued on the other side despite a clear lack of any sort of bridge to connect it.

Bratt, though, knew something the others didn't: This river didn't actually belong here and had been, at least the last time he was in town, Dorfeture Drive. The visitors would have known this fact had the signpost not been completely aflame.

The river was not actually made of water, either. Bratt, with his hand still over his nose, stooped to get a better look. Had he been able to smell properly, he would have noticed the familiar scents of hops and barley. Dorfeture Drive, which coincidentally led to the Brandeline Bragg's Beer Brewery, was flowing with a combination of porter, pale ale, stout, pilsner, bock, and lager. What the group couldn't see up the street was that every barrel of Brandeline Bragg's Beautific and Balmy Beer had burst, turning Dorfecture Drive into a river of sudsy alcohol.

What they couldn't see at the bottom of the street was that a gathering of four dogs, three deer, a small gaggle of geese, twelve rats, two cats, one skunk, nine squirrels, and a mule were all teetering on the verge of being the drunkest they'd ever been thanks to the free flowing beer.

That any of these animals experienced drunkenness before this day has nothing to do with the story being told, and if you want this tale to continue on, then it would be much appreciated if you didn't continue down side plots that have nothing to do with the overall narrative.

"It's not deep," Bratt said to his companions, the words muffled slightly through his fingers. "There's a road under there. It can't be more than a few inches."

He looked back to the flow in front of him.

"We have to cross," he said. "Both the mayor's house and the City Hall are on the other side. It'll be fine. A little beer never hurt anyone's shoes."

Vix would have begged to differ, having had several pairs of shoes that had been ruined by spilled brews over the years. However, this was neither the time nor the place for begging or for differing.

With a confident stride, Bratt stepped into the stream and immediately fell to his waist in the frothy suds. Yes, Dorfecture Drive *had* been in the place where this river of brew now flowed. Clearly, though, that road was no longer there.

Dorfecture Drive, by the way, had at this point been relocated with no notice whatsoever to Very Wide Way, which was an extremely narrow alley on the other side of town. For that matter, several other highways, throughways, streets, drives, roads, lanes and thoroughfares had also managed to uproot themselves from their original locations and wiggle their ways into the Very Wide Way.

Consequently, all the folks who lived and worked along Very Wide Way found it indubitably difficult to get about their daily business. The people were crowded with streets.

However, a short time after the bevy of roads had converged, the people found a few other things that made their daily business incredibly difficult, and the smarter of the town's people (those who were the most successful at monetary gains through insurance fraud) decided that day would be the perfect day to tidy up their cellars and not emerge for a while.

Those who didn't descend into cellar safety found themselves in quite the quandary indeed, as they either became sidewalk fixtures in the forms of scaly, black pillars, or they simply stopped existing altogether.

It was bedlam on a scale no one had ever seen before, and no one would ever see since – at least, not on this particular orbit of existence.

Chapter 59

Bratt stood in the gushing beer for a moment deciding if he should wade across to the other side of the street, hoping the river didn't go deeper. The current, though, was already quite fierce, and if he didn't decide quickly as to his next course of action, he may very well be swept away to the bottom of the creek where a menagerie of beasts were at work becoming industriously intoxicated.

One of those beasts, a mule, had wandered farther up the road so he didn't have to force his way through the crowd of animals gathered around flowing beer at the mouth of the river. The group heard it clop-clopping unevenly as it meandered into the light of a nearby burning signpost.

"Get out of the river, Bratt," Molly said as an idea popped into her head.

Bratt did as he was told, happy to have someone else make the decision for him so he didn't appear to be a coward.

Molly eyed the mule, the poor beast swaying back and forth in its drunkenness as it tilted its head down to the river for another drink. She glanced back to the group, all of them looking as though they'd just witnesses some unspeakable act of impoliteness with their hands and hankies covering their noses and mouths.

"I need you all to step away from the river. Go back down the street a bit and out of view for a moment," she said.

The four did as they were told. Bratt and October weren't sure exactly what Molly had in mind, but both Vix and Screech were already guessing at her intentions.

Molly stepped up to the river. She brought her right hand to the gauntlet strapped to her left arm and undid a snap. Beneath the layer of leather, there was a tiny copper key attached to a tiny copper hinge that was folded into the mechanism. If one were to see it without any context whatsoever, one might think it were a key to wind a clock or perhaps a tiny toy monkey that clashes symbols together and causes much annoyance. But this author has given you plenty of context, so there shouldn't be any confusion as to this tiny key's function.

Molly flipped the key up into position and gave it three quick turns. A tiny ticking began underneath the leather, barely audible over the sounds of gushing suds. She then pushed the key back down and snapped the fold of the leather closed. She looked around her for some quick materials. She strode to the base of one of the cherry trees and scooped up a handful of dirt. She then stepped to the river of beer and stuck her other hand into its depths. Molly stood again and rubbed the dirt and the beer together until they made a disgusting-looking paste in the palms of her hands. She knelt and, using the paste, drew an "X" on the cobblestone road in front of her. She then flicked some of the gunk back into the river. She stood, looked toward the burning signpost, before flinging a few chunks of the mud into the flames.

The signpost flickered and the mud sizzled in the fire. The group could no longer see what was happening, but they did hear the paste being flung into the flames and the hissing and popping noise that followed.

Bratt, October, Screech, and Vix, who were now standing around the corner of one of Bell's dozens of haberdasheries, listened in anticipation. Nothing was happening, or at least nothing sounded like it was happening. Then they heard the crash.

The group bolted out from their hiding place. They saw Molly glancing back at them with a terribly satisfied look on her face. Across the river lay one of the cherry trees, which had chosen that exact moment to fall over. It had managed to uproot itself from its position on the other side of the flow, and the top of its formerly blossom-festooned branches were now resting on the ground a few steps away from Molly. Coincidentally, it had fallen exactly on top of the "X" Molly had drawn onto the pavement.

About two meters down the river was the mule, still drunk but very much alive.

Molly's experiment was a success. She now knew she could create magic, at least a certain level of magic, by using her magnetic mechanism. Had her gauntlet not worked, you see, the life of the spell would have come from the poor, drunken mule. But the mule's life had been spared, Molly's device had worked wondrously, and the group now had a means of crossing the river of alcohol without fear of getting swept away.

The drunken mule, whose name was Todd, by the way, continued his inebriated ambling up and down the banks of the river, drinking his fill. If he were to die, it would surely be from alcohol poisoning and not from having his force sucked from his body by any close-by conjuring.

Molly looked triumphantly at her handiwork, then at her muddy hands. She glanced momentarily around for something on which to clean them, but found nothing. With a shrug, she wiped her hands clean (or as clean as she could get them) on the sides of her dress. She brought her left hand back to her nose to mask the smell of the tree and found she rather liked the aroma of beer and soil - at least in comparison to the noxious odor of the tree.

The group gathered around the branches, all of them wondering if this bridge was worth the trouble after all. In order to cross, they would have to touch the enormous spores across its branches where there once bloomed cherry blossoms. Up close, the mushrooms' pungency permeated even the most perfumed handkerchief, which happened to be Mr. Screech's.

"Oh blast that damned witch!" Vix said. "Couldn't she have enough sense to stop her silly spells when she realized they weren't working properly?"

Molly nodded in agreement. However, she wasn't exactly sure the pandemonium was entirely the fault of Madame Vermilion. She suspected all this anarchy was a combination of the witch's accursed spell casting and the event that had set these five people into action.

But forming a hypothesis on the genesis of the city's chaos and how daft certain witches can be were not getting the group anywhere. They'd have to hold their noses – both figuratively and literally – and continue on their journey by crossing a cherry tree bridge covered in disgusting fungi.

"Is there not a way to remove the putrefaction from this tree before we mount it?" October asked as he forced down the urge to vomit into the river of beer. "With whatever witchcraft you used to fell the tree in the first place?"

"I don't know what books you've been reading about how magic works, but it's not as simple as waving a magic wand and shouting some made-up words," Vix said before pausing a moment. "Well, at least not where we come from."

"Magic isn't some invisible hand that does the work for you," Molly interjected. "It's more like a gentle nudging finger that pushes things into motion that could happen without the aid of a spell."

October and Bratt, in response, merely looked at her.

"This tree," she said, almost pointing with the hand that was covering her face. She caught herself and pointed with the other hand instead. "It was going to fall over sometime, whether we were here or not.

The ground on the other side is loose. I don't know if it's because of the beer or if it's because whoever planted it was a shoddy arborist. My spell only sped up the process and made sure the tree fell in the exact, correct direction."

"How did you know that tree was going to fall?" asked Bratt.

"Actually, she didn't know," Vix said. "Her spell was designed to create a path across the river. The magic emanates into the ether, Molly's intentions find a foothold on whatever will work best, and, as they say, voila."

Of course, Molly *did* know the tree was the best option. It was her naturally occurring magic, and it was the reason so many of her spells were successful. But she held her tongue on this topic, though she didn't know if she was trying to keep Vix from sounding uneducated on the matter, or if she was trying to keep Vix from knowing how truly powerful she was.

"Spells like that are pretty easy, actually," Molly said. "Instead of trying to create magic that specifically causes the tree to fall, I create magic that looks for a way across the river. Then the spell finds the easiest way to get it done, and it gets done. Focusing on something as specific as removing hundreds of mushrooms from the branches of a tree, though, is far more difficult. It would require more elements, and more power. Even then, I can't say for sure that the work would be immediate. For all we know, the spell would cause the mushrooms to die in sunlight. I'm unsure what time it is now, but I'm guessing sunrise isn't for hours."

"In this case, it would probably be quicker shucking the disgusting things off ourselves," Screech said.

They were the first words out of his mouth since the members of the group had introduced themselves back at Dr. Cerulean's apothecary. Bratt, October, Molly and Vix were momentarily startled by this, having subconsciously come to the conclusion that Mr. Screech was likely going to stay silent during the entire endeavor.

They were all quiet for a moment. Whether it was to contemplate Mr. Screech's sudden vocal return, to mull over the mysteries of magic, or mere procrastination from the task ahead of them, none of them could say.

And none of them did.

October took a single step forward. It appeared he was going to be the first to either cross the tree despite the mushrooms or begin scraping the fungi off its branches. We'll never know his intention, though, because the air was suddenly sliced by a shrill scream.

October stopped in his tracks.

Chapter 60

The five looked toward the source of the screech, which sounded as though it came from across the river and further down Cherry Tree Lane. There, on the horizon, they could see a green blotch topped with a pink point barreling down the road. Someone - or something - was following.

Bratt was the only person among the five who recognized the woman running (or, rather, trotting) down the lane. It was Madame Veramilicent Vermilion. Hot on her heels was a scaly, black creature with vacuously black eyes. Its grinning mouth was full – too full - of long, sharp teeth. It was running after Vermilion. Chasing her.

No, Bratt realized. That thing wasn't running. It had two bulbous and knotty arms outstretched, looking not unlike the branches of the collapsed tree in front of the onlookers. However, where two legs should have been was instead the body of a snake. It was *slithering*. And it was a good thing, too. If it had actual legs, Bratt thought, it would have caught up to the fat little woman long ago.

As Vermilion and whatever was giving chase grew closer down the road, Bratt saw the monster was wearing tattered clothes. On its shoulders and torso, the thing was wearing a coat striped verdant and purple, which was ripped at the seams as though it were made for someone three sizes smaller. Around its neck appeared to be loosely tied cravat. And on its head, held on by the force of heaven only knows what, was a tattered purple bowler hat that was accented by a green floral printed hatband.

For a moment, Bratt wondered if this creature had devoured Mayor MacBritches and then decided to dress itself in his clothes. But no, he knew the truth.

The creature *was* Mayor MacBritches.

Behind the mayor was what could only be described as cracks in the wall. Wherever MacBritches' scaly body slithered, small fissures erupted outward, across the ground and into the air. The path behind him looked as though bolts of black lightning had been frozen into the night.

"Odds bodkins!" Mr. Screech blurted out. "How strong was that cursed heart?!"

"This goes beyond whatever enchantment was placed on the heart that woman ate," Vix said, barely holding back her hysteria. She tilted her head toward the ever-nearing witch and her serpentine pursuer.

"It's the event that's done this," October stepped up beside Vix. "I've seen that phenomenon happen in other places." He raised his voice to both be heard above Vermilion's approaching screaming and to be heard above what sounded like an approaching tornado.

"Which phenomenon are you talking about?" Bratt yelled with exasperation.

"That creature!" October shouted with an urgency that bordered on hysteria. "This Peculiarity has an effect on people!" Bratt couldn't help but notice October had glanced at one of the nearby scaly forms that stood silently on the street corner. "It changes them. It does things to them. Some of them become petrified. And some people, for some reason, are affected differently. This," he pointed at what had become of the mayor, "is one of them!"

"Those cracks you see are cracks in the very stuff that holds existence together!" he added, his voice raising an impressive octave that would have turned Bell's Operatic Alto Laureate green with envy. "Blast it all, I don't have time to explain right now. We have to find a way to kill it!"

"I have an idea," Vix said. "But we have to make sure Vermilion crosses the river safely!"

It was no sooner said than done, as that was the moment Madame Vermilion reached the tree. It surprised everyone, probably most of all Vermilion, as she scrambled across the fallen trunk better than any squirrel and was on the other side far quicker than the physical proportions of her body appeared to allow. She brushed every putrid piece of fungus along the way and didn't seem to care a lick.

She landed on her knees once she'd scurried successfully across. Her pointy pink hat was askew, dirty and dented, but still in place.

"IckGAHHH!" Vermilion's words vomited forth as she panted. "Ickgaaa EEEMEEE!"

The blackened snake mayor reached the upturned root of the tree. It appeared to struggle mounting the makeshift bridge as his tail-body couldn't quite gain purchase on the bark. The mayor-thing's incredibly wide shoulders seemed to throw his ability to balance on rounded catwalks that traverse rivers of beer into question.

Its dark eyes looked up at the group. Even from this distance, Bratt could tell. The eyes, a dark, purplish-blue spilling into black pupils, those were his eyes. Those were October's eyes. The mayor was now the second person Bratt had ever seen who now had the same, galaxy eyes as his own.

Intriguing, he couldn't help but think.

It opened its mouth and hissed, and Bratt's trance was broken. Inside the mayor-snake's mouth a disturbingly red tongue that flopped out to one side. The tongue particularly unnerved Bratt because he was expecting something long and forked, as one might find in an actual snake. Instead, it was wide and thick, as though a normal human tongue had been filled to capacity with jelly.

Behind the hideous thing, more cracks were appearing. Now the group could see that they weren't black. They were openings to something dark behind them. Bratt saw that there was some sort of space back there, and what was that in the darkness? A tentacle?

"Stop!" October shouted at Bratt. "Stop looking into the void. That's how he got that way!"

They all looked back at the mayor, who had now managed to get halfway across the tree, moving slowly with its arms outstretched on either side as if it were some sort of tightrope walker in a circus performed in hell.

"Stand back!" Vix said calmly but firmly.

The group did as it was told, with the exception of Vermilion, who was still on her knees gasping for air. Bratt and October each linked a hand under either side of the round little woman's arms (Bratt had to suppress when his hand plunged into the sweat-soaked material of her armpits) and dragged her away from the riverbank. Even among the chaos, Bratt couldn't ignore the repulsive odor of the old lady's sweat mixed with the obscene smell of the mushrooms.

Once the three were away from Vix an acceptable distance, Bratt turned his head away and let loose that day's lunch.

"Oh, really," October said, bringing his own handkerchief back to his face without realizing it was the same hand that had just been in Madame Vermilion's armpit.

Another pile of lunch then appeared at October's feet as well.

The mayor, in the meantime, was gaining. Vix didn't doubt the thing's ability to cross the tree – eventually. If it fell into the river of beer, it would most likely be swept away, but it would still be slithering around, creating breaks in the universe wherever it went. Vix was incredibly adept at many thousands of spells, but there was one she thought would be perfect for just this occasion. And it was one that came naturally to her without having to draw up any ingredients or shout out any magical words.

Before anyone could say another word or vomit another meal, the river of beer began to boil.

The snake mayor's eyes grew large with fear. Its dark irises looked like domino dots on the widened sclera. It looked down at where its legs once were and where its body was now perched. The scales nearest the river were starting to curl. The creature was being steam cooked.

It slithered quicker in an attempt to reach the end of the tree quicker, but in its haste, it lost its grip, and it fell into the roiling liquid.

There was a brief but bloodcurdling scream, part human and part beast, as the skin peeled back from the thing's muscles, exposing pink and sinewy innards that turned white as they boiled. The monstrosity writhed momentarily before finally going limp. What remained was swept away in the scalding liquid.

The trail of cracks left in the abomination's wake began to heal immediately, disappearing as though they were being rubbed away by an unseen eraser.

It takes a lot of energy to make a river boil. It takes even more energy when there isn't a magic ruby around to help out. And as Vix turned around to face the group, her look of triumph turned into a look of confusion - and then into a look of realization.

Poor Todd the mule had paid the ultimate price after all. And so had poor Molly.

Step 10: Should Your Travels Cause Chaos, Mend What You Can

"It is up to you, the traveler, to ensure you leave a place as close to the way it was as you found it. This will mean packing out what you have packed in, mending any machines or hearts you may have broken, and generally giving the dimension you've visited a good once-over to ensure everything is spit-spot."

— Dr. Gustopher C. Cerulean, as quoted in the copious notes of Bratticus L. Magleby.

Chapter 61

There were plenty of problems in Bell that night that had not been witnessed by Bratticus L. Magleby, October F. Magleby, Molly St. Mercalli, Artemis Vix, Byzantium Screech, or Madame Vermillicent Vermilion.

Where Mayor Rudy MacBritches' home once stood, there was now what appeared to be a giant black and green egg, which was broken and oozing a sickly yellow liquid all over the perfectly manicured lawn. That perfectly manicured lawn had grown hundreds of dandelions, all of them with tiny teeth.

Where Bell's best restaurant once stood (the restaurant was too chic to actually have a name), there was now a gaping chasm.

The Ridiculing River, where rapid and pristine waters once flowed, was full of a substance that oozed like honey – except it was black and smelled like the bottom of Bobbert Finn's chamber pot. Speaking of Bobbert Finn, inside his boot shop, shoes of all kinds had come to life and were tearing it apart.

Gregar Rumpkin's Candle, Candle Holder and Wax Fruit Emporium had melted altogether, including all the unmeltable pots and furnaces. In its place there was now a pool of gurgling mess, a conglomeration of wax, metal and wood, that looked as though it was ready to take on its own life, stand up, and walk away.

And all throughout the city, as what appeared to be nightmares sprang to life from every garden, townhouse, mansion, shack, and loo, there wasn't a single human to be seen save for Bratt, October, Screech, Vix, Vermilion and the late Molly St. Mercalli.

Vix knelt over Molly's body. She was never a sentimental person, and she wasn't about to start being one today. She did, however, feel a pang of regret at having lost such a talented protigé. She touched the young woman's face and wondered if it was actually too late to do something about Molly's very rude decision to suddenly die.

And then she remembered something else she knew about Molly – something Molly hadn't known that Vix knew. But Molly was dead now, so does it matter what she did and did not know?

"We have to get back up the hill," October said. "I've seen this many, many times."

"Oh, do explain," Screech said, his response tinged with annoyance at the very idea that any of this could have happened before.

"You do realize there's a universe right next to this one, don't you?" October barked back. "And that the only difference between that one and this one is how you, sir, decided to pass gas when we all first entered the city instead of waiting until you could hold it no longer when you saw that black snake creature?"

Mr. Screech was dumbfounded.

"He - he looked into the - into the hole in the sky!" Vermilion was in hysterics. "He looked into the hole in the sky! He stared into it, and suddenly his face turned black. He grew scales! SCALES!"

Bratt, who never considered himself a violent person, now felt a nearly unrestrainable urge to slap the silly woman back to reality – whatever reality was at that exact moment. He clenched his fists and closed his eyes instead.

Vix turned to look at Vermilion.

"Well, you're safe now. I'm very interested to hear about all this, but we have to talk on our way back to the apothecary." She looked back at Molly. "It appears we still have a chance to save Miss Molly St. Mercalli."

Molly had been drained of all her life force thanks to Mistress Vix's powerful conjuring. For all intents and purposes, she looked and felt dead. Whether it was because of the scientific augmentation strapped to her arm or whether it was some sort of power that came from Molly being a magical person herself, the energy that sapped the life from poor Todd the Mule had only sapped most of the life from Molly St. Mercalli.

"But in order for us to do something to save her," Vix said, standing, "I need one or two things from Molly's submersible."

"Couldn't we just use the walking stick to transport us up the hill?" Bratt asked.

October, never missing a chance to dress Bratt down - especially now that he had an audience - rolled his eyes theatrically so everyone could see his annoyance with the very thought.

"I'm surprised you worked all this time with a man who developed the ability of traversing time and dimensions, and you know nothing about how it works." Here he held up the walking stick, its handle directly in Bratt's line of sight. "The filter only works 13 times."

October thumbed open the panel that held the orb he'd taken from Cerulean's machine. He held it up between his thumb and forefinger. The light from a nearby burning signpost reflected into its shiny surface, making it appear as though he were holding a tiny ball of fire.

"See?" he said, pointing a finger at the side of the orb with the tiny puncture marks.

Bratt looked closely. There were, indeed, 13 of those tiny holes. One of them had been blackened around the edges, as the top of a tin stovepipe does after years of coal fires.

"We only have 12 more uses. Now," he waved his arm at the pandemonium of the city, "You see what's happening here? This means our little piece of the universe, and all the little pieces joining it, are deteriorating. Until and unless I can get another one, we need to conserve."

So Bratt looped his hands under Molly's armpits and October picked up her legs, and the group began their trek back up the hill.

Chapter 62

Here is what we learned from both Vermilion and October as the troupe carried Molly out of the hellish landscape that once was the neat and precocious City of Bell and back to the apothecary.

Vermilion, having cast a ludicrously lousy spell that backfired with a force she'd never seen, had Mayor Rudolph MacBritches' unrequited and undesired infatuation. She had thought she could remedy it with more magic, but none of her enchantments seemed to work at all and, in fact, led to even more problems.

As the City of Bell went haywire around her, MacBritches seemed not to notice, his attentions focused entirely on Vermilion. It didn't matter where she went, he was by her side. She had been trying to make her way back to the apothecary, but was continuously sidetracked by the Mayor, who pulled her into jewelry shops, dress shops, flowers shops, restaurants, cafes, diners, bars, and a store that specialized in nothing but second-hand bicycle horns.

He'd purchased all manner of items until Vermilion's hands were full of bags containing jewelry and clothes and one bicycle horn that was "like new." MacBritches' hands were full of bags containing every item imaginable for a lovely picnic in the park, where he fully planned to ask for Vermilion's hand in marriage.

It was a wonder the two were able to make their way in and out of shops in the first place, as there seemed to be issues everywhere they went. None of the shopkeepers were even remotely interested in selling items to shoppers, most of them having to deal with a variety of problems in their stores. The mayor wasn't put out, though, as he gathered everything he desired and noted, with each trinket or piece of food he placed in the bags he'd found behind the respective retailer's counters, that he was the mayor, after all. His credit was exemplary, and he'd pay each of the store owners back as soon as they had each regained their respective composures and finished flipping their respective lids.

But still, amid the city's veritable ataxia, nothing phantasmagorical had yet taken place. The streets were all where they were supposed to be, the cherry trees still had cherry blossoms upon them, and the mayor's house was still a house.

It wasn't until MacBritches dragged Vermilion to the hill in the park to watch the sunset that the city's terrestrial topsy-turviness turned to terrifying torments. That's when The Peculiarty became visible again, this time eclipsing the setting sun. Vermilion, having most of her faculties still about her, knew it was unwise to stare at the sun - even in an eclipse. MacBritches, though, having never witnessed a full eclipse of the sun, stared in awe.

Vermilion caught just a glimpse of the thing that blacked out the sun in her periphery, and she perceived it wasn't a celestial body covering it, but rather a paranormal force *opening* in front of it. As she looked at the mayor as he gaped at the sky, she saw his eyes blacken first. Then, like ink spilling across paper, the blackness spread over his face and down his neck. At first, his skin merely darkened, and MacBritches sat on the picnic blanket as still as a statue, his lips barely parted.

Then his skin began to change in texture as well as color. Following the same path the blackness had before, the man's epidermis began to pucker and harden, Tiny points poked through, puncturing the skin. There was no blood. The points flayed the skin, causing it to flap off in disgusting strips, exposing the shiny layer of scales beneath.

It all happened in seconds, of course, and once Madame Vermilion saw Mayor MacBritches' transformation begin, she was off the blanket and on her way out of the park as fast as her fat little feet could carry her. She didn't look back, but if she had, she would have seen the ground and the air around the mayor beginning to fizzle and break away, revealing the same void that had momentarily blacked out the sun.

The sun, mind you, had not been eaten away by the Peculiarity. But it had, at this point, set behind the western mountains, beginning a night of horrors not even the most deranged of minds in the City of Bell could have dreamed.

What once was the mayor, having made his full transformation, then resumed his pursuit of Madame Vermilion. It's true, he was no longer a human being by any stretch of the imagination, but the infatuation spell still remained. Vermilion had, at this point, trotted as quickly as she could toward the apothecary. That was when she heard the hissing, screeching noise of the creature. She looked behind her, and at the far end of Cherry Tree Lane, she could see it slithering toward her. She muffled a scream and darted into the closest building to hide: Mayor MacBritches' mansion.

What she couldn't see is what those tiny cracks left in the MacBritches thing's wake were doing to the landscape. As it slithered down Cherry Tree Lane, the blossoms fell from the trees in a domino effect, and the putrid mushrooms grew. When it undulated up the walk to the house, where Vermilion's scent was emanating, the grass on either side began to sprout tiny, sharp-toothed weeds. And when it entered the home, the structure began to transform from brick and wood to mucus and membrane.

Vermilion had found a place to hide in the mayor's basement. She didn't stay long, though, when the walls began to ooze with pus. She might have attempted to hold her breath and deal with it if a drop of the yellow liquid hadn't landed on the hem of her dress, burning a hole right through it. Frantically, she found the bulkhead doors that led from the basement to the mayor's side yard and was able to escape with only four more holes burned into her dress and one smaller hole burned into the back of her left hand.

Thus began the destruction of Bell. Wherever Vermilion fled, the mayor-thing followed. And where the mayor-thing slithered, the nightmares spread.

Chapter 63

October seemed to know plenty about what was happening in Bell, and it was never entirely clear where he'd obtained all this information. While he had mentioned, several times to several people, that his knowledge came first hand from his experiences traveling about this little corner of existence, it was hard for Bratt to know if this was the actual truth. There was something about October that wasn't entirely trustworthy; he seemed to have foresight into nearly everything that was happening - as if it were all written down in a story that he'd already read.

Nevertheless, October did divulge some very valuable information on the short walk back to the apothecary on the hill. The Peculiarity, this hole in existence, revealed something terrible beyond everything they knew. Looking into it and being completely consumed by whatever existed in the void outside caused changes, which apparently differed from person to person.

Mayor MacBritches, for example, was not only a pompous, self-serving, narcissistic buffoon, but he was also under an enchantment that was the byproduct of a curse. All these ingredients cooked together within the mayor, bringing forth the abomination that had helped plunge the city into the darkness in which it was now wallowing.

October said he'd seen such an occurrence not only in a universe next to the one they were all currently occupying, but also in universes spanning existence (he called it "The Bottle" several times) that housed them all. He'd seen men transformed into grotesque batlike creatures, he'd seen women mutate into viscous mounds of gelatinous gunk, he'd seen young boys transfigured into hairy, gnarly ape-like monstrosities, and he'd seen geriatric ladies metamorphose into giant, clicking beetles. All of these monsters, wherever they stepped or breathed, had a deteriorating effect on reality, as if they were releasing tiny, cosmic termites that munched away at the struts and girders of existence.

Whatever lurked outside the hull of reality was apparently infectious.

Most people, though, who were not affected by magic or narcissistic buffoonery, were merely transformed to into misshapen pillars of black scales.

October gravely explained that, unless a remedy could be discovered soon, this little pocket of the universe would cease to exist altogether. He suspected there was something even bigger beyond the border, but it, for one reason or another, wasn't able to make its way inside – at least not yet.

Vix also took this time to explain to Vermilion why none of her spells were working properly, and she made sure to chide the old witch for using magic that was never properly hers to begin with. Vermilion, having just been chased all around the City of Bell by a snake-mayor centaur, and then having just recalled every detail for the group, was too exhausted to argue.

Bratt asked no questions during the walk, but he was taking in every detail. Mr. Screech also asked no questions during the walk, but it might have been because he'd had the ability to speak scared out of him altogether.

Chapter 64

It was still night, and the moon was still shining, although it was now close to the western horizon. Bratt, October, Mr. Screech and Vermilion were all inside the apothecary, sitting in silence save for an occasional sneeze or unrestrained break of wind. No "pardon me's" nor "gesundheits" were uttered as the four waited and worried.

None of them had known Molly St. Mercalli long – save for Mr. Screech. So none of them had time to form an actual emotional attachment to Molly St. Mercalli – including Mr. Screech. But October had informed everyone that Molly was integral to whatever it was that needed to happen, and Artemis Vix was now inside The Presidio working magic on Molly.

Since it was only Molly who knew how to work the magnetic device on her arm, Vix had to hope there were enough raccoons about to power her spells.

Bratt assured her there was no shortage of the little bastards, but he still felt a twinge of unease when he finally shut the apothecary door and walked to the opposite side of the room and as far away from the energy-sucking magic happening in the submersible.

This in and of itself was a feat because it was the closest he had ever been to the northeast corner of the apothecary. October, Screech and Vermilion, who followed Bratt away from the door leading out to The Presidio, didn't walk as far as Bratt. Whether they realized it or not, the trio was deciding which fate might be worse: death by magical vacuum or the venturing toward the northeast corner of the Dr. Cerulean's apothecary.

Eventually, they satisfied themselves with a sort of halfway point, where they stood behind a large wardrobe that contained a few of Dr. Cerulean's best dress outfits, which he'd never worn and never intended to wear.

After about half an hour, Vix walked calmly back into the apothecary. Those hunkering down inside, hearing the opening and closing of the door, appeared from their respective hiding places. She had a dejected look on her face. Molly was not with her.

"She doesn't have the proper ingredients in her submersible," Vix said with some surrender. "I think there's something that can help, but it's in my home. We would need to use your device to get there, I believe."

She nodded toward October.

Mr. Screech broke his silence.

"Home?" he sounded as if he'd been holding the word in like a breath. He sounded downright giddy. "Back home? Now?"

"Now hold on a minute," Bratt said, walking back toward the center of the room. "What happens if we leave this place? Will it be consumed by this, this, whatever this is that's going on?"

"Perhaps," October said, looking at the walking stick in his hands.

Bratt waited for him to elaborate. The elaboration didn't come.

"Can you do it?" Vix asked.

"Yes," October responded, glancing toward Bratt. "It's a shame we don't have more filters. It would be nice to have a bit of insurance, wouldn't you agree?"

"Well, if Dr. Cerulean has any extras, I have no idea where they might –"

"I know," October interrupted Bratt. "I know that you have no idea. Well, time is not on our side, ironically, so it appears we'll have to travel to your world, Mistress Vix."

Mr. Screech's sigh of relief was staccatoed with bits of what was either breathy laughter or sobs. Vix didn't look directly at him, but she guessed he was probably wiping a few tears away from his eyes.

"To the submersible, then?" Bratt asked.

"We'll have to bring Molly out," Bratt said. "I don't know the risks of attempting to send an entire ship at once."

Bratt held his tongue, knowing that transporting a whole submersible was entirely possible given the fact that a whole submersible was now currently lodged in a pond at the side of Dr. Cerulean's apothecary.

Chapter 65

Molly didn't breathe. She had no pulse. Her skin, once the color of creamy coffee, now seemed as pale as Mistress Vix's hair. She was cold to the touch.

Bratt, who was versed in mathematics and not medicine, would have declared her dead. Although he had no formal schooling in what constituted as "deceased," he guessed a medical doctor would have arrived at that conclusion.

Vix, though, was adamant: Molly St. Mercalli was alive, somewhere in that corpse.

The group gathered outside the side door of the apothecary. The night was almost over. The moon had set, as it had a tendency to do after spending many hours in the sky, and a hint of morning light was barely cresting the eastern horizon, dimming the stars above the distant Procumbent Plateau (which was, in fact, a batholith that jutted vertically into the air).

October had flipped open another panel on his walking stick, located on the opposite side of the filter. Under the thin plate of metal, Bratt could see a series of clockwork mechanisms below four tiny, black dials. With precision, October adjusted each dial with a single finger and then snapped the lid shut.

"Well then," he said, straightening himself up and peering at the rest of those assembled. "I believe we're all ready to go."

Molly had been placed on the ground lying face up, her arms at her sides. The rest had gathered around her in a circular formation. To a stranger, it might have appeared some sort of séance was about to happen around the body of a dead woman.

But don't let's be ridiculous. They were simply preparing to travel to another world located in another dimension that existed in another time.

Bratt looked back down at Bell. The sign post fires had appeared to have gone out, and the city was dark. He wondered if there were any survivors. As October's walking stick sprang to life, it made a sound like electricity humming through a generator. Its faint blue glow engulfed the crowd in a perfect sphere of plasma. And as Bratt felt himself being pulled inward, he couldn't help but notice there wasn't a single dead raccoon to be seen near the submarine.

Chapter 66

It was a steam engine, and it shined in the bright morning sun of what felt like a chilly spring morning in the desert. Above, a vividly azure sky stretched eternally with hardly a cloud in sight. There were rolling hills of white and red dirt as far as Bratt could see, broken only by bushes of sagebrush, clusters of red sandstone formations, a range of purplish mountains in the distance, and the bright, blue gleam of the train.

On the side, printed in a bold, white font with black trim, was "The Trevithick," obviously the name of the beautiful piece of machinery. Behind it were what appeared to be two passenger cars and three boxcars, all looking brand-new, and all the same shade of brilliant blue trimmed with glossy black. There was no coal car, Bratt noticed, and he wondered what could possibly fuel the magnificent train.

For that matter, he wondered how that magnificent train got to where it currently sat, considering there wasn't a single railroad – or regular road – to be seen. Besides The Trevithick itself, the only other items that were clearly out of place in this desert were the six travelers - one of whom was lying on her back and appeared to be dead - and the patch of grass upon which they were situated. If one had observed the six people buzzing into existence on the soil of the near-barren landscape, one might have seen a raccoon crazy with fright darting from the electrical orb and out of sight.

Of course, there were no people in this area of the wilderness to witness the event – which was precisely the reason Mistress Artemis Vix chose this location to park The Trevithick.

"Do ensure all the sand is off your footwear before entering," Vix said without hesitation. She walked off the patch of grass and to the side of the passenger car as if the group's sudden transportation from the dark, grassy hill above the City of Bell to the bright, sandy desert was nothing more than a bump on a road during a carriage ride.

She left the remaining four to deal with Molly.

Bratt watched as Vix tapped the door to the car twice. When it sprung open and a small stepladder protruded from the train to the sand, he expected to see a servant of some sort inside. But there wasn't a soul to be seen in the entryway or beyond. After a second or two, Mr. Screech followed behind Vix. Vermilion took a look around and then waddled after Screech. October looked at Bratt, and the two resumed their positions at Molly's body - Bratt at the arms and October at the legs - and carried her to the coach.

The interior of the passenger car was extravagant, and it included many similar elements as Dr. Cerulean's parlour. Unlike Dr. Cerulean's parlour, though, the elegant coach was uncramped. Across the widows were drapes of a deep, burgundy velvet, which slid open the moment Vix entered. The morning sunlight poured into the windows and illuminated six crystal sconces. The small light fixtures were spaced neatly between the windows on either side. Their prisms cast rainbows across the interior.

The effect was not unlike the time Bratt accidentally chose the wrong mushrooms from the forest next to the apothecary to make a summer salad. He'd spent the next half-day watching rainbows flicker across every surface he observed.

Instead of rows of benches, there were two long couches on each side, each upholstered in white and royal blue damask.

"Place her there," Vix said, pointing to the bench on the right side of the car.

The men did as they were told, and Bratt carefully moved alongside a slender table in the center of the coach to situate Molly's head on a small pillow.

The table was covered in a cheery goldenrod cloth. Upon the cloth was a crystal bowl filled with green apples - which had to be wax, of course. They were each too perfect a shade of chartreuse, and there wasn't a blemish to be seen.

Vix noticed him eyeing the apples.

"You won't want to eat those," she said.

"They're wax, I suppose," he answered.

"No," she said. "They're real. And they're probably the most delicious apples you'd ever want to eat. But, alas, they are poison."

"Why would you keep poison apples in your coach?" October asked.

"They're just so lovely," Vix replied. "Plus," she added, cocking one eyebrow and casting a sideward glance at Bratt, "they come in handy every once in a while when there's a recreant step-daughter who needs to be dealt with."

The only person who might have found this comment funny was Mr. Screech. If he did find it funny, though, he didn't show it. He was not one to smile, and no one had ever seen him laugh. He'd likely never laughed in his life. In fact, I have it on good authority that he was born with a scowl on his face. When the doctor spanked his bottom, Byzantium Screech merely looked over his shoulder and let out an infinitesimal snarl.

As for Bratt, any similitude between Mistress Vix and fairy tale witches went completely over his head, as stories of jealous queens and tiny men didn't exist in his where and when. October smiled only slightly at the comment, though it was unclear if he actually understood Vix's joke or if he had been momentarily amused by something else. Vermilion didn't seem to be paying attention at all to the conversation and was far more interested in the fine furnishings of this, no doubt, very expensive, locomotive.

That Vix was joking was a sign she was back in her element. She'd been away from The Trevithick - her home - for far too long. But it was also an indication of something else, something no one present save for Mr. Screech would have truly noticed. Mistress Vix was happy about something more than just being home again, and if Byzantium Screech hadn't been so relieved to be back in his own realm himself, he might have noticed Vix's unusual jocularity.

"What's in the rest of these cars?" Vermilion wondered aloud.

"My personal quarters are in the next coach," Vix answered immediately, happy to shed some illumination on a possession of which she was very proud indeed. "The boxcars house my collection of magical artifacts, gathered from around the globe."

Vix and Screech and Molly's world, was, a globe after all, unlike the lens-shaped world of Bratt and October and Vermilion. Bratt cocked a curious eye.

"The globe?" he asked.

"The world, you silly idiot," Screech chuffed.

October stepped to Bratt and made eye contact with him – two galaxies staring at each other – and said in very audible whisper, "This world is round."

Bratt was flabbergasted.

Upon hearing about Vix's gathered treasure, Vermilion's eyebrows raised as her interest piqued. October, for his part, was noticeably unamused.

"Well," October said curtly. "I suppose we'll just sit around and talk about trains then, shall we?"

Vix's momentary elation at the chance to brag about her conquests was quickly quelled.

"Your point is taken, Mr. Magleby," she said. "Very well. Please, everyone, have a seat."

The four of them sat down on the bench opposite Molly. There was enough room to fit perhaps four more people. Bratt wondered if he'd ever felt so comfortable as his body sank into the cushioned damask. He fought the urge to close his eyes, and only then realized he hadn't slept for nearly two days.

Vix turned on her heel and opened the door behind her where the locomotive's engine stood beyond. Bratt could momentarily see into the engine's interior, which was not as he'd expected it to appear at all. Where there should have been levers, latches, pulleys, chains, wheels and cogs, there was simply a single wing-back chair that looked out through the windows, which gave a panoramic view of the desert beyond. He watched as Vix walked to the compartment where coal would be shoveled in an ordinary steam engine. She reached in and removed a giant gemstone, the color of ripe pomegranates, the size of a watermelon. It appeared to be giving off its own source of light.

She handled the stone with care, but she was also quick. As fast as she'd left the passenger coach, she was back inside again, closing the door behind her.

"The good news is that we won't have to be making any sacrifices - animal or otherwise - to work magic here," Vix said, placing the radiant stone on the yellow tablecloth. "The bad news is this could take some time."

She sat on the bench opposite Vermilion, Screech, Bratt and October, just inches away from where Molly's feet were lying lifelessly on the cushion. The sun through the window behind Mistress Vix gave her the appearance of an angel, her loosely-gathered pale hair creating a corona of white light around her face.

"Now," she said, speaking to Bratt, October, and Vermilion. "Magic is always more powerful with a coven of witches. Many hands make light work, as the saying goes. But, what use are many hands if those hands don't know what they're doing?"

The four sat on their bench, listening intently. Bratt felt as though he were back at university.

"I could either teach you all how to properly perform a spell, or Mr. Screech and I could do the work while everyone waits. Both scenarios will take time, but only one will actually work. Unfortunately, the only scryer we have in our midst is currently toes up."

Vix patted one of Molly's shoes unsympathetically.

"So the question is, should we rely on our energies combined to bring Miss Molly back from the brink and risk something going wrong? Or should only the two experienced among us work the magic and risk not having enough power to get the chore finished?"

Bratt, memories of being stumped in school now washing over him like a waterfall, wasn't sure if Vix was asking for the group's input or if she already knew the answer and was testing them.

The corners of Vix's mouth turned upward slightly in a grim representation of a smile. The rest of her face remained neutral.

"I think one of you knows the answer."

She looked directly at October. October looked back with an equally neutral look on his face.

"Young Mr. October Magleby," Vix finally said, "you seem to have an uncanny knack for knowing what's going to happen. Perhaps you know the correct path to take?"

October sighed dramatically, crossed his legs and leaned back, spreading his arms across the back of the seat. Bratt, who was seated to October's right, thought he meant to put his arm around him at first. But he realized October's melodramatic gestures were simply his way of communicating that he, like always, knew something that everyone else didn't.

He sat that way for a moment, and then he responded.

"It will work with you two," he nodded toward Vix and Screech, respectively, "and her," he pointed a thumb at Madame Vermilion, who was seated on his left. "Bratticus and I have another task to undertake, I believe."

Vix did not physically react, but only replied, "then let us begin."

Chapter 67

October had led Bratt out of the coach and away from the train. The two had walked about 30 meters away, over two sandy hills. The two stood on a third hill now, where they could see the locomotive clearly but were completely out of earshot.

The starkness of the blue steam engine was even more startling from this distance, the lack of any tracks even more pronounced against the vast desert. By now the sun had climbed a little higher, and the heat was on the verge of becoming stifling.

Bratt looked from the distant train to October and saw something he'd never expected to see in his doppelganger's face: fear.

"Egads," October finally said, an interjection wholly unexpected by both men.

"I believe it's about time you come clean with me," Bratt said.

"Listen," October said, bringing his voice to a whisper despite the pair's distance from the train. "Where I come from, that is to say, where I was raised," he stammered. It was completely out of character for him, or at least for the character Bratt had come to know over the last two days. "Things are going way off course from the letter!"

October had literal tears in his eyes.

"What letter?" Bratt said.

From his inside breast pocket, October produced an envelope with a wax seal that had been neatly broken. Bratt, having some knowledge in matters of sealing wax (he had, after all, been tasked with sending bills to all of Dr. Cerulean's clients), saw there was no deterioration at the edges of the broken wax, which meant it had only recently been opened. The envelope trembled slightly in the breeze.

Except there was no breeze. It was trembling because October was trembling.

Slowly, Bratt went to take the letter from October's shaky grasp. When October saw Bratt meant to take it, he clutched it hard, causing the envelope to fold nearly in half, and flung his hand back.

"No," he said, "you can't. It's - you're not allowed. I was given explicit instruction to ..."

October trailed off. A tear rolled down his left cheek. Gobsmacked, Bratt had no idea what to do or say at this moment. So he let his hand fall back to his side. He stood and stared at October and waited.

"I lied," October said. "I lied back there. I don't know about what will bring Miss St. Mercalli back. I had to. I had to get you alone because you're the only one I can trust now. I mean, we're the same, you and I!" he said with an air of hysteria, completely ignoring a speech he gave not too long ago about how different the two of them actually were. "Right? We're the same person!"

Bratt's eyes widened a bit, but he couldn't find the words to respond.

October took in three breaths and seemed to calm down slightly.

"This letter is from us," he said. "Well, that is, I mean to say" he stammered again. "This letter was written to me by another version of me from another timeline. His life is on a separate time loop than mine – ours. But it's all cyclical, you see?"

Bratt didn't see. He shook his head slowly and expected October to respond with exasperation, as he had before, at the very idea that Bratt wasn't grasping this concept.

But October surprised Bratt yet again.

"Well, uh, let's put it like this," he looked around the ground and found a slightly smooth portion of sand. Using his walking stick, he drew a large circle in the dirt. "This is everything - all of our timelines, all of our universes, all things past and present. Everything."

Bratt looked at the circle and nodded.

"This is me," here he drew an ellipse in the center of the circle, which gave his improvised chart a three-dimensional look. "And this is you." He drew another ellipse, which was slightly off kilter from the first.

"We're going around in a circle, you see?" He poked the cane twice into the sand, once on one ellipse and once on another, creating two dots that were almost touching. "We are aging, but our timelines are still spinning in an infinite rotation."

"Yes, I understand," Bratt said.

October drew another oval timeline, again off from the other two by a fraction. He poked another dot, this one placed on the new ellipse and at the opposite side of the encompassing circle.

"This is also us," he said. "A different timeline. But we've aged.

And we've lived through this. We've lived through all of this. The Peculiarity, the chaos at Bell, all of it. And we haven't stopped utilizing our ability to traverse time and dimensions, either."

He swiped an "X" at a point where all three of the ovals intersected. "Here is where you and I both crossed *and* diverted paths for the first time. Or, at least, versions of us who live in timelines near parallel to our own." He looked up at Bratt to see a new look of confusion cross his face. "Yes, it's all very difficult to grasp. Trust me. I have been grappling with these concepts since I first received the letter. But our meeting here," he pointed to the "X," "also included another version of us. One who had been through everything and had grown in years."

October straightened himself and squinted against the climbing sun. He shaded his eyes with the envelope in an unintentionally obtuse parody of a salute.

"He is the man who wrote me this letter," October said. "He gave me explicit instructions on things I needed to do and places I needed to be in order to stop The Peculiarity from happening altogether and saving existence - all of existence. Every possible macrocosm of life is at risk of being consumed. This letter is a roadmap on how to prevent it from happening in the first place - because it has been stopped before."

"So, you met the man – you met *us* – only older?"

"Yes," October said. "In fact, the man was at exactly the right place at the right time to discover me as an orphaned child. He was the headmaster at a university in my where and when, though he obviously had traveled to my universe from his own. He went by the name of Professor Purpureous P. Jones. He raised me.

"It was not until I received this letter that I understood the truth. He came to my universe many years before I was born to establish an environment where I could learn everything I needed to know in order to put this Peculiarity nonsense to bed once and for all. The letter is so specific. It told me exactly how I would come to the apothecary. It told me where to find the filter. It even told me that three witches would arrive while you and I were in conversation."

He looked down at the envelope in his hand.

"But that's when the accuracies stopped. The witches were early by nearly two hours. Our trek into the city was supposed to take place as the sun was rising. The other witch, Vermillion, was supposed to be dead when we arrived. Molly wasn't supposed to die at all! Vix's train - we're supposed to take it back to your dimension with us. But now I am questioning if we should."

He looked suddenly and painfully guilty, as though he'd just let loose a good friend's darkest secrets after being sworn to never reveal them. Another tear dropped off October's cheek. He didn't bother to wipe it away or conceal his breakdown in any way from Bratt.

"I - I don't know what to do," he finally said.

"Can we not visit the professor? Travel back to your timeline?"

October's surrender was pitiful.

"No," he said, his shoulders slumping. "Professor Jones is dead. And my ... my world is gone."

He breathed in.

"There is nothing left of my life back there."

The remaining tears finally broke forth, and October crumpled to the desert floor sobbing. He dropped the walking stick but held fast to the letter.

October's stoic and irritatingly pompous facade had broken. He was a man without a home. He had no support, no family and no friends. The letter in his hand had been his only light in the dark, and it appeared even it was dimming.

"Will you, please, let me read his letter?" Bratt asked.

"I can't," October said with a sniff. "It's the very first instruction given, and Professor Jones noted it was the most important. I can't let anyone read the letter - especially you. Besides, I've said too much already. I can't set things off course any more than they already have been. It would risk everything."

Bratt wondered if the "you" meant him in particular or if it meant any of the versions of him October might meet along his journey. He didn't ask, though. October had already revealed portions of the manuscript that he guessed Professor Jones would not have liked revealed, and it appeared October's fountain of information he was willing to share was drying up once more.

October gathered his faculties long enough to fold the envelope and return it to his inside breast pocket. He stood, leaving the walking stick in the sand. He wiped his wet face with the back of his hand, and then resumed his position of standing and shading his eyes - sans the cryptic letter.

"I am going to tell you one more thing from the letter," he said, "and I guess we'll see if it's a mistake or not to reveal it. But it's increasingly clear I cannot steer this ship by myself any longer."

Bratt nodded.

"We have to find a way to The Core of existence. It's the center that holds all these timelines together."

October appeared to have an epiphany. He looked down at his illustration in the sand and then at the discarded walking stick. He bent, picked up the staff, and drew a dot in the center of the large circle in the ovals within.

"It's the center of gravity," he said. "It holds everything in place, but it also fuels everything. And The Peculiarity - these holes in the skies that are leaking darkness and chaos into our worlds, is the direct effect of the damaged Core.

"We must go there, and we must fix it. We must use science, yes, but magic as well. It will be the most difficult thing any of us have ever done or ever will do – assuming we can survive long enough to get there, and assuming we can survive mending The Core after we arrive.

"And," October breathed in the warm desert air and let the breath out slowly and dramatically. "We're going to need a giant source of energy to do it."

There was a pause as both men looked down at the sand illustration.

"It is going to have to be more powerful than magic, though. Whatever that power is," October said.

Bratt gazed down at the scribbles in the sand. Three dots – representative of himself, October, and the elder October, also known as Headmaster Purpureous P. Jones. Each dot orbiting around a larger, center dot – The Core.

With the dot in the middle, Bratt realized the chart in the sand was, more or less, an image of the anatomy of an atom.

Somewhere in the distance, the hoarse screech of a hawk sounded as it swooped away from the desert floor with a fresh raccoon from another dimension in its clutches.

And then it was Bratt's turn to have an epiphany.

Step 11: Say Goodbye To Everything

"There are two very reasonable outcomes to traversing time and dimensions. The first very reasonable outcome is that things will turn out just peachy, everyone will be happy, and soon everyone will be having celebratory picnics in honor of you, a person who successfully traveled across existence and to other times and other spaces. The second very reasonable outcome is that everything will go to hell. In preparation of the very reasonable second outcome, it's best to say goodbye to everything and everyone you've ever loved before you travel — just in case."

— Dr. Gustopher C. Cerulean, as quoted in the copious notes of Bratticus L. Magleby.

Chapter 68

October's guess, as it turned out, has been the right one - or at least *a* right one.

Artemis Vix didn't pay much attention as the two men left her train and wandered out into the desert. Once the door had shut behind them, they were completely out of her consciousness altogether. She had more pressing issues that had to be dealt with.

Unlike October, Vix hadn't been provided a map of things to come. After witnessing The Peculiarity and the power it had over ordinary people, she knew she had to do something about it. Of every tool in her arsenal, she didn't believe a single one of them could do anything about the lurking void that had such a devastatingly powerful effect on the world.

If it punctured into their own, who knew how long they'd have before the streets of San Francisco were festooned with blackened forms that once were people. Or, considering the amount of residents she herself had cast spells upon, who knew how long they'd have before the streets were crawling with humanoid spiders or octopi with bat wings – or something even worse that none of them could fathom.

Of all the parts that made up the whole of Mistress Artemis Vix, one of them could be called altruistic. Admittedly, though, it wasn't a large portion of the sum. While an onlooker without knowledge of her intentions might believe Vix was heroic for her efforts at saving the world, the truth was there was more to her current motivations, not the least of which was that she still had much magic left to master.

For instance, for all her years and all her abilities, she was still unable to predict the future. To know which move to make next, she'd need precognition. And Molly St. Mercalli was the only witch she knew who had the gift of such sight.

Before all this nonsense, Vix thought, she never would have believed she'd have gone out of her way to save the likes of Molly St. Mercalli. The young woman showed a little too much promise and could, after two or three more years of study, be even more powerful than Mistress Vix herself. This irked Vix, considering she'd spent the better part of four centuries honing her craft, while Molly had been on this planet barely 21 years.

She needed her now though, if only for a little while longer. Besides, she'd found what she'd needed inside Molly's submarine, and she guessed it would be the catalyst to finally gaining what Molly had and what Vix did not.

Chapter 69

Bringing the young witch back from the brink would not be easy - even with Vix's powerful ruby. She'd need Mr. Screech's magical skills, of which there were few, as well as the magical skills of Madame Vermilion. Even then, everything was a gamble considering how magic had seemed to be sucked from the world as a sponge soaks up water. Vix knew now this had to do with The Peculiarty, but she was still uncertain exactly how the two connected considering The Peculiarity had not, to her knowledge, appeared in the world of Molly and Screech and Vix.

Vix had faith in Vermilion's abilities, and she hoped that since the old witch came from a different world, her abilities would not be hindered. However, they had to do something about that pesky curse first and foremost. Otherwise, any help from Vermilion would, at best, be futile, and at worst, magnify all the problems Vix and, by extension, the witches and scientists, faced.

"How long ago did you eat the cursed heart?" Vix enquired.

Vermilion exercised her talent at scowling, a talent, Vix mused, that rivaled that of Mr. Screech.

But this was no time for scowling contests, and witches' abilities to portray as sour a face as possible, while impressive, were not going to get them anywhere.

"Well?" Screech pressed.

"I believe it was perhaps two days ago," Vermilion relented. "Although, I can't say for certain because all this time hopping has gotten my grasp of things all jumbly-wumbly."

"No matter," Vix said. "It's new enough that we might be able to do something about it."

Vix disappeared through the door of the coach - this one leading to her personal quarter - leaving Vermilion and Screech momentarily alone together. Vix's giant ruby sat on the table next to the bowl of green apples. Vermilion and Screech exchanged several looks, the two of them engaged in an unspoken battle of grimaces. Neither spoke, and neither really understood what they had to scowl about. They only knew they must.

Vix returned shortly, holding a burlap satchel that was bulging with unseen items.

She paused for a moment, counting something in her head.

"With all this traveling, I do believe I've lost count of the days," she said. "Mr. Screech, do find out what day of the week it is."

"Very well, mistress," he responded. He stood and exited the door that led to the engine. He was gone only a second or two before he returned with a large, flat disc. It appeared to be made of wood.

He placed it on the table. It was a calendar, Vermilion could see. It wasn't a single disc as she'd originally thought. It was, in fact, three discs that had been secured at the center. The bottom was the largest, and it was etched around the edges with symbols foreign to her, though if she were a citizen of Vix's and Screech's dimension, she would have recognized them as the symbols of the Zodiac. Beneath the signs were written the months, though they did not line up exactly with the astrological symbols. The names of the months were also foreign to Vermilion.

The next disc, smaller by one-third, was notched around the edges, each groove accompanied with a number ranging from 1 to 32. The disc on top, the smallest of the three, was marked with seven symbols.

He placed it on the table, and when it plopped down, the two upper discs spun slightly in either direction, indicating they were attached on a swivel.

"Do you think the magic will work?" Screech said as he leveled the disc.

"This is a very minor spell," Vix responded. "If we've learned anything in the recent past, it's that these trivial magics seem to be fine. Just be glad we aren't trying to affect major change right now."

Vix studied the calendar on the table.

"We'd be lucky if today were Saturday," she said.

Vermilion looked from Vix and back to Screech with confusion.

"Saturday," Screech said with a patronizing tone. "Sa-tur-day? Saturn?"

Vermilion only stared.

"Good gods, woman," he said. "Saturn. The god of ending."

Vix sighed and placed the satchel on the table next to the giant ruby. "Saturday is the day for breaking spells. Now, I think we might be able to get the job done on any day of the week, but a Saturday would make the task quicker and easier. We might even be able to accomplish it in one try and with minimal bloodshed."

Vermilion's eyes widened, and Mr. Screech smirked. Vermilion turned to Vix, her expression declaring that, surely, this whole bloodshed business was a joke.

Vix reached into the bag and pulled out a knife and a white pillar candle.

"On with the spell, Mr. Screech," Vix said as she handed him the candle. "And don't look so terrified, you silly little thing," her latter comment was directed toward Vermilion.

Mr Screech produced a small, silver matchbox from his waistcoat pocket. He struck one of the matches with his fingernail and used it to light the candle. He didn't blow or shake the match out, as Vermilion expected he would. He instead handed it to Vix, who placed it in a small copper bowl she produced from the burlap sack. The match burned out on its own, producing the sweet smell of burning pine with a hint of sulfur.

In the meantime, Screech had dropped seven tiny beads of melted wax from the candle onto the center of the wooden disc. He then placed the candle on top of the melted wax, giving the whole conglomeration of discs and lighted wax the look of some otherworldly birthday cake, Vermilion thought.

Mr. Screech grasped the base of the candle lightly with both hands, and then dragged them up to the top. He muttered something Vermilion couldn't make out and then brought both hands together and snuffed out the flame, cupping his palms and fingers as if he were capturing an insect.

He quickly brought his hands near his face, opened them, and then blew the candle smoke he'd captured onto the calendar disc. A sudden desert wind blew and rocked the coach back and forth slightly. The crystals hanging from the sconces on the wall clanged together lightly like windchimes. The candle on the disc also rocked just a bit, and as it did, the two smaller discs spun slowly. The three watched as the wooden plates finally stopped.

"Oh drat," Screech said. "Friday."

"But, how do you know which of the alignments to read?" Vermilion said, looking down at the wooden mechanism, realizing there was no singular point that indicated a specific number or symbol.

"Because we know it's April," Vix said with a sigh. She tapped her chin with the blade of the knife, her expression one of deep thought. A moment passed before the tapping stopped and Vix refocused her eyes on the discs.

"I've got it!" she said. "We'll use a harmony angle to break the curse. Bring things back into balance, as it were. It's a perfect Friday spell."

"Of course," Mr. Screech said.

"So, does this mean no bloodletting?" Vermilion asked hopefully.

"Oh, pisshaw," Vix said. "We have to cut you open just a little no matter what day of the week it is. Now. Roll up your sleeve."

Chapter 70

In total, the trip burned away two more of the tiny pinpricks in the little globular filter.

October still hadn't allowed Bratt to see the letter, but he did divulge a few more of its secrets - one of which involved Mistress Vix.

According to October's letter, Vix might have well been the villain of the story. Rest assured, dear reader, that Professor Jones had only written a portion of the tale, and that portion was the one he himself had lived. And it was true that for his story - for Headmaster Professor Purpureous P. Jones' story - Vix had been the villain. But by now you've surely grasped how things work when one is a traveler of dimensions. One's story can differ in a variety of ways, from things as miniscule as a haircut to events as major as a transporting submarine, depending on which timeline one occupies. And while October had a full and firm grasp on this theory, it wasn't until his own timeline deviated from what was written on his precious letter that the seriousness of it solidified in his psyche.

Was Vix the villain of the story in which October and Bratt were currently a part? That remained to be seen. Nevertheless, October said Vix shouldn't be trusted with some things - especially when it came to sources of unprecedented power.

So the boys made the trip in secret.

When October and Bratt returned to the grassy hill overlooking the City the Bell, the first thing Bratt noticed was the large amount of dirt and sand next to the pond - the exchange from Bratt's first-ever trip across universes and time. He tamped down his amusement after realizing the apothecary was now a beach-front property.

The second thing he noticed was the shadow of Molly's submersible. The bright sun was beating down on the apothecary. When the group had left, maybe an hour ago at the most, the sun had just been rising. But now the sun was low in the west, projecting a hot army of photons onto the side of the building and throwing a long shadow from The Presido. He knew then that time moved much slower in the world of Vix and Molly and Screech than it did here.

The third thing Bratt noticed was that something was missing. His mind didn't quite grasp it at first because it was busy taking stock of the things that were present, just as his grammar school teacher did at the beginning of each class. It was only when an absent student's name was called that anyone really noticed the student was absent. This was how Bratt's brain was functioning at this precise moment. It was calling roll.

The apothecary? Present. The grassy hill? Present. Two goats? Present. The submersible? Present. The pond? Present. The forest? Present. The City of Bell?

There was no answer.

October had noticed, too. Now both men looked into the valley where the City of Bell once stood with its many residents, pompous and pretensions but good nonetheless, and saw it was only a city a quarter the size that it had been before, and in its center was a giant lake of substance – or maybe it was a *lack* of substance – that was neither white nor black nor any other color, for that matter. It appeared as though a portion of the town had been erased somehow.

October looked to Bratt, a look of pity and understanding on his face.

"It's happening," October said. "I've seen this before. It's what has become of my world."

"Well," Bratt said with dejection, "I suppose it's a good thing we decided to return sooner rather than later, yes?"

October nodded.

Bratt entered the side door of the apothecary and looked around at the bric-a-brac that had become his world over the past year. He contemplated what he could in the short amount of time he had, and then strode quickly to the doctor's workbench. He picked up a canister that still had a used filter stuck to it, and walked out of the apothecary, silently bidding it all farewell.

Outside came a crack of thunder, although it wasn't thunder at all. It was the sound of a dimension falling apart and being drained.

We cannot blame Bratt for his inability to focus. After all, would you have your complete faculties about you if you stepped outside your door tomorrow morning only to discover your entire neighborhood was now nothing but a void? Of course not. So let's not judge Bratt too harshly for completely forgetting his volumes of notes, hidden in a small chamber beneath his bed. And let's not judge him for thinking about Molly's submersible and how it might be crucial to the group's needs in the future. And let's not judge him for the very small amount of urine that leaked into his undergarments when he thought about the consequences of his dimension being torn apart.

The two men darted from the apothecary and to clear ground (they didn't want to accidentally transport any of the doctor's whatnots and bric-a-brac) and October set a course on the staff back to the desert.

Chapter 71

Around Madame Verimillicent Vermilion's ample bosom was now wrapped several yards of black silk ribbon. It had been tied at the front with a triple knot. Over the knot was melted a few drops of white candle wax (harvested from a different candle, as everyone knows a single candle should never be used in two different spells), and on the candle wax was a drop of Vermilion's own blood.

Vix held a bowl in her hand filled with a concoction made of Vermilion's blood, dirt, salt, and a splash of water from a clear glass bottle that had been in Vix's burlap satchel. She dipped her finger in and pulled out a clump of the gritty substance and then began to draw an "X" across Vermilion's face.

Vermilion wasn't expecting this and pulled her face back quickly, causing the first line of the "X" to become a zigzag instead.

"Oh, really," Vix said as she reached into the burlap satchel for a clean handkerchief. "We don't have all day, you know!"

She wetted the handkerchief with a bit of water from the bottle and then wiped the crooked line off Vermilion's face.

"At least warn me!" Vermilion spitted the words out.

"Fine," Vix said, gathering more of the sludge onto her finger. "This is your warning. Now hold still!"

She drew the line again, from the top right of Vermilion's forehead, down across the bridge of her nose, and to the jowl at where face and neck combined. Vermilion held as still as she could while she pressed her own handkerchief against the cut on her arm - the site of the bloodletting.

Vix drew the knife up once more.

"I did not agree to all this stabbing!" Vermilion bellowed. "How much more of my blood do you need, woman?!"

Mr. Screech and Mistress Vix exchanged looks. Mr. Screech's look said, "Use that knife and kill her and put us all out of our misery." Mistress Vix's look said, "I am trying to stop myself from doing just that."

But Vix did not kill Vermilion, despite every burning desire to do so. Instead, she held the black ribbon that was bound around the annoying little woman and, using the knife, cut it. The ribbon fell to the floor of the coach.

She wiped the blade clean with the cloth from the burlap sack. She placed the knife into her breast pocket rather than the back into the bag.

Vix glanced quickly at where Molly lay in her sleeping death. She was beginning to turn blue, and her skin had taken on a waxen look. There was no time for dillydallying.

"We're finished?" Vermilion said, her face wrinkled into a look of confusion.

"Finished," Vix confirmed.

"But I don't feel any different."

"Did you feel any different after you cast the spell that set the curse in motion?" Mr. Screech asked with a contemptuous tone.

With the point taken, Vermilion chose not to answer. However, she did think of a few choice words she'd loved to say to Mr. Screech at that very moment. She hoped he possessed some amount of telepathy so he could read her scathing thoughts.

He didn't. But he looked the little witch up and down as if he *had* known what she was thinking. He finally turned to Vix.

"We had better try her out, at least," he said. "We don't want the spell to go wrong. And we especially don't want it to backfire."

Vix scoffed at the idea of a backfiring spell. It might kill the other two, but if more than four centuries of life on this planet had taught her anything, it was that she was as close to being immortal as she could be.

"Fine," she finally capitulated. "Let's step outside and see how it goes."

Chapter 72

It didn't take Vix long to capture a rattlesnake that was sunning itself on a nearby rock. She even managed to sneak up on the poor creature before it had time to notice her and start its rattle.

She swooped down and grabbed the snake at the base of its head. The rattle then went crazy, and the serpent wriggled wildly.

"Now," Vix said, walking to Vermilion and Screech, who were standing in the shade of The Trevithick's engine. "Here's our bit of insurance."

She thumped the snake's head on the side of the engine, knocking it out cold.

"We don't have much time before this beast wakes back up," Vix said. "So, using your own powers, I want you to summon up a whirlwind just there." She pointed to a spot in the desert that was relatively free of sagebrush or rocks. She placed the snake at Vermilion's feet, and she and Mr. Screech walked several meters away.

Vermilion took a deep breath.

"You'd better hurry it up," Mr. Screech called out. "I see the snake is beginning to move again."

Vermilion looked down at the snake and, indeed, the rattler was begging to slide slowly back and forth in the sand.

She dug in her feet, looked toward the desert, and uttered a few words under her breath. Her thumb and forefinger on her right hand touched, creating an "O." She then blew through it.

It was slow going at first, but eventually a small dust devil appeared, swirling sand up into its funnel.

Vermilion exhaled with satisfaction. But her gratification lasted only a second before she remembered the deadly creature at her feet. She hitched up her dress, ready to bolt away from the snake as it awoke from its tiny concussion.

But the snake didn't budge. She noticed its rattler had stopped moving.

Vermilion looked up and toward Vix and Screech.

"Well?" Screech called back.

"Oh, do get a move on," Vix said impatiently, grabbing Mr. Screech's arm and leading him back to where Vermilion stood. "Obviously the snake is dead or else she would have come bounding toward us in terror."

"Did you kill it?" Vermilion asked Vix.

"Of course not!" Vix said in a huff. "Trust me. I know the difference between alive and dead. And that snake was alive."

"So, what does this mean?" Vermilion asked.

"Obviously it means the curse is broken," Mr. Screech said. "But it also means your powers are still drawn from an energy near you. It seems you've brought your own laws of magic along with you."

The three stood in the sweltering, dry atmosphere. None of them spoke for what seemed like a small eternity.

"This might actually a very good thing," Vix said to Screech. "It could mean that her abilities haven't been depleted as yours have. She just needs a source of power, right?"

Vix didn't wait for an answer. She led the other two back into the coach.

"Go clean yourself up," Vix said to Vermilion once the three were back inside. "You'll find a wash basin in my private coach. Just through there. The water is for washing up and *nothing* else," She said cryptically as she pointed to the door she'd gone through to fetch the satchel. "And, mind you, do not touch anything other than the wash basin. Trust me when I say you will not like the consequences."

Vermilion didn't move at first, unsure if she really did want to go into a room where touching things would lead to dire consequences.

"Hurry up!" Vix demanded as she took the bowl of apples off the table and set them on the floor. "Get cleaned up and come back in here at once. I can't stand the smell of you, and I fear it'll interrupt the spell."

Vermilion had never been ordered around so much in her life. But she did as she was told in that moment, hoping beyond all hope that she'd be able to adequately whip up a curse of her own for all the people who dared to inconvenience her.

Chapter 73

Madame Veramilicent Vermilion waddled out of the room. The door led to a short platform that connected the two cars. On either side was a neat little railing to keep one stable if one was moving from coach to coach while the train was in motion. She shut the door behind her.

The sun was blazing, and since the train engine was pointing south, there was no shadow between the two carriages. Madame Vermilion had never experienced a desert climate before, and she was wholly unprepared for the sheer energy of the heat. She looked out to the left and saw the dead rattlesnake less than a meter away. A slight breeze blew, but it only fanned the warmth, along with a bit of sand, uncomfortably onto her face. Some of the particles stuck to the "X" that was drawn there.

She cursed under her breath and hurried into the next car. As she stepped inside, she saw this vehicle was nothing like the one she just left. It was far more comfortable, and the air was a good 15 degrees cooler than it had been on the platform. The entire right side of the compartment was a bookcase. It was, as you might have guessed, full of books. Some of them looked as though they had been pressed and glued that very morning. Others appeared to have been ancient. On the opposite side was a wardrobe, no doubt full of clothes. Beside it was a small pedestal, upon which sat a large, pink ceramic basin. A matching pitcher sat inside the bowl, and the two items were reflected in a large, ornately trimmed mirror that hung on the wall.

At the far end of the compartment was a large four-poster bed, covered in a dark blue satin duvet with a large, coiling, golden Chinese dragon stitched on it. Two huge, fluffy pillows, also gold in color, sat against the headboard, which appeared to be made of ebony. The bed beckoned to her, calling for her to empty her exhaustion upon its soft surface.

Vermilion suddenly became very aware of how tired and dirty - and smelly - she actually was. She hadn't bathed or changed in days, and her green frock reeked of sweat, dirt, feted fungi and a hint of essence of snake-mayor. Her own odor was amplified in this room, which smelled pleasantly of lilacs.

She walked to the basin and looked in the mirror. She stifled a small scream at what was looking back at her.

It is common knowledge that the word "disheveled," which has its origins in a bastardized English translation of a French word, had gained footing in the common lexicon nearly 300 years before the moment Madame Veramilicent Vermilion stood looking at herself in an enchanted, gold-trimmed mirror that had been procured by a master witch. It is also common knowledge that the wizard and accomplished hairstylist Pierre Pelletier, who was looking in the same enchanted mirror exactly 127,750 days prior, had caught a glimpse of a woman staring back from the future and coined the word "deschevelé" upon seeing the creature that peered back at him.

However, though this story is chock full of magics and mysticisms, it is not focused on a bewitched looking glass that connects two moments in time when the conditions are exactly correct, so I will thank you to keep your attention on the plot at hand and not allow your mind to go wandering.

Vermilion saw her hair had come undone from its tidy bun and now appeared to be attempting to escape her scalp in every direction. Her once pretty pink hat was now dented on one side and covered in what could only be soot, although she couldn't recall running through any fireplaces recently. Her expensive green dress with the puffy shoulders was now torn in multiple places, revealing her cabbage-colored undergarments beneath. Her lipstick was smeared to the left, and sweat had run lines across her rouged cheeks, an effect that made her think of sliced tomatoes.

And that horrid "X" made her appear as if she were about to engage in a medieval war against a tribe of raucous Celts.

Disgusted, she lifted the pitcher out of the basin and poured the water in. It glittered slightly, no doubt with magic, Vermilion thought. She placed the pitcher to the side of the bowl and placed her hands in the water.

She felt a tingling sensation and looked to her hand. Not seconds ago there had been a disgusting blister where a drop of acidic pus had fallen onto the back of her hand when Vermilion was hiding in the mayor's basement. Now, the wound had healed completely, and there was only a tiny scar where the festering wound had been.

She scooped up more water and began splashing her face.

The solution was, indeed, some sort of magic potion. After just a few splashes, Vermilion's face had been cleaned completely and, surprisingly, her makeup had somehow reapplied itself in the correct places. She wetted her fingers and began to touch it to her flyaway hair. Her hair, when it came into contact with the water, immediately put itself back into place, looking like a thousand black threads being sewn tightly into a quilt. Vermilion gaped.

Her face and hair were now perfect. She looked at her wet fingers, and curiously dapped them onto her hat. It quickly popped back into its original shape, and Vermilion watched with fascination as the dark stains evaporated.

Over the ensuing minutes, Madame Vermilion found herself splashing water all over her body. It cleaned and mended anything it touched, and before long she was looking better than she had in years. She paused, looking at herself in the mirror once more, and wondered if the restorative powers of the water worked on the inside, as well.

She glanced over her shoulder. She was still alone in the room. She quietly brought the pitcher to her lips and began to tilt it back.

"Trust me, you don't want to do that."

Vermilion screeched and jumped as high in the air as a woman of her stature could possibly jump. The pitcher flew from her hands and dropped to the floor. She expected it to shatter and spill the water everywhere, but it held its shape. Interestingly, no water escaped, despite the fact that the pitcher was lying on its side.

Vermilion spun around. There stood Mr. Screech, his arms folded.

"I - uh - I" Vermilion's mouth felt like mush. "How did you? … But I didn't hear the door!"

"I've been here the whole time," Screech said nonchalantly. "Just because you can't see something doesn't mean it isn't there. You'd do well to keep that in mind."

Vermilion looked to the pitcher on the floor. She picked it up and went to place it beside the basin. It was heavy and full, she realized, and the basin was now empty and dry.

"What? What is this?"

"Just place the pitcher back into the basin," Screech said.

Vermilion, slowly, did as she was told. She was doing a lot of what she was told today, she noted to herself. It was utterly out of character.

"I suppose you think the water would have, what? Made you young again? Well, my dear woman, I doubt you were the exemplification of elegance in your youth."

Vermilion let out a small gasp of offense. The sheer audacity of this man had left her speechless.

"Have you ever heard the myth of Medusa?" Screech asked

Vermilion shook her head. Where she was from, there were many myths, but they differed greatly from the myths of this world.

There are an infinite number of parallel universes, you see, where existence continues side-by-side with another that is completely identical in every way save but for one tiny detail, some as miniscule as the difference in grains of sugar one puts in one's coffee. But then there are angular universes, also an infinite number, caused when a cataclysmic event creates so many changes at one time that two or more existences go shooting off in different directions, each of them changing drastically from each other the farther they go.

The universe of Madame Vermilion and Bratticus Magleby and the universe of Mr. Screech, Molly St. Mercalli, and Mistress Vix were once a singular entity millions of years ago. It's hard to say what exactly caused the universes to break apart from each other. Some scholars say it was a meteor, while others claim it was an enormous solar flare. I have it on good authority, though, that a small world passing got caught in the new planet's gravitational pull. In one timeline, the two tiny planets collided and then broke apart, creating a globe with its very own moon. In another, the passing mass merely pulled at the edges of the pliable little world until it cooled in the shape of a bulbous pancake.

Whether it was meteors or moons, the fact is the one world became two, each of them evolving in alternate ways. So of course Vermilion wouldn't know of the myth of Medusa. In her world, the ancient myths involved giant naked trolls that lived in the core of the earth.

"Well, to make a long story short, Medusa was a hideous gorgon who turned men to stone by simply looking into their eyes," Screech said, examining his nails for traces of desert sand. "There actually was no Medusa, but the myth had to come from somewhere, right?"

Screech looked at Vermilion for a sign she was understanding. Vermilion offered a semi-blank expression in return. He continued with the story.

"The ancient Greeks discovered a cave full of warriors, each of them turned to stone. Stories began to spread about a horrible creature that could turn anyone into solid rock with just a glance. Well," he chuckled, "wouldn't you know it? There wasn't a monster at all. It was actually the water from an underground spring that was causing the anomaly. The warriors, seeking shelter, had merely partaken of the water."

"That … that would have turned me to stone?" Vermilion goggled at the enchanted pitcher.

"Indeed," Mr. Screech said. "It's been drawn from what is known in contemporary nomenclature as the Fountain of Youth. Hysterical, really, that so many explorers believe it's in Florida somewhere."

Vermilion looked puzzled. She'd never heard of a Fountain of Youth nor this, what did he call it? Flowerida? Her eyebrows knitted, and she looked back at Mr. Screech.

"Don't you see?" he said. "The water *does* keep one young for, well, not forever – nothing lasts forever – but for a very, very long time. What lasts longer than stone, after all? But whatever magic is in that water is amazing for cleaning stubborn stains and polishing metal."

"And," he said, looking Vermilion up and down in appraisal, "it also mends things that are broken or torn. So make sure to thank Mistress Vix for allowing you to use what little amount of the mystical fountain water she has left."

Vermilion's eyebrows scrunched even closer to each other, creating what appeared to be a black caterpillar crawling across the surface of a white pumpkin.

"But there's a whole pitcher of the stuff!" she said pointing at the ceramic container that had failed to break and failed to empty. "And it's full! I didn't even–"

"Come along," Screech interrupted. "I hate to use a hackneyed cliché, but, really, we haven't got all day."

Chapter 74

When Vermilion reentered the passenger coach, she noticed Vix had removed the yellow cloth and placed Molly on the table. Except it wasn't actually a table, she saw. It was a shiny black stone of some kind, covered in runes.

There were four candles of different colors placed at various locations around Molly's body. Above her head was a green candle, and at her feet was a red one. There were also candles above her left and right shoulders, yellow and blue, respectively. On Miss. St. Mercalli's chest lay a sprig of pine.

Vix was seated on the bench where Molly's body had originally been placed. She smiled coldly as the two entered the compartment.

"All set, then?" Vix asked.

"What is it I need to do?" Vermilion asked, attempting to gather her concentration, which had been scattered in nearly every direction since learning she had almost been turned into a statue.

Vix briefly explained the process, noting that she had already cast a circle of energy around the train. Vermilion glanced outside and didn't see any sort of shapes surrounding the locomotive, circle or otherwise. But she, wisely, held her tongue. Vermilion was given a wand - a *wand* of all the ridiculous things, she thought - to use during the procedure. Vix had her long knife - the same she used to slice Vermilion's arm. Mr. Screech's tool, it appeared, was a long eagle's feather.

There was one more tool, as well.

Vix produced the gauntlet that Molly had been wearing. Vermilion hadn't even noticed it'd been removed from the dead girl's arm.

"Strap this on," Vix said. "This will remedy your little energy draining issue."

"But we don't know how it works," Mr. Screech interjected.

"No," Vix said curtly. "Molly *believes* we don't know how it works."

Chapter 75

There was chanting. There was moving of wands and knives and feathers. There was lighting of candles. There was burning of pine. It all felt rather convoluted, Vermilion thought, silently noting that it would be much quicker and easier to go find some desert creature and suck the life out of it first. And then there was stillness as the three witches waited.

Nothing happened.

Mr. Screech was the first to speak.

"Perhaps there is still an element of the curse present," he said genuinely.

Vix did not respond. She gently sat down on the bench and looked at Molly's face. It was still that ghastly shade of periwinkle.

There suddenly came a loud drumming sound, and all three jumped. Vermilion, having the second startle of the day, clasped her chest and let out a gasp.

"Hello?" came a distance voice. "How do we open this blasted thing?"

It was the voice of October Magleby. He had rapped on the train's door.

"Dammit all!" Vix spat. She'd completely forgotten about the two men. "The circle!"

"What circle?" Vermilion said, her heart still pounding.

"For Pete's sake, get that thing off your arm!" Vix commanded. "Hide it! Under the bench!"

Mr. Screech walked to the door of the coach, looking back to make sure Molly's gauntlet had been properly hidden. He turned back toward the door and opened it.

"In order for the spell to work, the circle must not be broken," Screech said as he stood aside to let the scientists in. "The energy around the train is to stay intact. That means nobody enters or exits." He nodded toward the two men, who no doubt interrupted the magical workings when they crossed the border of Vix's circle.

The two men, now inside the vehicle, looked at the stony faces of the three witches.

Vix sighed.

"Well, I suppose this is my fault. I should have guessed your errand wasn't going to take long." She stood and dusted her lap off, although the gesture seemed to be pure theater since there was nothing to be dusted off in the first place. "I guess we'll have to do it again."

Vermilion, whose attention was on Bratt and October, suddenly screamed as the hand of Molly St. Mercalli sprang to life and grasped her arm - right on the fresh wound Vix had cut half an hour ago.

"HELP," Molly's voice demanded. It was loud and monotone.

Vermilion's fear and unrelenting urge to wrench herself free from the corpse's grip and bolt from the train disappeared completely at that moment. Her face went slack, and she turned mechanically toward Molly.

Molly was still lying on the black slab of stone. Her eyes were open and staring at the ceiling. Both her arms were outstretched. One had found Vermilion's arm. The other was grasping at air.

Vermilion stood and steadied herself. She bent down over Molly, placing her free arm on the young woman's shoulder, and helped her first sit up and then stand. Molly's hand was still clenched on Vermilion's arm, but Vermilion felt no pain.

Molly didn't appear to be alive at all. Her skin was still pallid, and her eyes looked blindly forward.

"HELP," she said again in that droning voice. "THE GRIMBLENOX."

Molly took a step forward, her free arm outstretched. She stumbled forward a bit, and Bratt stepped forward to help steady her. Molly's left hand found purchase on Bratt's arm.

"HELP. STOP. THE GRIMBLENOX."

Bratt's eyes also went blank. He stiffened.

All of Bratt's thoughts suddenly became singularly focused. There were creatures beyond the walls of everything that has ever existed and ever will exist. They survived on energy as a human survives on food, water and oxygen. The energy came from The Core. The beasts were coming. They had to be stopped. He knew all these things and *only* these things. All other motivations were erased, and his body barely remembered to breathe as the whole of his concentration was now on stopping the Grimblenox. He must stop the Grimblenox.

"Stop the Grimblenox," he murmured without inflection.

"Help stop the Grimblenox," Vermilion said, her tone matching Bratt's.

October, eyes wide with terror, looked to Vix and Mr. Screech for answers. Mr. Screech had a comparable expression on his face, but Vix only looked annoyed.

"Get her hands off those two!" she ordered.

October and Screech exchanged glances of uncertainty and then stepped toward the trio. Mr. Screech was closest to Bratt, and he reached out and pulled the young man toward him. It took several tugs, but finally he was free.

Bratt shook his head quickly as if trying to shake water out of his hair.

"What," he said, his eyes darting around the room. "What happened? What ... what happened?"

October wrenched Vermilion free from Molly's grasp as well. Vermilion had a markedly different reaction than Bratt.

She screamed in terror and in pain. A dark, red spot was spreading on the sleeve of her newly-cleaned green dress where Molly's grip had reopened the wound in Vermilion's arm. Bratt, for the second time in as many days, repressed the urge to slap her.

Molly stood at the end of the black altar, her arms groping in the air. She looked forward at nothing.

"HELP. ME. STOP. THE. GRIMBLENOX."

"Don't let her grab you while she's wearing those gloves," Vix said.

Mr. Screech's look of confusion turned suddenly to understanding.

"What is this?" Bratt gasped. "What is going on here?"

Mr. Screech let out a puff of air and straightened his spectacles.

"The gloves are enchanted," he said. "Whomever she touches is forced to do her will."

"Which means she has a will to force upon others," Vix said. "The spell has worked. Molly lives."

Molly had been wearing the gloves when she first arrived at the apothecary, Bratt mused. What had been the witches' plan? Had they meant to use that power on him? On October? And to what end? Were these three sorcerers friend or foe?

"Does she, though?" October asked in exasperation, watching Molly as she stumbled about, looking at nothing, her skin still waxy and pale.

"Well, clearly she hasn't completely returned to us," Vix admitted. "But we're on the right track."

Chapter 76

The five of them sat around the black stone, which had since been recovered with the yellow table cloth. Each had a teacup in hand save for Molly. Her's sat on the table as Molly still hadn't regained the ability to do much of anything, let alone drink tea.

Molly stared straight ahead.

"So what now?" Bratt asked, placing his cup on the tablecloth after taking a sip and realizing he really didn't like tea at all. He had only ever drank it because it was so hard to come by in his world, and thus he never wanted it to go to waste.

But as Mr. Screech had brought the tea service into the coach (on Mistress Vix's orders, of course) Bratt saw an abundance of glass jars, each filled with darkened, shredded tea leaves. On each jar was a little label declaring the tea was "flavored with cinnamon" or "flavored with star anise" or "flavored with peppermint." One of the labels read "flavored with duck consommé," and Bratt knew then that these people perhaps had *too much* tea. In the end, he'd chosen one "flavored with cardamom," as it was a spice he particularly liked on his morning oatmeal. It turned out, when it came to flavoring brewed leaves, it wasn't really his cup of tea.

"Do we intend to just sit here and wait?" October asked, looking from Vix to Molly.

Molly sat upright in a position that would put even the most vicious of finishing school mistresses to shame. Her spine was perfectly straight. Her hands were folded primly on her lap. She looked straight ahead, her eyes unfocused. Or, rather, not focused on anything within the train car.

She had regained most of her color, and, thankfully, had stopped her monotone declarations of "HELP. ME. STOP. THE. GRIMBLENOX."

Mistress Vix followed Bratt's suit and set her tea down.

"While we await Miss St. Mercalli's return from the void, we need to discuss our plan of attack," Vix said. "Clearly the fates have brought us all together to do something extraordinary. The Fabric has been ripped, and we've all seen firsthand the consequences of that tear."

Bratt and October exchanged quick glances, knowing the horrors were far worse than what the witches had witnessed.

"But how can we form a plan of attack when we don't even know what we're attacking?" Vermilion piped up. "How do you go to war against an enemy you know nothing about?"

"I know about it," came a small voice, almost a whisper.

Molly had spoken.

Interlude 5: The Core, A Brief History

I'll issue you a warning, dear reader. You are about to learn about the things that happen once your spirit and your body have parted ways. This new knowledge might fly in the face of the philosophies that guide your own life. You may, if you wish, skip ahead beyond these next few chapters so as not to upset the very belief structure that holds you in place. However, if that's the path you choose to take, then let it be upon your own head when the story stops making sense.

Please take this warning to heart, because this tale, as you might have noticed, is barely making sense as it is.

Chapter 77

When a human dies, there are a variety of things that can happen. Nearly all of them are good.

Many people believe their consciousness will be reborn into another living creature. Again, the mind is powerful, and if it chooses to do so, then it absolutely can return to the mortal realm as a caterpillar or a dragon or even a writer of stories with very little effort.

Most people have a preconceived notion of a heaven or an afterlife of some sort. Since the power of the mind is the greatest force there is, these notions are usually forged into existence once the anchor of the mortal body has been unleashed.

The majorities of those who die and decide not to return in a new form end up existing free of pain and frustrations, and surrounded by the whole of their wildest desires, whatever they may be.

However, there are a few people who go to places most of us only see in our worst nightmares. This is a particularly bitter conclusion considering the horrible places in which they end up are purely of their own design. These are the people who lived life hurting others and knowing what they were doing was wrong. Deep inside, they know they need to be held responsible for their actions, so their psyche creates exactly such a punishment. Sometimes, these people realize they control their environment. This usually happens after their subconscious feels reparations have been made. Still, others live in that realm for as long as time exists, which, by the way, is *not* forever.

The power of the mind, after all, is more powerful than anything else. Imagination is the only force that can break gravity without combustion, that can fly without wings, that can dig without tools. Imagination can travel into the very center of a black hole and live to tell the tale, unlike several interstellar explorers in the not-too-distant future, whose stories the world will know in due time.

That time, though, is not now.

A very small percentage of those who die end up gathering their energy together and traveling to places they loved, visiting people they cared for, or voyaging to some destination in order to fulfill some sort of business that was never resolved during life.

Molly St. Mercalli, upon her death, did not go to a place of fantasy or a place of horror or into the egg of an unhatched platypus. Instead, her astral being traveled to the edge of everything that ever is, ever was, and ever will be.

It was her unfinished business, which, by the way, was complete news to her.

She remembered watching Mistress Vix step up to the river with her arms outstretched. She knew what she was going to attempt – it was, after all, Vix's favorite spell. But Molly didn't have the opportunity to remind her that magic, in that world, comes at a greater price.

Then it all went black. And then deep purple. Then a nice, comforting blue. Then onto green, and yellow, orange, red, pink, white. At least, that's the only way to describe the colors she saw after leaving her body behind.

The human eye's cones and rods translate color into the brain. However, most human eyes only possess enough rods and cones to see seven colors in varying shades. I have it on good authority that there are at least 472 additional colors all about you at any given time - you're just unable to perceive them. With the burdensome rods and cones left in her corpse, Molly was able to experience all these colors. And, sadly, as she found out later, she would never be able to describe them to another *living* soul.

But if your aim is to become versed on ophthalmology and whether or not humans possess the proper photoreceptor cells to see what lies beyond the visible spectrum, then I assure you there are a great many books on the subject – most with at least twenty times the number of pages of this one and twenty times the number of contributing authors. This tale, however, is not about the magic of sight, so please focus your attention.

Molly found herself lifting through this new and exciting ocean of colors, seeing planets and stars and gasses and comets as she rose. Falling upward, as it were, was exhilarating. What she experienced might be described in later years as "psychedelic" or "hallucinogenic," and Molly felt the only earthly experience to which it could be compared was the glowing, colorful sensation one gets when one's eyes are closed so tightly that it is almost painful.

But at the height of her euphoria, she suddenly passed through an invisible barrier of some sort that housed the atmosphere of colors, dividing it from an infinitesimal space that could only be characterized as the exact opposite of the spectral world she'd just left. Calling it a "space," though, still does not accurately describe the vast nothingness beyond.

It was without color. It was neither white, nor black. It was nothing. And it's something none of us who still find ourselves with beating hearts could ever conceive of.

She somehow knew that if a person who was still alive could reach this barrier, that person would not be able to pass through. However, she also knew that no living person would ever reach this barrier. It was impossible because it was the edge of existence. It was a place no person could ever reach, not with a million years or a million machines at their disposal.

Molly looked behind her as she drifted away from the barrier and out into the void. She could see the existence she'd just exited was a giant object, organic and alive. It appeared to be in a constant state of reorganization. It was in the shape of a very plump tire, Molly thought at first. But as the distance grew, she saw it had changed into what looked like a wine decanter of some sort, a portion of it bulbous with a tube that extended outward and then back into the other side. It flattened into a disk shape, and then took a form that resembled a giant sea turtle.

The transformations were slow. In fact, Molly was witnessing the reshaping of existence over a period of several millennia. But Molly was outside of existence now, where there is no such thing as time. She was able to perceive everything that is, and ever was, and ever will be, in one fleeting moment.

Within the pool of lights she could see a small orb, glowing brighter than any of the luminescent fog within. It appeared to move around inside, sometimes coming very close to the edges of the shape, and sometimes disappearing into its depths. She was reminded of a goldfish in a fish bowl. What was it?

She waited for the glowing ball to make its way back toward the surface, and she scoured the ever-retreating mass for a sign of its return.

It floated back into view, muted somewhat by a dark violet patch of fog housed within the existence. As if it knew she was watching it, it stayed put at the edge. It was the first time she'd seen it go static.

Everything in the mass before came from that orb of light. And that orb of light was the engine that kept the mass undulating. It was the entity that, somehow, powered existence itself.

Chapter 77

She could tell even through the membrane of outer existence that there was a single stain of darkness on the orb's surface. How big could it actually be that she could discern it from this distance? And what was this ball of energy that moved about within all of time?

Luckily for Molly, she was dead. And dead people often get the answers to secrets without having to do much legwork. For Molly, she had no legs to work at all, but her consciousness was alive and curious.

She was still out in the nothingness, but her vision traveled like lightning to another place. She was viewing the scene through a cluster of universes and timelines. It came into view slowly at first, sharpening as though it were emerging from a dense fog.

Molly first saw the back of a girl, perhaps 17 years old. She was sitting at a desk by herself in a bright room with a single, large window. The room came further into focus, and Molly saw it was furnished in a way that seemed alien. It lacked the ornate Edwardian details of which Molly was accustomed. The girl's chair had no embellishments and appeared to be in the shape of an oval. Her hair was not pinned up, instead flowing free across her back and shoulders. It was the color of sunlight through amber.

Her right hand grasped a fountain pen. Her left hand steadied a large piece of paper on the slick surface of the desk.

She was creating a piece of art, though Molly couldn't see the details. She came closer to the spectral young woman and peered over her shoulder. It was a drawing, that was for certain. The girl appeared to feel some sort of presence and glanced back over her shoulder. Molly's instinct was to duck, but the young woman couldn't see her. The artist returned to her work.

Molly was immediately distracted by the oddest of things. From the crown of the girl's head came a tiny ball of light, no bigger than the head of a pin. But it shone brightly. The girl apparently had no inkling whatsoever that her brain had just birthed a brilliant piece of energy, and she continued scrawling on the paper.

The light rose away from the girl and up into the nothingness. Molly watched it as it vibrated like the abdomen of a cicada. As it rattled silently, its brilliance brighter than the light pouring in through the window, it began to grow. As it did, the vibration slowed to a pulse, but with each pulse, it continued to enlarge. It emitted the same dust that appeared to have filled Molly's own existence, and within moments it had completely filled the room.

Molly retreated in a way only a person who is dead or dreaming can. She stepped back by about a mile, ignoring the world that materialized around her. She focused only on the ever-growing orb.

She barely took stock of the building in which the young girl was drawing. It was long and rectangular with not a turret nor gable to be seen. But even if the structure had a hundred turrets, they would have been impossible to see anyway; the energy of the orb had already consumed it, the glittering, gaseous substance now flowing freely and almost violently from it, like sparks from an axe being sharpened on a stone.

Around the orb of energy formed a membrane, which contained the orb's emissions. It continued to grow. Like a giant soap bubble, it rose away from the surface of the artist's world. It took on different shapes as it grew. A griddle cake, then a storm cloud, then a pearl, then a rod.

Molly witnessed an eternity's worth of evolution as the form before her expanded and broke free from its own ever-undulating existence in which the young artist lived. It grew, and grew, and grew until it was at least the same size of the artist's when and where. A scientist from another time might view this phenomenon from afar and conclude that it was mitosis.

Molly saw before her, with nothingness all around, two separate entities, each containing an infinite number of possibilities. They were nearly twins, floating about in the void. The new existence did not leave the side of the old; the two stayed together, nearly touching, with what appeared to be only inches between them.

She'd seen the birth of a new reality – new worlds and new timelines – and she knew then how these multiverses came into existence.

And all at once, Molly was back to where she'd been before silently asking the question.

Chapter 76

It was an idea. The Engine of Existence came from an idea. The young artist, whether she knew it or not, had created life with endless amounts of stories to tell within. Molly now peered back at her own collection of continuum, watching as its orb, its Core, floated gently out of sight.

Everything in her own reality came from the thought or idea of someone else, its intention so powerful that it literally took on a life of its own. And the idea was forever churning out the fabric of existence. Molly, she realized, was more or less the creation of someone else's imagination.

There was no existential crisis then, as only the living can experience such maddening trauma. She guessed if she had been alive, though, she might have driven herself crazy wondering who had dreamed her up and, more importantly, if she had dreamed up her own worlds without even realizing it.

The time for self-reflection was at an end, though, as Molly saw something else.

What was that white spot on the surface of her reality? If Molly had eyelids, she might have squinted to make it out. It appeared to be a pinprick in the skin of existence, and gaseous bits of rainbow were spilling out of it in a slow but steady stream. The particles, if that's truly what they were, floated about the object as oil does around a boat when spilled on the surface of water. It was a wonder she hadn't noticed the fine mist of purples and yellows and blues and oranges weightlessly dancing about in estuaries through the nothingness before.

It was so vast, though, so infinite, this spheroid collection of countless universes.

Now she was departing the vicinity of her existence, and she watched it as it appeared to grow smaller the farther away she got. Soon she had traveled too far away from the undulating form of reality to see details. The pinprick had to have been somewhere on the other side when Molly first withdrew from its containment. As the thought came to her, the substance transformed once again, this time into a corkscrew shape. The pinprick, and the entrails it was scattering, disappeared from sight.

Molly eventually lost view of the glowing shape itself as she sped further into the void. She looked around her to see where, exactly, she was taking herself. Then in the distance came another tiny light. As she got closer, she could see it was the existence she just left. Had she gone in a circle somehow? But no, it wasn't the existence she'd left. It was *a different* existence. A *different* conglomeration of universes. A *different* container filled with people and planets and stars, all zipping around inside on their own beams of light.

That's the funny thing about infinity, you see. One may reach the edge of the universe, but the universe is still encapsulated inside something bigger. One may eventually observe a subatomic particle, but what would happen when that particle is cut in half? There will always be something in the middle.

There is an edge to everything, she knew then. Perhaps even an edge to the nothingness? If so, what lies beyond?

But we won't bother ourselves with going mad over the concept of infinity, though, because Molly then saw something that would have chilled her to the bones - if she still had bones, that is.

Unlike the mists of her own reality, which were leaking out through a tiny hole, the existence before her had a mighty gash on one side The contents within were spewing out, creating an enormous lake of the brilliant mist. From behind this new existence, she saw a swarm of tiny, purplish creatures with hundreds of long legs – or were they *tentacles?* – feeling their way across the surface. They looked like little spiders scurrying over a misshapen light bulb, but she knew they had to be huge considering the size of the reality upon which they were scuttling. Some of the things were swimming into the gash, pulling it open. The things outside were cleaning the mist that was pouring out.

No, they weren't cleaning. They were *eating.*

One of the things then slithered into the laceration and emerged with a blindingly bright orb in its clutches. It was the source of all the light within the existence. It was the engine, Molly knew. It was the alpha of everything. It was The Core. As it was plucked from within, the husk of the reality before her withered and the lake of light dissipated.

The spider-octopus things swarmed at The Core, fighting over it. Their spindly appendages grabbed at the orb of light, pulling it apart into dozens of pieces that lost their luster as they broke.

The creatures devoured them.

She'd witnessed the birth of a new multiverse just a moment ago. Now, she had witnessed a multiverse's death.

As the remnants of the destroyed existence evaporated into the void, Molly somehow drew closer, and the spider-octopi things came into crystal clear view.

There have not yet been words invented to describe the horror Molly witnessed then as the beasts broke apart the last bits of the core and fought among themselves for the scraps. But she did know the beasts' name: The Grimblenox.

If she had to describe the Grimblenox, she would have said it had two prominent features. First were the tentacles, long, thin and terrible, that could reach around and into objects bigger than the human mind can fathom. At first glance, those tentacles looked like spider legs because of how grotesquely thin they were. They also lacked the fluid movement of a sea creature's appendages, instead moving stiffly as if connected by a thousand joints.

The second feature was the eye – its huge, green and yellow, bulbous, penetrating eye. Unblinking and with an iris that looked as if it was a slivery opening to a portal to hell, it bulged upward and outward from the body. If one weren't paying attention, one might believe the eye was the creature's head.

For a reason even Molly with her newfound infinite wisdom couldn't grasp, the things' single eyes faced up and away from the bodies, so the Grimblelnox couldn't actually see what it was eating. This resulted in some movements that disgusted Molly. As the things, using their hundreds of spindly tentacles held onto the piece of existence they were consuming. Then, in a nauseating gesture of contortion, the creatures turned their tentacles around until the eye was looking directly into the source of food. After a quick inspection, those horrific tentacles shifted the piece of matter back to below the Grimblenox's body, where its unseen mouth sucked it dry.

The Grimblenox was feeding. It's food was existence. After it had eaten, the existence was gone - without a trace of it ever being there. Molly feared it might see her, and she had a sneaking suspicion that if it were to consume her, she would cease to exist as well, and her consciousness would be erased completely.

Chapter 77

Molly then remembered. Had it been a year? Perhaps two? There was a person she loved, back in her own existence. It was a love she had thrown away in order to become a more powerful witch.

What of her now? Was she still in San Francisco? Was she still an alchemist? Was she as wonderful and as aggravating a person as she remembered? What would happen to her if the Grimblenox got through the edge of existence?

That infinite knowledge came again. She knew what would happen. She, along with anyone else Molly had ever cared for, would cease to exist. These creatures did not just kill. They *erased*. These things took the universes created by thought and completely wiped them out as if they'd never been thought of at all.

What could she do now, though? She was dead. Was there anything she could do? She didn't dare attempt anything just yet, fearing that if one of those things saw her, it would gobble her up and remove her from time and eternity. Period.

She looked back toward the swarm of Grimblenox, now floating lazily about after gorging themselves on who knows how many universes and lives and loves.

And then one looked at her. The top of its body, that one putrid eye, pointed directly at her. And for a moment, she looked right into its slit pupil.

A part of her psyche went black. She knew if she had a physical body, it would be unable to withstand the force of the gaze. It was a gaze that pushed the very hopelessness of the void into one's soul. This is what the Mayor of Bell must have felt before the power of that penetrating eye did to him what would be done to me if I were alive, she thought.

The disgusting creature skittered, and soon the other beasts noticed Molly and began skittering as well. Like long-legged spiders they swam mechanically through nothingness in her direction. They were fathoms away – they *had* to be. But they had seen her. They were hungry still. If they fed on the powers of the mind, then Molly St. Mercalli must have looked delicious.

And she thought of her lost love again. She couldn't let these things, these Grimblenox, to get her. But it seemed like there was nothing she could do. The essence of Molly, now suspended in the void beyond reality, seemed unable to move as the spindly, disgusting beasts plowed through the nothingness toward her.

Her terror piqued.

Chapter 78

Then something strange happened.

Molly felt her form being tugged backward as if some invisible rope attached to her soul were being winched. Taken completely by surprise, she didn't think to turn around to see what was pulling her. She only watched as the hideous creatures suddenly and quickly began to decrease in size as Molly retreated.

Traveling backward, she watched as the hideous, horrendous Grimblenox disappeared from sight. Although she was facing away from them, she could feel the presence of her own reality as she neared it once more. She wasn't dead after all, it seemed. Or, at least, she wasn't going to stay dead. Someone down there had found a way to bring her back. It was

Vix who orchestrated the spell, she knew, the answer coming to her in a flash. The fat, peevish little witch had helped, too. And so had Mr. Screech. And Vix used something of Molly's to bring her back. Vix was hiding something. There was treachery there. But what was it?

The ability to *know* was vanishing the closer she got to the reality she'd left.

The scientists – Bratticus L. Magleby and October F. Magleby – had not assisted. They had traveled, back to where they came from to retrieve something powerful. It was something that would ultimately aid them all in their crusade to stitch the fabric of time and existence back together.

The scientists and the witches were not going on the same path, though. She knew this to be true as sure as she knew she was about to come back to life. But what was the answer?

The *knowing* faded before she could discover all the answers she needed. If only she'd had the wherewithal to think of the questions earlier. But then again, she hadn't a clue she'd be returning to the land of the living.

And as she was dragged back into the atmosphere, her mortal thoughts took control. She began to forget all the things her infinite mind had learned. When she finally began tumbling into the membrane of existence, she saw something – briefly – in her peripheral vision: a tentacle.

Step 12: Knowledge Is Power, So Be Powerful

"As one traverses time and dimensions, one accumulates knowledge. Some may be content enough to simply know things. However, those who travel should be warned: Knowing things and using knowledge to affect things are two very different, well, things. To have knowledge of something and to not use that knowledge to affect positive change is a grave sin indeed."

— Dr. Gustopher C. Cerulean, as quoted in the copious notes of Bratticus L. Magleby.

Chapter 79

"I know about it," Molly said.

Her eyes focused now, and she looked around the room. They were all seated on the damask benches in the coach, including Molly herself. She saw there was tea and was suddenly thirstier than she'd ever been in her life. Or, come to think of it, in her death.

The group watched speechlessly as Molly grabbed a teacup and poured hot water into it. She didn't bother with any tealeaves. She drank it down, and the nearly scalding water didn't seem to bother her at all. She poured herself another cup and drank it just as quickly as the first. Her body, still trying to adjust to being alive after having become quite comfortable in a state of death, didn't register the hot water. She poured and drank another.

She exhaled dramatically. Water dribbled down her chin and wet the front of her dress. She drew in an enormous breath of air and held it in her lungs for a few seconds. She exhaled again. Her senses were coming back slowly but surely.

Then she remembered. Her eyes bolted to her left arm. Her gauntlet was not there.

She faced Vix. She couldn't gather the correct words, but when she stared into Vix's eyes, Vix knew.

"Oh really," Vix said dismissively. "We had to remove it for the spell to work. All those magnets were interfering with the magic."

"Don't worry," she added, "It's safe and sound."

Molly looked from Vix to Madame Vermilion to Mr. Screech. The stench of conspiracy was thick in the air, and Molly could smell it even though her olfactory receptors had yet to return to working order.

She looked to Bratt and October, both of whom looked uneasy as she made eye contact. Whatever was going on here did not involve the identical scientists.

"Treachery," Molly said at last. "You three." She pointed a stiff finger from Vix to Vermilion to Screech. "Treachery."

October and Bratt exchanged a knowing glance. Whatever was happening now had something to do with the mechanism Molly kept strapped to her arm.

"Molly," Vix said in a tone meant to sound reassuring, "You've just been plucked back from the void. Why, you're paranoid. That's all."

Vix had spent hundreds of years honing the craft of lying, and her skill at weaving falsehoods was better even than the most accomplished politician. But the thing about lying is that it becomes weaker and weaker the longer people spend time together. This is why a parent always knows when her child has sneaked out of the home after midnight to go gallivanting about causing mischief with chicken eggs and water-closet paper.

While Molly hadn't known Vix very long in the relative terms of Vix's lifespan, she had known her long enough to discern when the truth was being told. And at this moment, there was no truth.

Whether Vermilion and Screech were co-conspirators or merely pawns was not immediately clear. But Vix had taken one of Molly's most prized possession, second only to her submersible.

She would have considered the person she loved, wherever she may be, as her most prized possession, but Molly knew people weren't things to keep and to hold. Although, she did wish she'd kept her, especially now that she'd seen into the beyond and the dangers that were waiting there.

Molly sprang to her feet and wobbled, but only for a second. Vix stood as well, preparing for what to happen she did not know. Molly trudged to October and whispered something in his ear. October nodded, grabbed Bratt by the wrist, and the three nearly sprinted out of the coach's door and onto the hot desert sand.

"Wait!" Vix called after them. She stood in a momentary stupor as the two scientists and the young witch bolted from the train. Both Screech and Vermilion, stunned into rigid silence, watched as October, Bratt, and Molly ran out and away.

This turn of events was utterly unexpected.

Vix pulled herself together seconds later and began her pursuit after the three.

The day had grown long, and the desert floor had been cooking all day in the sun. The horizons wobbled through the lens of the refracted heat.

"Follow me," October commanded Bratt. He then took Molly's arm and the three of them darted quickly - or as quickly as Molly's legs would allow - away from The Trevithick and into the desert.

"Get her onto your back!" October shouted, thrusting Molly at Bratt. He hefted her over his shoulder like a sack of flour. October looked back and saw Vix coming after them. She wasn't running so much as she was gliding across the desert floor, as if she were standing on an invisible platform being dragged over the ground. Her arms and legs were not moving much, but she was still gaining on them. Her black dress, fluttering in the hot wind, was a stark contrast to the white and red sand beneath her.

The hot wind blew. Vix's black and wide-rimmed widow's hat cast shadows over her face.

"Run faster!" October said.

He thumbed open the panel on his staff as they dashed up and over a formation of red rocks.

"Keep moving!" he said as he reached out his free hand for Bratt's. The two grasped hands, and October pressed the tiny button on the walking stick's handle, and the three disappeared into a burst of blue and purple lightning.

Vix stood on the top of the rocks looking at the place the three had just been. There was now a tiny grove of trees, green and completely out of place on the desert's red rocks.

Chapter 80

"Get us to submarine. Witches are enemy."

The words spoken in October's ear solidified what he'd suspected – and what his elder counterpart Professor Jones had written: Artemis Vix was a villain.

He didn't hesitate to flee from the train, but as he was running, he contemplated the very real chance that Bratt's dimension was no longer there. However, he trusted that Molly learned something new on her journey to the afterlife, and he used the staff to take the trio back to the hill above Bell.

He had to make sure his calculations were off by just a fraction so the three wouldn't accidently trade places with Molly's red submersible, so he scrolled the digits inside the cane's handle three times, pointing their coordinates approximately three meters northwest from their previous location.

This plopped the trio right at the edge of the forest beyond the enclosure that once housed a llama named Gertrude and now contained two goats, a pond, a sandy beach a red submarine, and now a formation of desert rocks.

They scrambled once arriving, ignoring the scenery around them. October was glad to see the submersible, and he wondered if he would be able to transport the entire vessel if needs be.

October and Bratt had hoisted Molly up and into the Presidio. Once inside, they placed her on the slab of stone in the center of the deck. It was nearly identical to the stone in Artemis Vix's coach, Bratt noticed, though he had seen markings on Vix's stone that did not appear on Molly's.

As she was coming out of her fog, October and Bratt surveyed the interior of the submersible.

The large window was facing toward what was left of the City of Bell. The void hadn't grown since the two left earlier. Bratt had assumed it was like a fire, spreading and consuming everything it could. But now it appeared to be stagnant. The apothecary on the hill remained untouched. The sun, now setting, was still in the sky. The forest grew to the west (minus one small grove), and the Procumbent Plateau still jutted up in the east.

Bratt also noticed with a startling realization that there, at the very end of the room, was a stack of soiled socks and a bundle of sticks cut at such a length that they appeared to be useless. He couldn't dwell on the items too long given the current situation in which he found himself, but he also couldn't help but think of Dr. Cerulean and the calculations he'd made before disappearing into time and space.

October seemed equally entranced by the void's failure to grow. Bratt guessed October's own reality suffered a far worse fate.

Or perhaps he'd assumed it had been destroyed and it, like the dimension in which they all currently resided, was only partially torn away.

"Boys," said Molly.

They turned to look at her. She had shed her trance, and it was clear she was ready to talk.

Chapter 81

Mistress Artemis Vix had spent her entire life, which spanned centuries, collecting and perfecting the use of magical items. And until recently, she'd thought she had perhaps found everything there was to find, and her purpose in life seemed to be dissipating.

Then the magic in the world began to wane, and she began to feel as though there might be something else out there she could attain. At least, she knew, there was something out there that was capable of sucking the energy out of her fellow witches.

When she saw what had become of that mayor, the man who was transformed into some otherworldly creature, Vix had rediscovered her purpose. Her desire to locate and harness the power of whatever had created the abomination pulsed through her body, giving her more motivation than she'd ever felt in her life.

She had to get her hands on this power. She was not about to let something so great slip through her fingers.

So while the rest spent their time deciding how to fix whatever was broken, Vix has been mulling over the ways in which to *capture* whatever was creating the havoc. Fortunately for her, she had a few witches and two scientists at her disposal to help her reach her goal – even if they were unwilling participants.

Chapter 82

Molly's consciousness had now fully materialized in her body, although she was still shaking a bit of rigor mortis out of her elbows and knees.

She told them everything she could remember, from the feeling of pure elation being nothing but energy to witnessing the hole in existence as it spit out pieces of the universes within. She even tried to explain the hundreds of new colors she'd seen, finding absolutely no way to do it. But what was the most important part?

She was struggling to remember. She had seen something, something dark and evil. Whatever it had been had encased that portion of her memory in a cage of hard, black scales. She couldn't bring to mind exactly what it was, but she knew its name: The Grimblenox.

"There are things, creatures, beasts," Molly told the men. She scrunched her face in deep concentration. "I can't recall it in its entirety. All I know is that it, like every other thing that lives, has to eat. And it eats time. It eats The Fabric."

The two Maglebys sat at attention, neither of them questioning the facts or how she came to know them. She'd traveled to a place not even October's staff could take them, and she'd returned to tell the story.

"We know of holes in our Fabric, or at least, that's what we thought they were," Molly said, the tone of her words sounding like a young student attempting to recite an essay from memory. "It turns out it's just *one* hole. As we travel on our respective timelines, we've been encountering the hole when we get to it."

"Of course!" October said, punctuating it with a hard tap of his cane on the submersible's floor. "Each universe is traveling at light speed in an infinite loop within existence. So the damage is only done when a particular universe crosses in front of the Peculiarity. That explains why a portion of Bell is no more, but the rest of this world still lives."

"I guess, in a way, that makes a part of our task a little easier to tackle," Molly continued. "We only have one piece of the fabric to mend. But our task is also a bit harder. We have to somehow stop the Grimblenox from opening The Peculiarity any wider. I believe they're attracted by the essence that's spilling out of our little bubble, and I know they want badly to get to The Core. But the Peculiarity is, luckily for us, too small right now."

Molly skipped the details on the origins of Cores in an effort to keep the scientists focused. After all, she didn't want any of them to become distracted over whether they exist only because someone else dreamed them up. She figured that was a lesson they could learn after they shed their mortal coils.

"I believe the only way to fix the hole in the Fabric is to travel to the Core. We will be able to access every part of existence from that one spot. Then we have to combine our talents to make the repair and, hopefully, stop the Grimblenox from sniffing us out."

"By talents, do you mean the three of us?" Bratt asked. "Or do you think we'll need the powers of the witches we just abandoned?"

"Abandoned is a very strong word," Molly said. "Besides, Vix will be fine. Her train, The Trevithick, can go anywhere on land. She's enchanted it to run on rails that only appear where they need to appear, and they're gone as soon as the train passes."

Molly paused and reflected. "And that ruby," she began, but stopped mid sentence.

When it appeared she didn't intend to finish her thought, October interjected.

"That sounds like powerful magic," he said suspiciously. "You told us, not but yesterday, that magic in your world relies on gently pushing circumstances into place that would already happen naturally. Do spectral train rails have a habit of popping up naturally in your world?"

"To be frank, Vix is oftentimes the exception to the rule," Molly said. "The ruby, which she no doubt used to help bring me back from the threshold of eternity, has imbued her with eternal life. At least, that's my theory. And she has been honing her magical skills for many years. She's collected countless artifacts that she uses to increase her power."

"So, how old is she, then?" Bratt asked.

"I don't know," Molly shrugged. "And I don't think she knows, either. But I do know she was present for the beheadings of Anne Boleyn,

Blackbeard the Pirate, *and* Marie Antoinette."

She added pensively, "She always spoke of those occasions with such fondness."

October and Bratt looked blankly back at Molly, the two never having heard of such people.

"Well, be that as it may," Bratt finally said, "you still haven't answered my first question. Will we need her and the other two to complete our mission?"

"Maybe," Molly said. "But, then again, maybe not. I know you have something in that satchel that should do the trick."

Bratt had nearly forgotten the leather strap that was slung across his shoulder and chest. He looked down at where the bag was resting against his left hip.

"You know about it?"

"There are quite a few lessons I learned during my little holiday away from mortality," Molly said. "Now, we need to get to work."

Molly stood. She assessed the two men momentarily, and then decided if she didn't trust them both by now, then that trust would never come. She stooped to the floor and tapped it five times, the first time with her thumb, the second with her index finger, the third with her middle, and so on.

There was a small whispering noise like the sound of breath through teeth. Suddenly, a seam in the previously seamless floor appeared.

"My little secret," she said. "Vix has my electromagnetic gauntlet, but what she doesn't know is I have two more."

The seam became a crack, and the crack opened into a hatch. It was small enough that no standard-sized human could fit inside, but it was big enough to hold a sizable amount of secrets, whatever they may be.

There was darkness within. Molly laid on the floor and stuck her hand in. Her priggish expression morphed into one of confusion - and then anger. She bolted upright, almost knocking heads with both October and Bratt, who had bent over the mysterious hole in the floor to get a better look.

The hidden compartment was empty.

"She. TOOK THEM!" Molly yelled the final two words, and they reverberated through The Presidio's interior. "She knew!"

Molly began pacing.

"You idiot!" she scolded herself. "Of course she knew! She probably had that damned Mr. Screech in here with his damned blending spell."

"Blending spell?" Bratt interjected.

"Yes, yes, it makes the witch unnoticeable. They're in the room with you, but you just never really see them," she waved her hand as if she were shooing away a fly.

Molly continued to pace back and forth as she spoke. "But when? When could she have? She was with the group the entire time."

"Actually," October said, "she wasn't with us the *entire* time."

This stopped Molly in her tracks. She was facing only slightly away from October, but she still made a melodramatic show of slowly turning her head to look at him.

"What?" she said calmly.

"She said she knew how to bring you back, but she would have to do it alone - and in the submersible" Bratt said. "She was in here for … I don't know, how long was it, October?"

"It was long enough!" Molly interjected as she took two steps forward. She hesitated as she decided which of the two men she meant to grapple with. She drew in a deep breath.

"Of course," she said, "there was no way you could have known."

She collapsed back down on the altar. She placed her elbows on her knees and then hid her face in her hands. She wasn't crying. She was cooling.

Minutes passed in awkward silence. And finally, Molly emerged from her position. Her hair was slightly rumpled, and her face had imprints of her palms etched across them.

"I guess," she said with an unfocused stare out the giant window – reminding Bratt of a mad scientist if ever there was one, "we'll have to rely entirely on what we can find in the laboratory."

Chapter 83

After several hours, the three had given Molly's obsidian altar a mechanical upgrade. It was a blessing they'd been just meters away from the apothecary, or else they would have been wanting badly for parts.

Any hope of bringing Dr. Cerulean back from the brink, though, had been dashed, as many of the parts came from his dimension-traversing machine. Bratt had to force himself to postpone his mourning to a more convenient time.

Though, he realized while dismantling a section of levers and gears, he did have his copious notes still hidden in his own floor compartment and perhaps could – given enough time, ironically – rebuild the contraption.

October had issued a few, graphic words under his breath at having wasted a trip to the apothecary only to return to it hours later. Bratt had whispered a few, less expressive words of relief at having a chance to recover his notes.

Regardless of frustrations and gratitude, the trio managed to enhance the slab of black obsidian. Attached to the floor of the submarine, on either side of the slab, was now bolted a series of gears and pulleys. When activated, they tilted the altar up. Looking into the large window from the outside of The Presidio, one would think there was a giant mirror inside.

The underside of the black slab was now equipped with an array of wires, tubes, pistons, valves, aluminum sheets, nickel tiles, copper slates, and a case made of lead. The machine was, technically, incomplete, though. When the obsidian was hoisted into the vertical position, a thick, circular lid was exposed. When unscrewed, it revealed an empty shaft that was, by no coincidence, exactly the same size as the cylinder that Bratt had concealed in his satchel.

Molly had worked out what she called a mirror spell. In essence, it cast magic upon whatever was reflected in its surface. That magic could vary depending on the will of the witch. She'd used mirror spells many times before, although they were mostly cast to cause a woman to rethink leaving her home when looking at her reflection so she wouldn't interfere with Molly's work, or prodding a man to believe a conspiracy theory in order to start a war.

The latter spell had been cast on the orders of Mistress Artemis Vix, of course. Molly's desire for warring nations was utterly absent.

Besides her ability to work mirror spells successfully, Molly had used her most powerful talent - her inclination for divining the present and the future - to predict that the mirror spell would in fact be the best option.

The purpose of the added machinery was to give Molly's spell a blast of energy that she could not have mustered herself - even if she still possessed one of her magnetic gauntlets.

However, she thought with a simmering aggravation, she would have been far more confident if she'd had her device - even more so if she had all three at her disposal. But that was neither here nor there. Vix had them. She had all three. There was nothing to be done about that now. But at least Molly had two brilliant, albeit magicless, minds on her side, and one rigorously supercharged magic mirror.

Chapter 84

Mistress Artemis Vix stood in the heat of the desert, the dry wind blowing about her. Although she was dressed in black, she didn't feel a stitch of warmth. In fact, whether in arctic tundra or tropical jungle, Vix was never bothered by the atmosphere, having perfected an acclimation spell over decades of study. She'd enchanted her entire wardrobe so that, no matter the weather, she was always comfortable at a balmy 21.6 degrees Celsius.

Despite her physical comfort though, the vexation within her brewed hot.

The disappearance of the two men and her own protégé might actually be the means to the end she had been working toward. But then again, it might have just torn all her plans asunder in a second's worth of blue and purple electricity.

Her ability to know these things, though, had just traveled to another dimension. With Molly gone, Vix had no way of ascertaining possible futures.

For the first time in decades, Vix scowled in a way that rivaled Mr. Screech's sourest of expressions.

She turned on her heel away from the site of transportation and trudged back toward The Trevithick, where Vermilion and Screech were standing outside the door of the passenger coach.

"Back inside!" Vix commanded from afar. The two scrambled back into the train as Vix hitched her dress up to nearly her knees and marched through the sand. There was no need for graceful and dramatic gliding now.

The three sat down. Vermilion and Screech sat opposite Vix, who had composed herself during her short journey back from the desert and into the train. She was as calm and collected as she'd ever been, despite having to take the next step in her quest blindly.

"Vera, dear," Vix said, shocking both subordinate witches with the informal use of Vermilion's given name. "You wouldn't by chance have the ability to scry? To see beyond the veil of time and ascertain possible directions and the consequences thereof?"

Vermilion sat silently for a moment, mulling over her own story. If she'd had the talent to foresee the future, she most likely wouldn't have set out to kill her niece on that fateful day. She perhaps would have stayed home and brewed a nice cup of tea to wash down the heart she'd just eaten. (Of course, if she had done this, she would have missed out entirely on Vix and Company's curative magic for the curse she had also just consumed, but that was not necessarily a thought that popped into Madame Vermilion's mind at that particular moment.)

"No," Vermilion said flatly. "No, I do not."

"Then we'll have to continue forward," Vix said soberly. "We'll be stumbling blindly in the dark, I expect, but what better test of our magical prowess, eh?"

Mr. Screech looked back at Vix with an expression he hoped did not betray his lack of confidence. Vermilion didn't try to hide it at all.

"We don't even know what we're doing yet!" Vermilion spouted. "And you expect us to put our lives in your hands?"

"Who better than I?" Vix responded confidently. "After all, I've learned to live hundreds of years without dying. So I think I'd be the one with whom you'd feel most secure. Who amongst us can say she or he has survived multiple burnings at the stake?"

She looked at the two of them before raising her own hand.

"I have. And if I can live through that, then there should be no fear for the two of you."

Mr. Screech knew better. It wasn't that she was skilled at staying alive; it was that she was incapable of dying. He figured it had something to do with the giant ruby. But he guessed Vix couldn't die even if she wanted to. If she were quartered, and the pieces of her body buried at four separate locations on the earth, she would still live and it would only be a matter of time before happenstance brought the pieces back together. Just because a mortal stands next to Vix does not make him impervious to death.

Vermilion, though, was put a little more at ease thanks to her ignorance of the matter.

Let this be a lesson to you, dear reader. To be truly happy, you must know as little as possible. To remain blissful, as some saying somewhere goes, you should ignore all school lessons, disregard any advice from anyone in a position of authority, and only read books by this storyteller, as they are the only ones sure to leave you with even less knowledge than you began with.

But this is not a remedial class on the euphoria of uneducation, and you'll do well to keep your focus honed on the tale being told.

"To ensure we are in tip-top magical performance, we'll be utilizing these amazing gadgets provided by our own Molly St. Mercalli." Vix bent over and produced the two additional gauntlets from their hiding place beneath the damask bench.

"Well, I never!" Mr. Screech said. "She had more?"

"Indeed," Vix said, passing one of them to Screech. "And, I believe you still have yours, Madame Vermilion?"

The familiarity had passed, and Vix had returned to using surnames. Vermilion nodded, and reached below her own bench, nearly toppling over in the act. Soon, all three witches had the leather devices strapped to their arms. The brown hide looked entirely out of place on Vix's arm, clashing with the black of her blouse, dress, hat and boots.

"Drat," Vix said, noticing the fashion faux pas. She looked around the room, and her gaze settled on the tea service. She picked up the teapot and plashed a bit of the water into her left hand (by now it had cooled to room temperature). Then with her right, she reached up into her hat and pulled out the hatpin with the black jewel. She used this to stir the water in her palm before blowing on it. Some of the water sprayed, but most stayed in the cup of her hand. She then clapped her hands together loudly, causing the rest of the water to splash outward. Remarkably, none of it seemed to land on Mistress Vix, although plenty found its way into the faces of Madame Vermilion and Mr. Screech. Then with her right hand, she rubbed the gauntlet strapped to her left arm from top to bottom.

Vermilion watched as the air shimmered somewhat around the brown leather. It reminded her of the way the atmosphere danced on the horizon in the desert heat just outside the train. Once the fluttering stopped, Vix's gauntlet was the same iridescent black as the jewel atop the hatpin.

Vix replaced the pin in her black hat, and then she noted Vermilion's awe.

"Oh, do calm down," Vix said, shaking the rest of the water from her hands. "Its color hasn't changed. I've just altered the atmosphere around it to let only certain amounts of light through. It's a wholly uncomplicated glamour, I assure you."

"Can you make mine pink?" Vermilion responded, holding up her own left arm.

"No time," Vix said as she stood. "We must adjourn to the desert. I have a spell planned, and I need the three of you to learn it well."

The sun had set by now. Vermilion hadn't noticed the lights inside the coach had brightened slowly as the evening had become darker.

Chapter 85

"Can your staff transport The Presidio to The Core, do you think?" Molly asked October as he was on his knees making a few final adjustments to the altar.

"I believe it can," October said, turning a screw tightly into the mechanism that would tilt the obsidian up. "I've been mulling about that prospect myself." He made one last turn of the tool and then stood. He reflexively brushed his knees off, though the interior of Molly's craft was remarkably clean.

"The energy that moves our matter to another dimension is electrical, is it not?" He didn't wait for an answer. "Therefore, it can be conducted. If I ensure the staff is resting upon the metal hull of this vessel when it's activated, the hull should, in theory, conduct the energy throughout the entire craft."

"Although," he paused, "I'm unsure whether the whole procedure might fry us in our shoes."

"Well, none of us are wearing metal shoes," Bratt said. October looked back at him blankly. "Following the laws of electrical currents, it can only be conducted through metals. Well, as far as I can tell, we're all wearing leather on our feet."

October rolled his eyes. "Well of course I was about to get to that point," he said with annoyance. He certainly didn't like being bested by the likes of Bratticus L. Magleby in matters of science.

"I just wish I had my gauntlet," Molly said. "It really would help us in a bind. I mean, what if we were to meet the Grimblenox in our journey? Just one look could turn us to black pillars of scales in a best case scenario. At worst, one of us could be transformed into some hell creature that would promptly attempt to destroy the other two."

"We really should have some sort of contingency, just in case," she added.

"Could we not simply turn the mirror on the monster? Wouldn't it reflect the creature's own power on itself?"

Molly knew this wouldn't work. It was partly because of the way she'd encountered the beasts during her brief trip through death. But even if she didn't have knowledge of the monsters, she would have deduced a mirror would have no effect.

"There are more than one Grimblenox," she said with a shudder. Although her recollection of the swarm of creatures was still glazed over with the mental equivalence of black scales, her body reacted to the memory with disgust. "If they're not turning each other into crusty black masses, then we can make an educated guess that a mirror certainly won't do the trick.

"In addition, the spell we're generating here is a healing spell, meant to set The Core right. We most definitely do not want to throw a healing spell at that outer reality leviathan."

Each stood in contemplation for a moment.

She gave the two men a look that more or less told them they should have known the obvious from the beginning. "If the mirror *did* reflect a power back on the monster, we'd be taking the chance that it might turn into a more nightmarish creature. And a more nightmarish creature than the Grimblenox is not something I care to experience."

Molly sat back down on her altar and folded her arms gently. She looked out the window at nothing in particular.

"Besides, this isn't some ancient myth," she said wearily. "We can't just kill Medusa with the aid of a mirror."

Bratt and October exchanged glances. This was another one of those things the two could not understand since neither of them came from a dimension in which the ancient myth of Medusa existed.

The three sat in silence a moment longer before Molly leapt up from her seat.

"I have an idea!" she exclaimed.

Chapter 86

October was miffed, as there were only seven trips left in the staff. Wasting yet another one traveling back to the desert was incredibly annoying. Nonetheless, it gave him a chance to test the staff's ability to transfer entire submarines through time and dimensions.

He wished he had some extra time to go snooping around a few more parallel dimensions in search of another filter. However, as he'd discovered with much dismay, nearly all the other dimensions in this little pocket of time had been ravaged by The Pecularity – including his own. It was no small wonder that Bratt's was still, for the most part, in tact.

If October took a chance now by hopping to another timeline in hopes of finding a fully functional dimension there, he'd be risking not only burning away another portion of his own filter, but also finding himself in a place that no longer existed.

He very well couldn't go about saving all of reality by wasting his precious few trips jumping around to places that weren't even there, now could he?

The group took some extra precautions as they prepared to transport Molly's entire submersible across time and dimensions.

Before they left the grassy yard that now included a pond, a sandy beach, and a red rock formation at the forest's edge, Bratt retrieved a ream of leather Dr. Cerulean used to make belts (both for crankshaft pulleys in his mechanical inventions and for keeping up pants that weren't snug enough to stay up on their own). He'd cut three large pieces for each of them to stand on. He also cut an extra strip for October, which he used to hold the staff in place after activation.

Bratt thought he'd be more worried than he was at the prospect of being fried to death by electricity in an errant dimension-traveling experiment. However, having witnessed several horrors that would turn another man's hair white, and having witnessed several more horrors that would change that hair back to its original color, he found himself quite calm and collected.

October's theory was correct. The electrical current from the staff did, in fact, carry through the metal hull of the submersible, essentially turning it into a larger version of Dr. Cerulean's machine. It had the added bonus of keeping the energy confined to the vessel and the occupants inside. When it traveled, it didn't bring anything else with it.

When October activated his cane, the whole submarine transported quite nicely and didn't bring any grass or raccoons along with it.

In the forest there was a lucky raccoon that happened to be inspecting The Presidio at the exact moment it was transported away from Bratt's dimension. Had it been near the group as it traveled without the encompassment of an unsubmerged submersible, it very well might have been plucked from the dimension and chucked into the desert along with the travelers.

With the power of the staff being conducted through the steel hull and not into the atmosphere, though, that particular raccoon wasn't scratched nor scathed as the particles that made up The Presidio buzzed and shifted through the fabric of existence and into another dimension.

The poor rodent immediately died from fright, but still.

When The Presidio arrived, buzzing almost silently into existence right next to The Trevithick, the desert was dark. The silvery sliver of a crescent moon hung low on the horizon, and a river of stars lit the night like a fleet of ships on a dark ocean. The stars were the only way to discern the desert's horizon from the sky, the sand dark in the absence of moonlight.

The only other light that shone in the barrens was from The Trevithick. The lights were on in the train's passenger coach, though the drapes were closed. All the other cars were dark.

Molly was the first out of the sail. She stepped quietly onto the platform. Bratt followed, and finally October was out. The three of them looked at the train, seeing the warm, yellow glow around the edges of the curtains in the passenger car. In the distance, a pack of coyotes yipped wildly for a moment before falling silent.

The pack caught their prey, Molly thought. She couldn't help but draw a parallel between their own situation, except their prey was far bigger and had a more ferocious bite.

She'd come with a plan. Because she was a member of Vix's inner circle, she was one of the few who knew the magical passcode to enter the train. However, she'd only used it to access the passenger coach, and she wasn't sure if it would unlock Vix's personal chambers.

The three strained their ears listening for some sort of conversation within the train. Either the coach was well insulated, or the witches within were not doing or saying anything.

As October surveyed the scene, he became increasingly agitated. They had traveled between these two dimensions not once, and not even twice. This was three times, now. If their task at hand couldn't be accomplished in this trip, then he didn't know what his next move should be. It certainly wouldn't be long before he'd be unable to travel at all, let alone find a way to The Core.

Bratt was imagining how all of this could possibly end. If what

Molly said was true, then there were beasts – bigger than planets - which they would have to either destroy or immobilize, all while repairing an orb that somehow generates life itself.

"Well, it's about time," came the voice behind them.

The trio jumped as high as a trio can when perched atop a submarine in the middle of a desert in the middle of the night. Both Bratt and October spun as if on swivels. Molly also turned, but she did so with a bit more grace.

Mr. Screech stood in the sand below. It was nigh-on impossible to discern his features in the shadow of the submersible, but October and Bratt knew for certain he hadn't been there before. Molly now knew he had probably been standing there even before they'd returned to the desert. It was simply a fact that none of them noticed him until he spoke.

"Really, I'd thought you all would have returned hours ago. But, upon further reflection, I do see you came during the night in an effort to surprise us."

Molly couldn't see Screech clearly in the darkness, but she had a sneaking suspicion he was examining the cuticles on his nails in a gesture of superiority.

Bratt was suddenly overcome with a boiling dread that all their efforts were futile, and they - all of them - not just he and October and Molly, but also Mistress Artemis Vix, Madame Verimillicent Vermilion and Mr. Byzantium Screech - were now trapped in some nightmarish, infinite loop, doomed for eternity to travel between the apothecary on the hill at the end of End Lane in the City of Bell in the County of Muss in the State of Konfusion and The Trevithick train in the middle of the desert in the middle of a state of which he knew not the name in a country with which he was wholly unfamiliar.

It was enough to drive one mad, he thought. Though at that moment he was unsure of whether his definition of mad meant "crazy" or "angry." Both would suffice, he was sure. And both were inevitable.

October, for his part, had no such inkling. He saw their travels as finite - incredibly so, considering there were now only seven dimensional moves possible, and it didn't appear the group was going to be in a position to find a new filter for his staff anytime soon.

Molly simply called Mr. Screech a pair of words that none of those present had ever heard a woman say, or any civilized man, for that matter. October had only heard the adjective and noun coupled together once before in his childhood when Professor Friday F. Jones became incredibly honest after drinking nearly a full cask of 200-proof alcohol-based cleaning agent, which he'd mistaken for wine. (In Professor Jones' defense, though, the wine and cleaning agents were packed in very similar casks, and they both tasted relatively the same.) It was that day October heard Professor Jones tell Assistant Professor Reginald T. Jones exactly what he thought of him and likened him unto unmentional body parts on a person with unspeakable familial relations.

That was the day Professor Friday F. Jones died, October remembered. Everyone agreed it had to have been alcohol poisoning, and it was young October's job to clean up the wine and cleaning solvent cellar where Friday F. Jones apparently fell backward four or five times onto a large knife that had Assistant Professor Reginald T. Jones' name embossed in gold on its handle.

Isn't it interesting how small things such as a coupling of words can bring back such fond childhood memories? But why I keep allowing you, dear reader, to veer wildly off topic is a mystery. Take my word: If it happens again, I may just have to put an end to this tale until you're ready to pay full attention.

"Where did you learn such language?" Screech quipped from the dark, a rhetorical response if ever there was one. He didn't even wait for Molly to answer. "Come along, then. The three of you. Let's get you inside and out of this chilly air before you've all been infected by a wandering drekalo."

Neither Bratt nor October knew what this drekalo creature was, but Molly did, and the mention of it lit a small but fierce fire under her posterior. She hesitated only a minute, deciding which fate was worse. In a matter of one and one-fourth seconds, she made up her mind that she'd rather sit as a prisoner inside a comfy steam engine carriage than come into contact with a drekalo.

"Come along," she said to the boys. She mounted her submersible's ladder and climbed to the desert floor.

October and Bratt followed.

Chapter 86

A drekalo, dear reader, may look like a child, but it is not. It is a demonic beast that wanders the wilderness at night. From afar, one might think it is a lost youngster, and one might attempt to help it find its way home. Up close, though, the drekalo is a disgusting thing, looking like the corpse of a little boy or girl that has been decaying in the sand for months.

And if one looks into the face of a drekalo, one will become sick and die within days.

It's not a pretty sight, neither the death nor the drekalo.

So if you ever encounter a lost child in the wilderness, don't be fooled by its cries for help. Your best course of action will be to turn around and walk as quickly away from it as possible.

Chapter 87

Bratt noticed two things upon entering Vix's passenger car. The first thing was the liquor.

Vermilion and Vix sat opposite each other on the car's benches, each holding a glass of dark, burgundy wine. On the altar in the middle of the room, which had been re-draped with the yellow tablecloth, was an open bottle of wine and a decanter of a dark, brown liquid. Molly knew it was some sort of bourbon - one of Mr. Screech's favorites. Bratt, on the other hand, couldn't tell bourbon from mud, as he never really had a taste for the stronger spirits.

There were three empty wine glasses and an empty tumbler next to the bottles.

"I must say, you did take your time," Vix said as she took a sip from her glass. "Please," she gestured at the benches, "have a seat. Let's commiserate."

The second thing Bratt noticed was Madame Verimilicent Vermilion, Mr. Byzantium Screech, and Mistress Artemis Vix were all wearing Molly's gauntlets.

Molly sat first. Either she didn't see her inventions strapped to the arms of her now-enemies, or she didn't care. She plucked an empty glass and poured a generous amount of wine into it.

"You really should let it breathe a little, my dear," Vix said as Molly immediately brought the wine to her lips and guzzled.

Molly finished the entire glass without coming up once for air. As the last few drops drained into her mouth, she gulped in a quick breath of oxygen.

"Shut up," she stated while looking at the glass, although she was clearly talking to Vix. Molly grabbed the bottle and poured another. Meanwhile, Mr. Screech had put his hand on the backs of both Bratt and October and guided them - in a way not unlike shoving - gently toward the benches.

"Please," Screech said in a calmness that set Bratt's teeth on edge. "Have a seat."

The two men sat. Molly drank another glass of wine.

"There's plenty for everyone," Vix said, gesturing toward the empty bottles. "Well, Molly might just finish an entire bottle of cabernet by herself, but I do have an ample collection in one of the boxcars."

At the word "boxcars," Molly stopped drinking for a millisecond so indiscernible that it could have been mistaken for a tiny hiccup. Vix saw this and smiled.

"Speaking of which," Vix said, finishing the few drops of liquid in her own stemware before setting it on the tablecloth clad altar and standing.

"There's quite the collection of many things in this train, is there not?"

She walked to the carriage door that led to her personal quarters and placed her hand on the latch. She made no movement, but the click of something audibly unlocking reverberated through the passenger car.

"Oh, Mr. Screech," she said as she opened the door, letting the cool desert air inside, "aren't you forgetting something?"

"Ah, yes," he said with all the enthusiasm of a man who forgot his goggles on the drawing room table before heading out for a morning drive in his St. Louis Gasoline Buggy. "I'll need to hold onto this for the time being."

Screech plucked the staff from October's hands.

"Hey!" October barked, grabbing for the walking stick. But Mr. Screech was nothing if not sneaky, and he was able to whisk the cane away from October's grasp and then snake comfortably out of arm's length. October tried to stand but found he was utterly unable.

Panic began to boil in Bratt's innards upon seeing the look of pure horror in October's eyes. Bratt, too, tried to get up but found he was somehow bound to the seat. They both struggled, emitting grunts and exhaling breath from mouths that, considering all the circumstances, hadn't been cleaned in a couple of days.

Molly quickly finished her glass of wine. Her third? Her fourth? She slammed the glass to the altar and swallowed the last of it hard and loud.

"Stop it!" she ordered through a puckered and sour expression, waving a hand in front of her nose in the process. "If you have to strain yourselves in a futile attempt to get off these benches, at least have the courtesy to breathe through your noses!"

The two men stopped squirming and looked at Molly, both their faces now wearing looks of puzzlement. As soon as they calmed down, Molly nodded and poured the rest of the wine into her glass and then emptied it into her mouth in one, final gulp.

"Well," Vix said with amusement. "That *was* entertaining, I must say!"

Vix walked out the door without further comment. Both Bratt and October looked to Molly for some sort of explanation. Molly stared ahead at the drape-covered window across from her with a look of pure and utter annoyance. Mr. Screech was standing in the corner of the car, gently inspecting October's staff.

"You be careful!" October seethed. "That is our only ticket to salvation!"

Mr. Screech acted as though he didn't hear. He continued twiddling and fiddling and poking and prodding. October secretly hoped the despicable man would accidentally transport himself to the bottom of the sea. Then a deeper part of October shushed himself for even thinking such a thing. With the string of bad luck the group had recently found themselves tied to, Screech probably *would* transport himself to the bottom of the sea, either removing the dimension-traveling machine from the equation completely or taking the whole train with him in the process.

A third, even deeper part of October guessed that the train would magically keep them safe under water, and a fourth portion of October's depths thought that was poppycock - otherwise Vix wouldn't need the use of Molly's submersible. And so the thinking continued, down and down and down forever, like an infinite pillar of turtles balancing a world upon their chapter.

"What is this?" Bratt said, struggling again while trying his damndest not to breathe in Molly's direction.

"Just stop moving about," Molly said without looking at him. "It makes no difference. These seats have been charmed. Their electrons are now spinning in the same direction as ours. We're stuck until the magic is lifted."

"So," Bratt stammered, "So we've been ... magnetized?"

"Magnetic," October said blandly. "Magic. Magic magnets. Magnetic magic. Majnetic."

Bratt blinked at October's sudden and, honestly, surprising portmanteau. October did not look at Bratt. Bratt turned his gaze toward Molly who also didn't look back at him. He looked from Molly to Madame Vermilion, who was also seated on the bench. Vermilion looked back at him, smiled without happiness, and nodded.

"Yes, well, it appears magic and magnetism are really just different bits of the same machine, aren't they?" She said.

She set down her glass and stood without effort. (Well, without having to deal with magical magnetization, that is. She still struggled a bit due to her overall lack of grace.) Apparently whatever force was holding onto Bratt and October, and most likely Molly, although she hadn't exactly tried to stand, clearly wasn't affecting Vermilion.

Bratt stifled a "But how?" that nearly jumped out of his throat. He clenched his teeth and held it back in its little mouth prison. He knew that if it escaped, it would only be answered by Molly rolling her eyes, or someone saying, "Magic of course." He pondered for a moment why the little "But how?" chose now to try and force its way out, considering all the "But how?" opportunities that had come before.

"But hows?" are funny that way. They like to bide to their time, ignoring obvious moments to surface only to leap out when their presence is nearly unnecessary.

Bratt looked from October to Molly, hoping either would say something. October only looked dejected. Molly's face was unreadable. Sometime during Bratt's battle with the "But how?" that had now found its way back to where it came from, Molly had picked up the wine bottle and was holding it in her left hand. She continued looking at the drapes in front of her, though, and the whole scene reminded Bratt of old Mr. Kitterman back in Bell, who used to purchase bottles of wine, drink the contents straight from the bottle, and then sit on a street curb with the bottle in hand, looking very forlorn that his treat had been consumed.

The five sat in silence for a few moments, each engulfed in some sort of activity. Bratt's was looking from face to face with expectancy. Screech's was the inspection of October's walking stick. October's was attempting to see how far his face could droop. Molly's was poring over the pattern on the drapes. And Vermilion's was to reseat herself and munch from a little plate of cookies she'd retrieved when she stood up earlier - though it's not clear exactly from where she'd gotten them.

The door leading to Vix's personal car swung back open. She was holding a silver bust of a woman who appeared to be someone from ancient times. At least, that's what Molly would have thought. Bratt and October only saw the visage of a woman cast in metal, her long hair held back with a small laurel, her large nose protruding out elegantly and catching the light from the sconces on the wall.

"I'm guessing this is what you came back to get, yes?" Vix said with a smirk.

This popped both Molly and October out their respective trances. They each traded glances with Bratt, who couldn't help but arch an eyebrow in utter confusion.

Vix noticed their shared perplexity.

"You - you didn't come for the Ensorcelled Bust of Hypatia?" she asked, nearly dumbfounded that the group hadn't traveled back to The Trevithick to retrieve the powerful bauble.

If eyebrow arching were an ancient Olympic sport, Bratt, October and Molly would have surely taken the podium with gold, silver and bronze medals. All three were now practicing prolific arching skills in their unmitigated bewilderment.

Vix was immediately taken down two or three pegs in a harsh reminder of why she needed Molly so badly. Vix held so much power that it was almost ludicrous. But Molly knew how to scry. She could always point Vix in the right direction, and if Molly had been at her disposal, Vix would have known at least more about what was going on right now than what she'd assumed was about to happen.

Chapter 88

So what was it Vix thought the two scientists and the prodigal witch had planned?

It can be frustrating going through life and not knowing others' intentions and thoughts. For example, Molly, Bratt and October had no way of knowing what Vix thought they'd wanted the Ensorcelled Bust of Hypatia for.

But that's the way of humans. Sometimes, a thing can be right in front of our faces, as the bust was for our heroes, and we'll never know more about why it's there, what it's origin is, or what its possible function could be.

If we don't investigate further, or if someone isn't willing to educate us, then we have to accept that there are some things we may never understand.

Thus, Molly, Bratt and October, and by extension, you, dear reader, will never know why Vix thought they wanted the Ensorcelled Bust of Hypatia.

It's maddening, isn't it?

Chapter 89

Vix cradled the Ensorcelled Bust of Hypatia in her arms. She looked to the scientists and then to Molly.

"Then what, pray tell, did you come back here for?" she demanded.

Molly didn't answer. She only held the empty wine bottle in her left hand and swayed slowly back and forth. In her stupor, she'd recorked the bottle as if she were afraid any contents within would be spilled as she rocked in her seat.

October and Bratt exchanged glances. Neither of them knew what to say.

The two didn't have to answer, though, because it was at that exact moment that Molly's wine decided to catch up with the rest of her, and she tumbled forward onto the altar. Her backside held fast to the bench, but it wasn't enough to keep Molly's face from slamming to the altar's top. It appeared at first that she was going to steady and catch herself with her free hand. However, in her drunkenness, the only thing her free hand managed to do was to knock a wine glass straight into her face's path.

The glass broke, and Molly's cheek bounced into the pile of stemware fragments.

Everyone was still for a moment - even Molly. All eyes were upon her face, which was still resting on the altar. The cheery yellow tablecloth had begun to turn a deep maroon.

Then Molly screamed.

She bolted upright. Protruding from her cheek were two large shards of glass. Blood was pouring down her face. She began grasping and pulling at the pieces of stemware lodged into her face with her right hand. Her left hand still clutched the bottle.

"Good lord!" gasped Screech.

Vermilion scuttled up and away from the scene as if a million spiders had just broken loose. She backed against the door to the engine with a look of horror on her face.

"Molly!" Bratt yelled, trying again to stand but failing - and flailing - miserably.

"Blast it all, do something!" October demanded.

Vix's expression hardened at the sight of the blood on her yellow tablecloth. She stomped to Mr. Screech and shoved the bust into his arms. As he took it, he let go of October's staff, and it clattered to the ground. No one seemed to notice this as Molly's screams continued.

"Take this back to my carriage - and take her with you. Clean her up!"

Mr. Screech nodded and walked down the center of the car. He held the bust of Hypatia to his chest with his right hand. With his left hand - the one on which the gauntlet was strapped - he grabbed Molly by the arm, breaking the spell that kept her in place.

He guided her out the door and into Vix's car. Molly screamed the whole way. As soon as Screech and Molly were in Vix's carriage, though, the screaming immediately stopped.

October and Bratt looked at each other in alarm.

Vix was removing the items from the tablecloth, preparing to gather it up so she could get it soaking before the blood set into a stain. She didn't seem to notice the sudden absence of screams.

Vermilion spoke up.

"Eh, er, do you think we should check up on Mr. Screech?" she asked. "I ... I don't hear screaming."

Vix didn't look up from her work. She'd placed the decanter and the remaining glasses onto the floor, along with the bowl of green apples that had been the only item to adorn the altar when the group had first stepped foot into the carriage all those hours ago. She had begun bringing the corners of the tablecloth together, creating a basket to hold the broken glass.

"My carriage is spy-proof," she said, nonplussed, as she folded the tablecloth into a ball, set it on the floor, and then began inspecting the altar for scratches. "No sound goes in or out, and if you look into the windows, all you'll see is an empty room."

"Besides," she added with a grimace as she ran her finger along what appeared to be a new mark in the altar's dark surface, no doubt created by Molly's drunken foolery, "We have the gauntlets now. Molly is powerless."

As Vix went about her busywork, October looked toward his staff. When it had tumbled to the floor, the panel had popped open, revealing the orb-shaped filter inside. He thought he could have stretched his arm and retrieved it, but he didn't dare make a move with Vix in the vicinity.

He was worried less about Vermilion, though he probably wouldn't have made the attempt with her so close, either.

Although he didn't grab for it, he did examine it - the filter, in particular. He focused his eyes on the tiny vents, one of which would blacken after each trip. Thirteen in all, October counted the ones that had been singed during use. He didn't *have* to count them because he'd been keeping a precise tally in his head since installing the new filter.

In total, the staff had been used six times. There were still seven available trips.

So why, then, were there only five unscorched punctures? He knew for certain they hadn't traveled more than six times, and until this precise moment, the walking stick had never been out of his possession. There was no way anyone else could have used it.

He mentally checked his math, just in case.

Dr. Cerulean's trip - the one that seemed to have set all of this in motion - was the first use. When October, Bratt, Molly, Vix, Screech and Vermilion traveled to the train the first time, it burned a second puncture in the filter. October and Bratt had traveled back to the apothecary on the hill to retrieve the canister, which was trip number three. They used it a fourth time to return to the desert to get Molly. From there they made the journey back to the apothecary - number five - and then returned to The Trevithick with The Presidio in tow. Six.

He'd usually been careful to inspect the walking stick after travels to ensure nothing had been damaged along the way. The finite number of uses left in the filter was always at the top of his mind, so he found himself constantly thumbing open the panel to count the number of scorched punctures. Hadn't he counted the number of trips just before the three of them returned to the desert? Yes, of course he had. He'd counted five. So what had caused multiple punctures to burn out in the last journey?

His stomach dropped as if it had been flung from the top of the clock tower at Ansford-Upon-Uptonshire-On-Tees University. There was only one thing the group had done differently this time, and it was so obvious that October was surprised it hadn't occurred to him before they'd decided to take the gamble in the first place.

They'd brought an entire submersible with them. All that extra mass clearly took more energy to move. It was basic physics.

So now the group had even fewer chances to get the job done.

Chapter 90

October began doing more mental math. If they could get out of The Trevithick and back to The Presidio in time, that would mean an additional three units of the time filter gone - assuming they transported the submersible when they traveled to The Core. But they had to - absolutely *had to* - transport Molly's submarine. It was the key to finishing what they'd started.

His stomach sank further when he realized it would leave only two remaining punctures in the filter. That would mean the group would have to leave the submersible behind after they'd finished their chore. But where they were going, would it be possible to leave the vessel at all? October had not discounted the fact that leaving an airtight craft in an uncharted atmosphere could mean certain death.

He'd been paying so much attention to his cane that he didn't notice the door to Vix's personal car opening.

Vix was too busy on her knees, pulling out a new yellow tablecloth from a compartment beneath one of the benches to notice, either. Bratt was watching October, wondering why he looked as though he'd just been slapped by a woman wearing iron gloves. The only person to see Molly coming back into the passenger carriage was Vermilion. Vermillion's wits were not about her, though, and it didn't immediately occur to her that Molly's appearance without her chaperone, Mr. Screech, was in any way out of the ordinary. In fact, Vermilion only realized something was wrong when Molly stepped up behind Vix, lifted the wine bottle she still held in her hand, and brought it promptly down upon the back of Vix's skull.

Sometimes in stories, dear reader, wine bottles are used as weapons. And oftentimes, those wine bottles break. But let me assure you that in reality, wine bottles are quite tough. And it takes more than the bashing of skulls to break them open. However, even the sturdiest of wine bottles will fail eventually. Sometimes, though, there are certain circumstances that reinforce wine bottles, even to the point that they could never break - even if they were to be smashed against the hull of the densest of yachts. Such was the case in the passenger carriage of a magical train parked in the middle of the desert in the middle of the night.

The sound of the bottle echoed like a cathedral bell, its gonging punctuated quite pleasantly with the percussion of Vix's skull cracking. The ancient witch fell forward on her face. Her shoulders were slumped against the floor, but her knees, champions that they were, held their place, leaving Mistress Artemis Vix in a very embarrassing position indeed.

Vermilion looked at Vix's body, it's head and shoulders firmly planted into the plush rug of the carriage floor, and her bottom thrust up and out as if it were begging to be kicked. The master witch's moon-colored hair was now turning red as blood seeped from her scalp.

October, too, gaped at the sudden and severe way in which Molly had returned and dispatched Vix. Bratt, ever the gentleman, had averted his eyes so as not to gaze upon the woman's rear end, which was precariously close to his own face.

Several seconds passed before Vermilion decided she'd try to do something. She lifted her left arm up and began frantically fiddling with the gauntlet, completely unsure of what she was doing. Molly stepped over Vix, walked up to Vermilion, and proceeded with the same greeting she'd extended to Vix. Vermilion fell to the floor with a thud, her pink hat now dented yet again.

Molly turned on her heel and looked back at the boys. The two men were speechless, as men are wont to be when they've just witnessed someone crack the heads of two of their enemies with nothing more than an incredibly sturdy wine bottle.

"Well," Molly said matter-of-factly. "There you have it. And the two of you doubted I could pull it off."

She tutted at the two of them, still stuck on their seats. They looked at her, noticing the cuts on her face were now completely gone. Impressively, she was also now clean from head to toe, her clothes un-mussed, her hair un-tousled.

"Men," she said.

Chapter 91

Sometimes we are privy to the details behind the scenes. While we may never know why Mistress Artemis Vix assumed the group had returned to pluck the Ensorcelled Bust of Hypatia from her collection, we can at least take solace in knowing the exact reason Molly, October and Bratt returned to The Trevithick that night.

Let us travel backward in time to a few short chapters ago when Molly, Bratt and October were still in the submersible outside the apothecary of one Dr. Gustopher C. Cerulean.

"I have an idea!" Molly had exclaimed at the time.

In fact, she'd had several.

October, having been raised by a parade of pompous professors, made plans in one of two ways. First, a plan would be made based upon texts with specific instructions written by scientists, theologians, scholars, and philosophers who had come before and had used methods most scientific, theological, scholarly, and philosophical to hone and perfect said instructions.

Second, in the absence of texts, he would make plans based upon his own life experiences and knowledge, use a scientific method of determining what works and what does not, and continue forward with those plans until one of the plans eventually worked.

Unfortunately, October had found himself, for the first time in his life, without specific instructions provided by texts. His last bastion of formulating plans - the letter from Headmaster Purpureous P. Jones - had most recently proven to be not quite as reliable as he'd assumed. He'd never actually found himself in a predicament in which he'd have to resort to developing a plan based on his own life experiences and knowledge. So he was momentarily at a loss for contrivances.

Bratt's mind was awash with ideas. In fact, he was always coming up with plans for this and plans for that. Unfortunately, none of them had anything to do with the matters at hand. Although, if everyone got through this ordeal alive, Bratt had thought, he might go about exploring the northeast corner of Dr. Cerulean's laboratory.

Molly, though, came up with not one plan but three, and she formulated three separate plans that could be executed simultaneously.

Her first plan, which was the least likely to succeed but was worth trying nonetheless, was to walk right up to Vix's train, knock on the door, explain the situation, and ask for the witches' help. If the trio arrived at just the right time, Vix and Screech would be sitting down to their evening spirits, and the two were much more agreeable after a few drinks.

Her second plan, which had a slightly higher percentage of working than the first plan, was to sneak to Vix's personal carriage, where Molly would attempt to use the same spell that opens the passenger car. Once inside, they could snatch the item they needed and be on their way without having any interactions whatsoever with the witches. If the trio timed the nighttime thievery just right, then Vix and Screech would be sitting down to their evening spirits, and the two weren't quite as sharp as usual and might just miss any noises coming from Vix's car.

Her third plan, which Molly said would most certainly be the one the group would ultimately rely on, was to allow themselves to be caught by the sneaky Mr. Screech. The witches would undoubtedly be awaiting the return of Molly and the two Maglebys, and Vix would have Mr. Screech at the ready. If the capture was timed precisely, then it would be time for Vix and Screech to sit down for their evening spirits. Of course, the three would be invited to join, although no doubt the invitation would be the catalyst for some sort of enchantment. Molly couldn't see exactly what sort of magic the witches would use on them, but she said they should expect it. With the witches assuming they'd gained the upper hand, their guards would not be so strong and, hopefully, no one would think to relieve Molly of her enchanted gloves.

She assured Bratt and October that she would find a way to get into Vix's compartment, use the gloves to disable whomever chaperones her, and steal the item the group needed to complete their task.

Molly said she'd have to use a non-magical force to bring Vix down, as the master witch was near impervious to other spells, including ones emitting from enchanted gloves. But that wouldn't be a problem as long as she could get Vix's attention on something else, like replacing a tablecloth, for example, and as long as Molly had access to a blunt object, such as an empty wine bottle, for example.

After explaining the plans to October and Bratt, Molly took a moment to look at a few possible outcomes of the plans three. The two men watched in silence as Molly removed a bit of salt from one of the drawers in her bureau and sprinkled it onto the surface of her altar. They both winced just a bit when Molly used a glob of her own spittle to rub the salt around, eventually creating an oval on the black, reflective surface. She then went to her knees, her eyesight at the obsidian's edge, looking directly across its surface.

You see, dear reader, scrying is not unlike math. A statistician, for example, can make predictions on certain things based on numbers and formulas and odds. Scrying uses a very similar method – it takes the numbers and formulas and odds of certain actions and tells the witch what a few outcomes will be depending on the actions taken. A smart witch looks to several possible futures and plans accordingly.

Molly sat there watching for several moments before she stood up, used a piece of her skirt to wipe away the salt and spit, and then nodded.

"Our odds are favorable, gentlemen," she'd said.

Chapter 92

Actually, their odds were not favorable, and Molly knew it. But she also knew there was much energy in intent. It was, after all, the bedrock upon which all witchcraft was built - at least all witchcraft in her when and where. If there was no faith behind the deed, then the deed would surely fail. She had to make sure the Maglebys two believed they could not fail.

Molly formulated the plan of drunkenness and mutilating her own face on a whim. The idea hadn't come to her until she'd taken a seat and realized she wouldn't be able to stand again. If Vix had only a few tricks up her impeccably-tailored black sleeves, then perhaps Molly would have foreseen the possibility of the rump-holding spell that kept the trio glued to their seats. Unfortunately, Vix's arsenal of magic was as vast as the Pacific Ocean and twice as deep.

Molly had to improvise with the tools she had in front of her. She knew eyes would be upon her, so she couldn't remove her enchanted gloves that had been secreted away beneath her corset, no matter how stealthy she thought she could be. But she could make a show of drinking an entire bottle of wine.

This is the part of the story where an author provides background to why a person is immune to the effects of liquor. It's the part where we learn that the person in question had built up a tolerance to wine over years and years of practiced drinking. Or perhaps the person had taken a magical draught beforehand that quelled the fermented liquid's influence on the mind and body. Or maybe the person had slipped a bewitched herb into the wine to weaken its efficacy.

I'm sorry to disappoint you, dear reader, but I'm unable to provide you with any of those scenarios. The fact is Molly drank an entire bottle of wine by herself in the span of a few minutes. She hadn't actually eaten anything of substance since her miraculous return from the dead, and her stomach was more or less empty.

As everyone knows, people who have recently risen from the dead and are functioning on an empty stomach tend to get quite drunk indeed, especially when consuming amounts of alcohol that could have loosened the inhibitions of at least three people.

Please take a moment, then, to applaud Miss St. Mercalli's efforts to do everything she did considering the fact she executed her plan while simultaneously being as drunk as a skunk, as they say.

Although, this author has never witnessed a skunk drink any amount of wine, brandy, whiskey, bourbon, beer, moonshine, champagne, rum, vodka, tequila, port, or cooking sherry. Nor has this author ever considered the circumstances in which a skunk would find itself an opportunity to do so, as skunk cocktail parties are such an absurd idea that the very mention of them is too wild even for this story.

But there are plenty of books featuring animals that talk and wear human clothes and, yes, drink liquor. So if you're hell bent upon reading about beasts with appetites for intoxicants, then kindly close these pages and seek out those works. We are telling a completely different story, so be a gracious reader and stop digressing.

It was thanks to Molly's drunken state, though, that she was able to muster up the courage to shatter a wine glass in her cheek. Even then, she found it incredibly painful and regretted it immediately - which is sometimes the case when those who are intoxicated make decisions.

But her stunt did the trick. She knew Mistress Vix was adamant that her carriages remain as pristine as possible. As long as Molly could get her blood to stain the yellow tablecloth, then Vix would be thrown off her guard and - hopefully - escort Molly into the next car to use the Waters of Perdurability to clean and heal her face, thus releasing her from the binding spell and allowing her to pull on the enchanted gloves.

Her improvised plan actually went a little better than she'd thought it would when Vix ordered Mr. Screech to take poor, drunken, bleeding Molly to the next coach. Vix would have, no doubt, been on the lookout for foul play. But sneaky Mr. Screech wasn't as sharp, and this gave Molly an easier opportunity to use her gloves.

It was a good thing Screech was her escort, too, because in her drunken state, Molly surely would have revealed her attempt to free the hidden gloves from her corset and pull them on - especially since she still held a wine bottle in one hand. Luckily, Mr. Screech was not fond of blood, and he was trying his damndest to keep Molly at arm's length while attempting to avert his eyes from the sanguine fluids dripping off the young woman's face.

"Clean yourself up, girl," he'd said, shouting a little in order to be heard over Molly's cries, He prodded her in the direction of Vix's basin and pitcher.

With her back to Screech, and while still wailing, Molly wriggled her right hand into one of the gloves before switching the wine bottle from hand to hand and slipping on the left glove. She then spun around and grasped Mr. Screech's neck with her left hand and squeezed as hard as she could. He opened his mouth to scream.

"Shut up," she whispered, mustering up all the internal energy she could.. "Be still."

His eyes glazed over and he did as he was told. The gloves had worked. Molly had hoped there was still enough magic inside them to do the trick, and there was.

Molly didn't release her grip, though, as she had to steady herself to keep from falling over. She waited a moment or two as she gathered herself.

"You," she slurred, pointing a finger in Mr. Screech's face and nearly poking his eye out, "stay here until I've left the train."

If she hadn't been so tipsy, she might have chosen her command with a little more care. But she was trying with all her might to remain as focused as possible, and at the moment she'd thought the command to be quite adequate.

After stabilizing herself, she turned back to the pitcher. She glanced up momentarily at the mirror hanging above the basin and saw the horror in front of her. The gash on her cheek was still dripping blood, and the very sight of her epitomized the very definition of the word "horror."

She stuck her tongue out and made a face at the wizard and accomplished hairstylist Pierre Pelletier, who was no doubt watching her from the same mirror approximately 350 years before. The wizard and accomplished hairstylist Pierre Pelletier, who was in fact watching Molly in the same mirror from a distance of three centuries, looked at the face she made and cursed under his breath that he hadn't invented the word "horror."

Molly poured a small amount of water into the basin before scooping some of it up with her cupped, gloved hands and splashing it on her face. She looked back into the mirror to see everything was back in order, and the gash on her cheek had healed quite nicely. She took another few seconds to rub water across her hair and on her clothes, watching as the mystical liquid stitched everything back into perfection. She had to pull herself out of a momentary drunken stupor in which she marveled at the water's powers, something she wouldn't have normally done in a state of sobriety.

She wished the water could cure drunkeness, but she was not too far gone to know not to drink it. Instead, she placed the empty wine bottle on the tabletop, popped the cork, and began pouring the water into it, spilling what seemed like gallons of the stuff all over the place. The pitcher never seemed to empty, though, and eventually Molly got the wine bottle full.

In the process, the faded label on the wine bottle became brand-new, the small table upon which the basin had been set was clean as a whistle and perfectly polished, and the rug beneath her feet now looked as if it had been dyed and loomed just yesterday.

After one or two tries, Molly was finally able to recork the wine bottle. She managed it after scrunching her right eye closed and bringing the neck of the bottle about a centimeter away from her face. She straightened herself up, shook her head back and forth a couple of times in an attempt to shed some of her drunkenness, and proceeded back to the passenger carriage.

The wine bottle would be an apt weapon, she knew. The water inside would make the glass impervious. When she re-entered the car, she saw fate had smiled on her as Mistress Vix was in an absolute state of vulnerability. Molly was able to stumble right up behind the so-called master witch and club her - or, rather, *bottle* her - on the back of the head so hard that it should have killed her.

Molly didn't waste much time worrying about the ethics of blasting the back of Vix's skull with an indestructible bottle because she knew Vix would be up and about sooner or later. Instead, she turned her attention to that vile little thing that dared to call herself a witch: Vermilion.

The blow wasn't as hard this time. Molly pulled the power of it just a bit; she actually didn't want to kill the piggish little woman, though she wouldn't kick herself if there were some lasting mental damage. As Molly was going in for the strike, she couldn't help but smile to herself as she watched the wretched little creature attempt to use Molly's own device to activate her magic. Even in a wine-induced fog, Molly remembered that Madame Vermilion's magic came from sucking the energy out of some nearby living thing, and had Vermilion dained to use her own, original power against Molly, then Vermilion surely would have won the battle *and* taken down either Bratt or October - or perhaps even both - in the process.

Well, that's what you get when you cheat your way to the top, Molly thought as she brought the wine bottle down on the side of Vermilion's head, making sure to take aim at that stupid, pink pointed hat she insisted on wearing.

Vermilion fell with a satisfying thud, and Molly triumphantly turned to scold the men for doubting her abilities, although neither man actually had.

Chapter 93

It was at that exact moment in time, with Mr. Byzantium Screech stupefied in the next carriage over, Mistress Artemix Vix lying prostrate in a pool of blood, Madame Veramilicent Vermilion unconscious in a heap, the Maglebys Two dumbstricken in their seats (which they were no longer stuck to, by the way, thanks to Vix's very sudden lack of concentration), and the Ensorcelled Bust of Hypatia's dead eyes a witness to it all, that Miss Molly St. Mercalli's wine decided it'd had a pleasant evening and the party was enjoyable but it's time to leave, thank you kindly.

Even though there was broken glass and an ever-increasing puddle of blood on the rug, Molly's instinct was to not vomit inside the passenger compartment. There were two options when it came to letting loose the contents of her stomach. The first was to make it back into Vix's personal car and use the chamber pot beneath the bed. The second was to simply exit the passenger vehicle and expel the wine into the desert sand.

With the passenger carriage's door not but a meter away, she chose the latter option.

Bratt and October, both of whom still believed the bottom-sticking spell was still in place, watched Molly stumble and trip her way to the exit and fling open the door. They couldn't see exactly what she'd done next, but they could hear both the sound of retching and the sound of liquid being projected onto the ground.

The two men sat in stunned silence for just a moment before the door leading to Vix's coach burst open. There, fuming and disoriented in the doorway, was Mr. Screech. This caught Bratt and October completely off guard, as they had assumed Screech had met the same fate as the two witches who were now either unconscious or dead at their feet.

October's response to seeing Mr. Screech alive and well was to grab for his walking stick. As he did so, he found himself totally unglued from the bench. Since he'd expected to be anchored to the seat, the sheer force of his lunge sent him toppling nearly head over heels in the direction of the staff. Luckily, Vermilion was there to break the fall.

With surprise, October sat bolt upright, looked up as Mr. Screech bore down on him, grabbed the staff, and sidestepped not a moment too soon. Screech, who had had the wherewithal to step over Vix's body, wasn't quite as prepared for Vermilion. As October moved aside, falling back onto the bench, Mr. Screech's foot caught hold on Vermilion's skirts and he went flying forward, knocking his face into the door that led to the engine.

The force, though, was not comparable to that of an indestructible wine bottle thrashed against the back of the skull. The impact of his face against the door knocked out nothing more than one of his teeth.

With their posteriors no longer adhered in place, October and Bratt both jumped up and ran for the door. Luckily, Mr. Screech had found the sudden loss of one of his teeth incredibly perplexing, and he sat on the floor of the carriage feeling the new gap in his mouth while simultaneously scanning the immediate area for the tooth. With his attentions focused on finding pieces of himself that had been pitched during the collision, the Maglebys were able to escape the passenger car and spill out into the desert night.

October was able to avoid Molly's little wine pond, but Bratt wasn't quite as lucky. His left food had found itself directly in the center of the muddy gunk. By the light cast through the open doorway, he lifted his foot and looked at the caked dirt stuck to his boot. The aroma was offensive and strong.

"Come on!" yelled October, who was already several strides away.

Bratt looked up and saw October running toward The Presidio. Molly was there, leaning against the side of the submersible, her face pressed against the cold steel.

"Go!" October called to Molly. "Get inside!"

Molly opened her eyes and looked around her, finally seeing the two men running toward her. It dawned on her then that she'd commanded Mr. Screech to stay put until she left the train. She sucked in some of the crisp night air, and then looked to her hand to make doubly sure she still held the bottle. She did.

With barely a stumble, Molly mounted the ladder leading up to the deck. She climbed as fast as one can when one is carrying a bottle while simultaneously dealing with the effects of having too much wine. All things considered, she was doing a decent job.

October had reached the ladder and was now below Molly. He would have disagreed with the assertion that Molly was doing a decent job, though. She was climbing entirely too slow, and with every step she seemed like she was going to slip and fall.

"Pass me the bottle!" he shouted up at her.

Molly looked down at October. She knitted her eyebrows together in an accusatory manner.

"Oh good gracious," he said. "Give me the bottle so you can use both hands!"

She thought on it for a few seconds and then began to hand the bottle to October. It slipped from her grip and banged October squarely on the nose before falling to the sand. October spewed some choice vulgarities as his nose spewed blood. Bratt, who'd by now made it to the submersible, picked up the bottle.

"I guess it'll be easier to tell us apart now," Bratt quipped when he saw October's clearly broken nose.

October merely glowered before continuing his climb. Bratt followed.

Soon the three were inside The Presidio. October began to set his walking stick, a pang of worry striking him as he remembered again how transporting the vessel had burned away multiple journeys at once. As he went to roll the dials into place, he realized there was no way he could know where it was they were supposed to be going. Only Molly had the answer.

Molly appeared to be steadying herself against the obsidian altar. October winced. Was she in any sort of state to help him figure out the coordinates?

He used the back of his hand to wipe another trickle of blood from his nose.

"Molly," October said. "I need you to tell me how to get to The Core."

"But, I – I don't know the directions," she replied, more lucidly than October had expected. Apparently the effects of the wine were ebbing a bit. "How can I find it?"

October let out an exasperated sigh. He'd need to give Molly a crash course on how to navigate time and dimensions using the cane. He strode quickly to her, opened the panel, and pointed.

"These," he said, indicating a row of 13 numbers, "is where we are now. And these," he pointed to a row below, "is the place we've just left. Bratticus's dimension."

Molly's eyes were wide, and October was too engrossed in the lesson to see she was not going to comprehend the machine at this point.

Let me make one thing absolutely clear, dear reader. Miss Molly St. Mercalli was not a dullard. She was, in fact, probably smarter than both

October and Bratt in many areas. And given an hour or two, there is simply no doubt she not only would have fully comprehended the workings of the dimension-hopping walking stick, but she also would have mastered it and thought up two or three improvements, as well. But an hour or two was not a commodity currently at hand, and Molly herself was still coming out of a fairly severe case of drunkenness.

Bratt saw any lessons on interdimensional machinery was a fool's errand, and he set to work on a plan that would play to Molly's strengths.

Then it came to him.

Chapter 94

Mr. Screech disregarded his quest for the missing tooth when he realized all three members of the opposing fellowship had escaped The Trevithick, one of whom was carrying a bottle of the Waters of Perdurability.

He stood and surveyed his surroundings. One of the two unconscious women at his feet began to stir. It was Vix.

"Oh, blast it all," he heard Vix say in a struggling tone, her words muffled by the blood-soaked rug. "My ... my carpet!" She pushed herself up and looked dismally at the ground. "They don't even make these carpets anymore!"

Any trace of timidity had now gone out of her voice, and she stood quickly as though she'd never been injured in the first place. She was a frightful sight, Screech thought, seeing her once snowy hair now a dark and matted umber. Her face, too, was half covered in coagulating blood.

Of course, he couldn't see his own state of disarray – a middle-aged man with hair sticking this way and that, a front tooth missing and his own collection of coagulating blood – his starting to crust on his chin.

Vix looked around the carriage.

"Where are they?!" she demanded.

"They've fled," Screech said, his words coming out with a slight whistle thanks to his missing tooth. "They're inside Molly's submarine." He pointed.

Vix ran to the door and looked out. She paused a moment, waiting for The Presidio to vanish in a flash of blue and purple electricity, but nothing was happening. She growled.

With eyes of fury and crusty red, brown and white hair encircling her face like a thicket of thorns in winter, she slammed the door shut and stampeded past Mr. Screech, nearly knocking him over in the process. She kicked Vermilion's body aside as best she could and then flung open the door to the engine. The sound of The Trevithick's boiler sprang to life, pulsing like a beating heart.

If one were to observe the situation from afar, that person would have seen the trackless train begin to glow a palpitating blue, lighting up the desert sand in thrums of sapphire that reflected off the red metallic surface of the nearby submersible. One would also observe the sudden appearance of two tracks of bright, blue light suddenly appear in front of the train.

And, if one were truly watching all of this happen from a distance, one would have gasped as the train lurched forward on the tracks of light and barreled at breakneck speed toward a submarine that had no business whatsoever being in the middle of the desert, and one would have turned around and began walking back the other way knowing full well that this was not a situation one wanted to walk into while strolling through a remote desert in the middle of the night.

Chapter 95

"Your gloves. Do they only work on humans?" Bratt asked, taking Molly's hand in his. It struck him that, barring their interactions during the actual act of traversing dimensions, this was the most intimate the two had been thus far.

Molly looked into Bratt's universe eyes and began to lose her concentration. Recognizing that telltale look of sinking into the depths of his stare, Bratt averted his eyes to Molly's black, lace gloves. He took her other hand and brought the two up into her line of vision.

"I mean, could you command a machine to do your will?"

Molly blinked several times and appeared to shake off her momentary trance. She looked to her gloved hands, both gently but firmly held in place by Bratt's.

"I — I have never tried," she said.

"Only you know where to find The Core," Bratt continued. "And I have a feeling it's not somewhere that can be reached by dialing in a few coordinates."

October made a sour face in Bratt's direction, but Bratt didn't see it nor would he have cared if he'd noticed.

"Could you use these gloves to tell the cane where to take us?" Bratt asked her.

Molly peered down at the gloves. Their black lace was thick and, thanks to their recent bath in the Waters of Perdurability, in perfect condition.

She had used her enchanted gloves many times on people, persuading them to see her point of view (and, yes, to do her bidding). She had never imagined using them on a machine, though. But magic was not exclusive to humans, she thought. She used magic on inanimate objects all the time. She glanced down at the altar upon which she was sitting and mused for a moment on how this giant slab of stone, not alive but somehow living, was about to be part of one of her greatest feats of magic - if she could pull it off. If she could manipulate things like mirrors and gloves and altars, and if she could manipulate humans, then she was positive she could manipulate a machine.

Yes, she thought, she could use her gloves - as long as she concentrated hard enough - to convince a device to do her bidding as well.

Molly mentally kicked herself as her inebriation melted away. Why hadn't she thought of this before? She knew the answer, though. Her enchantment was created specifically for navigating the perils of a world controlled by bull-headed, boorish and imbecilic men. It was the gloves' purpose, and there was no reason to assume the bewitched accessories should be used for anything else. Their magic was strong, though. It had to be to penetrate the thick skull of a man whose mind was made up based on his extremely narrow worldview. Convincing a device that is free from sexism, bigotries, privilege, senses of superiority, god complexes, and facial hair to do her bidding would no doubt be far simpler. Besides, does she not use similar magic to pilot The Presidio?

She only hoped there was enough magic left in them after the amount of power she pushed onto Mr. Screech. Magic was draining in her world. She didn't have her gauntlet, and there was no way of knowing if there was any enchantment left in the gloves to convince a machine to take them to the nearest lake, let alone The Core.

She looked up and back into Bratt's eyes, his gaze no longer having a mesmerizing effect on her. Molly looked directly into his pupils, and Bratt thought she was the only person to ever do it without falling into a stupor. She stared at him a bit longer, a test, in her own way, to prove that she had more power than any machine – or any man, for that matter.

Not even those hypnotic, eternal eyes could sway her. And at that moment, that last effects of the wine left her body completely. She was in total control.

"Yes," she said confidently. "Yes. I can do it."

"Fine then," October said, resigning himself to the situation.

One of three things was about to happen, he knew.

First, this plan was going to work famously, and The Presidio would be transported to The Core where the group could execute their plan, save the day, and leave any third-parties observing their actions through the pages of a book completely satisfied.

Second, the plan would fail miserably, and The Presidio would be launched into some unknown part of reality where the three of them would be forever trapped, or, trapped until The Grimblenox sucked every particle of existence from the bubble of all there is, was and ever will be.

Third, the plan would not have a chance to succeed or fail given that The Trevithick had just come to life and was now advancing at a preposterous speed upon two glowing, magical railroad tracks that apparently only appeared when the train was good and ready to go somewhere.

"Well, we best have at it, then," October said, shoving the head of the cane between the faces of Molly and Bratt. He had activated it, and the tubing was alight with the soft glow of blue energy. "It's now or never. And I mean that literally." He then pointed the cane to the window.

The two broke eye contact and looked.

All three now could see the train was just seconds away from crashing into the submersible. Bratt had just enough time to mentally curse October for being dramatic rather than simply stating, "There's a train about to hit us."

Molly gasped, grabbed the cane, and yelled "TO THE CORE!"

She couldn't beat the speed of the train, though, and before she could cast her spell, The Trevithick collided into The Presidio.

Interlude 6: The Peculiarity, A Brief History

I'll issue you a warning, dear reader. The news I'm about to tell you will likely frustrate you and possibly drive you to the brink of madness. Alas, there is no other way to tell this story, so please forgive me.

Throughout our tale, there has been much chaos, disorder, turmoil, confusion, commotion, havoc, bedlam, tumult, anarchism, mayhem, some mix-ups, a few mix-downs, countless non-sequiturs and utter, utter pandemonium. However, there has been a constant throughout: The Peculiarity.

I've saved telling you its origin until the latter portion of these accounts because its beginning is also its end.

Chapter 96

Clearly, something subsequent had happened following the collision of The Trevithick and The Presidio, as you might have guessed considering the amount of pages left to read. As you might have also guessed, Molly was successful in convincing October's interdimensional device to transport the submarine to The Core. And, if you've been paying attention to how things have been working in this story, you also will have guessed that Vix's train, having been made of metal, and having come into contact with The Presidio just as the staff was sending its electric current through the hull, was also transported.

The two groups - the witches in their train and the gallimaufry of the trio in their submersible - despite their separate means of transportation, arrived at The Core at precisely the same moment, which was a marvelous feat considering the infinite amount of moments available in which to arrive.

However, though the two vessels were more or less connected at the time of transport, they didn't arrive at precisely the same place. It was a more mathematically probable situation given the infinite amount of places available in which to arrive.

And what of this place? How to describe it?

Let me ask you a question, dear reader. Have you ever had a dream? Statistically speaking, the answer is probably yes. Think to those dreams now. Do you remember how your brain shows you images, and they're dark because there is no light entering through your closed eyelids? But because you don't need light to see thoughts in dreams, you still know what those images are? And remember now how sometimes in dreams you know you're dreaming, and you can control what happens around you. And I ask you now to remember how sometimes you're not aware that you're dreaming, and the events, however absurd they may be, continue on, jumping from topic to topic and scene to scene, with you believing everything you're seeing is actually happening. Sometimes in your dreams you are you. Sometimes in your dreams you are someone else. Sometimes you can see yourself as if you were watching the flipping picture cards through a nickelodeon. Sometimes you only see events rushing past you. Because your body is lying still, your mind sometimes doesn't allow you to move in dreams. But sometimes you can fly. Your dreams are colorless, except when there is color, in which case you see it vividly and can recall the exact color you saw upon waking. There are times when all these things seem to happen at once, and your dreams are simultaneously lucid while your mind is convinced the events are actually happening. There are pleasant dreams, and oftentimes there are nightmares. And every once in a while, you wake up in your own bedroom, absolutely sure your dream or nightmare is over, only to find out your mind is being a tricky little bastard and you're actually still asleep and dreaming.

That is the most accurate description I can give you for The Core.

The Presidio blinked into being on one side, and The Trevithick popped into place on the opposite side. When one is at The Core of Existence, one can't exactly say which direction is east or west or up or down, so forgive me for being unable to provide those details. In fact, I can't say they'd be entirely relevant to the story, so I'll ask you not to bother about arbitrary directions in a directionless domain.

The two vessels slowly orbited The Core, and even the most cynical of the travelers - October - had to admit, if only to himself, that it was simultaneously the most beautiful and terrifying thing he'd ever laid eyes on.

They found themselves within a sort of chamber, vast and globular, like being inside a snowglobe the size of a city, Bratt mused. It was an enormous pocket at the roots of reality, its walls composed of a deep and dark blue ethereal substance with wisps of gray clouds that sparkled like stardust. Some might have surmised it actually *was* stardust. On the other side of the gossamer material that encapsulated The Core, universes stacked upon universes were barely visible, their supernovae, galaxies, black holes and nebulae all stitched together by some dark force that was only visible through the horizons of a gravitational field. The cacophony of it all shone dimly through as if it were nothing more than the embers of a dying fire.

Between the film that encapsulated the chamber and The Core itself, time and distance didn't hold the same shapes they did elsewhere. Bratt could see The Trevithick in orbit in what seemed like a thousand meters away while simultaneously perceiving it as being near enough The Presidio that he could jump from one craft to the other if he so desired. It was all like a dream, he thought, where an object can be both far away *and* incredibly close, and a destination that is within arm's length is totally unreachable as the distance somehow continues to stretch with every ounce of effort put in to reaching it.

And like a dream, the two groups found the spaces around them difficult to manipulate. Gravity still existed in one form or another within the cavern, but it apparently behaved differently for each person. Within the submarine, Bratt, October and Molly each found themselves pinned to a different part of the craft's interior. Molly's feet were planted firmly on the floor. Bratt's gravitational pull placed him on the ceiling. And October had rein of the walls. Molly, at first, thought the wine was having a second, more drastic effect on her. But when she realized - and forgive me for the ill-conceived but necessary pun - the *gravity* of the situation, she found that she was at that exact moment more sober than she'd ever been in her life.

With people hanging from every surface of the interior, Bratt couldn't help but feel the same claustrophobic sensation of being in Dr. Cerulean's foyer.

In the train, Mr. Screech was clinging to one of the passenger coach's benches, unsure of which way he might fall should he let go. His tooth rested on the compartment's ceiling. Mistress Vix, for all intents and purposes, was standing upright in the context of The Trevithick, and she was peering out of the engine's front windows at the intense sight before her.

Madame Vermillion had lost her gravity completely, and was slowly bouncing about the interior like a helium balloon on the verge of losing its levity. She had only now regained consciousness, and upon realizing her situation, she began to flail her arms in an attempt to grasp something and stabilize herself, failing miserably with every effort. She made no sound, though, as if she feared the very vibrations would send her reeling from the vehicle and into the uncertainty beyond. Her expression was one of mixed terror and confusion, made all the more ghastly by the lines of dried blood that streaked across one cheek, thanks to Molly's forceful wine bottle blow.

Vix peered back through the windows of the two doors that separated the engine from the passenger car. She saw Vermilion bouncing about and decided to test her magical abilities in the strange and new place. She brought her fingers into the air and made a sweeping gesture inward until her hand closed into a fist. The ruby in the boiler glowed a little brighter for a moment. Vermillion then gently hovered toward a corner of the cabin where she managed to gain her footing, although her body stood at 45-degree angle to the floor.

Her magic had worked, but Vix did not feel certain about anything. She blinked twice, craning her neck to make sure Vermilion had made purchase. Seeing the old woman had stopped bouncing about, Vix blinked again and then returned her attention to the goings on outside the train.

The atmosphere pulsed like an arrhythmic heart, as if someone with no sense of tempo were trying to keep time by tapping on the glass of an aquarium. It didn't necessarily make a sound, but it definitely had a vibration.

Or was this simply where every vibration began?

All eyes went to the center of the chamber, where the engine of reality, The Core, burned in phantasmal magnificence.

It was brighter than any sun, although the onlookers didn't have to shield their eyes from the strength of the light. The brilliance, Bratt knew without reason, was not caused by photons, but by something undefined by science. It was electricity sparked by something other than friction - a force different than the ionization of particles. Upon its surface, swirls of a yellow, purple and magenta substance shifted rapidly, bubbling and popping. Droplets burst from the surface, creating arcing caterpillars of light before joining midair like quicksilver and falling back into the globe. Beneath the outer layer of luminous liquid glowed hues of glittering blue and a green more pure than the first shoots of grass after a winter thaw. All the colors radiated as the tip of a poker radiates after being left in the fire too long. And from the main globular mass of energy came streaks of lavender and white plasma, which arced and danced outward to the chamber walls. The bursts of spidery light were multitudinous, and dozens made contact with the steam engine and the submarine, though neither craft seemed to be affected in any discernible way.

Nearly all of them considered for a moment that they might be dead. Molly knew differently, though. Had the group been killed, she knew, the colors manifesting from The Core would be endless and indescribable. She took a some solace knowing her very limited mortal eyes could only perceive just a few of those colors right now.

Despite the discord, the space around The Core was completely silent save for the barely audible noises of the witnesses as the sight took their collective breath away.

While the dazzling sight of the Engine of All That Exists was enough to send any person into awe, it was the sight of something horrible, something repulsively out of place, which had the attention of both witches and scientists alike.

On one side of The Core, spaced directly between The Trevithick and The Presidio, was a black crater emanating a hideous shaft of darkness. All things being dreamlike in the cavern, Bratt couldn't guess the size of the puncture. No, not a puncture, he thought. A *wound*. But he guessed if Molly were to maneuver The Presidio to the tear in the Core, the craft could have easily fit into its gaping maw.

The blackness pouring out from the hole pierced the brightness as a beam of light would if a hole were suddenly drilled into the wall of a cave. It behaved as photons would through the darkness. It was a negative. The opposite of light. The shaft stretched out, breaching the translucent enclosure of The Chamber and continuing on through the universes beyond. It blackened out even the darkest parts of the space outside The Core's cell.

"The Peculiarity."

Molly's were the first words spoken. They sounded odd and hollow, the words coming out correctly though in a way none of them were used to hearing, as if someone were playing a recording of a person talking backward – only the phonograph was being played in reverse, creating the illusion of words. And with those words, the six travelers began to understand just how precarious their situation was.

It echoed across the space, and the passengers aboard the Trevithick could hear them perfectly, despite Molly's distance and location inside The Presidio. The atoms of every piece of matter were connected here, Bratt thought, like the strings of a piano connect the keys to the hammers. When one end was plucked, the vibration could be heard at the farthest reach of the strand. Even as this epiphany came to him, he perceived the interior of The Trevithick as if he were inside. Was he simultaneously existing in two places at once? He wasn't sure, but he guessed perhaps vision, like sound, behaved in an altered way here.

Or maybe perception and sound in this place was at its purest form, and he had only been experiencing a muted version of both outside the walls of The Chamber, Bratt thought.

"If we wish to save the very Fabric of all that exists," answered Vix in that eerie tone, her voice as clear to the passengers of The Presidio as if she were standing next to them, "we must work together to plug the hole."

She spoke with authority, though the others detected a note of fear. Bratt could see her face clearly. Her once entrancing visage was now haggard, her usually wistful and wavy hair dead and crusted with blood. He opened his eyes wide as her expression came closer and closer into view, and then it was gone as fast as it had come. In its place were countless clusters of buzzing insects. No, they weren't insects he realized, but particles. He was looking *into* the ancient sorceress, and he could see and hear the very atoms that had banded together to create her skin.

Bratt gasped and, as a lucid dreamer would, forced himself outward and back to his body with what felt like massive effort.

Were the others experiencing this, too? Yes. He knew they were even though none of them moved. The string of fabric on which he was standing was the same piece of string upon which all them stood. He felt what they felt, as they felt what he felt.

Madame Vermillion, who was the most objectionable of the gathered assembly, nodded her head in agreement with Mistress Vix. Vermillion's motives had always been purely self-serving, as even the sight of The Core could not change who she was, but those selfish motives corresponded with the motives of even the most altruistic member of the travelers at this very moment. The others could feel her contempt, and they knew how much cooperation displeased her.

"You tried to kill us," October's voice was accusatory. "How are we to trust you?"

And October got a flash of Vix's intentions at that very moment. His thoughts traveled up the same piece of string on which Vix's thoughts were perched. He couldn't decipher the details but he did see two things. First, Vix did not intend to hurt the passengers of The Presidio. The second part was that she didn't intend to harm them because she needed them for some greater plan. Was it her plan to heal The Core? Vix, wielding hundreds of year's worth of control, put up a tiny shield against October's prying.

"We came armed with a plan," Molly said, speaking to the passengers of the steam engine.

Did she speak, though? Or were her intentions merely shared through the connection of The Core's energy?

"As did we," responded Mr. Screech soberly. "Though, upon inspection of the depth and breadth of the task before us, I am ... having doubts."

The Core's plasma burst silently around the two vessels. The shaft of darkness peeled through the light.

So, Bratt thought as he reflected back on the hours of work he, October, and Molly had put into their magic mirror and into their plot, the three witches had been using their time to formulate plans, as well.

Screech glanced through the windows and into the steam engine at Vix without flinching, although his eyes betrayed his fear of retaliation at suggesting the master witch's strategy was flawed. It was a very human reaction in a place where such a thing was completely obsolete. Vix didn't return the look, and only stared into The Core with an expression of stone. The others knew she could not disagree with Mr. Screech's assertion.

Vix reached her arm back and touched her ruby.

After what seemed an eternity (or was it a millisecond?) in The Chamber where time didn't exist, Vix finally spoke.

"We witches three have power, true, but the spell we brought with us will not be enough," she conveyed, though through thoughts or words no one could tell. "I believe there may be a way to boost our energy. It would mean having to abandon my engine."

Silence again. Each person experienced the others' trepidation. Bratt wondered what the synapses of his own ideas looked like as his brain buzzed with activity. No, he realized, it was October who wondered about the electrical impulses inside the mind. Bratt was only sharing the desire because of the string that connected them. He looked anyway and saw the pulses of thought as they fired across his brain (*October's brain?*), popping like chandelier bulbs in a house that had just been struck by lightning.

How long was he inside his own head? Was it his own head? Was it October's? Bratt focused his attention back with effort, his intentions seemed to slow as if moving through molasses.

It was all like a very dire hallucination brought on by days without sleep and meals consisting only of strange mushrooms and buttons of peyote. This was not a place meant for them, and Bratt knew - or at least he knew someone else knew - that they would all go mad if their stay was prolonged within the dreamlike state of The Core.

"Can your vessel carry us back?" Vermillion asked, her words directed at Molly.

"No." It was October who answered.

There was silence then. The Core continued its fiery boil of energy, a shaft of nightmarish darkness pouring out and into the ether. Everyone's attention focused on October. He looked down at the walking stick. Had he flipped open the panel without realizing it? No matter. It was open now. The power of bringing both The Presidio *and* The Trevithick across space, time, and reality and into the depths of where they all converged, had burned away everything. All the punctures of the filter had been scorched. Not even one of them could escape now.

Five of the six each realized in turn that he or she had left lives behind where either no one cared enough about them to mourn them, or there was no one left to care. So they each mourned for themselves. Only Molly felt sorrow for a person she truly loved, though that sorrow was muted because, having been to the other side, she knew that connection would not matter once she was gone. The others did not feel what Molly had felt, and they could not perceive it, at least not yet.

With their fates sealed, there was only one thing left to do, and that was to do what they came to The Core to do in the first place.

Chapter 97

"What is your plan?" called Bratt, a little louder than necessary. He realized after he spoke that the question itself was unnecessary.

"A sealing spell," Vix responded. Did she respond? Or did Bratt simply know what she knew? "We expected to patch a hole in the Fabric of Existence. We were not prepared to fix the loom."

"We are prepared to fix the rupture in The Core," Molly's intentions transmitted. "I think we can do it if you can use the sealing spell to fend off the darkness for a moment."

"It's our only option," Vix said.

Here she finally looked away from the awesome power of The Core and peered into the boiler of her engine. Within it glowed her precious ruby. It emitted soft pulses of crimson light, perhaps the souls of the thousands whose life force charged it through the centuries. Bratt could see into its core, and its bloody history was written within. He saw the particles that stitched the magic gem together were culled from the atoms of thousands of people. Its shape was constantly changing at a molecular level as it gathered new power from viable sources - and shed the spent energy - across the years.

"We'll bolster our magic with the power of the stone," Vix said, looking first into the eyes of Mr. Screech, and then to Vermilion.

The master sorceress stammered – perhaps for the first time in her life, she thought. *The group thought.*

"I – I know not what will happen once the ruby's power is exhausted," she said, taking in a deep breath in an attempt to shore up her emotions. It was a futile action; her emotions were transmitting into the sphere like electricity through copper. "But I can guess that the force keeping us safe within The Trevithick will deteriorate once the gem is spent."

Bratt's mind had been both inside The Presidio *and* The Trevithick during the group's time in The Core's cavern, as had the minds of all the other travelers. Could they use the string connection to physically transfer their bodies from one vessel to the next?

"But how?" asked Vermillion. Whether she was responding to Vix's audible proclamation or to Bratt's inaudible thoughts was not clear.

Mistress Vix touched the window of The Trevithick. The others felt the cool surface of the enchanted glass in their fingertips. October knew at that moment that he had been correct during his philosophical stupor earlier in the train. Its walls and its glass were magical. It would have kept the water at bay had it driven into the ocean. It would have kept its passengers cool had it driven into a forest fire.

Vix looked over the tumultuous Core to The Presidio, unsure if it was miles or inches between them.

"I believe we can physically bring the two machines together," she said. "Our vibrations are traveling without issue. I'm certain harnessing whatever is connecting us will be easy enough."

Easy, each person knew, was a completely relative term. Drying one's clothes after a swim is easy if one jumps into an oven, but then one has to worry about being burned to death.

Was this Bratt's thought? No, it was October's. But it was shared across the chamber.

"We will handle it," Mr. Screech said aloud in response. "How to get inside is a different story."

But Bratt had been inside the steam engine multiple times since the group arrived. Hadn't he? No – it was his mind that was there. It was not his body. This sudden epiphany gave him a sort of hold on the chaos. The power of the mind was the driving force behind his transportations in this place. It was thought that slowed his own time down. It was thought that magnified atoms. Their physical forms - likely - were not in multiple places at one time. Their minds, though, were. Bratt grasped the concept like a rail in a darkened stairway. He still couldn't see where the steps led, but he was at least stabilized for now.

He could feel his realization being shared. No human in the history of time or space had ever had a mind that stayed in one place. Even you, dear reader, are not 100% in the present at this very moment. What was that sound you just heard, for example? And are you really going to eat the same thing for dinner today as you did yesterday? And what of tomorrow? You have a list of things you need to get finished, you know.

Determined, both Vix and Molly attempted to maneuver their respective vehicles at the same time, both hoping to wield some sort of control in this place of chaos. Both hoped they could bring the vehicles together.

Molly used her thoughts to steer The Presidio as she might while under the sea. Vix used her thoughts to set The Trevithick upon magical rails as she might in the desert.

Both attempts were unsuccessful. Either their magic wasn't working correctly, or they were unable to adequately focus their powers on controlling their machines.

The six fell silent, each racking his or her mind for a possible solution, and each finding it difficult given the significant priority ahead of them. Six different brains powering through an infinity of outcomes, all of them shared. But the discord had been tamped slightly as the group came to grips with how things worked in The Core.

They would have to physically leave The Trevithick and get inside The Presidio. Given the behavior of gravity, though, this was incredibly risky. The group would be unable to complete their task if three of them had suddenly been pulled away in different directions and into the space beyond The Core. And none of them knew if it was even possible to breath outside the confines of their respective vehicles.

Both October's and Bratt's minds went to work. Their thoughts and life experiences blended into one and created a shared experience abundant with knowledge of traversing time and dimensions. October experienced the work of Bratt and Dr. Cerulean as they built the doctor's contraption. Bratt underwent the education of October and his knowledge of traveling.

Wait, thought Bratt. Was that Dr. Cerulean he saw with October? Yes, it had to be. Working with October to build the staff. No, it couldn't have been. But the doctor was there, wasn't he? Bratt couldn't grasp it before the answer buoyed violently to the top of the ocean of the two men's shared knowledge.

"Yes," the two said at the same time.

"There is a way," Bratt said, holding back his hysteria as best he could. "The electromagnets each of you are wearing on your wrists."

"It is the same device Molly wears," October continued.

"Yes," Molly said, the revelation striking her.

"It will work," Bratt said, unsure if he felt pleasure or dread. "It will work."

And the logic was now shared with all.

Both the train and the submersible had within them powerful magnets. In The Trevithick, those magnets were worn on the arms of the three witches. How interesting it was that the very tools they needed now had been the very tools stolen from The Presidio not but hours ago.

The Presidio itself was powered by electromagnets, but Molly was unsure if the power that charged the magnets was functional amid the arcs of plasma that skirted across the chamber's inner atmosphere. But October and Bratt knew there were two magnets on board that could do the trick. The first was currently stuck to a canister that contained a device meant for splitting an atom. The second was now housed inside the handle of October's cane. Artemis Vix knew she could use a relatively simple spell - the same one that kept the Maglebys secured in their seats while aboard the The Trevithick, in fact - to help the two magnetic powers attract. Of course, she'd have to use her ruby to amplify the magic, given the distance now between the train and the submersible. Was the distance that great, though? Blast having to decipher distances in a realm where distance is immeasurable, and blast having to attempt to describe it in words to a reader who has yet to travel there.

Bratt stooped and retrieved the leather satchel that contained the canister as October flipped the filter open on the side of his walking stick. They both moved at the exact same time and at the exact same pace. And at the same time and pace, Vix, Screech and Vermilion unsecured the brass fasteners that kept the magnets inside their leather holsters. It was all like a bizarre but beautifully choreographed dance.

"Cast your spell," October said.

"Yes," Vix answered as she turned around, plucking the enormous red crystal from the boiler of The Trevithick's engine. The ruby, bigger than her head, was balanced in her left palm. Its pulse had now evened into a bright and steady glow. Vix brought her right hand up to her left forearm, clasped the magnet inside, and removed it completely. Vermilion and Screech did the same.

The witches three and the Maglebys two all removed their magnetic objects at the same time. Each person held his or her own magnet for a moment. The air was silent but brilliant with The Core's emissions. Not one of them moved.

Vix was the first to let out her breath, and as she did the magnets fired to life. The three slabs of grey, rectangular objects flung from the arms of the witches and clung fast to the inner walls of the train. The two orbs in the submersible flew from the hands of the Maglebys. The one that had, until now, been fastened to the cylindrical canister unlatched itself and stuck to the giant window that looked over The Core.

The witch's charm traveled across the invisible string that connected all things inside the chamber, and they could feel the thread tighten suddenly. The connection was made, and like a fisherman's line reeling in a beast from the depths, The Trevithick began moving rapidly toward The Presidio.

It should be noted here, dear reader, that in fact these magnets were pointless because their physical properties within The Core were not magnetic. Their use in this manner was strictly a placebo. But, human minds being what they are, the six travelers had to find a way to convince themselves of a plan to bring the two vessels together. The group didn't realize it was their intent doing the work, not a few lousy pieces of rock and metal.

If it's your wish to attempt to convince someone of something they would never believe, then be my guest. For the purposes of our story, though, we'll allow the scientists and the witches to believe the magnets were working so that we can continue our tale.

Perception of depth and distance was still somewhat difficult for all of the travelers, but they could see that the area between the two vessels was diminishing quickly. Unlike the behavior of their respective worlds' moons, their trajectory was not affected by The Core. Vix, having not thought of the laws of physics either one way or another, still wasn't expecting the two vehicles to come together in a straight line. But instead of bending with a gravitational force and around the mass between them, as the path of some celestial object might bend as it neared a larger, more dense celestial object, The Presidio and The Trevithick moved directly toward each other as if there was no giant, undulating object at the center to create a force of gravity.

All of them shared the thought: What will happen when we crash into The Core?

And they found out.

Chapter 98

One of the most asinine and ridiculous elements to this story is about to happen, dear reader, and I know that's quite the feat considering everything that has happened so far. But what I'm about to tell you is the absolute truth, and I only wish I could provide you with something that has even an ounce more of believability.

Unfortunately, believability is not something The Core of Existence provides. Believability only comes into being after energies shed from The Core and become hardened and rigid as they pulsate outward, eventually becoming notions as palpable and as boring as the chair in which you're sitting right now.

I invite you to brace yourself, as Bratticus, October, Molly,

Veramilicent, Byzantium and Artemis did at that moment.

The travelers witnessed aghast as the steam engine, the submersible, and all the contents within - including themselves - blew apart silently and slowly as each passed into The Core's surface. They all shattered into an immeasurable number of particles and floated outward on invisible waves. Then, as quickly as they had been spread out, those particles imploded into a single spot, just above the bubbling mass of the Engine of Existence. In its place was a microscopic sphere, burning bright and hot. It shone like the fire of a bomb, forced through a pinprick in a dark quilt. Compared to The Core, it was miniscule – barely there. But it was there, no matter how it sized up to the machine that powered existence.

And then it was over. The Core did what it had done since it acme into being: it created. The groups were together now in one vessel. Somehow, The Trevithick and The Presidio had merged into a single, round piece of machine. It had come together in the shape of an orb, as most things tend to do as they become new creations in a vacuous setting. It had several windows looking this way and that, none of them square or rectangular or octagonal or hexagonal. They were instead the shapes of craters and starbursts. The Presidio's huge window remained more or less intact, and its edges had taken on the appearance of an iceberg jutting into a metallic ocean. The hull itself looked as though it had been patched together from fabrics of red and blue, although a close inspection showed the metal had no seams and instead faded together as the light of a breaking dawn fades into the purple of a night being chased away.

Everything had merged, it seemed, with the exception of the people themselves, and whatever had been in direct contact with the people's skin. Each witch and scientist was still dressed in his or her own attire. The modified altar, which Molly had steadied herself upon when The Presidio lurched toward The Core, remained as it had been when the submersible and the train were two separate vehicles. She was holding something in her left hand, too, which had made it through the splicing.

There was one item, or rather a pile of items, that also made it through the transformation without any observable change. It was the pile of socks and sticks, which was still sitting in the same shape it had been back in The Presidio, though now it was in a place directly above October and to right of Vix. None of them truly took note of the sticks and socks, though, and can you blame them, dear reader? Would you take notice of a collection of branches and a few pieces of cloth footwear if your molecules had just been separated and then stitched back together inside a whole knew contraption?

No. No, you would not.

Vix's ruby, unchanged, now returned to its previous, thrumming glow.

Bratt held the cylinder in his hands. October's cane, too, had been unmarred. The magnets they'd used to bring the two ships together had apparently fused into the hull of this new vessel.

Vermilion had lost her pink hat in the journey. As she looked dazedly around inside this new object, she could see a little spatter of pink mixed into the surface of the metal orb a meter away from where she was standing now.

In fact, there were spatters of many colors, they could now see. There were pieces of the walls that looked like diamonds stuck into earth where the crystal sconces had fused with the hull. On a patch near the large window was a smattering of yellow that Vix guessed was once her prized tablecloth. And in a beautiful, grid pattern just to the left (or right, depending on the angle at which you were looking) was a cluster of colors that had, no doubt, been Molly's collection of bottled magical ingredients.

Vix didn't realize it at the time, but there were no indications that the boxcars carrying her prized collection of magical objects had been fused into this new conglomeration of materials.

All the travelers saw gravity was inverted but uniform here. Rather than a unique gravitational pull for each person, they all now stood upright in their respective places across the inside of the orb, each with his or her head pointing directly inward.

Somehow, the grafting of the vessels had, in a way, solved - or at least eased - the problem of their awkward gravity situation.

The six stood in their respective positions for a moment, all of them taking in the impossible circumstances that had led them to this point. The word has not yet been invented for the feeling of confoundment they each felt. Confoundment, in fact, doesn't even come close. Not but moments ago they had clashed as two separate forces in a desert at an unfathomable distance and time away, and carefully plotted plans by both parties had been dashed away like sandcastles in a hurricane. Now here they were, in a single, hodgepodge vessel at The Core with no way to escape.

All was silent and still.

Chapter 99

If one were to observe this scene from afar, one might believe the combined Trevithick and Presidio was a tiny moon orbiting a sun that splashed plasmatic rainbows and shot bolts of purple electricity — and so happened to have a column of anti-photons bursting out from one side.

Now, you might be wondering how the two vehicles became one, knitting together at an atomic level, while Messers October and Bratticus Magleby, Madame Verimilicent Vermilion, Miss Molly St. Mercalli, Mr. Byzantium Screech, and Mistress Artemis Vix remained unscathed. Some authors might put the answer to this query later in the story, hoping to keep the readers on edge. If you've been paying attention, though, you'll have noticed a great many unresolved plotlines, so tying one loose end up at this juncture isn't out of the question.

The fact is The Core was a place of a creation. Things *began* there. So even the destruction of something would lead to the creation of something. The Core, knowing it was damaged, pushed for the creation of something that could help. The Core wasn't necessarily sentient, mind you, but it knew that there was hope for repair from these wayward travelers. It knew like water knows to flow downward and into the sea (thus preventing the problematic issue of humans walking face-first into random, floating ponds each day). It knew like human bodies know to grow their vital organs on the inside rather than the outside (thus keeping hearts and livers safe from scavenging buzzards). And in this natural knowledge, The Core gave the congregation of scientists and witches a nudge in the right direction.

That energy, though, was finite, as more of The Core's power was being drawn out from its wound. And after their short-lived contemplation, the group came awake with their task heavy on their minds. Scenarios of "what if's" and "could be's" played out through their imaginations.

Madame Vermillion's face was sourer than usual, her eyebrows knitted together in a show of extreme displeasure at the thought that she would be doomed to remain in this maddening place. Perhaps the gem could retain enough power to help get them out of the sphere once their chore was complete, she thought. But they all felt the hopelessness from Mistress Vix of such a thing occurring.

"Ahem," Byzantine Screech's quavering voice broke the silence. "Perhaps we'd better get a move on, then? Do what we came here to do?"

He spoke the statement as if it were a question, as though he were asking the others if they thought eliminating The Peculiarity at this point was even worth it.

In a silent answer, Bratt shook himself out of his momentary daze. He looked to Molly, who nodded, and with determination began cranking the gears attached to her obsidian altar, turning its polished surface toward the entropic brilliance of The Core.

"Aha," Artemis said, eyeing the mechanics that allowed Molly's alter to stand upright to face The Core. "A mirror spell!"

"Yes," Molly said, taking her place beside the obsidian. "But I have some extra power, too, thanks to the boys."

October was almost horizontal to the stone's now vertical placement, relative to the Trevithick-Presidio thing's inner surface. The top of the obsidian now almost reached the ceiling, where Bratt stood.

October reached out and opened the hatch of the lead cabinet built into the back of Molly's obsidian. He held out a hand, and Bratt stretched his arm and handed October the canister. October then screwed the cylinder into place and latched the heavy lid.

"We'd best get to work, then," Vix said, looking to the pulsing red light of the stone she held in her hand.

With her right hand, she pulled a piece of chalk from her coat pocket and knelt. She scratched a large triangle onto the floor-wall-ceiling, which was located to the left of the obsidian, taking care to leave room for it to do its work. Inside each angle, she scribbled a different symbol. A crescent moon at the point facing The Core, a widdershins spiral at another, and the head of an owl at the third. In the center, she drew a large, open eye.

In the pupil of the eye, she placed her ruby. It faltered slightly at first, as if it were deciding to roll in one of the myriad directions inside the orb. Mistress Vix cast it a stern look, and for all intents and purposes, it obeyed her condemning expression and stayed put.

"A witch for each point," she said.

Molly, Bratt and October looked on at the emblem scrawled onto the metal. So, they all thought, their realization shared, this was the plan devised by the witches three while Molly and the Maglebys were busy augmenting the obsidian altar.

Both Screech and Vermillion tested their ability to walk toward Vix's triangle and found that they could, though the going was treacherous, and Vermilion ended up going to her hands and knees, deciding crawling would be less precarious. She got just near enough that she could touch the triangle with an outstretched arm.

Mr. Screech, too, found he was close enough to touch his point of the triangle by standing on the tips of his toes. Thankfully, the metallic orb in which they were all housed was big enough for the black altar, but had its circumference been just six inches larger, Screech would not have been able to reach the magic symbol.

Something within The Core sputtered, and the black shaft suddenly developed what Bratt first thought were holes. Dozens of tiny specks of light shined in the darkness. It was an illusion, though, as Bratt realized almost immediately. They weren't holes in the blackness. They were pieces of the core, shedding in tiny flakes like skin after a particularly egregious sunburn.

It was the first simile that sprang to Bratt's mind, dear reader. Don't let's lay blame on the storyteller for such an absurd metaphor. It remains in this story because it was more apt than any of those aboard The Presidio-Trevithick knew. The Core *was* shedding like skin. It *had* been burnt somehow. Something had damaged it so badly that it was now beginning to break apart. Unlike the average human's epidermis, though, there was no fresh layer of Core beneath. As the flakes turned to pieces and the pieces to chunks, all six travelers could feel its power draining.

Chapter 100

The pieces of glowing Core were firing like bullets away from the sphere and into the void. Behind the ship, unseen, the tip of a burgundy tentacle attached to some demonic cephalopod, the suckers on its dactylus a sickly pink, made its way slightly through the ever-widening hole in The Core's cavern.

"Go, dammit! GO!" October bellowed as he repositioned himself near the obsidian.

Vermillion stretched and placed her hand on the spiral. Screech's two fingers pressed against the owl. As the three witches finally came in contact with Vix's chalk emblem, it began to glow a dull blue – the same color as the particles in October's staff, Bratt noticed.

"We have to get into the line of that shaft of darkness," Molly shouted. "The mirror has to reflect it!"

But she hadn't been able to control her ship before it merged with Vix's train. Would she be able to steer this new, globular vessel?

Molly gritted her teeth and concentrated. She used a low, psychic power to steer the ship, and she hoped the same effort would help power the orb. She mentally pushed, and then pushed harder. She felt her consciousness start to slip just slightly as she willed every part of her to move the ship.

The vessel began to advance, but very slowly. Molly's nose began to bleed, making Bratt the only person among them now without blood on his face. Vix looked toward her former apprentice and saw the struggle. She shot a glance toward her own ruby, which was the fuel for her train. She willed the gem to life in the same way she would have if she were commanding it to push The Trevithick into motion.

Vix, too, found the work hard going. Still, she squeezed every drop of effort she could. The chalked triangle dimmed a bit.

The orb moved quicker now. The dark beam was just feet away from the enormous glass window of the vessel. The shards of Core cast streaks of light across their faces.

"The words!" Vix yelled. "Now!"

The trio of witches began to chant in an ancient language. The entire orb began to glow the dull, light blue of the chalked triangle. The same blue of October's cane. The same blue as the electricity that buzzed atoms from one dimension and into another. Vix held up her right hand with its palm facing toward The Core. Her left arm reached to the center of the triangle where she grasped the ruby. Tiny sparks, barely visible through the brightness of The Core, discharged from her outturned palm.

Their chanting grew louder, and the others could now hear the words.

"Na'arrurum en. Tizqarum. Ziturum. Zakjum. Izuzzum, izuzzum, izuzzum."

"Na'arrurum en. Tizqarum. Ziturum. Zakjum. Izuzzum, izuzzum, izuzzum."

"Na'arrurum en. Tizqarum. Ziturum. Zakjum. Izuzzum, izuzzum, izuzzum."

Something began to happen at the edges of the crater on The Core. Where the darkness had created a stark boundary from the glowing mass of energy to the pitch black of its wound just moments before, Bratt now saw a soft blue light. It was the same blue of the witches' triangle, and it appeared to be blending – or perhaps mending – the edges of the cavity.

The shaft of darkness began to fade. The shreds of glowing

substance subsided completely. The trio's spell was impressive.

Vix's ruby had faded. It was no longer the brilliant red of a gemstone. Now it resembled a piece of basalt, nearly black and entirely unremarkable. Vix panted as though she'd just finished running a race. The once-powerful stone rolled from the triangle and across the hull with a series of echoing clanks. Vix, too, dropped to the floor. From the ducts in her eyes trickled small rivulets of blood. No one noticed her, though.

"Do it now!" October called.

The Presidio-Trevithick moved into place with one final and determined push from Molly, and the entire craft was briefly bathed in the blackness that joined the hole in The Core to The Peculiarity. Bratt shivered. It wasn't due to the temperature, either. His very soul was trembling in terror at being doused with whatever this black matter was. The moment was over as quickly as it started, though, as Molly guided the submersible until the beam was flowing directly at the polished surface of the obsidian slab.

The vessel rumbled as the mirror caught the dark energy.

Molly paused momentarily. "My device! It can't –"

"The cylinder will make up for it!" October cut her off. "Do it! Cast your spell! I'll activate the mechanism!"

Molly nodded brusquely. She began yelling her spell - something in English, and something that rhymed - though Bratt couldn't make out exactly what she said over the shaking of the metal hull. Molly's spell was not an ancient one, like Vix's. Hers was new and state-of-the-art.

He wondered how much more the ship could take before it broke apart completely.

But as Molly finished her incantation, the craft steadied itself. Molly looked at October.

"Now!" she exclaimed.

"Look away from the mirror!" October yelled as he pulled the lever that activated the cylinder. Inside the tube, the suspended atom was split, and the energy housed within channeled into the reflective tablet.

They all screwed their eyes shut and looked away.

Chapter 101

The drama, the sounds, the thoughts, at that moment, paused completely. Time held still as the atom was pulled apart, and it released the energy of a tiny star. Noise, light and matter imploded around the canister, just briefly, before the group heard a colossal "whoomp," as if an enormous tapestry doused in fuel had suddenly been lit with a match. The altar began to blaze with hot, white light. The force of the blast went outward and away from the travelers inside the orb in a focused ray, shattering the giant window. All of them suffered a certain amount of burns to their clothes and skin.

The initial blast was powerful and blinding, but it was over in a moment. The six could feel the heat receding, and they each in their turn dared to look.

The altar now glowed a dull orange, and from it was pouring a beam of soft white light. It was focused directly at what once was a tear in The Core. They all saw with a moment of horror that the glass between the orb and the atmosphere of The Chamber had been breached by the spell. Curiously, they were all able to breathe, and they hadn't felt any dramatic changes in pressure - discounting the atomic blast, that is.

None of them had expected The Chamber to contain oxygen. And in fact, they were all correct. There was no oxygen there, but it didn't matter because their bodies were not being powered by oxygen or nutrition or even a even a snuff of cocaine, which Mr. Screech usually kept handy for occasions of sapped strength and weariness. It was the mind that powered life at the Engine of Existence, so as long as each continued thinking, then each would continue existing.

Consequently, it was favorable that none of them came to this realization just yet. You see, had they known that they would simply continue on, forever, without death to end their misery, they might not have attempted to heal The Core. With October's dimension-hopping cane now out of order, the lot of them would be doomed to spend eternity in The Chamber with only each other as company. And if you've ever had to spend even a fortnight with a small group of people and no other interactions whatsoever, then you'll know the monotony of it all can leave one longing for the sweet release of death.

Where the hole in The Core had once been, there was now only the same, swirling, colorful glowing substance that covered the rest of it. The sphere appeared not to have lost a bit of its power, but it glowed. It glowed gloriously. It sputtered and boiled, alive and unfettered.

They could all feel it. They could feel the healing. Its almost medicinal power pulsed outward, healing their burns and giving them new life. And with it came a new resolve and a new energy.

"Let's close the other hole!" Mr. Screech said, breaking the silence that had once again engulfed them.

Molly reacted immediately. She focused on steering the orb, and it began to turn immediately but slowly. The Core was getting its strength back, and Molly felt hers returning as well. Vix, still weak, her skin now the same pale color as her hair usually was when not caked with dried blood, refocused on steering the vessel. The orb picked up speed quickly, throwing everyone off balance momentarily. Vermillion fell to the floor. Screech's arm was flung back. The triangle stopped glowing.

"Back!" Vix yelled as the splendor of The Core swept out of sight. "Back to the corners!"

Vix had found her gem and was grasping it in her left hand again. But there was no red glow now. Its power had been completely spent. The witches three had each scrambled back to their original positions, stretching their arms and placing their hands to the points of the triangle. The chalk symbol resumed a dull brilliance, though it was a far cry from the blue shine it had emitted during the first spell. With no ruby, and without the aid of Molly's gauntlets, the only thing left to power the magic was each witch's energy.

They each in their turn hoped they could glean enough power from the newly healed Core to get the job done. Vix found a bit of extra determination in what she hoped would happen next. Now that their energies were about to focus outward, she smiled. This was going to be her chance to get her hands on whatever it was, whatever power that thing from beyond wielded. She would add it to her collection. She would be the most powerful person ever to have lived.

She clutched her ruby. It had stored the powers of hundreds of thousands of souls – perhaps even more. All she would need to do is get the blood of the thing. Just a drop. Give it to the ruby. It would hold the power. It would boil it down to its essence. It would replace all the power that had just been drained.

Vix held fast to the blackened gem. Her other hand remained on the triangle's tip, but she was ready, even in her weakened state, to grab at the knife tucked inside her jacket – the same knife she used to draw blood from Vermilion - in order to stab the thing and allow its blood to drip on her mother's ruby. It had been bathed in the Waters of Perdurability. It was indestructible and could cut through anything.

Vix took a breath in anticipation, licked her lips, and prepared the command to begin the witches' chant once more. And she prepared to become a god.

The others, for the first time, began to understand Vix's intentions as the string of their shared emotions and thoughts strummed louder with The Core's regained strength. All of them looked at Vix with shock and contempt. Vix continued to look outward through the hole in the orb that had only moments ago been covered with thick glass.

And then Vix began to scream.

Chapter 102

She dropped the gem and it clattered to the vessel's floor. This was not what she had in mind. This Grimblenox was not at all what she had pictured when Molly came suddenly back to life. A beast, yes. Huge, yes. But this thing before her was the size of the moon. Perhaps bigger. She could see its form through the walls of The Chamber. A thousand skinny tentacles spewing out from all sides, It's huge eye was not yet in view. Instead, through the hole made by The Peculiarity, Vix could see three dozen of its appendages wiggling their way inside, looking like black and purple snakes, whipping violently back and forth, feeling their way along the inside of the structure.

Vermilion was the next to bellow in fear. She removed her hand from the triangle and fell back against the wall. Screech opened his eyes to see the horror just outside The Presidio. His arm flew from the triangle as if it were a hot stove. Molly's concentration faltered. The orb began to wobble, and they were all thrown off balance yet again. October cried out the worst obscenity he'd ever learned. Bratt discovered he no longer had a voice, and he teetered on unconsciousness at the sight before him. He struggled to stay present.

Molly had seen the creature before, but whatever power it had to turn living things to pillars of black scale had also put a black veil over her memory of the beast. Now, the memory returned to her in a flood of terror.

"Do not look into its eye!" Molly cried.

But it was at that exact moment that the eye came into view, and it was too late. While Molly, Vermilion and Vix had all quickly averted their collective gazes, October, Bratt and Screech – all of whom were men therefore weren't wise enough to immediately follow directions from women who were smarter than they were – couldn't help themselves but to look just as the eye was passing across the hole.

And nothing happened to October or Bratt. They both made what could only be considered as eye contact with The Grimblenox. Each of them looked into the depth of its terror-inducing, almond-shaped pupil. And Bratt and October, collectively, knew then that their strange eyes, the very eyes that had gazed upon this same creature on the day they were born, was what had kept them safe. They were impervious to the beast's disease because they'd been dosed with a tiny bit of the virus before. All these years their bodies had built up strength, and those unique, dark blue and purple eyes of theirs, were shields against the creature's power.

Mr. Screech, on the other hand, wasn't quite so lucky.

The Grimblenox's eye had passed away from the punctured

Chamber, and now its huge, disgusting mouth was covering the hole.

The Peculiarity was still too big for the Grimblenox to get through, but fissures were emerging along the edges of The Core's chamber as 50 more of the thing's hair-like tentacles wiggled their way in and pulled on the opening. The Chamber's walls, which had once looked like delicate gauze, now appeared more like cloudy glass, its stability tottering beneath the weight of the abomination.

The cracks spread.

Mr. Screech's eyes were the first things to change. Had any of them looked into his eyes in those first moments, they would have seen they were now identical to those of Bratt and October. Screech's face then began to turn black, the darkness seeping over him like ink spilling across a linen sheet. Molly watched on in horror as the man began to transform into a pillar of black scales.

Only he didn't remain a pillar of black scales.

The hole in The Chamber was now surrounded by tendrils of undulating cilia at the edges of the creature's maw. The Grimblenox's mouth was a grotesque oval, with rows upon rows of long, thin protrusions that could only be teeth spiraling inward. A serpentine tongue, which looked like a knotted length of intestine, whipped violently around the exterior of The Core's chamber. It was as long as the monster's tentacles – perhaps longer.

The beast's viscous skin was not scaly, as one might have assumed. Instead it appeared spongy and black, with huge patches the color of a drowned cadaver, a mix of sallow purple and a yellow seen only on infected sores. It was pocked and covered with pustules. Some of them were ruptured and oozed ichor, which dripped and leaked off the creature's body and into the atmosphere around it, forming into putrid globs that meandered around the edges of the chamber like the seeds of some mutant dandelion drifting in a breeze.

It rattled, a sound like a thousand consumption patients simultaneously gasping for air. The tip of its disgusting tongue found its way into the hole and past the ship.

Bratt saw then that it wasn't a tongue. It was a proboscis.

It began to suck, and the metallic, glowing liquid of The Core began to break loose once again. This time, instead of being thrown to the void, it was being consumed by the nightmare made real before them. It was relishing it.

The group within the orb, though, now had another obstacle, as eight long, spindly legs had sprouted from the thing that was once Mr. Screech. His mouth had cracked back open, though now was situated on his belly, elongated and running the length of his torso. Dozens of eyes had opened on the other side of the mouth, and inside were large, tombstone teeth that looked perfect for pulverizing bones. Where Screech's missing tooth had been was a gaping crater that dripped a black, oily substance.

A few drops fell onto the ship's metal hull. The metal sizzled where they landed.

This new, abhorrent spider thing let out a series of wheezing noises, its many eyes wide and looking in multiple directions at once. The long legs had spread out, touching multiple surfaces within the ship, until it was in the exact center. Two of the legs ended in what could only be described as human hands that had been dyed black and pulled through a taffy stretcher. Two of the legs ended with long, black toes with toenails that looked like vulture talons. What was even more disturbing was that two of the legs ended with what were once Mr. Screech's ears. And it was unclear what was at the tip of the remaining two legs, but an educated person would have guessed it was something Mr. Screech had two of. An optimistic person would have hoped they were his nipples.

His clothes, which had been crusted over in black scales, were now in tatters across the floor.

Outside the orb, The Grimblenox fed.

There was nothing they could do now. The atom within the cylinder had been split. Vix's gem was spent. The walking stick was out of power. The gauntlets had been absorbed by the ship. And one of the group was now a hideous beast. All their work to heal existence's engine had been for naught.

The Screech spider scurried about, picking one leg up at a time in an effort to lance the remaining people. Its long mouth opened and shut like a bear trap, its teeth gnashing. Vix, Vermilion, October, Bratt and Molly each in their turn scurried and darted away as the tips smashed into the ship's interior.

Those legs began to poke holes through the metal.

The Grimblenox's repugnant tongue bumped The Presidio-Trevithick, sending it spinning again until the window pointed back toward The Core. The Grimblenox appeared to care nothing about the six travelers who had come to save all that there is or ever will be. They must have seemed like nothing more than insects to it.

They now had The Core in full view. It was, once again, beginning to dim as the beast drank its essence greedily.

Molly looked to her hands and then to the Screech spider. Her eyes widened.

She rolled her body toward its nearest leg and grabbed hold with her right hand. Her left hand was still wrapped around the item she was clutching before The Presidio and The Trevithick had merged. Molly wasn't expecting the spider thing's scaly exterior to burn, but it did. It burned in a chemical way, and her black, lace glove began to deteriorate. She screamed in pain. And then she screamed a word.

"DIE!"

Molly's gloves had been charged by the power of The Core, and the Screech thing obeyed. It died. Its eight grotesque legs held their places, and its body went limp in the center of the core. The multiple eyes, which didn't have eyelids, went a milky white – a sight even more disturbing than when the spider creature was alive.

Molly pulled her hand away with a gasp, and couldn't help but let loose a series of painful sobs. It was all for nothing, Molly realized, as she looked down at her now scorched and blistering palm.

Her glove had melted into her skin. She lifted it up to her face to inspect it, and saw some of the black scales had stuck to her burned flesh. She looked back Screech's leg, and could see bits of her skin fused to it, as well. Beyond the window of the ship, she could see The Core dying, looking no brighter now than bonfire in an immense swamp.

The Screech spider's scales began to scatter. Some of them fell through the giant window, and the remaining witches and scientists watched with a small amount of wonder as the black pieces of Screech floated serenely through The Chamber's atmosphere, as if someone had tossed black rose pedals into a gentle breeze. It was beautiful. It was disgusting.

And they all shared the same emotion in that place of dreams where all minds are connected: All hope was lost.

Chapter 102

How odd it was, then, that a sudden burst of blue electricity popped and sizzled where the pile of socks and sticks lay, momentarily brighter than The Core, it seemed. It wasn't a ball of light, though. It had a shape. It was the silhouette of a tall man in a slick, high hat. The arcs of buzzing energy took form into a human, whose height was exaggerated by the six to eight inches of a feather plucked from some exotic bird.

Stupefied, the witches and scientists looked on as the form took shape and the sticks and socks, which none of the assembled had truly noticed before, disappeared completely.

Outside the ship, the sounds of the chamber rupturing sounded like thick ice atop a giant lake as it cracked amid warming weather. The group couldn't see how much more of the Grimblenox had made its way through, but now there was a horrible stench from the beast that permeated the atmosphere. Hundreds more tentacles were feeling their way inside the Core's Chamber.

The man lay on the floor. All eyes were upon him. They couldn't tell if his eyes were open or not because a pair of dark goggles hid his face above his nose. A huge mustache concealed his face below his nose.

After a moment, though, he stirred. He coughed. He reached out and moved one of the Screech spider legs out of his way. His head looked around the interior of the vessel. Beyond the broken window, The Core roiled and hummed. It was the sound a giant tuning fork might make, Bratt thought.

The man looked around the interior of the orb, and his mouth fell open slightly – a look of utter astonishment. He then turned his head toward Bratt.

"Oh, tits," the man said, dejectedly.

Chapter 103

No one spoke.

The man reached up with two gloved hands and removed his goggles. His eyes appeared to be nearly black. Upon closer inspection, they could see the edges of his pupils barely defined against irises that were dark blue and purple, flecked with strands of gold and white. They resembled a dark galaxy being manipulated by a black hole.

Both October and Bratt gaped, their eyes - the same eyes - poring over the man.

It was Dr. Gustopher Cerulean.

Chapter 104

"D - doctor!" Bratt said breathlessly. "Dr. Cerulean!"

Further words escaped Bratt yet again. Cerulean had the same eyes as Bratt – and the same eyes as October. October saw this, too, but didn't look so surprised.

Something bumped the Trevithick-Presidio again, sending it spiraling away from The Core. Everyone held tight as the vessel slammed into the chamber wall. The collision resulted in the sound of what could only be described as the interior of a giant cathedral bell. Every person brought their hands to their heads as the cacophony nearly burst their eardrums. All of them except Dr. Cerulean.

He, instead, inched toward Madame Vermillion. As the others were shaking the ringing from their skulls, Cerulean stood up and began speaking to Vermilion. She listened, her eyes wide. Her head whipped toward Bratt, looked him up and down, and then looked back at the doctor. After a moment, she responded not with words but with a look of abject understanding. She nodded. Cerulean nodded back.

The ship was once again facing the disgusting mouth of The Grimblenox. It was so close now that, if the ship drifted the length of two cricket fields, they would all be inside the creature.

October looked at Dr. Cerulean, and then took a deep breath, letting it out in a rush. He suddenly made his mind up about something. A look of stony determination crossed his face.

"Well," he shouted, "There's a reason we had a backup plan!"

All faces save for those of Dr. Cerulean and Madame Vermilion turned toward October as he reached out and snatched the wine bottle Molly still had clutched in her unburned fist.

"Wait!" Molly screamed as he plucked the bottle from her hand.

October, though, did not obey.

He let loose his beloved cane, and it clanked to the floor of the ship where he had once stood. He leapt from his position and used his free hand to grab at the edge of the window, which was just a meter away. There were still a few shards of thick glass protruding like railroad spikes there, and the metal at the edges were still hot from the blast of the mirror. Still, he held on with an iron grip. Blood began to spill out from his palm in tiny red droplets that floated lazily outward from the ship, and the skin on the heel of his palm began to blister. October pulled himself out the window, and whatever force had kept him in place while inside the orb had now let go. He steadied himself on the exterior of the ship, and then shoved himself upward toward the Grimblenox. The motion pushed the Presidio-Trevithick gently away from the creature's mouth.

Bratt's inability to speak seemed to be his greatest talent these days. He looked back toward the others. He glimpsed Vermilion, who had ignored October's sudden penchant for heroism. She was making gestures with her hands. Bratt had seen this before. It seemed like years ago, although looking back, it had only been days.

She was casting a spell. One of *her* spells. Not one of Vix's or Molly's spells. Not the spells that require ingredients and symbols and incantations. No, this was one of the spells that happened by using the life force of some unfortunate creature.

October, meanwhile, flew through the electrical arcs that buzzed from the surface of The Core and to the edges of The Chamber. Many of them struck him, though they appeared to have no physical effect on him - at least one that manifested itself in intense burns, charred clothes, singed hair or screams of pain. When all is said and done, dear reader, those bolts of energy were in fact feeding poor October's ability to send himself directly at the monster. Thought and intention are the most powerful forces in all existence. More powerful than a raging hurricane, more powerful than an inferno, more powerful than floods, earthquakes, and even more powerful than the horror and pain caused by slamming one's large toe into the leg of a bed after waking up to use the chamber pot in the middle of a dark night.

It's thought and intention that raises great pyramids, thought and intention that builds mighty dams, and thought and intention that guides masses of humans wherever they may be to act with kindness and generosity as they build empires and industry with a place and part for everyone. Unfortunately, it's also thought and intention that coerces and lies to those same masses of people, which can - and often does - result in empires of division and people who believe they are somehow more exalted because they happen to look a certain way or belong to a certain family or faith. These are the empires that destroy others for not conforming to their own structures. They destroy lives before ultimately destroying themselves.

It was that power of intention – the power of creation and destruction used simultaneously – that October was using now.

He glided without effort through the space between the ship and the beast's mouth, his look of determination only faltered when he had to shield himself from a few globs of Grimblenox pus.

He glided, and glided, and glided. He was an arrow, and there was no way for him to miss his mark (a mark which would have been impossible to miss considering it was the size of a continent). He had a weapon in his hand, determination in his mind, and the guidance of all the terrible and wonderful thought and intention that was the very essence of The Core.

And then, he was gone. He had done it. He had jumped, or flown, as it were, into the creature. Into the Grimblenox. Bratt felt a pang of sorrow - and a tiny prick of regret that October's enigmatic letter from himself to himself was now gone with him.

The group had not seen him as he disappeared into the throat of the abomination, but as he was sucked into its disgusting orifice, October reached down and uncorked the bottle, and the Waters of Perdurability began to splash down the Grimblenox's stinking gullet.

Chapter 105

There were a million sounds happening now, but once again, Bratt couldn't help but feel everything had gone silent.

The hundreds – *the thousands* – of tentacles began to slow their movement. The proboscis' serpentine movements began to wind down. And the color began to change. Those sickly, scabby pustules the colors of rotten grapes and bananas now began to go gray, and then white. The pigmentation from the ropy tongue faded into a marbled, ashy color. The cracking sound of The Chamber's walls stopped, replaced now by the noises of a new cracking: that of stone.

Molly, Vix, and Bratt, eyes wide with wonder, watched as the proboscis snapped with a loud report that echoed through The Chamber. The giant, tubular piece of rock broke again, and again, until it was nothing more than a thousand small stones floating freely around The Core.

The tentacles began to follow suit. Outside The Chamber, they could hear a wailing, gasping noise as the Grimblenox turned to stone - a process that sounded very painful indeed. Those screams, if that's indeed what they were, would haunt Bratt for the rest of his life, he knew, whether he lived for only a few moments longer or for an eternity.

Vermilion, however, had her attention elsewhere. She was now holding in her hand Dr. Cerulean's pocket watch and was studying it profusely, though no one actually witnessed the doctor passing it to her. And then Bratt turned to see what she was doing.

He watched in silence as Vermilion held the watch in her left hand and, with the pinky and thumb on her right hand pressed together, making it look as though she were indicating the number 3 with her fingers, she made a spiral motion over the clock's face.

And as quick as a snap and without any warning at all, Dr. Cerulean fell down dead, having only uttered but two words out loud throughout the entirety of this story. Those final words, unfortunately, were not necessarily the kind to be published in some overpriced university text or engraved as part of an epitaph upon some stone memorial somewhere. Luckily for the poor, dead doctor, not a single one of the people who were there to witness his demise would ever remember those words.

It wasn't just the power of Dr. Cerulean that fueled Vermilion's magic, though. Even Bratt could feel the spell sucking magic from each of the witches, and from the witches even beyond The Core. Vermilion, using the strength of The Core as a lasso, was harnessing all the magical energies available to perform this spell.

It was at that moment that the witches in the dimension from which Molly, Vix and Mr. Screech hailed began to lose their magical abilities as their timeline spun incredibly close to The Core and Vermilion used the passing energy to fuel her spell.

Vermilion had her tongue slightly out of her mouth, and she was biting on the tip as she mustered pure concentration. That concentration broke only a moment when she noticed Bratt looking at her. She looked like she remembered something.

"Get his feather!" she yelled at Bratt.

Flabbergasted, Bratt had to shake himself out of the trance he'd put himself in.

"Grab it!" she ordered. "The feather! From his hat!"

Bratt scrambled, reached, and plucked the cerulean feather from Cerulean's hatband.

As he did, things began to fall apart across existence as the structures that held all things together began to falter without the stabling effects of the power being used. Vermilion held tight to the pocket watch, which burst suddenly with blinding white bolts of electricity, more powerful than had ever emitted from October's cane. The Presidio-Trevithick and all its passengers flew violently away from The Core, bursting through a tunnel of light and out of The Chamber. As it did, the power from the spell blasted the pieces of stone beast into oblivion. And with nothing actively forcing the hole in existence open, the shell began to heal itself.

Of course, none of them saw this as they had all been lobbed light years away from that place. Vermilion had done it. She had used her own Core-strengthened witchy powers, fueled by the life of Dr. Cerulean and pieces of magic from across existence, to send them away from The Engine of Existence.

Certainly, none of them saw anything anyway because the magical blast sent them reeling into unconsciousness as their vessel appeared to disintegrate when its speed exceeded that of photons.

Chapter 106

There was something else at The Core that the group did not witness. They did not see that the power of their exit, a combination of the nuclear fallout and magic that had burst from the spot where the Presidio-Trevithick had been, had ricocheted off the inner walls of The Chamber. That blast, strong enough to destroy a Grimblenox, barely missed the slowly decreasing hole in The Chamber. It bounced off the walls just near the edge of the opening and then plummeted into the center of the cavern - and into The Core.

The damage was unnoticeable at first. But on the far side of the Engine of Existence, a tiny hole had been ripped. And through it seeped a small and nearly undetectable shaft of darkness created by wayward magic, scientific byproduct, and the tainted bits of stone matter left behind by the obliterated Grimblenox. It contained just enough corrosive material that, once it gained enough strength from The Core, could - and would - puncture a hole in The Chamber, through incalculable timelines and dimensions, and through the edge of reality, where it would capture the attention of the beasts that roamed beyond.

You see, the group of witches and scientists banded together in a place where time does not exist to destroy The Peculiarity that they themselves created when they destroyed it.

And somewhere, a reader went mad, furious that a story had the effrontery to introduce a paradox.

Step 13: When In Doubt, Employ A Deus Ex Machina

"There will come a time when all may seem lost. This is the time in which to use a Deus ex Machina maneuver, which will involve all manner of planning that will, at first, seem most convoluted. But, in time, a traveler will, forgive the pun, thank God that such a strategy was devised to begin with."

— Dr. Gustopher C. Cerulean, as quoted in the copious notes of Bratticus L. Magleby.

Chapter 107

The Trevitick-Presidio thing was bobbing slightly now, gently rocking with its large, blasted window facing a blue and cloudless sky. Bratt was waking.

The slight curve of the vessel under his body was smooth and surprisingly comfortable. He opened his eyes and looked upward at the azure beyond the edges of orb. He could hear water splashing calmly outside. He came to life a little more and looked around him. He was alone inside the vessel, Dr. Cerulean's feather still clenched in his fist. The only other item he could see was the doctor's pocket watch. It was now entirely blackened. Whatever force singed the machine's filters with each travel across dimensions had now scorched the entire thing.

He reached for it and grasped it in his hand. It was cold and hard. He half expected it to disintegrate into a puff of ashes, but he could feel the weight of it and was surprised to realize it was - charred appearances notwithstanding - completely intact.

He turned over and got cautiously to his hands and knees and found the ship rocked - though only slightly - as he moved about. The perfect globe offered nothing with which to steady himself, so he gradually advanced positions to his knees, and then to one knee. Finally he was on his two feet, his arms outstretched in an attempt to keep his balance amid the wobble.

Bratt had the appearance of a magician about to perform some amazing feat of prestidigitation – one which involved a large, blue feather, which he grasped in the fingers of his left hand, and a blackened pocket watch, which was clenched in his right hand.

He paused for a moment, contemplating his next move. He realized he could hear birds chirping outside. A cool breeze wafted into the orb, and Bratt thought he had never felt anything so wonderful in his entire life. He shut his eyes and let the air circulate over his face. There was no direct light coming into the ship, but he knew if he could manage to pop his head through the giant opening, he would no doubt see a sunrise, wherever he was. Bratt looked up and saw a flock of birds, too far away to be distinct, fly in an undulating formation back and forth a few times before finally soaring out of view. He cocked his head and could hear the splashing of water.

But it wasn't splashing, was it? It was lapping. The sound of lapping water, which meant he was where a body of water met the land. By the sound of the even and smooth rhythms of water making contact with a beach or a bank, he could tell he was either in a lake or a very wide river. If he had been in an ocean, he guessed the movements of the Trevithick-Presidio would have been far more violent, and the sounds of waves most definitely would have been much louder.

He remembered, suddenly and with pain, like an unexpected punch to the gut whilst carrying on a benign conversation, Dr. Cerulean's lessons on dimensional displacement. Whatever body of water he was currently in was now overflowing just a bit in a nearly immeasurable way due to the presence of the orb. His view of the ship's interior doubled as tears filled his eyes.

Like the river of beer blasting down the street of Bell not too long ago, the tears came forcefully and without control. He cried for his life with the doctor, which he'd enjoyed so much. He cried for the people of Bell, whom he didn't necessarily get on with, but nobody deserves to be transformed into a pillar of black scales, do they? He cried for October, the unlikable and contrarian version of himself who, in the end, literally saved the multiverse. He cried for Molly, whom he'd realized could have been an amazing friend.

He was quite the sight to see, this man standing inside a metal globe, his arms outstretched to keep his balance, a feather in one hand and a watch in the other, with tears rolling down his face. He went to wipe them away with his left hand at one point, but the movement caused the orb to rock, and Bratt slowly moved the hand with the feather back to its original location. He leaned forward just a little to allow the tears to fall off his face.

He sniffed and watched the drops plunk silently to his shoes. A few dropped near some scorch marks where the Screech spider's drool had dripped.

Not one of those tears was shed for the other witches, though. And when he began to think of Vix, Vermilion and Screech, his eyes dried, and hot blood began to blast into his face. Unconsciously, he began to bring his left hand to his face once again in an attempt to dry the tears that had soaked his cheeks. The orb, again, cautioned this move by tilting to the left.

He looked around. There were a few holes in the hull here and there where the Screech spider had punctured through with its deformed legs. Light shone through them. A few of them leaked as the orb rocked them below the surface of the water and then back up again.

Bratt held still, looking up at the hand that held the feather, noticing it for the first time - really *noticing* it. Dr. Cerulean had never been without this feather (since he'd never been without his hat), but Bratt had never had the opportunity to study it.

Was there something written on calamus? Yes, there was. Words, very tiny words. Bratt slowly brought the feather closer to his face, shuffling his feet around to regain balance. The print was nearly microscopic, but there were three words larger than the rest: "Read this, Bratt."

He knitted his eyebrows and looked out toward the sky again. He would need some sort of magnifying device to read the rest of it.

Confusion began to set in. Why did he even have this feather in the first place? He knew it was the one that Dr. Gustopher C. Cerulean always worn in his hatband. And he knew the doctor was lost in time and space somewhere, right? No, that wasn't correct. He wasn't lost, he had been found.

And there was something about the doctor, some realization Bratticus had come to. Did it have something to do with the doctor's eyes? He couldn't remember. It was important, but blast it all, he *couldn't remember.*

Bratt began wracking his brain. Something had just happened. Something before. He was there. It had happened to him, dammit! So why couldn't he remember? Why was it escaping him?

Chapter 108

If you'll recall, dear reader, The Core is a place powered by thought and intention, and is more mind than matter, and thus everything about it behaved more like a dream than actual, physical reality. And like a dream, the details were slipping quickly away the more time lapsed.

Nothing is more expansive than the mind, you see. There are miles and leagues and eons of time and space within one human brain, and whole universes, if folded just correctly, can fit inside with room to spare for a nice badminton court and perhaps a field for some nine-wicket croquet. This is why dreams are fairly clear to the dreamer in the moments right upon waking, but those dreams fade away and become nothing more than abstracts from some vast scholarly journal lost to the ages. You see, we do not forget our dreams. We merely lose them among the infinite libraries that are our minds. Our brains keep certain information handy, most of which centers around the physical things we encounter. Those other ethereal tidbits, like the things encountered in dreams, are stored away for later, when we're no longer constrained by mortality.

It's all quite scientific, I assure you.

So because The Core was not a physical place in the sense that Dr. Cerulean's lab was a physical place, or the Trevithick-Presidio orb was a physical place, then the memory of it began to find its way into the warehouse of Bratt's mind, the same vast area that stored all his other dreams. He was able to recall almost perfectly all the events that led up to Molly's spell that forced October's cane to take them to the Engine of Existence. But after that, like those dreams we all experience, only a few major points stuck out to him.

He remembered that October had saved the day somehow, though grasping the specifics was like trying to capture the fine smoke that rises from a piece of incense. He knew that their plan to use a combination of magic and science to fix whatever was wrong actually worked. And now, after putting those pieces back into place, he knew that Dr. Cerulean had been there. Yes, and he had done something that surprised Bratt. Something to do with Madame Vermilion.

Bratt looked at the feather again and then out at the sky. At the edge of the window, he could see some sharp pieces of glass protruding from the metal. In one area, there was a large maroon stain that had the appearance of brush strokes. It was obviously blood, smeared by the fingers from which it had bled. His mind brought up that fleeting image of October again, his face a portrait of pain as he grasped the edge of the broken window.

The picture of October's terror and tenacity flitted away as quickly as it had come.

Bratt sighed.

With careful determination, he slowly stepped forward. The orb rolled slightly. He stepped again. The ship rolled once more. Soon, Bratt had rolled the window low enough that he could see more than just the sky.

He was at the bank of the Ridiculing River. He could see the sun rising far in the east over the Procumbent Plateau. On a hill between the distant batholith and the banks of the Ridiculing River, a green hill with a ramshackle and enormous apothecary was visible.

Bratt rolled the ship until water began spilling in through the Screech spider's punctures and then through the hole that was once The Presidio's window. He steadied himself and leapt through the opening. He expected to jump into the shallow water and walk to the bank, but he ended up tripping on the edge of the window and falling face-first into the river. The cold water blasted his senses. His hands each tightened around their respective objects so as not to lose them in the lazy waves.

Soaking wet, Bratt found his footing once again and stood. He had a smile on his face for what he realized was the first time since this entire ordeal began. He turned around and saw that the orb had lost its purchase in the sand of the banks, and now floated out to the where the waters flowed fast and deep. He watched it as it drifted quickly downstream, around a bend, and out of sight.

Cold, wet, and optimistic, the young scientist then began his trek back to the apothecary.

Chapter 109

The Peculiarity had been cured, to be certain, and with that cure came some pleasant side effects, one of which was apparently the return of waters to the river he'd just left. The last time he saw it, the Ridiculing River was flowing with sludge. Whatever force had found its way through that rip in existence that had transformed the rapid flow of pristine water to a disgusting tar-like substance had since been defeated, and the Ridiculing River was once again as it should be.

Several miles down the river, though, the gunk that had once formed thanks to the obnoxious powers of the Grimblenox had gathered into a dam of sorts, and in just a few days time, there would be a new lake perfect for swimming, fishing, boating and, yes, the occasional drowning.

It was by sheer luck alone that the only thing that would be destroyed by the creation of this new lake was the home of a miserly businessman who had got it into his head that he should run for mayor of nearby Bell, considering its former mayor had had the audacity to go and get himself transformed into a hideous snake creature. It was lucky because this businessman, who himself drowned in the middle of the night because he was unable to undo the multiple locks that held his door shut against imaginary intruders, was entirely unfit for any political office. Had he won the mayorship, he would have decimated the already partially-destroyed Bell since his goal was to use the power of the office purely to add more money to his own coffers.

Good riddance to bad rubbish, as someone somewhere once said.

As Bratt passed the edge of Bell, he could see that no longer were the cherry trees sprouting with disgusting fungi that reeked of dying flesh. The trees at first glimpse appeared to be bare, but upon closer inspection, one could see they were at the early stages of budding leaves.

Beneath the trees were piles of what looked like round, wooden shingles but were, in fact, the now dead and dry spores that had once been growing from Bell's trees. Their putrescence had vanished completely, and in due time, survivors would find multiple uses for the dried mushrooms. They made excellent hand fans for extra hot days (though any sensible Bellian would have it painted and adorned with some sort of crystal or gilded embellishments, of course), and many folks found they made more than adequate paving stones for citizens who desired a more rustic look for their gardens. Mostly, though, residents of Bell used them as shingles.

However, other unfortunate circumstances seemed to have been more permanent. Bratt could see the pillars of black and shiny scales standing intermittently throughout the streets. And while he didn't notice it at first, there was a whole section of the city that was completely missing. Bratt came to this realization when he walked past Dernier Cri Boulevard only to find the next road over was Terrace Throughway. He had paused then because he knew there were 13 streets between Dernier Cri and Terrace. The catastrophic events of the days prior had shuffled themselves out of their little shelf in Bratt's memory and popped directly into the forefront of his mind.

Yes, he had seen what The Peculiarity had done to Bell. He'd witnessed it being, for lack of a better expression, *erased*. And now the parts that had been affected – that had been sucked away by The Grimblenox – just weren't there any more. The remaining pieces of the world had knitted themselves back together seamlessly, and there wasn't a single trace of the things that were there before.

Bratt finally made it to End Lane, the road that led up the grassy hill and to the apothecary of one Dr. Gustopher Cramden Cerulean. However, End Lane now lined up at the edge of Bell with St. Sabnock Street, the rest of what once was End Lane having been removed from reality altogether.

At Cerulean's apothecary, things were just as they'd left them, raccoons and all. There was a time not too long ago the Bratt thought he'd be saying goodbye to this place, his home, for good. Being back brightened his spirits a bit after realizing a good many Bellians had met their fate and at least four exemplary sweet shops had disappeared from time along with everything else between Dernier Cri and Terrace.

He immediately ran to the workbench, pulled open a drawer and dug through a variety of tools, utensils, gadgets, and devices until he found the doctor's microscope. With a melodramatic movement, Bratt used his arm to sweep away everything on the tabletop. The gadgets, gizmos, doodads and whatchamacallits all clattered to the floor, making more than enough room for the microscope, the feather and the pocket watch.

Bratt dashed to the kitchen area, pulled a tiny tealight from the cupboard, snagged a box of wooden matches, and returned to the workbench. He lit the candle and placed it in the microscope's apparatus, which in turn reflected the light beneath whatever object was to be observed. Bratt placed the calamus portion of the feather under the lens.

"Read this, Bratt" jumped out immediately. He adjusted the feather and turned a dial on the side of the microscope to zoom in to the three words that followed: "Write with me."

Bratt looked up from the microscope. He was confounded and, for the first time, wished October was there to point out his stupidity. He guessed October would have known exactly what the message meant and wouldn't have minced words at how obvious the solution was.

He shivered a little. He was still drying after his fall into the Ridiculing River.

"Write with me," he said aloud, as if speaking the words would have helped bring the answer into view - which speaking words aloud often do. "Write with me."

He looked into the microscope once more just to make doubly sure he hadn't misread the words that had been printed so neatly by some unknown means.

"Write with me," he said again.

Chapter 110

I'm sorry to report, dear reader, that even after all of young Bratticus L. Magleby's adventures, and even though he gleaned much knowledge from the events and people he encountered, he was still just dim enough that he couldn't put two and two together. That, in and of itself, was a damn shame considering he'd graduated university with high honors for his mathematical skills.

You may have guessed already what Bratt should have done with Cerulean's feather, but it took the doctor's intern an entire week to figure it out.

In the meantime, he'd set about making repairs to the apothecary as needed, and he began a proper tidying up and organization of the huge room within the laboratory. The job would have taken days even without constant pausing for moments of pondering, so Bratt actually didn't make much progress.

He started his efforts in the southwest corner of the laboratory (of course, leaving the northeast quadrant for the very last - or perhaps he wouldn't venture to that area at all) and he'd make his way through one or two piles of knick knacks, paddywhacks, and even the occasional bone before he'd stop and think about his one-time companions and what became of them. By now, he'd almost completely forgotten what the Grimblenox had looked like and how it had died, but he wagered he'd never totally lose the memory of what the beast could do - or that it was October who managed to incapacitate the creature at the cost of his own life.

And what of Miss Molly St. Mercalli? This firebrand of a human, who was so impatient but so kind, with an intelligence that rivaled all she encountered. Did she survive? If so, where was she now?

His mind had filed away the fact that it was Vermilion who managed to get Bratt back to where he belonged. I can tell you with certainty that it did this because Bratt hated Vermilion so much that the very idea of her saving anyone's life, let alone his, would have driven him mad. He hoped that whatever had happened had killed her and that she'd never bother anyone ever again.

He found himself indifferent to the fate of Mistress Vix, though he couldn't help but wonder if she made it out alive. October had a letter that reported Vix was a villain, and that she'd had some sort of plan. It had appeared, at one point, that the letter was correct. Molly, too, knew something about the ancient witch that was never properly shared with Bratt. Now, he'd never remember what Vix had been up to, he supposed. He would resign himself to the ignorance of Vix's motives and return to work cleaning and organizing the laboratory.

And after a few moments of finding a place for everything and putting everything in its place, he'd fall into a trance of contemplation again, and he'd start wondering what happened to Molly and what happened to the corpse of the Screech spider and how he hated Vermilion, and the whole cycle would start again.

After five or six tries at being productive, he realized it just wasn't something of which he was capable at this juncture in his story. So he set about doing other things instead, one of which included polishing up Dr. Cerulean's pocket watch as best he could. He was unable to get it going again, but he still attached it to a nice, shiny fob and kept it in his waistcoat.

Eventually, Bratt dared to meander back to Bell. After all, he did have to eat, and he was in no shape to bring out one of the doctor's many ancient blunderbusses to go hunting.

Over a period of two days, he made several trips into town for supplies, and in the process of doing so found that the Bellians who'd had sense enough to hide in their cellars when The Peculiarity made its most damaging pass across the timeline had no recollection of the pieces of the city that had been engulfed by the Grimblenox.

He never named the beast or gave any indication that he knew exactly what had happened, mind you, but he did mention in passing how he'd miss Mrs. Ratherty's Candies and Cocaine cart, which had frequented one of the disappeared streets. Not a single Bellian had known what on earth he was talking about, and when his back was turned, they all exchanged glances that in no uncertain terms declared Bratticus to be as dotty as the late Dr. Cerulean.

As for the doctor, the townsfolk assumed he'd met the same fate as many of their fellow residents, whom they'd decided must have caught some fatal, outlandish pox that caused the skin to form black scales rather than red rashes. Never mind that it wasn't just the skin that had scaled over, but the clothes as well, and never mind that there was no indication any of them had been sick leading up to the nastiness nor were there any instances of folks falling ill afterward. The fact was that insurance didn't cover acts of God, but it did cover unfortunate medical ailments.

So citizens across the city declared their loved ones had been tragically taken by a new disease, collected a great many payments, and carted off what remained of their family and friends to be thrown into the new lake that had formed just a few miles away from town.

Mayor MacBritches' body, which had been boiled into an even more grotesque visage, had been discovered next to what had once been Dorfecture Drive. The residents merely tutted at the sight and noted to each other that the mayor must have made some very poor life choices to end up in such a state. Secretly, of course, they were all happy to be rid of him merely for the fact that each resident in his or her own turn had been tired of either having to adjust their front doors or set elaborate tables in their front yards merely to satisfy Rudy MacBritches and his absurd demands.

If this story has taught you anything, dear reader, it's that Bellians despised absurdity.

So they carted off the snake mayor along with all the other poor souls and threw him into the lake. Four generations later, Bellians wouldn't remember why the body of water was called Snake Lake, but they accepted it because dwelling on names of lakes is reserved only for cartographers and the very mentally disturbed.

The townsfolk were blissfully ignorant of any other signs that something supernatural had happened in their fair town. Brandeline Bragg's Beer Brewery was empty, you see, because a pack of wild animals must have broken in and drank up the entire contents of every cask. One needed only look to the forest in the hours following the scale plague to see creatures of all sorts absolutely stupid with drunkenness. And Very Wide Way had *always* been the crossroads of the city, didn't you know? So of course it should include at least four streets, which it did, plus four or five more. And Dorfecture Drive? No, there is no such place. It had always been a ditch and would always be a ditch, though there were no drains that emptied into it, and for some reason the entire length of it smelled strongly of beer. All the burnt signposts, you say? Why, it was nothing more than a passing lightning storm, a phenomenon as common as noses are on faces.

And of course that giant, dry, crusty egg that sat where once there was a mayor's mansion was the fossil remains from some ancient reptile, probably. It wasn't long before Bellians were charging tourists to take a peak at the monstrocity.

Bratt theorized that as the Grimblenox sucked matter out of space and time, it must have sucked it out of existence completely, meaning those things that were now gone had never been there in the first place. So of course none of the Bellians would have remembered how things were – because things were never that way to begin with.

The only explanation Bratt could muster for why he was able to know the history before The Peculiarity was that he, by way of dimension-hopping machinery, had stepped out of existence and become more of an observer than of a partaker.

Of course he was absolutely correct in that assumption, which makes it all the more frustrating that he couldn't figure out what to do with Dr. Cerulean's feather.

Chapter 111

It wasn't until he stopped at the grocer, which was run by Samuel S. Store, an ex military man who went into the market business after the State of Konfuson and the State of Schock made peace following The Great Tuna Maiming of '66, that Bratt finally found insight.

Out of habit, Bratt had always requested a receipt from General Store's General Store so he could properly be reimbursed. He made the request that day, even though the man who would have normally taken the receipt and added its total to Bratt's wages was now dead. General Store obliged, pulled out a thin strip of paper, whipped a quill out from behind the counter, dipped it in a well of ink and began to scribble.

Bratt's eyes opened in astonishment, and then he laughed loudly with a single burst. General Store was so startled that he upset the inkwell, spilling black fluid across the wooden countertop.

"What in blazes, man?" Store said as he stooped to find a rag from one of the bottom drawers. "I say, what in *blazes?!*"

"Write with me!" Bratt yelled and laughed again.

Store popped up from behind the counter, a rag in one hand and a look of confused anger on his face. Bratt reached across the counter and took Store's lapels in his hands and pulled him close. Ink smeared across the fronts of both their jackets.

"Write with me!" Bratt barked in his face. Store was too startled to respond. And with that, Bratt let loose Store's lapels, left his groceries, money, and his partially-completed receipt on the counter, and dashed from the general store. If the doctor's pocket watch hadn't been secured to Bratt's waistcoat by the new fob, it probably would have been left behind as well. Instead, it fell from his pocket and bounced continuously as he sprinted the entire way back to the apothecary, somehow finding a way to run even faster on the grassy hill's incline.

Chapter 112

With not a care for errant raccoons, Bratt burst through the apothecary door and left it standing wide open. He ran to the workbench.

Bratt pulled one of the drawers open with such force that it went flying from the cabinet and onto the floor. He dropped to his knees and began sifting through the spilled contents until he found a pen and an inkwell, which had luckily kept its stopper amid the chaos.

He righted himself, bringing the objects to the workspace top. Bratt had placed Cerulean's feather in a glass cupboard above the work bench for safe keeping. The feather had definitely seen better days. Thanks to being plunged into the Ridiculing River, its once sturdy and stately barbs had wilted, and somewhere along the way its plume had been singed.

Bratt plucked the nib from the pen and forced it onto the tip of the feather's calamus. It was nearly a perfect fit, but there was some twisting and grunting that occurred as he joined the two.

He popped open the inkwell, dipped the nib inside and then realized he'd forgotten one of the most crucial elements to writing: paper. Bratt stood there, his head darting this way and that in search of a piece of paper. Oddly, there wasn't a single sheet to be found. He dropped the feather to the workbench's top and made his way to his personal quarters, hurdling over the random bric-a-brac that littered the apothecary.

Bratt fell to his stomach at the side of his bed, tapped open one of the stones beneath, and reached into the hidden compartment. Inside were his many books full of notes detailing the workings of Dr. Cerulean's contraption, as well as copious notes on all matter of experiments, observations, ventures, research, procedures, analyses, notes, jottings, marginalia, and shopping lists.

It was the first time he'd ventured to the hidden compartment since the day the doctor traveled out of this dimension. The sudden feel of one of his leather-bound notebooks in his fingers sent a sudden and shocking sadness through him as memories began to flood in of Dr. Cerulean dictating to the studious apprentice who transcribed every word and sketched a great deal of diagrams.

He pulled out the closest book, which just so happened to be the journal that hadn't yet been completely filled. With the book in his hand, he got back to his feet and made his way back to the workspace, although his speed had slowed somewhat due in part to the onset of new mourning.

At the bench, he set the book down and opened it to a random blank page. He picked up the feather, which had been spattered with black dots when Bratt hastily dropped it with the nib's reservoir completely full of ink, and he put the tip to the page.

The nib made contact, and Bratt wondered what it is he should write. He supposed it didn't matter, so he began to record the events following Cerulean's disappearance into space and time. He wrote approximately three sentences before the nib had to be refilled. He stopped writing, dipped the feather in ink once again, and returned the makeshift quill to the paper.

While getting his thoughts into the journal was therapeutic, nothing spectacular was happening. He'd half expected the feather to begin singing, or perhaps even fly from his hand and point the way to some hidden artifact. The only thing it was doing, though, was transferring Bratt's thoughts to the page.

Is this what Dr. Cerulean wanted? For Bratt to journal the experience? The doctor was nothing if not obtuse, but would he actually go to such great lengths to hide a tiny message on his feather only to motivate young Bratticus to record the events following a scientific experiment? Surely there were other ways of conveying such a request that didn't include time travel, death, and printing teeny, tiny letters upon the shaft of a feather. Why, Cerulean could have simply made the request aloud before projecting himself through dimensions.

As Bratt mused on the situation, he realized Cerulean would not have made the request to begin with, because it was Bratt's job to record the details of all the doctor's scientific studies, so it seemed downright ludicrous that Cerulean would have even thought that Bratt needed such a reminder.

Of course, after Bratt found Vermilion in Cerulean's place, he hadn't actually had the time to sit down and make a record of what had happened, nor had he had the opportunity to take notes along the way.

Perhaps he *did* need the reminder.

What a way to go about it, though, Bratt thought. If Cerulean's note had been taking the scenic route to getting to the point, as it were, then this was the equivalent of a years-long cruise around the world.

Besides, there were far better instruments with which to write than a feather. Why, the invention of metallic pen nibs had long since made sharpening the point of a feather's calamus obsolete. Those metal reservoirs lasted far longer, and the ink could be easily wiped away instead of drying and clotting to the organic substance of a feather quill. So why would the doctor insist Bratt use the feather to write with instead of a more functional fountain pen?

He almost poked his eye out then as he brought his writing hand to his forehead with a slap. Instead, the metal nib stabbed itself neatly into a piece of flesh just above his eyebrow, and ink splattered across the right side of his face. He felt the pain but didn't care. He dislodged the metal from his face and put the pen down only long enough to wipe the concoction of ink and blood from his eye.

He asked himself how he could have been so blind and so stupid, a question you yourself have no doubt also asked about our dear Bratticus L. Magleby through the pages of this story.

Bratt pulled the nib off the feather. He scanned the ground where the contents of the flying drawer had spilled for something sharp. He saw a straight razor that had slid partially beneath the workbench, bent down, grabbed it, returned to the top of the workspace. He opened the blade from the handle and used it to cut the tip of the feather's calimus into a wedge and sliced a strip into the tip for a reservoir.

It was crude, but it would work.

He re-dipped the pen into the ink and placed the tip of it to a new page in the journal. Dr. Cerulean's cerulean feather, like the planchet of a witchboard that Vix or Molly or Screech might have used, began to move on its own.

Chapter 113

The words flowed from the quill.

"My dearest Bratticus," the message began, *"It was my sincerest hope that you would not be reading - nor writing - this letter. Alas, you are, though, and I have failed at my task of preventing The Peculiarity."*

It was a confusing way to start such a letter, Bratt thought, because The Peculiarity had been fixed. Hadn't it?

"As you have now surmised, my name is not Gustopher Cerulean, although I cannot deny that I have, indeed, earned every degree I have listed upon the signage of The Apothecary, my business cards, my resume and my stationary."

Bratt had to stop to refill the quill. As he did, a memory from the dream surfaced. Dr. Cerulean's eyes, the ones he'd kept hidden behind those dark goggles for the entire time Bratt knew him, we're dark purple and blue with specks of gold that looked like stars. The irises looked like black holes. There were only three other people he knew of in the entire multiverse who had those eyes. Two of them were versions of the same person - himself and October. The third and was Mayor MacBritches, who only acquired them after looking into the eye of the Grimblenox.

If Bratt had looked into Mr. Screech's eyes before he transformed into the spider thing, he would have added a fourth person to that list.

Suddenly, he remembered sharing a thought with October back during the dream that was The Core. He had seen Dr. Cerulean through one of October's memories, though the Dr. Cerulean he had seen was different somehow. Yes, instead of an impressive mustache, he had a full beard. Instead of goggles, he wore dark spectacles. He realized now that it wasn't Dr. Cerulean at all. It was Headmaster Purpureous P. Jones, who it turned out had actually been an older October Magleby from a parallel universe. It was Jones who had written a letter - no, they were *instructions* - to October detailing the events to come and how to react to them. It was those very instructions that gave October so much insight into events that were about to happen - although it also sent him reeling when those events strayed from the contents of his letter.

It appeared, Bratt noted mentally, that he himself was now receiving instructions of his own.

He returned the quill to the page.

"I have dedicated every waking hour of my life - from the moment I first read the letter you're reading now to the day in which I entered the machine - to education. I have spent the last 30 years mastering chemistry, biology, metallurgy, philosophy, physiology, zoology, engineering, technology, humanities, mathematics, entomology, pharmacology, oncology, medicine, surgery, divination, parapsychology, journalism and piano.

"I believe I have accomplished more this time around than I did the previous time. It's my hope you'll do the same.

"My name is Bratticus L. Mableby."

Bratt stopped writing. For once, he had come to the correct conclusion before it had to be spelled out for him, which in this case was happening quite literally.

He took a deep breath, dipped the quill again in the ink, and returned to writing.

"You, my dear boy, will never comprehend the paradox in which you find yourself. However, you will come to live with it, even if it does drive you slightly mad. This is to be expected, so fear not when your eccentricities become too much for your peers to handle. Once you've earned all your degrees (and please make it your goal to earn more than I did), you need not mingle among those who do not understand your plight. You have the apothecary, and all your financial needs will be met through your services to the citizens of Bell.

"Of course, you cannot stay there forever, a point which I shall revisit later in this letter.

"I cannot explain everything about the life ahead of you because, as you well know at this point in your adventure, even the slightest change can set you on a completely new course.

"However, there are several things you absolutely must know, and one or two things you positively must do to ensure you are equipped to take on the task of eliminating The Peculiarity when the time comes. You see, my dear boy, if you are reading this letter now, it means you have traveled the same path I have, and that you have healed

The Core and destroyed the beast. But alas, in destroying the Grimblenox and healing The Engine of Existence, you and your companions also created The Peculiarity.

"I am sorry to be the bearer of such frustrating news."

Bratt forced the quill to stop its movements. Was it true? Had they been the cause of the very thing they'd worked so hard to fix? The thing for which October sacrificed his life? How could it be? More importantly, though, how could Dr. Cerulean - how could *Bratticus L. Magleby*, from an alternate dimension, older and using a pseudonym - know that it was the cure that caused the disease? If indeed the elder Bratt had made a similar journey in his own time, how could he have known what had happened at The Core? Bratt, and everyone else still alive, had been blasted from The Chamber by some sort of magic (though Bratt's mind still refused to acknowledge it was thanks to Madame Vermilion).

He hadn't witnessed the events following his departure. How then, could his elder counterpart have such information?

The quill returned to the paper.

"You may be wondering how I am in possession of the knowledge of the events following your abrupt exit from The Core. Again, I am sorry to report the no-doubt discouraging circumstances of paradoxes, but I only know of this fact because I read it in a letter that was written to me by an older version of myself from an alternate dimension. Therefore, the reason you now know how The Peculiarity both began and ended and thus began is because I, that is to say you, have educated you, that is to say myself, on the facts. You may stop writing now for a moment in order to reflect."

Blast this automatic quill, Bratt thought as he paused for a moment to ponder on the nature of paradoxes, though he made a conscious effort not to mull over the philosophy too long as it would have driven him to lunacy right then and there. It truly was a "chicken or the egg" scenario, though its implications were far more dire. He quickly returned to writing in order to halt his mind from wandering too far down the path of contradictions and the nature of creation.

"The list of things you must undertake is short, but crucial.

"First, you must return to the place of your birth, the Village of Wax, on the

day that it was destroyed. Since you are transcribing this letter now, I know for certain that you are in possession of my pocket watch. Worry not. I know you have examined it and determined it has been taken out of commission, but I assure you it has one good trip left in it. The motor barrel bridge has been blasted a quarter of a centimeter out of place. If you make this one adjustment, you'll find the watch to be in temporary working order. The watch will likely not work for the purposes of traversing time and dimensions following this task.

"Now, please brace yourself for what you are about to write and what you are about to read."

It was an adequate time to remove the quill from the journal, both because Bratt did indeed wish to brace himself, and also because he needed to refill the quill's reservoir and turn to a new, blank page.

He began writing again.

"It is imperative you stop your parents from surviving the catastrophic volcanic eruption that day. They must die."

And with that sentence, Bratt stopped writing again.

~~~

He had taken a small break from transcribing the words of the dead doctor through the aid of an exotic blue feather, the mechanics of which he'd still yet to understand. He wanted to be adequately fed before the remainder of the letter was revealed to him.

So he set about making a fire in the cast iron stove, heating some water in the kettle, and mixing a bowl of porridge along with a healthy helping of butter, some ground cinnamon, and two or three spoonsful of sugar. He looked at the contents of the bowl and decided to add about a pint of heavy cream, since he had his health to consider, after all.

He also boiled a pot of coffee and poured himself a cup to which he added a healthy helping of unlabeled brown liquor. Though, considering the proportions, the drink would more accurately be described as a cup of unlabeled brown liquor with a healthy helping of coffee.

He ate. He drank. He could see through the apothecary's open side door. He still hadn't closed it since bounding back into the laboratory following his epiphany at General Store's General Store, the midmorning had evolved to early afternoon. It was a gorgeous day outside.

Inside, though, it was a different story. There was a storm of sorts brewing, and Bratt had to shore up his emotional levees before the gale began. The liquor laced with coffee seemed an appropriate tool.

Now, adequately full and only slightly drunk, Bratt resumed his position at the workbench where he re-dipped the quill into the ink and began to write once more.

"Yes, it is shocking, but perhaps the bitter pill is easier to swallow now that you've sufficiently lubricated your senses with the bottle of bourbon I kept in the kitchen area."

He only paused to shake his head in disbelief.

"Be forewarned: I did not believe myself when I read this very same note I'd written all those years ago. I loved my parents very much, and I refused to follow my own instructions. So I traveled to that time and place in an attempt to stop myself from this devious act under the assumption that my parents would be lost to me if I didn't.

"Of course, this would be impossible because I grew up with both my parents fully intact, as did you. So it would be scientifically infeasible for our timelines to be altered as such. No matter how much I learned in my adventures traversing time and dimensions, my ability to grasp certain truths was still rocky at the best of times. It seemed counterproductive - and downright horrible - that I should travel through time to ensure my own parents died, even if they were the parents of some other version of me.

"If you do not travel back and ensure your parents perish, then the alternate timeline of our friend October will never exist, and we will never learn the secrets of traversing time and dimensions.

"You see, it is October, not you, who will discover and perfect the secrets to opening up those means of travel. But in order for him to be placed on that path, he must be an orphaned baby discovered by a group of professors, one of whom will be an older October himself from yet another dimension. And how is his eventual wisdom of traversing time and dimensions imparted upon us? Well, I only know of the mechanics of

it all because an older version of myself dictated the knowledge to me, which I then recorded in a series of journals.

"So, yes, you must do it. You must make absolutely sure that the baby in the Village of Wax becomes an orphan that day. You'll have one problem, though, and that problem is I.

"As I noted earlier, as a young man I'd still yet to grasp the concepts of what needed to be done. So rather than traveling to make sure October became an orphan, I traveled to make sure Bratticus could grow up with two parents. So be forewarned that I will be at the village attempting to keep them all alive.

"I will have arrived earlier than you and readied the family's balloon for travel. Use this to your advantage, though, because it is how the baby October will escape the blast. You'll most certainly have to physically restrain me in my attempts to keep mother and father from dying a horrible, painful, and tragic death.

"Although you have not yet done this task, I know for certain that you will do it. I know because otherwise the feather wouldn't be writing you this letter because everything will have ceased to exist.

"Oh, yes, and if I were you, which I am, I would make sure your pocket watch latch release is adequately oiled. We wouldn't want it getting stuck as our parent's home is blown to Kingdom Come, now would we?

"Your second task will be to send Molly and her submersible back to the dimension from which she came. I know that you have grown fond of her, but she has her own life to live, and there is a person there whom she loves very much, and that person in return loves her. This will be relatively achievable by extending the positively-charged cable from the top of the contraption and attaching it to the hull of the submarine. The charge will transport Molly's entire vessel. Of course, before she goes, you must have her enchant a feather, which will later pass on your knowledge to a younger version of yourself if indeed The Peculiarity paradox continues."

And Bratt stopped writing once again.

Molly? But Molly was not with him. Not a single one of his traveling companions had made it back to the apothecary. And as for The Presidio, well, it had stopped being The Presidio somewhere along the way. It had morphed into some new vessel, though Bratt could not remember the details at this point.

He remembered October's breakdown when it was clear not everything was happening according to the letter Headmaster Jones had written. It came to him then, and Bratt was momentarily proud of himself for coming to the conclusion completely by himself and without any help whatsoever.

Something had changed. Something in this paradox in which versions of himself have seemingly, eternally been fighting The Peculiarity had changed since Dr. Cerulean, or rather the Elder Bratticus L. Magleby, had undertaken his own quest. Progress was made somewhere along the line, perhaps. And this gave Bratt hope. It was, at least, proof that he was not doomed to repeat the same futile tasks over and over with no possible way of altering the outcome.

Wouldn't that be an astonishingly discouraging way to finish his story?

Perhaps there was a way to remedy this paradox after all.

Besides, Bratt thought, feeling an arrogance he'd never felt before, he didn't need Molly to enchant a feather to get a message to his younger self. Why make it so difficult? A pen, a few sheets of paper, and a sturdy envelope would suffice. He smirked a little, looking not unlike October when he knew something no else did. Bratt brought the quill, which he now understood was powered by Molly's magic, back to the journal paper.

"Of course, you may see fit to find another way to communicate the information to your younger self - should your younger self need to know it. But I would strongly advise not relying on using common paper. This message is something you will need to carry with you and have at the ready. Letters written on paper can be read by anyone, and they have an annoying tendency to burn up when they come into contact with errant sparks. And as you very well know, and as the bin full of scorched jackets can attest, we are constantly in the company of sparks due to our many experiments.

"I implore you to find a means to transfer this knowledge in a message that cannot be discovered by anyone other than your younger self - and using a device that won't be lost or accidentally destroyed."

Bratt wondered then if he should put off further contemplations until the letter had fully written itself, considering the magic quill was constantly answering his own questions. And although the trash bin, which indeed had been full of jackets sporting a variety of holes caused by their catching fire, was obscured by all manner of furniture, he couldn't help but steal a glance in its direction to confirm the doctor was correct.

He made a silent promise to himself to withhold further speculation. He dipped the quill, turned the page, and resumed writing.

"Third, you must make the very best of the next 30 years. You may choose to remain in Bell for as long as you like between now and then, but I must caution you that you will, eventually, have to move yourself to the next dimension over and leave the apothecary behind. After all, you must establish yourself there to prepare the Bratticus L. Magleby, whose timeline is exactly 30 years behind your own (as mine was exactly 30 years ahead of yours), for his journey.

"Hire yourself as an apprentice, and impart upon yourself as much wisdom as is possible without revealing the future. Think to the time before the machine was built. Had you known what was about to happen, would you have accepted the job at the apothecary? All things considered, with you being me and so forth, I know the answer is no. You would have turned your backside to Bell and sought out much safer employment. If this were the case, then the fellowship of scientists and witches would not be formed, you would not travel to The Core, and The Peculiarity will have continued unchecked, thus resulting in the destruction of everything we know."

Bratt couldn't help himself here. He had to pause and wonder if he could prevent The Peculiarity from ever happening by simply doing nothing. Could it be that simple?

Pardon me, dear reader, for thinking such a query to be incredibly hilarious given the overall lack of simplicity in everything that's happened so far.

The writing continued.

"Do not think that you can ignore this chore completely in an effort to prevent The Peculiarity from ever happening. As you are reading this, The Core has already been ruptured and The Peculiarity has begun. It is the very Peculiarity that darkened your eyes as a babe as you, an innocent soul, looked into the infinite horror of the Grimblenox eye.

So unless your eyes are the color of some run-of-the-mill human being, then you can rest assured that The Peculiarity has already been set in motion.

"We, of course, must count ourselves lucky that we observed the beast from beyond while newly born. Had we looked into the creature's eye with even a month longer of life under our proverbial belts, the Grimblenox's power would likely have had the effect it has on most other people, and we would have been nothing more than a bundle of black scales from the get go.

"Granted, there's literally no possibility of that happening since it was I, that is to say you, who gave the Grimblenox the opportunity to peer inward in the first place. So if you, that is to say I, were transformed into a mass of a black scales at a young age, then the beast couldn't have looked into our existence in the first place.

"I hope you can see now, my dearest Bratticus, why I have been driven to such eccentricities in my last years.

"Speaking of The Peculiarity, the reason it was present at both the time of your birth and the day of my disappearance is quite elementary. Our realm of existence is housed within a container that has no edge. It is an existence with infinite possibilities confined into a finite space. Infinities travel in circular patterns. I cannot say the exact shape our existence takes, but since our infinities travel in circles, they often line up even if they're seconds, years, millennia, or even dimensions apart. As you witnessed in The Chamber of The Core, the magic that ruptured the engine created a singular line of energy, which penetrated to the walls of the cosmos. As each timeline races around those walls as a horse does on a track, that infinite line of blackness had the opportunity to blast through multitudes of them simultaneously.

"It just so happens that the ray of light upon which you traveled as a human new to this world and the same ray of light two decades later happened to intersect at the same point.

"So while it may have seemed that The Peculiarity happened in multiple places in multiple universes during multiple times over the years, the fact of the matter is The Peculiarity happened in a matter of minutes, and the Grimblenox discovered the puncture in existence moments afterward. You and the others traveled to The Core and healed it just moments after that. It just so happened that these different timelines spinning eternally around in this shape we call existence all lined up at the precise moment the witch's magic burned a hole in The Core.

"*Again, you may ask, 'How does the doctor know this?' And again, I shall answer, 'Because I found it out in a letter written to me by myself.'*

"*Now, once you have established yourself in the next dimension, and after you have hired yourself and you have built a new contraption, imparting your wisdom upon your younger counterpart so that he, too, may one day have the knowledge to fix and build his own machine, there are some things you'll need to keep front of mind as the time draws nigh.*

"*Firstly, you'll have to keep your eyes to the sky for The Peculiarity. It will appear some time just after the blossoms begin to open on the cherry trees and some time just before the cherries themselves are plucked from the branches. You'd be better off if you marked your calendar for exactly 30 years from the day that I stepped into the machine.*

"*If you see The Peculiarity, and I have no doubt you will, then you'll know it is time for you to set your coordinates and ensure you are transporting yourself to the very spot where the pocket watch was enchanted with a powerful spell that managed to send you and Molly back to the apothecary. I'm sure you'll recall how to track where the watch has been, and if you can't, rest assured that the detailed instructions remain on Page 442 of Volume 6 of your copious notes. Since there is no physical coordinate for The Core, you'll have to rely on this method, and build those directives into your new pocket watch.*"

As Bratt paused here to refill the quill, let us also take a moment, dear reader, for a tidbit of explanation. You see, Dr. Cerulean's pocket watch, as you may recall, was the mechanism he used to return to his fixed point in space. As you have just learned, there were multiple volumes and thousands of pages of instructions on how to build and program the device. I could transcribe those volumes in their entirety onto these pages, but what good would it do? It certainly wouldn't further our story, and I think we can all agree that this story has had enough asides, evasions, non sequiturs, digressions, departures and tangents as it is. So you'll simply have to take my word that Cerulean's watch, when tinkered with adequately, could find its way back to a place it had been before.

"*When you are transported to The Core, do not succumb to hysterics. It is my prayer to whatever sadistic creator is out there that this will be the point where it all ends. If by even the slightest chance your younger self and his companions have somehow managed to heal The Core, destroy the Grimblenox, and transport themselves away from The Chamber, then you'll merely appear within Molly's submersible back in the*

Ridiculing River, and you'll never have to reveal the truth behind everything that has happened - if you choose to do so, that is. However, if you arrive at this point and either the beast lives or The Core has not been repaired or, God help you, neither has happened, you must turn to Madame Vermillion."

No, Bratt thought, not Vermilion. But as the words etched themselves on the journal's page, Bratticus L. Magleby's mind library moved a few files around and shuffled through some stored boxes before it pulled out a memory it had actively tried to suppress.

It was Vermilion who saved him. Dr. Cerulean had told her something. She had cast a spell. And she had made sure that Bratt had possession of the doctor's feather.

Madame Vermilion, whom Bratt had disliked from the moment he laid eyes on her, had saved the day.

The quill was dipped, and the writing continued.

"She knows not her own strength, and through the tutelage of her newfound friends, she is even more powerful than she was in her native land. But she must pull energy from an incredible source of life. At this point, no doubt, all of your party will be drained, which is why you will be projecting yourself to this moment. You will be full from your breakfast. You will be well slept. Your body will be at its fullest energy, and it is this energy that will prime Vermilion's pump, so to speak. She will use your life to begin her spell, a spell that will gain power from the very energies that make up existence as it gains strength. And through that strength, she will be able to transport the entire submarine and all of its occupants away from The Core.

"Unfortunately, I cannot tell you what becomes of Vermilion or Mr. Screech or Mistress Vix. Vermilion's spell sent us, Molly and myself, back to the river. And I can only assume the others were returned to their own wheres and their own whens. Though why Molly ended up back in the County of Muss in the State of Konfuson is an enigma, and since this information was never relayed to me through a letter, then it is information I do not have."

Another pause. Bratt knew the fate of Mr. Screech. It was another change, perhaps another reason to be positive that things can be different this time around.

"Yes, Vermilion's spell will kill you. You will die, as I have died. After 30 years preparing for that moment, I have found peace, as you shall, too. Besides, the very blast from the canister that housed the atom will have had a sickening effect on you. Or, at least, it did on me. If I didn't die saving existence, then the end of my mortal journey would not have been too far afterward thanks to the sickness that has been growing inside me since the atom split.

"Most importantly, before you travel to The Core, you must communicate somehow to Vermilion that she has the power to finish the task and send everyone back home. She needs to know that she must use her own, ill-begotten witchcraft, and that you will provide the energy.

"I have written this letter to the best of my recollection, but things may have changed. I hope things have changed. With each time this adventure begins, I hope we move closer to our goal of ending The Peculiarity once and for all. There may be infinite timelines and infinite possibilities, but there is only one Core. We must protect it at all costs.

"Please destroy this missive so as not to set in motion the possibility that everything continues on in exactly the same manner. If there is one important lesson I learned from October, and believe you me, there were many lessons, it is that a letter such as this should not be used as a road map to the future. I will never forget the day his own instructions stopped being useful, and it was the day he himself stopped being useful, too. I believe with all my heart that had October made his own way through this venture, he would not have felt the need to sacrifice himself and would have realized that a bottle of liquid that magically transforms things to stone does not need a human vessel to find its way into a hole as big as an ocean.

"But I have no worries that you'll ensure things happen correctly and that you will dispose of this lengthy memorandum. If you're reading this letter, it means you've already followed these instructions. After all, if you hadn't followed instructions, I wouldn't be dictating this letter to a magical feather, now would I?

"Yours truly, Dr. Gustopher Cramden Cerulean, MPharmS, MD, PhD, LDLP, ASAP, a.k.a., Bratticus L. Magleby."

Bratt placed the feather upon the workbench's tabletop, stood silently, retrieved the bottle of unlabeled brown liquor, and proceeded to finish the rest of it on the spot, eschewing the use of a cup entirely.

Outside, the sun was setting, and nocturnal creatures began to stir. A raccoon made its way cautiously to the open door and peered inside the apothecary. All was still.

Bratt then began to decide, in the absence of Molly, how he would go about imparting knowledge to a version of himself he would meet in a few short decades.

Pre Epilogue

How kind it was of Dr. Cerulean to leave such a lengthy message for us, dear reader, as it seems to have tied up many loose ends, wouldn't you agree? Unfortunately, as you have perused this manuscript, you might have observed a plot point or two that may not have been satisfactorily concluded. I wish I could provide you with further insight, but alas, I cannot. For as the Grimblenox sucked streets in Bell out of existence altogether, so did it erase many aspects of this tale, as well as tales all over the multiverse.

Why, even now I dare you to recall exactly what happened on the fourth day of your third year in grammar school. The memory is gone, of course, and I'm sorry to tell you that it has not been stored away within the infinite library of your mind. It has been erased from existence altogether. I apologize that I must be the bearer of such tragic news, but the fourth day of your third year in grammar school has ceased to exist in time, and there's simply no way to retrieve it.

Other narratives and general nuts-and-bolts aspects of our story might have changed, since we collectively traveled all over, setting who knows how many actions and inactions into play. Why, this storyteller promised you the cerulean feather introduced at the beginning of our tale wouldn't be a significant object that would come into play later. Obviously, somewhere along the line, we jumped into a parallel dimensions a nanosecond to the left where in fact the feather was quite critical.

As for the rest of the unknowns and the unexplained? Well, there are a few additional items of note that this storyteller can reveal to you, of which Dr. Cerulean had little or no knowledge.

Miss Molly St. Mercalli was indeed transported back to her home of San Francisco, California, in the year 1906. After the deed at The Core was done, she had been blasted to the shores of the bay, in between two rickety piers. She was soaking wet, and the last thing she could remember was standing near Mistress Artemis Vix. There was another witch in another dimension where nightmares had come to life. Vix was casting a spell, and then everything went blank.

Her voyage beyond the realm of existence, her adventure at The Core, and the events that happened in between, were now shelved in a dark corner of her mind's library.

She stood on the beach and looked up toward her beloved city, which was now in shambles thanks to the force of Dr. Cerulean's machine. The blast that sent her beloved Presidio to another dimension had sent ripples of energy through the city, breaking buildings, cracking streets, and, yes, killing citizens.

Molly's heart fluttered in fear at that moment. For in the city was the love of her life, a woman whom she hadn't seen since the day she had placed a forgetting spell on her, believing it was for the best. Now, though, she realized all the magic in the world was nothing if it can't be shared with someone she loved.

Miss St. Mercalli plucked the remnants of her skirts into her hands, and marched toward the city in search of her love, hoping the woman hadn't perished. She felt a pain in her right hand as it clutched the fabric, and she looked down to see it had been badly burnt.

She hesitated on the beach trying to remember. After a moment or two, she made up her mind to do her remembering while she walked.

Molly's story continues on, and it is nothing short of marvelous. However, that story, wherever it is being told, does not continue here.

Molly's cousin, Archimedes Mace, whom we mentioned only in

passing, eventually found himself in London, where he'd gone down a far darker path than that of his sister. Having grown up under the tutelage of Mistress Artemis Vix, he'd taken a certain liking to her view of things. I cannot say exactly what brought him to Europe or how he'd made his way as one of the region's most successful necromancers, but I can tell you one thing for certain: His story, wherever it is being told, does not continue here.

Vermilion's powerful spell latched onto the magical memory of Vix's once-powerful ruby. As Dr. Cerulean's pocket watch would be used to return to The Core, so was Vix's ruby used to return to its place of origin - although that journey was wholly unintentional.

Artemis Vix found herself back in a desert, though it was not the desert where Vix's beloved Trevithick had been stowed. This desert had enormous dunes that looked like golden ocean waves frozen in time. A hot wind blew sand horizontally across her face. Vix recognized it immediately.

The hot sun beat down, and the whipping winds did nothing to cool her. Her pale skin would not burn, she knew that much, but the power she gleaned from her ruby – the now dead ruby – had ceased much of the automatic enchantments Vix had placed on herself so many years ago. She could actually feel the heat, her heavy black dress soaking it in like bread on a plate of gravy.

For the first time in hundreds of years, a bead of sweat dropped from her forehead.

She began to work her way through the sands of Sahara Desert, near the Cradle of Life on this particular world, where Vix's own mother had unearthed the ruby eons ago.

What a coincidence it was, Vix thought, that it was near the place from which the ruby had come that she'd hidden the one object that could help her now.

She hoped she would remember exactly the place she buried her mother's head. If she could start getting the pieces back together, she could enlist her dear mother's help. Of course, her mother would no doubt be tremendously grumpy, especially given the fact that it was her own daughter who divided her up into multiple parts and spread those parts across the world. But Vix found herself in her own incredibly sour mood given her plans to harness the Grimblenox's power was so rudely interrupted when October flung himself into the creature along with a bottle full of the Waters of Perdurability.

Like the others, her memory of the events was not precisely in tact. She had forgotten her sheer terror and complete abandonment of any plans when she first glimpsed the behemoth. Now, all she could think of was how much magical power had gone to waste.

Her ruby, useless now, was left in the sand. She'd have to find her mother soon, she knew, because without some magical help, she might not live much longer now that her precious gemstone had been used up. And as she walked, Vix began to age.

In three separate places on the globe, there had crashed three separate boxcars, each full of one-third of a magical treasure collected over hundreds of years. They were treasures their collector had assumed were gone forever. But like the power that drove her back to the desert from whence her mother's ruby came, the magical items gathered from around the planet also found their way home, albeit in a trio of boxcars.

Vix's story continues on, and it is nothing short of scandalous. However, that story, wherever it is being told, does not continue here.

Madame Verimilicent Vermilion, the very unlikely hero of this tale, managed to transport herself back precisely to the moment she'd left the State of D'Kay. There she was, looking up at the House of Vermilion where her niece, Prime Minister Margaret, the only ruler left in the land, was now standing at the open door.

Margaret, seeing her estranged Aunt Vera looking very bedraggled indeed, standing next to a pile of kindling, finally snapped herself out of mourning and pieced the puzzle together. It was Madame Vermilion, Margaret now knew, who was the cause of the State of D'Kay's now state of collapse.

And just like that, Margaret called upon the Prime Minister's Secret Service who promptly arrested Veramilicent Vermilion and jailed her, all while ignoring her assertions that the entire universe should be grateful for her and that she had helped stop the Grimblenox.

Vermillion, whose magic had been nearly drained during that final, important spell, could now offer no proof she was an existence-saving sorceress. Whe she tried to use a spell to free herself from the prison, she only succeeded in creating a few patches of rust on the bars.

Later that evening, as one of the custodial staff was cleaning up, she shuddered as she swept up two dead cockroaches.

It was clear poor old Madame Vermillion had gone quite mad indeed, so rather than prolong the punishment by keeping her locked up for years, Margaret chose to put her conniving, and apparently now crazy, aunt out of her misery. The old woman was beheaded the next day.

Vermilion's story does not continue on, and it ends here.

Epilogue

Please do not take offense that all the characters that encountered you throughout this story were afraid of your very existence, even if they didn't say it aloud.

As we watched their adventures, we had the advantage of many angles and points of view. We were able to see up close and far away. Why, we were even able to observe, to a degree, the life after life as Molly made her fateful pilgrimage to the place beyond death. Watching these things from such vantages hardly ever raise the hackles of those who are being observed.

However, there was one setting in which we spent a major amount of our time that didn't exactly provide us with an abundance of options from which to watch the goings on. So while in Dr. Cerulean's vast one-roomed laboratory, filled with a cacophony of belongings, we had to make do staying put in the northeast corner of the apothecary.

As is the case with any person lurking in the shadows, those who are being observed can feel the eyes upon them, even if they're unsure whom or what is watching them. While we have attempted to let this tale play out on its own, unfortunately there were moments when our presence was felt - and feared.

I will take this moment, dear reader, to thank you for not interfering in the story, even though you could have reached out from the darkness of the northeast corner and literally plucked the feather from Bratticus's hand. I am glad you didn't, as it would have upset him greatly and most likely would have led, one way or another, to the total demise of existence.

Your cooperation was much appreciated.

Postscript

This may not feel like a happy ending to you, but then, there are no happy endings because there are no endings as long as The Core is functional. I will tell you, though, that Bratticus L. Magleby lived a life of which any of us would be envious.

True to Cerulean's request, Bratt set out to learn everything he could about the world, earning degrees from great, prestigious universities and tiny, inconsequential colleges. He dedicated the next 30 years of his life to not only making himself a better person, filling his vast mind library with all the knowledge he could get his hands on, but he also did all he could to make others' lives worth living, too.

He was kind to those who didn't deserve kindness. He helped those who didn't deserve help. He made it his mission to break away the stones that encased so many human beings' hearts, driving them to hate each other and chalk up their differences rather than count all the things they had in common.

He was beloved in the City of Bell – (the one in the dimension next door, where he switched places with a pile of socks and sticks cut at such a length that they were completely unusable) - and he came to be known as the fun loving and learned old doctor who, yes, was a bit loony. And though he lived through an event most cosmically bewildering, he only allowed the aggravating paradox to drive him only slightly bonkers.

Bratt made a decision one year before The Peculiarity appeared above the apothecary. He decided this time around, things needed to change – for better or for worse. And when the younger Bratticus answered the advert, the elder Bratt met him without anything covering his eyes.

It had not been that long ago, after all, that he'd made himself a promise. If he ever met himself again, he'd be much less ruder to himself than October had been to him.

So the two Bratticuses met. And the elder told the younger *everything.*

ABOUT THE AUTHOR

Mateyo Jakobi has been creating art since he was a child.

One of his very first memories was the day his father, who also loved to create art, brought home a new set of markers. Young Mateyo wasn't allowed to use them, no doubt because of how expensive they were, so the boy attempted to convince his father to leave the room so the child could surreptitiously use the fascinating and colorful medium to create his own work of art. His attempts were futile.

Mateyo's *other* early memories included the ghost of the Man in the Tall Hat who haunted his childhood home, a Victorian-style pioneer house in southern Utah. At night, without fail, a group of strange, black, thin creatures, as tall as the house itself, would gather outside his second-story window after the family had gone to bed. They made noises, muffled and ominous, but they never got inside - either because they didn't want to, or there was some magic that kept the glass impervious to their efforts. To this day he still hasn't figured out what they were or what they wanted.

He has dedicated his life to telling stories, whether it be through illustrating and painting, through writing and journalism, through acting and singing, or even through the lies he often tells merely for his own entertainment.

Mateyo Jakobi currently resides in northern Utah with his husband, Rus, and their two dogs - a pug called Devin, and a dachshund called Karen.

The four of them spend their spare time time-traveling after they achieved immortality by bathing in the blood of ancient pagans.

They also enjoy going to the movies.

For more, visit www.mateyojakobi.com.